And Still the Earth Turns

And Still the Earth Turns

Muhammad Ali Bandial

The Book Guild Ltd

First published in Great Britain in 2023 by
The Book Guild Ltd
Unit E2 Airfield Business Park,
Harrison Road, Market Harborough,
Leicestershire. LE16 7UL
Tel: 0116 2792299
www.bookguild.co.uk
Email: info@bookguild.co.uk
Twitter: @bookguild

Copyright © 2023 Muhammad Ali Bandial

The right of Muhammad Ali Bandial to be identified as the author of this work has been asserted by them in accordance with the Copyright, Design and Patents Act 1988.

All rights reserved. No part of this publication may be reproduced, transmitted, or stored in a retrieval system, in any form or by any means, without permission in writing from the publisher, nor be otherwise circulated in any form of binding or cover other than that in which it is published and without a similar condition being imposed on the subsequent purchaser.

This work is entirely fictitious and bears no resemblance to any persons living or dead.

Typeset in 11pt Minion Pro

Printed and bound in the UK by TJ Books LTD, Padstow, Cornwall

ISBN 978 1915603 340

British Library Cataloguing in Publication Data.
A catalogue record for this book is available from the British Library.

Special thanks to Saba Akbar (@thelocaltrails) for providing the image for the cover.

To Sania, who found me when I was lost

Book One

The Chickens Are Coming Home to Roost

1

Another day in paradise

Anarkali, Lahore 2007
5:50pm

Survivors would later say that there had been an eerie sense of calm and stillness in the air a few seconds before it happened.

Perhaps it was God giving the people one last glimpse of peace before it packed its bag and left. Just as it had been threatening to do for the past couple of decades. But nobody had paid any attention to the distant rumblings of unrest.

All that changed.

For good.

A thousand years of blessings followed by three minutes of carnage.

The equation could not have been more poignant.

The irony of it all was not lost on Jabbar Kaleem.

It had to be on a Thursday, the busiest day of the week at the shrine.

Only a Muslim, a fellow devotee, a believer, would know all that. That was what made it all the more heartbreaking; *the chickens were coming home to roost.*

Some would say the bomber was a little boy, barely in his teens, while others would claim there was an older man involved as well. But to Jabbar Kaleem, or Chacha Fauji as he was known to everyone in the mohalla, the details no longer mattered, as he sat glued in front of the cheap Chinese rip-off plasma TV in his dilapidated house deep inside the old city.

Jabbar's wife Fatima was busy making tea in the kitchen, her remedy for every calamity. Over the course of the last half-decade, she had seen her fair share of those, enough to make her an efficient tea maker.

That night, however, even her skills had been put through the wringer as she kept coming back to the living room, stealing glances at the TV for more news on the tragedy. The fact that the day's episode had thrust her in the middle of the 'drama' that she usually watched from afar, was only gradually beginning to dawn on her, and with it, perhaps for the first time, she acknowledged the true depth of the terror gripping the rest of the country, that had seemed distant and alien until then.

A sombre TV anchor repeated the news that had already spread through the city like wildfire: "The shrine of a renowned Sufi mystic was rocked by two bombs and a firecracker on its busiest night of the week. Two back-to-back suicide bombings followed by a cracker blast killed forty people and injured over 175 and still counting inside the crowded shrine on a Thursday, when the city's poor and impoverished gathered for free food and devotion."

The two terrorists had been wearing vests packed with explosives, weighing around twenty kilograms. They had made their way into the heart of the complex, mixing in with the surging crowd of humanity that had come to pay their respect, receive blessings and, in the case of most of the homeless, get a hot meal for free.

The first attacker had blown himself in the basement, while the second entered the courtyard before detonating his explosives after an interval of two minutes. The details were sketchy at that point, but the reporter said that according to the police, both the bombers were about twenty to twenty-two years of age. A grenade shell had also been recovered from near the *wuzukhana*. Fatima moaned and turned her face away as the TV showed the aftermath of the blast site, which presented a horrifying scene with bodies and remains scattered over a one hundred-metre area.

"How can they show that?" she whimpered as she kept her back to the screen. "Those are someone's brother, father, children."

Jabbar said nothing, as he continued watching. The slight trembling in his hand as he brought the cup to his lip was the only indication of how he felt.

The first blast had ripped through the walls of the *wuzukhana* in the basement and sent flames and acrid smoke through the premises. In the ensuing fire and chaos, the second bomber had detonated, exponentially magnifying the damage.

The sound of the teacup slipping from Jabbar's trembling hands made Fatima turn around. Without another word, she stooped to hurriedly clean up the mess as Jabbar got up, handed her an old rag and took the remains of the shattered cup. Fatima sat down on the scrubbed but worn-out floor of their home and mechanically cleaned the spilt tea, her eyes still riveted to the glaring TV screen. Her furrowed and creased face betrayed the thoughts going through her mind.

Jabbar silently berated himself for having ruined his doodh pati that had, over the years, come to be an addiction.

"We need to get word of the boys and get them back as soon as possible; there is no knowing what the situation will be right now," he muttered.

A chill went up Fatima's spine. She started praying under her breath as Jabbar dialled. Her fingers mechanically counted the prayer beads of the tasbih as her lips mouthed the words silently.

Jabbar punched the numbers and waited.

For the second time that day, the world seemed to stand still.

Fatima muted the television. In the silence that followed, the caller tune for network failure sounded eerily morbid, like the wail of an animal in distress. Jabbar hung up and tried again and again, always with the same result.

The old soldier looked up helplessly at his wife in the silence, his eyes mirroring the vulnerability in hers. As the old grandfather clock that Fatima had brought with her dowry struck 6pm, the lights went out. "Come hell or high water, these *haramzaaday* won't forget load-shedding," Jabbar snorted cynically.

Fatima got up off the floor, her fingers expertly running over the familiar landscape of the room as she navigated her way to the kitchen in the darkness. She returned with a lighted candle which she tilted on the mantlepiece. She placed the candle on fast-solidifying wax. Jabbar felt an overwhelming wave of love for his wife, who suddenly looked lost and vulnerable in the flickering light. He got up and clasped Fatima's hand in his as they stepped out onto the terrace overlooking the old bazaar.

She rested her head on his shoulder as they gazed out onto the fluttering lamp lights of the city they had lived in their whole lives.

"*Allah meray bachon ko apny amaan mein rakh,*" she said in a quivering voice.

Jabbar grunted in agreement.

*

6.05pm

Two blocks away, the sound of the blast, muffled in the din of the city, was carried through the humid air to a pair of teenagers locked in a tight embrace. The couple was so engrossed in each other that they had no awareness of what was transpiring in the world around them. When the first blast had occurred, Ijaz had dismissed it as a kid firing off some firecrackers as he buried his face in the velvety darkness of Nida's hair and ran his hands all over her warm, soft skin.

He would have ignored the second, much louder, blast too, had Nida not pulled away and shrieked in unfiltered fear. He was about to reprimand her for raising a noise and drawing attention to them when he looked over to where she was pointing. Over the rooftops, a little off in the distance, the bottom edge of night sky where it met the buildings was glowing with an orangish tinge.

As Ijaz's heartbeat returned to normal, he could hear the chatter of people all around him. In the darkness, he could see people in surrounding buildings leaning over railings and balconies and enquiring.

Ijaz made another attempt to rekindle the moment by reaching out to grab Nida, but she moved away effortlessly, adjusting her dupatta as she gave him a bored look.

"Do you know, Maulvi *saab* lets me give the Azaan now?" he said excitedly.

Nida yawned. "You know, you look really silly with those three strands of hair on your chin."

Ijaz bristled. "You just wait, Nida, I'm going to be the muezzin at our masjid and Baba and your father all will be impressed by me," he tried but could clearly see that the moment had gone.

Nida opened her mouth to say something but then shook her head, which made Ijaz feel even more stupid. He seethed with rage at the object of his affection for not sharing his vision to be a big man.

"I have to go now," said Nida as she avoided his outstretched arms, making her way to the door.

"Wait!"

Nida turned with one hand on the doorknob, fixing him with a look that made his knees go weak.

He fished out the red and green glass bangles that he had got from the bazaar that evening.

In one fluid motion, Nida was back in his arms as she planted a kiss on his cheek and darted away with the bangles, leaving him grasping at air.

Sometimes I don't understand girls at all, thought Ijaz. When, last summer, she had come over during Ramzan with her parents, she only had eyes for him as she baked samosas for him and passed him notes when their parents weren't watching. Over the next weeks and months, she would find an excuse to be near his madrassah or smile and wink at him when he would come to her house with his friends to collect *chanda* for the masjid. He thought she would be impressed with how an important religious authority he would soon become. Everything he had learned to do had been to win her over. But lately, she had these moods, and she would completely transform into another person.

Ijaz adjusted the turban over his shoulder-length hair and fixed his clothes as he climbed down the water pipe and made his way to the madrassah, dreams of raising an army of kids with Nida swimming in his head.

*

Anarkali police station
6.15pm

In an impressive career spanning three decades, there were not many who could lay claim to having seen Shahzad Zafar lose his temper. The youngest in his Common Training Programme batch in the Civil Services, he had risen through the ranks of the bureaucracy, snagging critical appointments through a razor-sharp ability to see openings and an even stronger ability to keep his emotions in check no matter the situation.

However, as he ate up the distance from his car to the entrance of the Anarkali police station that evening, he was seething. Shahzad couldn't remember the last time someone had dared to break his concentration while playing bridge. The fact that he held a winning hand and was enjoying the look of discomfort on his batchmates' faces as he reclined in his usual spot at Lahore Gymkhana, crossed his mind again and he gritted his teeth, the carefully kept veneer of calmness threatening to slip away.

Somebody better be dead, he thought as he was led by a scared-looking constable – with a paunch that fell over his belt and bounced against his knees as he ran to keep up –inside the station and up the two flights of stairs to the interrogation room.

The entrance was blocked by two muscular men with arms folded who stood before the door with blank looks. Shahzad groaned as one of them grinned and stepped forward to touch his knee as a mark of respect.

"How are you, Bhola?" he asked as he lightly tapped him on the shoulder and tried to move past. But the other goon stepped forward, blocking the way. At that moment Shahzad felt like ramming his fist down the dhoti-wearing goon's throat but, just then, the door opened, and his junior came out, relief washing all over his sweat- and blood-streaked face as he saw Shahzad.

"Sir, I'm so glad to see you. *Oye*, out of the way." He pushed aside the two goons as he led Shahzad inside the room, which reeked of sweat, blood and human faeces. In one corner, Shahzad spotted a lifeless body lying spreadeagled in a pool of blood. He had seen too many corpses in his time to know that his worst fears were confirmed. His train of thought was broken by the sound of someone washing their hands from a bucket in a corner. As he turned around to grin at him, Shahzad groaned and turned to his junior.

"Why the fuck did you call this guy over?" he hissed, but his junior, Khawaja Zaheer, DIG Punjab Police, could only stammer.

"*Koi massla nai, sirji*," said Raja Niaz as he wiped the blood from his face and beard with a rag. "We're both part of the same team." He held out his hands. Shahzad noted the bruises on the knuckles.

"No, we're not, Raja *saab*," he said icily. "Frankly, I'm surprised you needed my help if you had the federation at your disposal," he said to Khawaja as his eyes tore into his junior.

"*Sirji*, Khawaja *saab* had no choice, I was asked to help him get the job done," continued Niaz affably.

"And you seem to have done remarkably well," said Shahzad, motioning towards the dead body.

Niaz guffawed, throwing back his head. "What's one dead Christian in a city filled with them?" he said. "In fact, it helps our case, one less from the colony."

That's when Shahzad grasped the situation. His junior had been asked by a certain politician to help him clear up a Christian colony in a lucrative spot in the city. Everyone within the bureaucracy had heard the rumours through the grapevine. *So, it's true*, thought Shahzad.

Shahzad could add the rest together. In return, Khawaja had been promised a choice posting. To get the job done, he had acted the only way the police had trained him to do. They had picked up a local Christian youth leader along with his younger brother and tried to convince them to agree to persuade their community to vacate the area. However, things hadn't gone entirely according to plan and, in their desperation, they went overboard.

Khawaja took him to one side. "Sir, I really need your help," he said. "The minister has washed his hands clean of the whole thing; this could ruin my career."

Shahzad nodded and consoled his friend. "Don't worry, Khawaja, we'll manage."

"There is one more thing, sir," said Khawaja as he pointed to his right. Shahzad looked at the window which led down to the side alley and into the slums. He knew even before his junior said the words. "The other boy escaped through the window. He's injured but he went through the glass and ran away before we could get to him."

Shahzad nodded, stroking his chin as a plan started forming in his mind.

*

Defence Club
6.30pm

Being the glass-half-full type all her life, Asma Zafar thought, *there is still something positive to be taken from the last three hours.* With nothing to do, and having been abandoned amongst strangers, she had found clarity and could finally see her relationship for what it was.

A sham.

Things had changed between them. It had been a long time coming while Asma had tried to put her finger on it. But it was only that night, when she had finally realised.

She didn't love Walid.

For Asma, the last three hours had been nothing short of hell as she had moved around in small circles for the sake of her fiancé, making small talk about inane stuff that she had no interest in whatsoever. But she had gone along for the sake of Walid, whom she had been dating for three years, waiting for him to pop the question, so that they could formalise their union, a task which he suddenly seemed reluctant to do ever since his father had won the MPA's seat in the recent elections.

As Asma cradled her cranberry juice in one hand, while listening to the chief secretary's wife lament about the latest lawn collection, she realised that she had never really given her relationship with Walid much thought. Beyond the fact that they had known each other practically their whole life, going to the same school and hanging out in the same social circles, they had never connected on a personal level. It had always been presented to her as a good match on paper; their parents knew each other, and in a society that judged you on your connections, this was just the right ladder to climb to the top of social status.

But lately, she had started questioning her choices. Like when she had proposed the idea of pursuing a degree in law, her own mother had discouraged her, telling her to concentrate on getting married to Walid first and then to focus on other trivial matters. The idea that her own journey was not in her own hands rankled her, even though she liked Walid. Or she thought she did.

But do I really know Walid?

At that moment, someone had mentioned the bomb blast and, for a moment, there had been a pause as everyone made perfunctory remarks about the poor people and how religion was being misused. And then somebody called for a fresh round of drinks, and everyone clapped.

Although everyone said they looked good together, had common friends, they really had nothing to say to each other when they were alone. And lately, the thought that the person she was going to marry might not be someone who shared the same ideas had started rankling at her. She had disregarded it as cold feet and had never given it much thought.

But that night, she needed reassurance. She wanted Walid to tell her that he shared her dreams and wanted her to be her own person and that she was not going to be some trophy, to be paraded around and kept in a gold cage.

She looked around the room but could not locate her fiancé. She remembered last seeing him when the waitress had offered them drinks. With a pang, she remembered the way Walid had looked the waitress up and down right in front of her.

She walked out onto the patio, down the flight of stairs and onto the lawn. As the noise from the party faded away, she could hear the sound of laughter coming from a wooden pergola. She could make out two dark silhouettes. As she made her way over the wet grass, she finally saw Walid sitting with his arm encircled around the waist of the waitress as they both sipped champagne and passed a joint between them. If Walid felt he had been caught, he certainly didn't show it. He tipped the champagne glass towards her. Asma noted the white powder marks on his nose and her jaw clenched.

"Hey, sweetheart," he patted the floor beside him, "come join us, we're celebrating Dad's appointment as the Minister for Investment."

There was a lot that Asma wanted to say, but she suddenly realised that she no longer needed someone's permission to say or do what she wanted. The feeling felt liberating. She took off the Tiffany diamond promise ring that had been a gift and flicked it towards Walid who, for the first time, looked incredulous as he watched the ring go sailing off into the darkness.

"What the hell did you just do?!" he shrieked like a little boy as he got up, throwing the waitress off the pergola in the process. "How am I supposed to find the ring in the dark?" he whined to Asma's retreating figure.

"Why don't you sniff it out," said Asma over her shoulder as she laughed for the first time in a long time.

*

6.35pm

As Sharoon lay in a pool of his own urine and blood, he looked back at the day that had started with so much promise. It seemed inconceivable to him that only four hours ago, his elder brother had picked him up from the factory where he worked and taken him to a restaurant where they had celebrated.

"We are not going to have to sell our land," Isaac had said. "This has always been our land, our city and the minister *saab* has finally seen the truth of our demands. He promised all of us in the meeting that there would be no shopping centre made here."

Sharoon had hugged his brother as they had made their way out, arm in arm. There had been three police vans waiting for them when they arrived in their street. In a matter of seconds, amidst shouts and protests, they had been handcuffed and whisked away.

The next three hours had been the longest of his life. And yet, there had been no time to think. Sharoon had seen the life go out of Isaacs's eyes as Niaz continued to pound him with murderous intensity. The beating had finally ended when the police constable who had picked them up from the colony, on a false charge of stealing electricity, had rushed in and pushed Niaz off the body.

There had been a brief argument in which the constable had threatened to call the DIG as Niaz had turned his focus towards Sharoon. In that instance, the door had opened, causing the constable and Niaz to look away. Using all his remaining strength, Sharoon had lifted himself off the floor – although his hands were tied, they had left his legs free – and jumped out the window. As he felt the glass shatter and break beneath the weight of his shoulder, Sharoon had felt the welcome feel of the wind on his face as the air was filled with shouts behind him. He fell head first through the air, but luckily the branches of a tree broke his fall. As he made contact with the ground, Sharoon felt like a giant metallic clamp was chomping down on his shoulder. He reached to touch his shoulder and felt the bone jutting out of the skin at an awkward angle. With adrenaline pumping through his veins, he felt no pain as he got off the ground, clambered over the barbed wire and ran into the darkened alley that led to the slums.

It was dark, and the ground was uneven as he ran. Behind him he could hear fast-approaching footsteps. As his mind raced, he noticed the sewerage gutter nearby. With his heart racing, Sharoon lowered himself down into the river of filth and slid the manhole cover over him, leaving a tiny sliver open for air.

2

Aftershocks

6.40pm

The ringing of the phone broke the stillness of the night. Fearing the worst, Jabbar picked up. It was Qasim, their middle child, calling from the hostel.

"*Abu* I just heard the news, is everything OK?"

"Yeah, I hope so, *beta*, so far, no news from your brothers, but I guess no news is good news, heh?" Jabbar tried to play it down as Fatima squeezed his hand encouragingly.

At the other end, Qasim could not help but grin as he heard his father's age-old philosophy repeated. Whenever he used to complain to his parents for not calling often enough when he first went away for studies, he would be given the same reply. But this time, in spite of his father's stoicism in the face of odds, Qasim could tell that the roles had been reversed and it was him who had to reassure his parents.

"Of course, *Abu jee*! You do not have to worry about anything; I talked to Mustafa *bhai* a couple of hours ago," he lied, playing for time.

"Mustafa *bhai* was at the shop; he said he had already paid the local police constable the weekly *hafta* as you had told him to. So, you should not worry about him; he must be at the shop, which is quite far away from the shrine anyway."

It was a shot in the dark and Qasim had no way of knowing if his words had the desired effect on his parents or not. Only once he heard Jabbar exhale at the other end did he allow himself the luxury of a smile. "It's OK, *Abu jee*," he repeated. "Don't worry, and tell *Ammi* that I am coming on Sunday; I want her to cook her special nihari for me, just like she always does. Abu, I have to go now, *Allah hafiz*."

"Will do, *beta, Allah hafiz*."

Jabbar pretended to scratch his jaw as he wiped away the tears. Fatima looked up at him and smiled. After all these years, it still never ceased to amaze Jabbar how the one person he had never counted upon could become such a pillar of strength for him.

All he had ever wanted was to join the army. But no matter how many push-ups he did, no matter how many times he sang to Noor Jehan's 'Aye Puttar Hattan Te Nai Wik De' or learned the lyrics of 'Aye Rah-e-Haq Ke Shaheedon', he could not imbibe in him the missing spark that the selection panel was looking for. Each time he was rejected, he became a little more defeated, a little more eroded. In time, life had consumed him, and he forgot his dreams and put his head down and plodded on. He had never wanted another son, his disappointment in Mustafa, and his realisation that somewhere down the line, it all boiled down to his own failure as a father, had left him completely disillusioned. However, the birth of Qasim – a completely unplanned and unwanted event – had changed him thoroughly. Like an answer from above, he had come into his life and from day one, ever since his tiny fingers had wrapped themselves tightly around his hand, Jabbar had found new strength and hope. The youngest of the three, Ijaz had grown up completely neglected by his father, relying on his elder brothers and the masjid Imam for guidance.

For Fatima, the birth of Qasim and the change it brought in her husband was proof of her faith. Right before her eyes, she saw each day her husband of old returning from the abyss. The cynicism and hopelessness had been washed away and he came back closer to her and to the family again. Jabbar found religion again. As all women are prone to, Fatima too knew without being told that both her other two sons had disappointed Jabbar, not living up to his dreams and aspirations, and she had prayed every night to God to bring her family back together.

Qasim had been the answer.

Jabbar had always wished for his first son to join the army. He had used all his connections and had got Mustafa, his eldest, inducted into Pakistan Military Academy Kakool as a junior cadet. But hardly a month in there and he had been expelled on the grounds of lack of discipline and possession of drugs.

The news had shocked and devastated Jabbar. He had had his first heart attack. Though he ultimately recovered, the wedge that had been forming between father and son for decades, was finally irrefutable and permanent. The two could not communicate directly anymore, all the years of neglect, of not being there, of not having a proper father-son relationship had transpired into an insurmountable wall that now could never be breached.

Although Jabbar had reconciled to the fact that his son would never share the same love for the army as he did – maybe it was testimony to the changing times and perceptions – but he could not bring himself to forgive him. On his part, Mustafa still held a grudge with his father for not letting him be his own man and for burdening him with the weight of expectations that Mustafa felt were unjustified.

It was the love for his mother which forced the middle-aged Mustafa to reach a compromise where he agreed to help his father at the shop. In time, a working relationship had developed, that was completely professional. Both Jabbar and Mustafa had tacitly reached an arrangement where they did not have to communicate with each other except through a third person, who was usually Qasim or Fatima.

The elder Kaleem would tend to the shop from morning till

noon and then he would come home, and Mustafa would take over; that way, both could also avoid having to be in each other's presence for too long. The situation ate at Fatima's heart, and every night she prayed for a way to mend the tear that had appeared in her family and to find a way to bring the two men in her life closer. And she waited for an answer which she was sure would come one day.

*

6.50pm

Inside Anarkali Ki Mashoor Fauji Tikka Shop, Mustafa had heard the blasts and felt the reverberations as they shattered one of the side windows. In spite of himself, his first thought had been for his father and mother. He laughed at his deep-rooted love for his father.

Well, what do you know, I still have feelings for Fauji, he thought.

Although he was smoking a joint, his mind was sharp enough to assess the situation. He came to the conclusion that keeping the shop open would be not only futile but also dangerous. He had seen plenty of shops and people being looted during the ensuing chaos after a terrorist attack. In fact, on more than one occasion, he had accompanied some of his drug addict friends during these activities when he needed some quick money for his needs.

But that was all in the past now. He had promised his mother to give up his former life of hard drugs, sticking to *chars* and homemade liquor. And although he did veer off the path on occasions, for the most part, he had parted ways from his past, acquaintances and all.

As he picked up the phone, Mustafa saw that the battery was almost finished. No sooner had he thought of staying inside the shop long enough to charge his phone, he was forced to veto it as the electricity went out. Mustafa shook his head, muttering a few choice expletives as he pulled down the shutters and locked the shop.

Out on the street, there was chaos everywhere. Out of the mayhem, he was able to find out that there had been two blasts at the Sufi shrine. Suddenly, Mustafa's usually stoic face went pale. "Oh my God! Ijaz!"

Throwing the half-lit beedi on the road, he started running in panic towards the shrine and soon got lost in the sea of humanity. Smoke continued to billow into the air from the sight of the blast.

*

Christian colony
7pm

The light was on in the one room that Sharoon, his mother, three sisters and Isaac shared with another family of four. As he peered in from the side window, everything seemed normal except for one key ingredient. The room was empty. The mattresses lay across the room just like his mother and sisters used to do. As he peered closer, he saw an overturned plate of rice and schoolbooks strewn about. It seemed that something or someone had made the occupants of the room leave without warning.

Feeling a hand on his shoulder, Sharoon whipped around and was about to plunge the shard of glass in his hand deep inside the stranger when he stopped. It was his youngest sister Jia, who was only six. Her face was tear-stained, and her hair had come loose from the pony that their mother used to make. She gave him a gap-toothed smile and hugged him tightly, in spite of the smell emanating from him.

"Jia." He held her tightly as he saw lights coming on in some of the adjoining rooms as neighbours poked their heads from behind windows and doors.

"*Bhai*, they hurt *Ammi*, asking about you, they even hit Jia," she croaked in a cracked voice that said more than her words could.

She must have cried and wailed until her voice had gone hoarse as none of the people he had grown up with had come forward to help her. Nobody wanted to tangle with the law.

In-between sobs, she told him how a police car had come to their slum and had asked specifically for him. When nobody could tell them where he was, they had taken both the families away. The only reason she had escaped was that she had been using the common latrine in the back.

Sharoon knew that it was impossible to spend another second in their home. With his shoulder throbbing with pain, he went inside and fashioned an arm brace with a piece of cloth. Then, carrying his sister in one arm, he was about to leave his home for good when his eyes caught something on the portable black-and-white television that had been left on. The news reporter was saying that the head of one of the suicide bombers had been recovered from the site and it had been identified. Sharoon's knees buckled when they showed the lifeless face of Isaac, naming him Muhammad Naeem. While Sharoon was still recovering from the shock, the reporter continued, saying that the police were on the lookout for a third bomber who had escaped.

Sharoon knew that his life hung by a thread when his own face flashed on the screen. Taking one last look at his home, Sharoon and his sister disappeared into the night.

*

Punjab University Hostel, Lahore
8.30pm

Qasim paced his room, a coursebook held absent-mindedly in his hand. His roommate – who had come back an hour ago looking crazy-eyed and smelling of blood and urine – looked up at him from his bed. Raja Niaz, a third-year student of political science and the president of the student body federation for the past seven years running, could not take the worry in his younger friend's countenance any longer.

He dropped the magazine he was browsing and got up. "That's it! Come on! Let's go." Being a local student body influential, authority and assertiveness came naturally to him.

Qasim stopped dead in his tracks; he had so far been unable to decipher the reason for the sudden liking that the feared and revered student leader had taken in a mere nobody such as him. So much so that he had managed to get a room in the hostel in his first semester which had been no mean feat. However, Qasim still trod carefully around his much bigger and volatile admirer who, only yesterday, had shown what happened if someone crossed him. Raja Niaz had beaten a boy to near death for merely talking to a girl that he fancied. The poor boy had only been exchanging some notes.

Niaz and his followers were quick to espouse the ideology of the federation to anyone who cared to listen; boys and girls were different species, who may sit under the same roof but could not and, more importantly, should not, interact. Unless it was after marriage, but that was not of much interest to Niaz. The university was his universe, and while you lived in his kingdom, you had to abide by the rules. Many had realised that the only way lay in either following the rules to the letter or joining the federation and becoming a foot soldier under Niaz, which brought its own set of privileges and demands. It was this single-track ruthlessness and tenacity to the task that had seen Raja Niaz rise up the ranks from a mere enforcer to now being the head of the student body of one of the largest national universities. It was his task to be on the lookout for and to recruit like-minded individuals who would come in handy for the party later. For Niaz, the party was the be-all and end-all of everything that mattered.

It had provided him, a mere nobody, with respect and shelter.

And he intended to repay that trust. No matter what it took, no matter how many bones he had to crush, how many fledgling romances he had to trample upon. It was all for a cause that he believed in.

And that was all that mattered.

"What, Niaz *bhai*? Go where?" Qasim asked cautiously.

"Let's go for a ride to the shrine, and anyway, I cannot stand your incessant walks anymore; I know you are worried, let's put them to rest," he said as he slipped into his shoes and walked out of the room as if the matter had been closed and decided.

Qasim had no time to argue as he quickly followed his roommate downstairs. Within seconds, he was holding on for dear life as they sped towards the shrine.

*

Anarkali 1996

It was mid-afternoon; Ijaz was playing hide-and-seek with the other kids in the street while Qasim watched, as he wrapped a cloth around the handle of his makeshift cricket bat. A while later, Qasim looked up to see four-year-old Ijaz sitting pensively beside him, deep in thought. He knew immediately that something was bothering him.

"Why aren't you playing with your friends?"

Ijaz shrugged and rubbed his toes in the mud.

"Come on, tell me what's wrong," he said as he stretched out his arms. Ijaz jumped up and ran into his embrace, hugging him fiercely.

"I don't want to be lost," he mumbled; his face pressed tightly against his elder brother's chest.

Qasim pulled his head back and looked at him. "What are you talking about?"

Ijaz would not meet his gaze. "Like *Abu* says Mustafa *bhai* is lost, I don't want to get lost so that no one can find me."

Qasim smiled and hugged his brother tightly. "You will never get lost; I promise you."

"But what if I am?" Ijaz was not convinced.

"No, you will not, you know why?"

"Why?"

Qasim reached inside his shirt and pulled off the silver chain from around his neck and placed it around Ijaz.

Ijaz's eyes went wide. "This is your tawiz," he whispered.

"Yes, it is," said Qasim solemnly. "*Ammi* put it around my neck when I was born so that nothing ever happens to me; her prayers are in here," he said as he showed Ijaz the leather pouch.

Ijaz nodded, transfixed. "And now I am giving it to you," said Qasim as he tucked the tawiz inside Ijaz's shirt. "As long as you wear this, I will always find you. You will never be lost."

Ijaz smiled, showing his gums as he hugged his brother tightly, then ran away to join his friends.

*

2007
Data Darbar
8.35pm

A group of turbaned youngsters in long, flowing white robes stood a little distance away from the media circus that had engulfed the Sufi shrine as each channel news anchor vied for the best vantage point to deliver the most bombastic version of the incident in their report with the medical ambulances carrying the dead and wounded away in the background. The police and other security officials tried unsuccessfully to push the crowd away from the scene of the blast and to salvage some of the evidence. But it was a losing battle and one they gave up easily once they realised that whatever evidence there may have been on the ground was now pasted under the soles of hundreds of feet.

Ijaz sat with his friends and watched the whole scene unfolding before his eyes. As he looked at the crowd that continued to grow, he saw people breaking down, crying and tearing their hair out as they caught sight of their loved ones. There were people coming in hordes from the nearby mohallas as they helped the emergency carriers in recovering the wounded from the rubble. There were long lines of media cars with crews jostling for space. And then in-between the melee, there sat a man outside a dhaba, calmly sipping his tea. It almost seemed as if he was an artist surveying his magnum opus. There was an air of calm serenity with which he was tilting the chair back on its rear legs as he rocked back and forth, as if giddy with delight. From across the road and over the heads of the people milling about, the stranger and Ijaz locked eyes. It was only a second, but to Ijaz, it seemed like there was no one else but him and the stranger. He felt as if the stranger could see right through all the layers, into his heart. It was Ijaz who looked away first. When he looked back at the spot, the stranger was gone.

As he searched, suddenly Ijaz's eyes caught a familiar figure pushing and shoving worriedly through the crowd. For the most fleeting of seconds, he lost his composure as he recognised his elder brother looking frantically for him. In that moment, he was once again a crawling toddler vying for affection. In the next moment, he brought his emotions under control again as he casually got up from his place and walked over.

"Mustafa *bhai*!" He put his hand on his brother's shoulder as the latter looked around frantically.

The relief falling across Mustafa's face was palpable as he whirled around and saw Ijaz. He crushed his younger sibling in a bone-crunching embrace.

"*Shukar hai Khuda ka*," exhaled Mustafa. "Where were you

Ijaz? I feared you would be at the shrine too." Try as he might, he could not hide his immense relief.

Ijaz shook his head and sighed; no matter what he tried, he was unable to make his family members see what was clear as daylight to him. "*Bhai* this is a Barelvi shrine! That is not true Islam; I thought you listened to me," he smirked. "These Sufis and shrine worshippers deserve what they got."

Mustafa had never been an orthodox practising Muslim himself, offering the occasional Jummah or Eid prayer, but even to him, the cool and nonchalant way in which Ijaz had dismissed the killing of innocent lives came as a shock. Before he could control himself, he slapped his younger brother, sending the turban flying off. His other madrassah friends bristled and surrounded him. But Ijaz motioned them off and quietly picked up his turban and took Mustafa by the shoulder. He knew that his elder brother meant well.

"Come, *bhai*, let us go home, *Ammi* and *Abu* must be worried," he said tactfully, trying to defuse the situation. He knew that this was not the time to get into an argument. His heart also went out to his brother for having come all the way to look for him. Mustafa could tell when he was being manipulated and controlled, but Ijaz was the one person in the world against whom he could never muster up the resistance. He was already regretting raising his hand at his brother. He forced a smile and put his hand on Ijaz's cheek, where an angry red welt was fast spreading.

"Ijaz *meri jaan*! I'm sorry; I lost control; I was worried about you," he began sheepishly.

"*Bhai*, don't worry about it! You are my elder brother; forget about it; let's go home." Ijaz motioned to his friends and walked away with his brother.

"Look at your hair," said Mustafa, trying to change the subject as he playfully pulled at his younger brother's shoulder-length locks. "You look like that girl in our mohalla you really liked – what was her name? Rani? Saima?"

"I was not interested in any girls," said Ijaz, reddening as he tried to hide his face.

"Nida!" exclaimed Mustafa, pleased with himself. "You always insisted on being her husband when you little ones would play *ghar ghar*." He beamed and poked Ijaz.

"I'm not interested in any girls, *bhai*," he repeated, albeit a little tentatively.

If Mustafa caught the nervousness in Ijaz's voice, he didn't show it. With one arm around his younger companion's neck, the two brothers started walking towards home.

*

8.45pm

Jabbar and Fatima had waited as much as they could. No longer able to stay on the terrace because of the mosquitoes and the stifling heat, both had decided that the only recourse was to take a walk and try to get some news. There was nothing more reliable and faster than the local grapevine when it came to news and gossip. The electricity had still not returned and was not expected to be back for another couple of hours.

As they walked down the stairs, a newly married couple from Gujranwala, who had rented out the lower portion of the house, greeted them. The husband ran a small dahi bhalla cart that his wife cooked for him every day, which he moved about all over the city. It was a meagre existence and sometimes the couple were late on rent. But Jabbar and Fatima enjoyed their company and overlooked such inconveniences. The house had got too big for them ever since Jabbar's brother had moved out and now, with Qasim gone and Ijaz hardly ever at home, it made sense economically and also socially to have the young family as tenants.

"*Assalaam Alaikum*, Chacha Fauji, where are you and *bari*

Amma off to at this time and tonight of all nights? Have you not heard what has happened?" Riaz, the husband who was just wearing a vest due to the humidity and heat, hurriedly tried to put on his sweaty and tattered kameez, wearing it inside out in the process. His wife brought the candle in one hand and carried their two-month-old daughter on her hip.

The little girl cooed playfully at Fatima, who took her and cuddled and smothered her in kisses as the child giggled.

Jabbar lit his cigarette as Fatima clucked disapprovingly. "Yes, we heard; we were just worried about Mustafa and Ijaz – we have been unable to get any word from them."

"Oh *acha*." Riaz nodded understandingly. "Have you tried their mobile?"

"Yes, but it's not getting through, *Allah na karey* something bad has happened."

Fatima and Riaz's wife both looked up worriedly.

"Oho, Chacha, *aap fikr naa karen, inshallah kuch nain hoga*." Riaz tried pacifying the older man as he could tell that the urge to smoke was more out of anxiety than need.

"Come! I will go with you, and we will try to find out, no need to make *bari Amma* walk in the dark."

Fatima patted him on the back and sat down with his wife as the two men walked out into the night.

*

8.50pm

Qasim tried to keep his mind on the road as Raja Niaz bent and swerved the motorbike at breakneck speeds in-between vehicles. In spite of the life-threatening situation he was in and despite the overbearing worry of his little brother, Qasim's mind kept drifting back to earlier that day.

It was the last lecture of the day. The weather was hot and humid, and the old fan creaked and groaned overhead, trying vainly to stir the heavy air. They were discussing the legal system of Pakistan and how it needed to be overhauled, considering the flaws in the terrorist prosecution system.

Qasim was sitting in the front row, vehemently explaining his point to the professor, oblivious to everything and everyone, his white starched shalwar kameez now all crumpled and soggy with sweat as it clung to his back. But if he was aware or uncomfortable, he did not seem to show it.

"Sir, my whole point of view is that our prosecution fails precisely because there are flaws in our judicial set-up; we need to make amendments and change the laws in accordance with the rest of the world."

The professor smiled, proud of having awakened some interest in one of his students. He nodded and looked to the rest of the class. "Well? Does anyone have a counterargument?" he asked.

From somewhere to his right, a hand had instantly gone up. Qasim bent forward to have a look. The girl, still with her hand up, looked back at him, her eyes blazing with fervour and something else that he felt but didn't recognise. The professor motioned for her to speak. As she began, Qasim turned around in his chair and looked at her, his expression hard to read.

For a second, Asma felt all choked up, and she could not utter a single word. As the seconds dragged on, she felt the eyes of the whole class on her. Qasim smiled encouragingly and nodded. And suddenly, she felt buoyant and confident about herself again.

"I agree with the premise that our law needs to change with regards to terrorist prosecution myself. I think right now, the definition of terrorism is too broad and as such, too many frivolous cases, such as kidnapping for ransom and acid-throwing, also get charged in the anti-terrorist courts and these are burdening the courts with too much workload, which then translates into a backlog of cases that hinders speedy justice." Asma found herself out of breath and looking at Qasim instead of the professor for approval.

He nodded and smiled encouragingly and turned towards the professor, who shrugged. "Hey don't look at me, she is asking you – what do you think about it?" The class laughed. Asma blushed.

Qasim turned back once again to face Asma.

He cleared his throat and began. "OK, what you said is actually correct, and I do agree with it, in essence, but that is not our main concern right now. The parliament, or whoever makes the decision, can change the definition of terrorism whenever they want to, bu—"

"How can you say that?!" Suddenly, all nervousness was forgotten as Asma found herself being drawn into the argument. "The case and proceedings flow from the definition of the crime; if you spread yourself too thin, you are bound to lose focus and the perpetrators of the crime slip through the loopholes."

"True, true." Qasim nodded encouragingly and Asma felt like a child being coaxed and cajoled into solving a tricky problem on her own. "But even though you have the right concept, I'm afraid you are missing the point here. We do not have to reinvent the wheel; once we get the proper amendments in the law, these wide definitions would solve themselves and such cases would no longer be dealt with under the anti-terrorist law."

Flustered at being treated like a child, Asma lashed out wildly and threw the kitchen sink at Qasim. "How can you say that?! Do you think that acid-throwing is not a form of terrorism? That is such a male chauvinistic thing to say! Would you rather have all women in burqas and not leaving the house?"

Qasim was flabbergasted. He sat up straight and looked around helplessly, all his confidence and poise of a few seconds ago, gone.

"No! Not at all, that is not what I meant."

"Well, you certainly implied it."

"I was merely talking about updating the mechanism of how evidence is gathered and what sort of evidence is admissible in the court."

"You do not think that terrorism against women is of any national importance," Asma said in a mock grave tone as her eyes twinkled.

"I assure you that that was not my intention. I have the highest regard for womenfolk; I was not even discussing this topic!"

"Of course, you weren't!"

"I mean, not that it's not important."

"Just that you are not interested in it."

Qasim tried to speak but nothing would come out anymore; beads of perspiration had formed on his brow. Asma smiled and nodded encouragingly. Something about the glint in her eyes or a telepathic connection made between the two at that moment gave her away. The realisation that it had all been a set-up suddenly dawned on Qasim, and he smiled back.

Just then, the bell rang, and the class dispersed. As the students all left the classroom, Qasim saw flashes of Asma through the milling mass of students as he sat in his seat, looking at her.

*

9pm

They had been walking for an hour as the pain in his shoulder had left Sharoon in a trance where he was only conscious of putting one foot in front of another in his desperate bid to put as much distance between himself and the police.

"*Bhaiya*, I'm hungry," said Jia in a weak voice. He patted the back of her head and tried to force her back to sleep, but she refused and started to cry.

"*Buss buss, acha*," he comforted her. He looked up to get his bearings. He recognised the dry fruits and kite ships of Mochi Gate. He smiled as he set his sister down on the ground and fished in his pocket for his wallet.

His face fell as he remembered the ordeal he had been through. The police had his wallet along with his daily wages and his identity card. He looked down at his sister, who was looking up at him with big eyes. He forced a smile. "What would you like to eat?"

"Jalebi." Jia beamed.

He grinned. "Jalebi? At this hour? How about some pulao?" he asked as he noticed a man distributing plates of pulao among the people from the back of a van.

Jia nodded. "OK, wait here; I'll be right back," said Sharoon as he made his way into the large crowd that had gathered around the van. As he waded into the crowd, he realised immediately that it was a bad idea as the pain in his shoulder sent bolts of electricity throughout his body. People closed in on him from all sides. There was no way to protect his broken shoulder as he was punched, pushed, kicked and clawed from all sides. The image of his sister waiting for him to bring food kept popping before him as he forced back his tears and persisted through the agony.

After what seemed like hours, he finally made his way to the front of the crowd. Grabbing hold of the back of the van, he looked up at the man who had been distributing the pulao.

The man tilted the large pot to him. It was empty.

Sharoon let go of the van and fell back on the ground as the van sped away. He sobbed as his hands dug into the ground. Finally, he got up and turned around. There was a man sitting with Jia, as she pointed straight towards him. Forgetting all about his pain, Sharoon leapt off the ground and ran across the road towards his sister.

When he got close, he saw that she was smiling and holding onto two bright orange pieces of jalebi in her grubby hands. A full plate of steaming samosas lay on the table in front of her.

"*Bhaiya!*" She smiled at him, proudly showing him the jalebis.

Sharoon looked at the man, a knot tightening in his stomach. The man smiled back at him and pushed the plate of samosas across the table towards him.

"Don't worry; you're safe," he said in a calm voice that seemed to convey that he knew more about Sharoon than seemed possible.

"Who are you?" whispered Sharoon as he fought with himself to just give up and gorge on the food or to keep up his guard and protect himself and his sister.

The man leaned forward and patted Jia's head as he placed another jalebi on her plate. Then he looked up at Sharoon. "I'm a friend," he said.

*

Defence Phase 4, Lahore
9.15pm

The dog had been running for three miles as the Land Cruiser chased it over the deserted road. Every time it tried to escape, the jeep would swerve and cut off its path, the beam from the headlights acting like a cage. Its ribs poked from its side, its tongue rolling out, the whites of its eyes showed fear as it struggled to stay away from the menacing tyres of the vehicle which threatened to run it over. Whenever the dog would slow down or look back, it would be shot with air gun pellets, making it yelp and howl in pain as it tried to get out of its predicament.

Finally, its body riddled with pellet marks, lungs heaving against the ribcage, the dog crumpled in the middle of the road as its legs gave out from under. Its ears pinned back, and with its teeth barred, it looked at the idling jeep a few feet away, awaiting its death.

"Come on, get up," shouted one of the boys, poking his head outside the window and throwing an empty beer can towards the exhausted dog which didn't have the energy to dodge as the boy and his friends proceeded to throw stones and bottles at it. Some of them found their mark as the dog yelped in pain, but it had no energy to run anymore.

"Well, this sucks," said one of the girls.

"Who's in the mood for some taka-tak?" said the boy. The suggestion was met with cheers as everyone got back in the jeep. Suddenly, a shot rang out from the darkness, shattering the windscreen, sending shards of glass into the night. The girls shrieked and even the boy looked scared.

"What the hell?" All the bravado seemed to have gone out of his voice.

"Let's get out of here." One of the girls had started crying.

As he started to turn the jeep around, there was another shot and one of the tyres burst.

"Oh my God, what's happening?" the girl shrieked. There was another shot as the second tyre burst.

"Hey, who is this?" said the boy in a shrieky voice. "Come out and show yourself."

They were in an undeveloped part of DHA (Defence Housing Authority) with no street lamps, the headlights from the jeep throwing back emptiness and shrubs that dissolved into darkness. There were two shots as the headlights of the jeep were shattered, pitching the area into complete darkness.

The shrieks of the girls rang out into the night, coming back to them accompanied by the howls of jackals in the distance. With trembling hands, the boy switched on the torchlight on his phone. He flashed the beam in a wide arc, stopping mid-motion as he spotted something that had not been there before.

Standing directly in front, as if he had been there all the time, was a man, dressed from head to toe in black, sitting on a black motorcycle. The boy mustered up the last dredges of courage and said: "*Oye Chu...*" The boy stopped dead in his tracks. He had not seen the man move, but suddenly he was looking down the barrel of a gun that was aimed straight at his head.

There was a red glow in the darkness as Deemu puffed on his cigarette before throwing away the stub. He got off his black Kawasaki 250 and smoothed down his kameez. He stopped near the dog, bent down, patted the dog and took out a biscuit from his pocket which he put in front of it.

"Hey, fuckface!" The boy felt like he was losing face in front of his girlfriend and others and made a last attempt. He approached Deemu with disdain and contempt. "Do you know who I am?"

Whatever he wanted to tell about his family connections and influence got shoved back inside his mouth with force as Deemu got off the ground with lightning speed, bringing the barrel of the 9mm Glock crashing against the nose of the boy and sending him sprawling into the dust.

There was stunned silence as the boy tasted blood and dust; he opened his eyes to see the dark figure towering over him. With the gun pointed directly at him, the boy could feel something warm and wet trickling down his leg as he felt real fear for the first time in his life.

"You are someone who likes to hurt helpless creatures," said Deemu in a soft voice, as he cleaned the blood off the barrel against the side of his leg before pointing it at the boy again. "Who among you can finish this phrase, 'barking dogs…'?" There was pin-drop silence. After a minute, the second boy raised his hand and said, "Seldom bite?"

Deemu nodded approvingly. "Good," he said. "You get to keep your shoes."

Deemu turned to the boy, who cowered as Deemu leaned down and patted him on the head. "Well, unfortunately for you, this one bites," he whispered.

"Please, I beg you," the boy wailed. "I'll do anything – what do you want?"

Two hours later, when a group of blindfolded students, all belonging to powerfully connected families, were found half stumbling, half running on the road, in bleeding bare feet – with the exception of one boy who still wore his trainers – and clad only in undergarments, they had no name or description for their tormentor who had made them leave their clothes, shoes and wallets in the Land Cruiser and set it on fire.

As for the dog, the last they remembered was the stranger scooping it up and putting it on his bike as he followed them, shooting at their feet whenever one of them would slow down.

Nobody could remember when he had disappeared off into the night.

*

11pm

By the time the men arrived, both women had already run out of topics. The little girl who had been making 'small talk' with her antics had long fallen asleep in Fatima's arms.

Seeing her husband and sons back gave new energy to Fatima. She wanted to jump off the chair and hug her children, but the arthritis in her bones wouldn't let her.

Eventually, Qasim had to step forward to help his mother. Seeing the family reunited, Riaz and his wife bid goodnight and retreated to their portion of the house.

Whether it was the heat or the enormity of the event, no one could sleep that night. For the first time in many years, the whole family sat together in the living room and talked. For once, the walls were down; the shock was too much for other emotions to find a place.

After the first hour, the candle burnt itself out, engulfing everyone in its strangely welcoming and soothing darkness. The effect of the darkness was almost instantaneous; somehow the invisibility leant a cloak of intimacy that let down the self-imposed walls, and everyone talked more openly than they had in a long time.

For Fatima, the time spent in pitch-black darkness and stifling heat were the best three hours she had experienced in a while. Finally, one by one, all the boys bid goodnight and went to sleep until it was once again just her and Jabbar left in the darkness.

After all these years, both could read each other's moods and expressions even in the darkness.

"What are you so happy about tonight of all nights?" Fatima could hear the smile in his mock gruff tone.

"Even you have to admit that our family has not been together like this in a long time."

The thought had crossed his mind too, but he playfully continued to tease his wife. "Don't tell me you think this is God's way of bringing us together."

Fatima had never approved of her beliefs and faith being mocked, but this time she knew that Jabbar was only teasing her and so she refused to take the bait.

"*Nain naa*, you know what I mean, what has happened is terrible, we both know it, but pessimism is haram in Islam and there is always something good in God's actions; you cannot disagree that this incident has brought all my family together under one roof after the longest time, and not only that, but we have also talked."

Jabbar picked up his things and touched Fatima's cheek lovingly as he went into the bedroom, a sign that he completely agreed with what she had said.

"I hope you are right, Fatu." He called her by the name he had coined when they fell in love, bringing a smile to her face. What he said next chilled her to the bone.

"But make no mistake about it, tonight was not God's decree – it was man killing man."

3

There will be a reckoning

The next day
Mayo Hospital, Emergency and Trauma Department
5.30am

It had been a slow night for Ahmed, the doctor on call, and he had got a good nap, while also making use of the free minutes on his mobile package to talk for an hour to his fiancée who was studying in Karachi.

But all that had changed an hour ago when he had been called by the attending nurse. After he had promised to call back his soon-to-be wife, the young doctor had gone to the reception to find a dirty, ragged mutt, with pellet marks all over its body, lying on his table.

"What is the meaning of this?" bellowed the young doctor. "Nurse! Come in here immediately." He raised his arm to strike the dog when he heard a calm voice behind him.

"I wouldn't do that if I were you."

The doctor whipped around to find a tall boy his own age standing in the corner. The angry words that had been about to come out of his mouth sputtered and died inside as he made eye contact with the stranger.

Deemu cocked his head towards the table. "Jeera needs your help."

The doctor gulped, turning and pointing towards the dog who was chewing on a file as its tail wagged absent-mindedly.

"Jeera?" asked the doctor.

Deemu nodded. "He's had a rough night."

"But, but, I'm… I'm…" The doctor wanted to say something to the stranger, but something in his calm, almost amused, expression told him not to step across an invisible line.

Deemu cracked his knuckles and stretched his arms to yawn as the doctor caught a glint of steel and saw the gun tucked in his waistband. Suddenly, all the doubt was gone as the colour rushed from his face.

"Nurse," he said in a quivering voice, "get the operation theatre ready, now!"

Deemu nodded approvingly and tilted a chair against the wall as he sat down.

*

Anarkali Bazaar
6am

Two crows basked in the early morning sunshine on a broken streetlight, their cries ushering in the new day. Underneath their watchful eyes, the bazaar slowly wobbled unsteadily to its feet like an old person, brushing the sleep out of its eyes. Two dhoti-clad men, carrying a large plastic bag between them, made their way nonchalantly across the single-lane road which, in a few hours, would be choked with cars, rickshaws, tongas, trucks and a sea of humanity. Off to one side, the municipality worker went through the motions of picking up yesterday's refuse, trying to reclaim some portion of the road that had been buried under decades of refuse and rubbish.

The fruit seller eyed both sides of the road suspiciously as he carried his day's business on his head. Some of the early morning risers, who had already opened their shops, winked and waved at each other as they nodded at the shopkeeper, who had recently set up his fruit cart outside the Atom Bomb Chicken Cholay. There were rumours that he was applying some sort of polish on his foot-long bananas, making them extra appealing in order to compete with the older and more established Haji Fruit Shop that only sold the tiny dotted local bananas, owing to a patriotic streak that he harboured.

Haji Ramzan, the owner, pretended not to notice his competitor as he buried his face in the morning newspaper. Sadiq, his second in command, sat at his feet, feverishly brushing the mangled and pulverised piece of *miswaak* against his teeth and sporadically flashing a grin to check out the progress in the reflection of his Honda 125's sparkling spoke.

Further down the road, two boys were bathing beside the British-era hand pump that still worked due to the regular upkeep and maintenance that had been amicably agreed upon and divided between all the shopkeepers who used its water along the road. Once the shorter of the two boys had washed off all the dirt and grime and donned his tattered kurta, he climbed on the back of the milkman's cart and was off to make rounds. The boy waved at a couple of his friends from the mohalla who were busy climbing the spiked gates of a government school and jumping back as the guard ran up and rattled his baton against the metallic spikes. The elder brother watched from afar, pouring the steel glass mechanically over his head after he had filled it from the bucket. He took his time and finished only when he could see Hakeem's barbershop down the road opening as his uncle arrived and unlocked the shutters.

The sounds of the gola ganda cart rolling into the market had already brought some early morning risers out of their beds and into the bazaar. They stood and waited patiently with their grandparents as the ice candyman shaved the ice, stuffed it into a plastic cup and poured different coloured syrups from the many bottles that stood glittering on his cart. Next to his cart, the shikanjabeen seller eyed his rival with unbridled jealousy and looked skywards at the sun, willing it to fasten its ascent so that his business could also start booming. He vowed to himself that the cool drinks he made that day would be extra cold and sweet so that no one would ever dare think of choosing a gola ganda over his mashroobaat.

Done with his Fajr prayer, Jabbar and Riaz made their way down the bazaar, pausing beside the open tents of the Landa bazaar that held the clothes, shoes and other belongings of generations of people – old, new, foreign and local – who had never imagined that one day a part of them would be on display outside a tattered tent in Anarkali. Just yesterday, Jabbar had got Fatima a pair of brown joggers that the shopkeeper, a boy not older than Mustafa, had assured him had been worn by Princess Diana when she had come to Pakistan at the request of Imran Khan.

"Chacha *ji*, I'm telling you," he had said as he thrust the shoes in Jabbar's hands while snatching the hundred rupee note from him simultaneously, "she was so sad to let these shoes go, but her baggage was over the limit. *Aapko tau pata hai, jinnay Laorenai takkiya o jammiya ee nai.*" He grinned, showing a line of red-stained teeth.

Fatima had smiled and clapped like a little girl when he had given her the shoes, accompanied by the backstory which had made her eyes pop out like saucers with excitement. It never ceased to amaze him how the little things always made his wife happy. Jabbar looked at the rows of shirts and jackets that hung from the roof of the tent and contemplated on buying something for himself. But then he caught a whiff of the pooris being fried over the large pan and his grumbling stomach made the decision for him. He shuffled down the road towards his shop, stopping only to lift his hand and motion to the boy making the pooris to send a plate of *nashta* to him. The boy nodded without breaking his motion of swirling the pooris in the boiling hot oil and fishing them out with his large spoon, without spilling a drop.

It never ceased to amaze Jabbar how quickly life returned to normal, no matter how big a calamity.

Was man really that insensitive? Was that not wrong? There were times when he felt cornered in his own mind by scepticism. *If only Qasim were here*, he thought, *he would make my thoughts go away with his logical arguments.* Jabbar smiled to himself. Thoughts of his favourite reminded him of the meeting that day at his brother's house, and he got up to leave. As if on cue, the mobile rang – it was Fatima telling him to hurry up as she was ready to go. Telling Riaz to look after the shop, Jabbar walked home.

*

6.10 am

With her stomach full, Jia had fallen asleep in the warm comfort of the space between the stranger and Sharoon as they drove through the streets. All around them, the city was slowly waking up.

Sharoon gritted his teeth as the pain in his arm throbbed with each turn and brake, but he kept his mouth shut and his eyes open. The stranger had fed them and promised to help them, and although Sharoon knew enough not to trust strangers, he agreed to go along since he had his sister to care for.

Presently, they pulled up into the parking of the Mayo Hospital. As they walked inside the Emergency Department, the stranger told them to sit down while he went to talk to the nurse at the reception. Fear at being handed over to the police again gripped Sharoon's heart for a second, but then a combination of tiredness, worry for his sister, a lack of options and the pain in his shoulder convinced him to push the thought out of his mind.

As soon as he sat down on a plastic chair in the waiting area and closed his eyes, Sharoon fell into a fitful sleep. There were people chasing him even in his sleep, and they were gaining on him as he found his feet suddenly turn to lead. He tried to shout but found that his mouth had been stitched shut. In his panic, he thrashed his broken arm and woke up with a scream of pain. As his hand fell on the empty chair beside him, he realised that Jia was missing.

He jumped out of his chair and was about to shout out his sister's name when he heard a squeal of laughter in the far corner of the empty room. Relief washed over his face when he saw Jia kneeling in front of a heavily bandaged dog and feeding it jalebi which she had saved in her pocket. There was a tall boy, a little older than him, standing watching them. Sharoon looked over at the reception where the stranger was still talking to the nurse and a doctor and pointing towards him. The stranger nodded at him and gestured five minutes. Sharoon nodded and made his way towards his sister.

The tall boy was leaning against the wall and chewing a toothpick as Jia sat on the floor patting the dog and talking excitedly.

"What's it called?" she was asking when Sharoon reached them. The tall boy turned towards him and gave him a quick look. Sharoon was worried that he might recognise his face from the news last night. The boy's expression was imperceptible as his sharp eyes bore into Sharoon. His expression did not change, and after a couple of seconds, he nodded at Sharoon, who exhaled and nodded back.

"Why don't you pick one," said the boy from the side of his mouth.

"Jeera," Jia squealed with delight. "Jeera blade?" she added.

The boy kept a straight face as he nodded, but his eyes laughed as he reached inside his pocket to take something out and extend towards Jia in one smooth motion before Sharoon could react. As he opened his palm, Sharoon saw that it was a candy which Jia quickly grabbed with both hands and gave a huge grin to the boy who was already walking out the door.

As Sharoon and Jia looked at the empty doorway, there was a whistle from beyond and then the sound of paws on the floor as the bandaged dog bounded across the room and out through the doorway after the boy.

*

6.20 am

Asma had been driving aimlessly all night when finally, her vintage 1969 model, navy blue with two white stripes, Volkswagen Beetle sputtered to a halt, bringing her back to reality. She looked out the window and saw the imposing figure of the Lahore High Court in the distance. She tried to turn on the ignition, but the engine would die down after a few sputters each time.

"No, no no," she said as she banged her hands on the steering wheel.

"You're out of petrol," said a voice outside her window, making Asma jump with fright.

"*Ji bohut shukriya.*" She shielded her tear-stained face with her hand and turned away from the window, wishing the stranger would go away. From the corner of her eyes, she could see that he had not left.

"Please *aap chalay jayen* I can handle this," she said as she tried to start the car.

"You'll die out the battery," shouted the stranger over the noise of the sputtering engine.

What is this guy's problem? thought Asma as she finally looked up with hatred towards all men spewing out from her eyes.

"Would you please get the fu..." She stopped short as she recognised the boy from her class standing outside her window.

"Fine by me," said a red-faced Qasim as he turned around and made his way back to the bus stop.

"Wait! Please stop," shouted Asma as she got out of the car. This was the first time she had called out to someone and they had not come running back. Qasim was standing halfway between her and the bus stop, looking at her with a bemused look, his pack slung over his shoulder. Inexplicably, Asma found herself walking towards him.

"I think I'm out of petrol," she said when she reached him.

Qasim thought about it for a second and then nodded. "I remember saying as much," he said with a deadpan expression that Asma found both endearing and irritating.

"I'm in your class," she said.

"Good for you." He puffed and pretended to check his nails.

"Urrghhhhhh," groaned Asma. "Such little boys you are," she muttered as she composed herself, then turned towards Qasim. "I'm sorry for shouting at you; I really need your help." She held out her hand. "I'm Asma."

For the briefest of seconds, he seemed to consider; then he clasped her hand in a firm shake. "Qasim," he said. "There's a petrol pump a few kilometres down the road, although," he added as he looked at her high heels, "I'm not sure you are dressed for the occasion."

"*Ji nahin*," said Asma as she took off her heels and stood up on tiptoes excitedly. "Whatever you can do, so can I."

"I never said you couldn't," smiled Qasim as he started walking up the road.

"Oh yes you did," shouted Asma as she ran to catch up.

*

6.30 am

As had been her practice ever since she had been a little girl in her parents' home, Fatima had got up at the break of dawn. Without making a noise or turning on the light, she had moved about the house in total darkness, her acute sense of direction and her calloused but firm hands guiding her through the walls of the abode she had come to call home.

With a loving glance, she looked at the indentations left on the bed where Jabbar had slept. Like always, he had already gone to the mosque to be the first one to open the door and make the call to prayer. Fatima felt an overwhelming feeling of love for her husband and the life they had been able to build. It had all been possible due to the strength of belief Jabbar had in himself and in what he felt they could achieve. Her constant companion and rock for the past four decades. Lately, he had started showing signs of slowing down as age had finally started catching up to Jabbar. Fear gripped Fatima's heart as she thought of the future, but then she relaxed as she remembered the decision she and Jabbar had come to a couple of days ago.

They would ask for Nida's hand in marriage for Qasim. It was the perfect match. Not only was Nida's father a well-established businessman of substantial standing in the area, but he also ran a successful dry fruit shop. Fatima had practically raised Nida as she lived in the same street and had grown up playing with her children, especially Ijaz, who was her exact age.

Fatima knew that Mustafa was the eldest and he should have been the first one to be married, but she had cried plenty of nights over how Mustafa had changed from a bright, cheerful boy to a resentful drug addict right in front of her eyes. It was her love that kept him still under her roof and making an effort to help around the house and at the shop. As a mother, she would always hold out hope and pray for a miracle. But beyond that, Fatima could not bring herself to ruin some poor girl's life by marrying her to Mustafa; he was too far gone.

The first streaks of dawn were creeping across the sky as Fatima poured a large cup of doodh pati for herself and sat down on the balcony, feeding bits of her paratha to the birds that landed on the ledge. Ten minutes later, as she was dunking the last bite of the paratha into her doodh pati, Jabbar called to her from downstairs. She smiled and waved back. Draping a shawl around herself, she joined her husband downstairs as they got inside a chingchi rickshaw and made their way out of Anarkali.

After half an hour of weaving their way through the early morning traffic, they reached the bridge overlooking the Ravi. Jabbar paid the chingchi driver and they made their way down the bridge to the river. At that time of the day, there were only a few people near the water, as a couple of boats lazily floated in the middle. But Fatima had no time or patience for sightseeing. Holding firmly to Jabbar's hand, she led him confidently along the riverbed to the farthest corner under the bridge where an old man sat under a makeshift tent. As they got closer, Fatima could see that the old man was bare from the waist up, his skin pockmarked with lesions and cuts and pores filled with pus from swimming in the toxic waters of the river. Her heart fluttered, but she was determined and kept walking.

When they got up close, the old man looked up and gave them a distant look, showing his bleeding gums with a solitary long tooth hanging in the middle. A young boy was sitting at the feet of the old man, massaging his legs with mustard oil. The boy fished around in his pocket and took out a half-burnt cigarette which he lit up and placed in the corner of the old man's mouth. After a couple of puffs, the old man straightened and focused his eyes on the couple.

Fatima nodded as she held the cover of the shawl in her teeth, hiding the lower part of her face. The old man nodded and held out his hand. Fatima tugged at Jabbar's sleeve and motioned with her head towards the outstretched hand. Jabbar shook his head but didn't say anything as he took out the hundred rupee note from his breast pocket and handed it to the old man, who in turn handed it to the boy, got up and, without another word, started walking towards the river. Fatima, Jabbar and the boy followed. At the edge of the water, the old man spread out a prayer mat and prayed for five minutes as the other three watched. After finishing his prayer, the old man snubbed out the cigarette with his tongue, stuck it behind his ear and beckoned Fatima and Jabbar towards him.

Through signs and bits of broken words, he made them face the water and close their eyes. Then the boy handed Fatima and Jabbar two plastic bags filled with raw meat which they were to throw over their heads behind them. They were told to dream of what they wanted and to pray in their hearts. As Fatima's hands went inside the plastic bag again and again, she dreamed of Qasim's wedding to Nida and the happy future of their family. Her heart stopped as she felt the presence of a large being land behind her. She could smell the meat as its talons dug into it and then she could feel the bones and flesh being torn apart as something colossal and deathly devoured it. In spite of being told not to, Fatima opened her eyes and turned around. She saw a huge shadow blocking out the sun and she smelled the putrid stench of death and the fluttering of wings before she felt light-headed and fell down on the sand.

When she came to, they were sitting in the back of a rickshaw and Jabbar was fanning her face with a crumpled piece of paper. There was a scared look on his face, and he kept asking her what had happened.

"It was just the heat." She patted his hand and looked away before he could see the fear in her eyes.

Back home, Fatima could still not shake off the sense of doom and despair that had enveloped her ever since the incident at the banks of the Ravi. She could sense the lull that preceded a storm. She could feel the stale breath of death hanging in the air.

Invisible, yet very much there.

Waiting.

As she got up from her seat by the window, where she had been shelling peas and watching the muted television screen, she winced as her knees made loud cracking noises on her way to the kitchen. The change in the weather had aggravated the pain in her arthritic knees, and it was especially worse today. Grimacing and gritting her teeth, Fatima made her way to the kitchen and took out a large pot. As if on an invisible timer, the door knocked just at that instant.

As she opened the door, Gogi the milkman greeted her with his buck-toothed grin.

"*Assalaam o Alaikum, Amma jee!*"

"*Walaikum salaam*, Gogi, how are you?"

"*Bilkul theek, Amma jee*, how are you? Jabbar Chacha *kaisay hain*? He has become very religious; I just saw him coming back from the mosque."

She chuckled. "*Buss*, you know your chacha, he has these sudden changes of heart, but *Allah ka shukar hai*, this is a good one; let's hope it stays."

"Inshallah, *Amma jee*," said Gogi, as he deftly poured the milk in the pot.

"Gogi, the milk has not been good of late – it's almost like water – you haven't been mixing it again, have you?" She fixed Gogi with her sternest look of disapproval.

Gogi squirmed uncomfortably. "*Kaisee baat kery hain, Amma jee*, I would never do that with you; you know the weather is very hot these days, so the buffaloes spend most of the time in the water; maybe that is why some of it gets mixed with the milk," he finished sheepishly.

Fatima laughed in spite of herself and slapped him lightly on the shoulder. "Just like your father, you always have excuses! Don't mix the milk, *beta*." She softened her tone. "How much more money will you make that way? It is not worth it."

"*Jee Amma jee*," Gogi mumbled as he handed her the pot.

Fatima grasped the pot but, for some inexplicable reason, her hands seemed to be clutching at air and the pot slipped, spilling most of the milk on the floor.

Whether her eyes were playing tricks on her or the arthritis in her bones, Fatima could not be sure, but at that moment the milk changed colour right before her eyes, and she saw the floor soaked in blood. She shrieked and staggered back, as Gogi held the pot with one hand and tried to grab her with the other.

A few minutes later, as Jabbar entered the house, he witnessed a scene that shook him down to his core. It was not Gogi, the milkman, making tea in the kitchen, his milk pots and pans lying by the door side. It was not Riaz, sitting at the doorstep, mopping the floor where some milk had spilt, nor was it Riaz's wife sitting in one chair, their sleeping baby cradled in her arms. Even the sight of Mustafa up at this hour, his bloodshot eyes now laced with worry, did not surprise him as much.

What shocked him was the sight of Fatima, his pillar of strength, sitting on the sofa, sobbing and crying like a little girl. As soon as she saw her husband, whatever little self-control Fatima had, evaporated, and she went into another bout of silent sobbing and shuddering. In a second, Jabbar was by her side and tried to comfort her and asked her what the matter was.

In-between sobs, she finally gasped, "Death is at our door; I saw the Angel of Death."

*

5pm

The day had been a mixed one for Mustafa. He had been able to score some hash from his supplier for a cheap price. He now had enough to tide him over for the week. On the other hand, the episode with Fatima had shaken him to his core, making him turn to drugs for comfort and putting his carefully rationed supply in jeopardy. Never one to really delve too deeply into religion and faith, the morning's fiasco had made him question his mother's frame of mind. And he was angry at himself for that. For Mustafa, his mother was the sole person still keeping him at the house.

Sitting at the shop, Mustafa took out a joint and lit it up absent-mindedly, his mind pondering over many things at once. As the hash slowly took effect, he began to relax, reclining on his chair as he gazed sleepily outside the window.

Just another day.

The day gave way to dusk, as a few customers and some window shoppers came and went. He watched them all through a drug-induced buzz, relying on muscle memory.

Mustafa smiled cynically. Death or no death, people just could not get enough of food, he mused as another old lady and a girl, most probably her daughter, entered the shop and asked for the deals being offered.

As Mustafa got up to reach for the menu card, Jabbar walked in, barely nodding at his son, indicating that his time was up and that he would take it from there. Mustafa stopped in his tracks, did an about-turn and, after picking up his few things from the chair, walked out. The episode at the house had again brought them closer for a moment as they both worried for the most important woman in their lives. But as always, after the initial bout of worry and apprehension wore off, there was an added air of indifference and aloofness between the two, as if both were embarrassed at their own vulnerability and the presence of some shared feelings still.

As Mustafa passed by Jabbar, the two almost touched shoulders in the cramped doorway of the shop. The latter caught a whiff of hash in the air as his eldest son went out the door. Jabbar almost turned to catch Mustafa by the scruff of his collar and ask him, but then he checked himself when he realised that he was no longer dealing with a boy but a man.

A man that more and more he did not even recognise.

And then there were times, like that morning, when, even if for a brief moment, he saw himself in Mustafa. Jabbar shook his head, as if clearing his mind of the noxious fumes, and then hurried to attend to the customers.

*

Jamia Rehmania Madrassah
9pm

Ijaz spent most weekdays at the madrassah, learning religious education from the resident maulvi and the nights praying and exchanging views with his fellow students. Over the course of time, he had got used to seeing newcomers all the time. And he had come to accept it as a given that at any time, some of his friends might disappear one day and, after a couple of days, new ones would be there to take up their places in the classes and on the prayer mats.

But even Ijaz was forced to pay more attention to his new bunk mate who came during the dark of the night. As he turned over in his bed, woken up by the light in his room and the noise, Ijaz saw the maulvi standing with another bearded man wearing dark-green-coloured shalwar kameez with a camouflaged vest that bulged with something heavy.

The man wore dark glasses in spite of it being night. His hair was flecked with strands of grey, gelled back and parted from the centre. As he rubbed the sleep out of his eyes, Ijaz suddenly realised that it was the same stranger he had seen at the blast at the shrine. He was at once transfixed. The stranger stood at a right angle talking with the maulvi, and Ijaz stared at the man, taking in his mysterious detail and appearance. Without turning his head or even moving his lips, the stranger suddenly spoke in a voice that seemed to come from everywhere at once.

"*Assalaam o Alaikum biradar.* My appearance disturbs you?" As Ijaz's cheeks flushed with embarrassment, he realised that all this time the man he had been gawking at in fact had coolly been appraising him.

"*Wa'alaikum Assalaam*! N-n-no I was just looking," he finished lamely.

The man turned completely to face him for the first time and took off his glasses. Ijaz could feel a cold chill pass down his spine.

The man had only one eye.

The other socket was a gaping black hole that seemed to drown the whole room in darkness. Ijaz had never been made to feel more insignificant or powerless before. In that moment, the stranger could have made Ijaz do anything without a second question.

The stranger flashed a smile, showing red gums and flashing white teeth with the front two chipped, giving him an added air of danger.

"No harm in looking, *biradar*, I am Gul Nawaz." He thrust out a hand, not making an effort to come any nearer.

Without knowing it, Ijaz felt himself being pulled out of bed by an invisible force, and in a moment, he was standing in front of Gul Nawaz in his bare feet, as his hand was enveloped in the giant's paw.

"I am Ijaz... I mean Ijaz Kaleem," he stammered.

Gul Nawaz gripped his hand tightly and fixed him with a piercing look that entered Ijaz's soul and located his deepest fears. His face was still smiling, but there was nothing warm in that one-eyed stare, and Ijaz knew at that instant what it must feel like for a prey, knowing that it wouldn't take two seconds for this man to kill him and feel no remorse afterwards.

"Sorry to wake you up at this hour, Ijaz *saab*; I have a youngster who has come from very far and needs a place to stay, and your maulvi *saab* tells me you are a *momin*."

Ijaz flushed again in happy embarrassment, surprised at the

same time, that this total stranger had such an effect on him that a word of praise from him would make Ijaz go to the ends of the world.

Gul Nawaz stepped back and Ijaz saw a dark-skinned boy his own age, with one arm in a sling, standing at the door for the first time. The maulvi prodded the boy. "Come on! Introduce yourself to your new *bhai*."

The boy stepped forward as if in a trance and shook hands with Ijaz. "*Assalaam o Alaikum*, I am Sharoon; I mean Shoaib," stammered the boy as he looked up at Gul Nawaz with a scared look. Gul Nawaz did not acknowledge the boy and proceeded to clean his ear with a matchstick. Signalling the end of their conversation, Gul Nawaz turned and walked away, talking in an indecipherable undertone with the maulvi. After Ijaz had prepared a mat for the new boy to sleep, he switched off the light and got back into bed and fell into a fitful sleep, dreaming of a one-eyed giant that roared.

4

Crossroads

Punjab University Campus
8am

It had been a strange week for Asma. When she had left the party that night, the only thought in her mind had been to put as much distance between her fiancé and the docile, timid version of herself as she could. She had no idea that it would lead to her meeting with Qasim, someone she had seen on campus and in her class but never would have imagined interacting with.

Ever since she had bought the Volkswagen from an old couple, her father had made sure that she drove only under the supervision of a driver. This had rankled with Asma's rebellious nature, and she had slipped out that night after paying off the driver to keep his mouth shut.

The only daughter of Shahzad Zafar, a high-ranking government officer father, and Nighat Zafar, a boutique owner mother, Asma had been brought up in a world that revolved around her whims and demands.

The first time Asma Zafar had seen Qasim, there had been no sparks or birds and flowers. She remembered an intense, quiet young man who seemed indifferent to her presence and continued to pore over his second-hand tattered law book. The incident had been shocking to her, having become used to being the centre of attention of both sexes wherever she went. Instead of annoying or repulsing her, she had been drawn towards this anomaly of a man and she found herself trying different ways to make him look up and notice.

Asma had seen him numerous times in the first semester as they both had many of the same classes. There was something very raw and honest about him. From his medium-length, neatly brushed, dark brown hair, his freshly shaved, square-jawed face, those full, pouty lips, down to his starched, buttoned-down shirts with the sleeves always carefully rolled up as if he was about to get engrossed in some physical activity, to his ironed jeans, which on anyone else would have been a major turn-off, but here Asma found it endearing.

She had surprised him and herself with her angry tone, but unlike most boys who felt threatened by her or her background, he had not run off, instead coming back at her with friendly banter, helping her to also loosen up.

After that first meeting, it had been impossible for them to avoid each other. Both had fallen into a silent game in which each chose a strategic seat in the class from where they could sneak looks at the other as their private game continued where actual conversation still remained the final boundary which needed to be crossed.

Until one day, in the evening, as she was headed towards her car, Asma had spotted Qasim walking out of the mosque, taking off his prayer cap and running a hand through his thick mane. She had changed course so as to make sure their paths crossed and waited as he walked towards her, his head bowed, absent-mindedly kicking an empty can in front.

As the can came to rest at her feet, Qasim had looked up, surprise giving way to something genuine and warm, and Asma had praised herself for having taken the initiative.

They had taken a long, slow walk around the library, talking about life in general. As they circled around the building, each trying to slow down as much as possible so that they could spend more time in that magical moment in which everything outside their circle ceased to matter and exist, they had discussed their dreams and deepest fears.

Qasim had realised that he had met someone who shared his thoughts on life in spite of their different backgrounds. He could never have imagined that words would roll off his tongue as smoothly as they did in front of this modern girl who had nothing in common with his background. But as they finished the sixth circle around the library block, Qasim found that not only had he told her all about his childhood, his mother, father and brothers but also about his own dreams of joining the Civil Service and escaping the small world of the inner city and the limited avenues it provided. What had been more shocking to Qasim had been the ease with which Asma seemed to know what he was talking about before he himself knew what he was saying.

And just like that, those long walks became a necessity. Something to look forward to.

*

"Come on, tell me," chided Qasim as Asma dug her head into his shoulder and would not meet his eyes.

"No, I said it already; what more do you want?" She blushed. "I told you that I like you, dumb-ass," she said with mock anger.

Qasim rocked back his head and laughed out loud.

They were sitting in the shade of the large bay window outside the academic block. As the students trickled out of their evening classes, the two surveyed them from their vantage point. Ever since they had openly declared their undefined feelings to the university, there had been a certain freedom that both had enjoyed.

Qasim, though, could feel the eyes that made their way over to them from time to time. Being a boy and having grown up in a community where every action is under a hundred eyes and ears, a part of him knew that what he was doing would end badly, mostly for him. He had found out that Asma's father was a high-ranking officer in the government, something that made him slightly jealous of her for an instant before it gave way to concern when she recounted the obligations she was being placed in by her career-oriented father and her mother.

He knew that nobody would dare touch Asma because of her father, but as far as he was concerned, it was open season. Qasim had a feeling that the verdict on him would be decided on the whims of his notorious roommate, Raja Niaz, the student federation leader. But until that time came, Qasim was not going to let his life be held back by someone else.

"Hey, I like biryani too, so what?" He smiled.

"Oh, stop it, you know what I mean." Asma punched him on the shoulder as he let out a yelp which made one student turn around and then scamper off.

Asma and Qasim both laughed.

"We are going to get in so much trouble," said Asma.

"I know," said Qasim solemnly, "so why don't you at least make it worth it by telling me why you like me."

"You are so cruel," she said as she turned to face him. Without making eye contact, Asma continued, "OK, so I like you, one, because you are not like anyone else. Two, you always carry a notebook and a pencil in your pocket." She smiled.

"Hey, those are for my notes," said Qasim defensively.

"And you tuck the back of your jeans under your feet when you wear sandals." She laughed as she wiped away the tears of mirth at the corners of her eyes.

"Well," Qasim's face turned red, "well, I don't want my feet or my jeans getting dirty; I have to pray," he finished lamely.

"Four, you know all the names of the chief ministers and secretaries and famous government officers," she continued.

"Oh, so now it's a crime to know about the Civil Service," he said with mock indignation.

"No, that's not what I'm saying," she said as her hand shot out to caress his face then stopped in mid-air as she realised that people could be watching.

"Yeah, yeah," he said. "I'm a nerd who doesn't know the difference between a croissant and a donut," he sneered.

"No, you're not listening," Asma said in a low, husky whisper that made Qasim look into her hazel eyes as he leaned closer. "I like that you wear starched collared shirts, sleeves rolled up, no tight-fitting glittery T-shirts that every other boy here is wearing, desperate to show off their biceps," she said, looking deep into his eyes.

"What else?" he whispered, drawing closer.

"All right," she said as she closed her eyes. "I love the way you notice everything. How you enter the classroom and take in everything, not lingering and yet never in a hurry, how you make time move according to your speed," she continued breathlessly as she could feel Qasim edging closer.

"Proud – no – bold, confident," she whispered as she felt his lips brush her cheek. They both sat up straight as the sound of footsteps broke the spell.

"Well," said Qasim as he mopped his brow, "that was…" He looked at her.

"Yeah," said Asma as she jumped off the ledge. As her feet hit the ground, she darted forward and kissed him full on the lips. "Well now you know," she whispered as she ran off.

Qasim sat there, his lips parted, still recovering from the shock, a big grin appearing on his flushed face.

*

Anarkali Bazaar
12pm

More so than most, the city of Lahore speaks to those who care to listen. If one is able to shut out the noise of the cars, the street vendors, the bickering husbands and wives, the giggling children, the chirping birds and the groaning beasts, the dead and the dying, you can hear the city speaking.

She is young. She is old. She is timeless.

Be yourself, she seems to be saying, *for I have you safe in my embrace.* If you look up, you can see the sky and the clouds. Yet hidden in plain sight is the dome of protection that cocoons Lahore and its inhabitants from the glare of the outside world. As the city expands and grows, the cocoon of protection tears at the seams, threatening to shred. But like a doting mother, the city always comes back to darn and stitch the torn piece back together again.

In the aftermath of the blast, the inner city had been torn. But slowly and surely, it was stitching itself back together again. If one were to take a bird's eye view of the bazaar in the day, the chances of mistaking it for a beehive or an anthill would not be low. As if spurring them on, the heat seemed to increase the tempo of the activity and hustle and bustle in the bazaar. There were numerous food and drink stalls strategically positioned outside the busiest streets as families, laden with the day's shopping, came huffing and puffing out into the stifling heat.

Sitting behind the counter, Jabbar took a moment's respite from his work. Business had been good. The marriage season always brought with it a fresh horde of gushing bride- and groom-to-bes and veteran mothers who knew exactly what should be on the menu to win over the in-laws.

By now an expert in marriage menu preparation and the meats and delicacies for each and every occasion, Jabbar knew exactly what to show a typical customer, but just the same, he made the proper pauses and stops to let the old ladies put in their suggestions on which he acted all surprised and awed. It was a testament to his success that the single-room shop that he started from had expanded into a sprawling three-room shop that had become the most sought-after place for wedding caterings, amongst other things.

He sighed as he took in the sea of humanity milling in and out of the labyrinthine streets of the inner city, each housing hundreds of shops containing everything under the sun. If you wanted something cheap yet reliable, chances are you would find it in these cramped and suffocating shops, provided you could endure the sea of humanity. From perfumes to spare parts, from clothes to cutlery, there was nothing that was not available.

All you needed was an acute sense of adventure to walk through the slithering and meandering streets and a high heat threshold, especially in the present weather. But what the bazaar lacked in outdoor air conditioning, it more than made up for in refreshment stalls. Every few feet there was a stall boasting the latest, tested and proven remedy for surviving heat and humidity. There was lemonade, plum juice, falsa juice, sugar cane juice and, the pride of the city, the common man's white wine: lassi.

As their womenfolk went about excavating each and every shop, the men headed for the nearest juice or lassi stall and dropped down on the readily available chairs and gulped down glass after foot-long glass of nature's ultimate coolant. This being peak wedding season, there was a higher demand for cold drinks, as more men than usual got tagged along to choose sherwanis and other groom-related things. Sensing a business opportunity, Jabbar had offered Riaz a spot in front of his shop to sell his dahi bhalla. Ever the entrepreneur, instead of charging rent, he had used half the cart to sell lemonade which Fatima had made at home. Ijaz and Mustafa took turns selling the lemonade, or 'shikanjabeen' as it was commonly called, with the other one running back home to regularly refuel the cooler with more juice or ice, sometimes even both. The purpose of the venture was twofold; the extra money was obviously welcome, but in his eyes, Jabbar was driving the point home to his boys that physical labour was always a man's pride, and even if they had achieved some success, they should still not forget where they had come from and what it had taken.

*

Punjab University Hostel
2am

As he looked at the unslept bed across the room, Raja Niaz knew he had a problem on his hands. He had been kept informed of the developing romance between his roommate and the daughter of Shahzad Zafar. So far, he had told his men to keep an eye out but not to engage. Ever the strategist, Niaz knew that if he played his cards right, there was leverage to be had from a good working relationship with the powerful bureaucrat who seemed destined to reach the highest office in the province.

But first, he had to make sure that he had Qasim's confidence. In order to do that, he had to first break him before he could put him together again. Niaz scratched his chin as a plan started germinating in his mind. He took out his phone and dialled Deemu's number.

*

Mall Road
4.30am

"Where are we going?" asked Asma gleefully as Qasim gunned the Volkswagen down Mall Road. It was early morning and most of the roads were empty. The old car hummed along quietly, the gentle night breeze flowing through Asma's hair as she stuck her head outside the window.

"Well, you said you were hungry," said Qasim as he drove with one hand on the wheel, the other outside the window, floating on the waves of the sudden emotions that had overcome him in the past few weeks.

"Yes, I am starving!" shouted Asma. She had stayed for the night in her friend's room in the hostel on the pretext of an assignment but had snuck out after a couple of hours when her friend had gone to sleep. Qasim had been waiting for her outside the hostel and the two had driven out in her car for a slow, casual drive, something that had become a regular routine that both of them looked forward to.

"Well, your wish is my command," said Qasim as he parked the car at the edge of a narrow street. "We're going to have to walk from here on," he said as he got out.

"Your wish is my command," mocked Asma as she draped the shawl she had taken from her friend around herself and covered her head.

Qasim arched his eyebrows. "How very thoughtful of you," he remarked.

"Not my first time amongst the savages," she teased him.

"We're not that backwards," he shot back, knowing that she was just egging him on.

They arrived outside the shop. The light was still on inside. Qasim told her to make herself comfortable and then went inside the shop.

Ijaz looked up from the newspaper he had been reading, surprised at seeing Qasim at that hour.

"Aren't nice, educated boys like you supposed to be in bed?"

"And aren't religious boys like you supposed to be praying?" he teased back as Ijaz hurriedly turned over the entertainment section he had been reading.

Qasim leaned over the counter and nudged Ijaz. "That's the girl I'm going to marry." As soon as Qasim said it, he knew it was true.

Ijaz followed his gaze to look outside at the young girl sitting alone, looking down at something on her phone. He looked back with surprise at his elder brother. "Well congrats, *bhai*," he said with genuine affection. "What's her name?"

"Asma Zafar."

"Aren't you going to introduce me to her?"

"Not yet, she's just got to know me; let's give it some time," he said and ducked as Ijaz threw a mock punch at him.

"Fine, go sit with your modern girlfriend, while I help you seal the deal with the best barbecue your friend has ever tasted," said Ijaz as he went inside the kitchen.

"That's what I'm talking about."

*

9 am

As she paced about in the street outside her home, a million thoughts swirled in Fatima's head. The black burqa stifled all the air and, from time to time, she had to lift up the veil to take a big gulp of air, if only Jabbar would for once hurry up and get here.

The tonga driver, who also lived in the same mohalla, looked at his watch but said nothing, in absolute fear of the old matriarch. He was of Mustafa's age and had spent many evenings playing with Fatima's eldest, so he dared not now show any sign of impatience. It was an unspoken code of respect that old people were to be treated with the utmost respect. However, he was losing time here, and time meant money. He stole a glance at her and snorted some air out of his nose just loud enough for her to hear but not too loud to seem impertinent. Fatima, on her part, was for once thankful of the burqa veil and pretended not to have noticed and kept looking away.

Finally, at the far end of the cobbled street, she spotted the familiar figure of her husband walking. She got up on the back seat of the tonga and told the boy, "*Chal* shabash, Mehran! Your uncle is here – let's go – we will pick him up on our way."

Mehran sighed inwardly and clicked his malnourished piebald horse into motion. It groaned and grunted its way forward, stopping near Jabbar who sprang up on board beside Fatima, belying his age. She looked away, annoyed with him for making her wait. Jabbar grinned sheepishly and winked at Mehran who had turned back in his seat to pay his respects.

"How are you, Mehran, *beta*?" Jabbar patted the tonga driver on the back. "Give my regards to your *abu*."

Then he turned to Fatima and playfully poked her as she winced and moved away. "I told you a hundred times that we had to be at Ahmed's at two and yet you still were late." She pouted.

"Oho, baba! We are only going to Ahmed's place, not to some commissioner's office, relax."

"But it does not look good – we are going to ask for Nida's hand, and already we are making them wait."

"You think too much; Ahmed will not think anything; he knows I was busy at the shop – I'm sure he would be too."

After a few weeks, the incident that had happened at the Ravi and its aftermath had all been forgotten, and both Fatima and Jabbar had once again started planning Qasim's wedding with Nida.

Both knew that nobody in their right mind would say no to the proposal. The only matter that remained was Qasim's consent, but both Fatima and Jabbar laughed it off as having no significance. Qasim was their angel. He was the answer to their prayers. Finally, Fatima allowed herself to relax, and she smiled at Jabbar, letting him know that she had forgiven him for being late. He chuckled and hummed a favourite Lollywood song of theirs under his breath as the tonga made its way through the streets of the bazaar.

*

Something seemed to be bothering Asma during the whole lecture. After spending so much time together, Qasim could pinpoint her every move and gesture. He could tell what a particular frown or a nervous foot tap meant. And today she seemed to be showing the classic signs of a majorly catastrophic day. He did not say anything until the lecture was over, and they were seated in the cafeteria.

"So, some morning huh?" said Qasim, referring to their latest morning adventure, which had involved driving to the 'phattak' for breakfast.

"Yeah, I never knew they had such delicious breakfast in such a filthy place," said Asma as she twirled the necklace that Qasim had fashioned for her that morning. 'Phattak', as it was commonly called, referred to the slum dwellings adjacent to a railway crossing. The area was also popular for its roadside dhabas that provided simple meals throughout the day. The simplicity and deliciousness of the food was heightened by the regular passing of the train and the accompanying sounds and activity. Most of the regulars at the food joint were blue-collar workers who wanted satisfying food with no frills. After her first bite of the spicy 'anda omellete' and 'paratha', which she washed down with a thick and creamy doodh pati, Asma knew that she was a fan. The crowning moment had been when Qasim had placed a fifty paisa coin on the track with a small, pointy rock in the middle.

"What are you doing?" she had asked, to which Qasim had just looked at his watch and then pointed in the distance where a train seemed to be approaching. After the train had sped off, Qasim had picked up the flattened and enlarged silver coin which now had a hole in the centre where the rock had pierced through. He had placed a string through it and tied it around her neck.

"Happy anniversary," he had whispered, reminding Asma that it had been three months since they had first met.

After ordering two plates of samosa chaat, a Pepsi for her and a cup of doodh pati for himself, he sat across and looked directly at her, waiting. She looked away, feigning interest in the hockey match being played on the television hanging from the ceiling.

"So, great lecture today, eh?" He changed tactic, cautiously.

"Mmmhmmm."

"That whole debate about circumstantial evidence not being admissible was totally an eye-opener for me."

"Mmmhmmm."

"What do you think? Doesn't our 'Qanoon-e-Shahada' law need to be amended?" He tried to get a little more out of her.

"I don't know, I guess, yeah." She shrugged and went back to looking at the screen.

The cafeteria boy brought them their order. Asma only nibbled on her samosa chaat, sipping absent-mindedly from her Pepsi bottle. Qasim put down his cup. "What's wrong?" Genuine concern showed on his face.

For the first time, Asma looked at him; she had been holding back tears, but now, a couple gushed out. She quickly took out a tissue and dabbed at her eyes and managed to grin through the tears. "Aah, it's nothing – it's my contacts; they've been messing with my eyes all day."

"Wouldn't it be easier just telling me what the problem is?"

"But would that be fun?"

"From where I'm sitting, yeah!"

"Well, that's too bad then."

"What are you talking about? Quit going around in circles, and just tell me!"

"Shhhh! Could you say that a little louder? I don't think that guy across the room quite heard that."

Qasim slumped in his seat; Asma decided that she had tortured him enough and smiled, taking his hand in hers.

"Oho OK! It's nothing, just the usual stuff, I told you *naa* my mum is on my case to get married to one of her friend's sons."

Qasim stiffened. "Oh *acha*, hmmm so what's the problem? The boy has a weird moustache or something?"

"No, nothing like that; the boys are all good, it's just that I'm not interested."

"You aren't?" Despite his best efforts, Qasim could not suppress the grin.

"No, I'm not, you big doofus, now smile!"

Qasim flashed a fake grin.

"But I was not joking about my mother's intentions, Qasim; she has got her mind set, and I'm not going to marry anyone but you."

Qasim looked down at his plate; his emotions had always been very deep-rooted and did not come to the surface very easily. That was until he met Asma.

"I know; I feel the same way. I don't have to tell you that, but you know how it is; you know my family background – I'm here on a scholarship; my parents cannot even afford my fees."

"That does not matter – it's my happiness that matters, and my parents would want me to be happy."

"But I don't even have a job; I have to at least graduate and get a job so that I'm able to take care of you."

"Don't give me any of that! I will wait no matter how long it takes, but both our parents should also be told that we are committed – this daily mental torture of being presented in front of aunties and uncles and their sons is killing me." She dabbed the already soaked tissue at her eyes again.

"OK, OK, we will do just that – don't you worry; I won't let anything bad happen. I promise," he reassured her.

"You promise?" She perked up at once.

"Yes, I promise, you big drama queen. Now, let's get out of here; the next class is about to start."

Both laughed and left the cafeteria.

In a corner, Deemu and Niaz sipped their tea and watched them leave.

*

"So that's the boy." Deemu sipped his doodh pati from the saucer.

"Yes, that's him, but do like I told you, only some roughing up; I don't want him badly hurt, only scared," Niaz reminded his protégé.

Deemu wondered why Niaz would not do it himself; he had seen Niaz in action and it was a scary sight. But he said nothing. His job was to do what he was told; he left the thinking to Niaz, and so far, he had not been disappointed.

Deemu nodded. "Where do you want me to do it? In the open or somewhere else?"

"I think it's better if you do it in the open; these days love is a little too much in the air – we need to send the message to these other lovebirds too." Niaz sneered at the couples sitting at the booths and walking around outside in the lawns.

"They have to know that the federation still rules this place." He banged the table for emphasis and the cup bounced and was about to fall off when Deemu caught it and put it back on the saucer in one fluid motion, like a feline.

If anyone else noticed the whole incident, they did a great job of not showing it. Everybody knew Niaz, and only a person with a death wish would go up to him in one of his dark moods, something of a rare occurrence over the last couple of months. There had been rumours that he had left the federation or had gone soft or did not have the support within the organisation that he once enjoyed. The truth of the matter was that Niaz had killed a boy four months back, and he had turned out to be very well connected. It had taken all of the federation's clout and influence to bury the matter. These last couple of months he had been sternly advised to lay low and deflect attention.

But Niaz had rested long enough; it was time to remind

everyone who was boss here. If that meant making an example out of Qasim, a very popular figure amongst the students, so be it. In fact, if he played his cards right, he could still kill two birds with one stone.

*

Sometimes it amazed even Qasim himself how fast their relationship had blossomed and progressed. So much so that it had now become almost impossible to hide it from the world. Already, his close friends had started teasing him. He had always been the most grounded one of the lot; he had to have his priorities sorted out. Qasim did not want to end up like Mustafa. Growing up in the same house, he had noticed how the dreams and aspirations of his parents had been shattered by both his brothers. And even though he loved and respected them, somewhere along the way, he took it upon himself to right all the wrongs that his brothers had committed. He felt that he owed that much to his parents.

In that regard, he had it all planned out, four years in university, get his law degree and then become a lawyer. Practice law, maybe even take the Civil Services exam and become a government officer, who knew. He had kept his options open; all that he was dead set on was that he had to work in the government. All his life, watching his father grovelling in front of lesser men for permission had shown him the light. Wearing a uniform or flashing a government card gave men so much power that they could do anything. Power made monsters out of men. Qasim had seen it on more than one occasion. He had seen policemen demanding protection money from his father, so that his shipments and shop were not 'looted', linemen showing secret arrangements on how to reduce your electricity bill, for an extra 'baksheesh', obviously. Qasim wanted to change this; he still believed in Pakistan and making a difference. And it had to happen through his personal example, which was why he needed to first get into government service. At least that was the plan, until Asma came into his life.

Everything seemed to have taken a back seat now to Asma. He knew that she was the one for him, and he needed to do right by her and marry her. And this obviously raised a lot of obstacles and hurdles, not the least of which were his parents. They no doubt wanted him to move up the social ladder, but they had their own plans, and marrying somebody out of their own social boundary was not an option. Qasim knew that the strongest objection would come from his father, and the only one to counter that was his mother. For the past few weeks, he had been looking for a chance to broach the subject with her and to get her on his side.

The good news is that, at least they haven't started thinking about my marriage so far, he thought to himself, *that gives me some time as I told them just last month that I needed to finish my degree and get a job before I can think of settling down.*

Dropping Asma off at the car park, Qasim walked back to his hostel deep in his thoughts when somebody bumped against him. He looked up to see a tall, slim boy his own age, dressed in black shalwar kameez, blocking his path.

"Do you think the university is your private mansion, frolicking around with girls?" He hissed the words through clenched teeth.

Growing up in the inner city had given Qasim a mental edge that usually lay dormant underneath his calm and cool exterior. He quickly assessed the situation and realised there was no walking out of this one.

He grinned.

He could sense the activity halt as the crowd started gathering up on the balcony and around him at a safe distance.

"I'm sorry, was that your mother or your sister?" he snickered.

The last thing Qasim heard before Deemu charged him was the laughter.

*

As soon as he saw Deemu's swollen left eye and torn lip, Niaz knew that not everything had gone to plan. Intimidation was not going to work on Qasim. Deemu told Niaz that he had beaten Qasim just as he had been told to do until Qasim had passed out and some of his friends had come to protect him.

"What happened to you?"

"He punched me. This one fights back." Deemu looked down sheepishly.

Niaz sighed. "You're getting soft *bachay*." He peeled off a five hundred note and gave it to Deemu. "Go get yourself fixed up; you did a good job."

Deemu murmured thanks and left.

Niaz analysed the situation. That he had misread Qasim was now crystal clear. The fact that he had fought back meant he would not come to him for protection. In that case, further intimidation might spoil his case; Niaz wanted to recruit more followers, not further alienate people, when the federation in general and Niaz in particular were going through somewhat of a slump.

For the moment it would be best to just wait and watch, let the mice play.

For now.

*

There was something otherworldly about the bazaar at night. The lights and noise of the inner city drowned out the honking of the traffic and the neon lights from the metropolis, leaving one with the feeling that they had somehow travelled back in time.

An air of homeliness hung in the air; shopkeepers and vendors took time out and were to be seen lounging outside their shops, just batting the breeze and exchanging the latest gossip doing the rounds. Politics was always high on the list of topics as round after round of tea was consumed. Families and children ran about in the street; there was the smell of freshly cooked pakoras and samosas in the air.

For Qasim, coming home over the weekends was always a very cathartic process. Spending a whole week away, he needed this reminder, through the smells, sights and sounds of where he came from, his roots and why he was doing what he was doing.

As Qasim entered the bazaar, he caught sight of his father sitting on the steps outside the shop with his paternal uncle Ahmed, the tenant Riaz, Mustafa and Ijaz, having tea and sharing pakoras on an old newspaper. Jabbar's face clouded over momentarily when he saw the marks on his son's face. But Qasim shrugged apologetically and hugged his father, telling him that it was a cricket match that got ugly. The other two men nodded in acknowledgement; cricket did things to you. Everybody knew that.

"I'm so glad you're back, *beta*, and just in time too, we have great news," beamed Jabbar.

"*Oye chotay!*" he shouted at the little boy across the street who ran the tea deli with his father.

"*Ji saab ji, aik aur* doodh pati for Qasim *bhai*?" he shouted back, waving at Qasim in the process who reciprocated the gesture with a smile.

"*Haan, te chaity ker shabash mera puttar,*" added Jabbar affectionately in Punjabi.

Riaz emerged from inside the shop with a chair that he placed near Jabbar for Qasim to sit. He offered his own chair to Jabbar but, the old man refused by saying that he preferred sitting on the ground. Qasim sat down, although he would have preferred to sit on the stairs himself but did not want to appear rude to Riaz.

"It's good to see you after such a long time, *beta*, now we have to keep meeting regularly, since you are my *beta* now," said Ahmed.

Qasim smiled and looked quizzically at his father.

"*Oye pagal Mubarak ho,* you're engaged to Ahmed's Nida! You're a man now!" roared Jabbar.

Nobody noticed Ijaz's seething look amidst the hugging and back slapping.

Late into the night, mother and son sat silently in the living room. All around them the house slept, the sounds of a million inhabitants of the inner city drifting out on the wind. Everything was peaceful and serene as the bazaar recuperated and prepared itself for the next day.

Qasim too needed some time to prepare himself for what lay ahead. He had argued and fought with his mother, the only outlet for him. And it had been a losing battle. The decision had been made, his father had given his word, and that was the end of the discussion.

And Asma's family was the final nail in the coffin as far as Fatima was concerned. Much as she loved Qasim, she did not approve of his choice in that instant.

"We just don't merge; they have their own culture, and we have ours, and there is no assimilation." She tried to make him see reason. It came as a shock to Qasim that even his religious mother was a mere mortal after all, susceptible to societal norms and unable to escape the boundaries of class and caste.

All of his pleadings and arguments fell on deaf ears; she was not backing him on this one. Refusal would completely break Jabbar, not to mention her too, and if Qasim really loved this new girl so much, he might as well bid farewell to his family that had borne him, nurtured him, loved him.

How does one argue against that logic? Qasim thought as he slumped in his chair. For all his modern education and progressive dreams, the fact remained that his life was still not his to choose. Like his mother had said, marriage was not just a union between two persons, rather in the antiquated culture that they lived in, it was an alliance between two families, and compatibility and background played a huge role. But not just of the individuals, rather of the families.

As Fatima patted her son on the back and wished him goodnight, Qasim walked out onto the balcony and looked down below at the sleeping city.

The image of their first stolen kiss under the mulberry tree still flashed before his eyes. He remembered the feeling of absolute bliss he had experienced as he had looked deep into the almond-shaped eyes of the girl who had made a home in his heart. As he looked back on the memory that would forever be tinged in his mind with heartbreak, Qasim recalled her looking back earnestly up into his eyes, all her walls down, completely vulnerable and exposed.

"Are we moving too fast?" she had asked in a timid little girl's voice that had made his heart break into a million tiny shards, and he had pulled her closer, nestling her head under his chin, and had assured her that they were not.

Somewhere out there Asma slept, unaware that their love story had ended, through no fault of their own.

*

Over the next week, Ijaz found less and less reason to go home or to talk to anyone from his family. His heart was burning with hate for all those who stood between him and his Nida. He had slipped out one night and climbed the water pipe to see her, but Nida had refused to open her window and he had cried and banged for hours to no avail.

That night, when Qasim had called him, Ijaz had ignored the call and turned off his phone. In his heart, he blamed his brother for his heartbreak. In his misery, he had found an ally in the new boy, whose actual name he had found out was Sharoon.

"Revenge is the only answer," said Sharoon as he dangled his legs from the roof of the mosque, looking up at the stars.

"Gul Nawaz promised that he will pay your family and take care of your sister?" asked Ijaz, still trying to digest all that his roommate had told him.

Sharoon nodded. "Gul Nawaz is a man of his word," he said, "which is more than I can say for a lot of people we know."

Ijaz nodded as he thought of all the people who had hurt him. *Someone had to pay.*

*

Next morning

It is as if the whole house has been bathed in white, thought Mustafa as he came out of his room. The floor had been covered in white sheets, and there were turbaned students sitting at every available seat or place in the room, reciting the Quran. Their voices rose and fell in unison, amplifying the effect into a loud humming noise. Ijaz looked up from his place as his elder brother entered; he smiled and shifted slightly, making room for his brother to sit beside him. But Mustafa quickly reached out and put a hand on his shoulder, making him remain seated. He motioned with his hand towards his mouth, making the sign of a cigarette, to tell him that he was going out for a smoke.

Stepping over and around the boys, he playfully knocked the praying cap off Qasim's head as he went out. His father, distributing dates around the room, shook his head disapprovingly and looked towards Fatima, as if to say, that is what your love has done to him. She pretended not to have seen Jabbar's look and bent her head further over the Quran.

As he walked down the stairs and out into the street, Mustafa noticed one boy in a white robe and green turban just like Ijaz, walking in front of him.

His first thought was to call out to him, thinking that he had also come down for some reason, perhaps for a smoke or to relieve himself and now had lost his way back. For the inner city had streets that took years of learning, and if you were not a local, the chances of getting lost were pretty high. However, the boy seemed anything but lost, far from it in fact. His walk was very purposeful, and quick. Once or twice, he turned around to check if he was being followed. Mustafa kept on walking cautiously, just another pedestrian. As he passed by, he stole a furtive glance at the boy's face. He was dark-skinned and seemed to be favouring one arm which was slightly bent. Mustafa caught the strong smell of niswar – a powerful drug he had dabbled in himself – on the breath of the boy, which also explained his heavy eyelids.

As their eyes met, the boy stopped dead in his tracks and crossed his arms over his chest, as if protecting something.

*

Sitting in a roadside tea stall, Gul Nawaz put his cup down on the table as his mobile started to ring. The call was from one of the handlers – he had arrived at the place appointed and was waiting for Sharoon. Gul Nawaz told him to sit tight and to keep in touch.

Gul Nawaz tilted back his chair and surveyed the buzzing rush of humanity all around him as he took out a small packet containing the dark green niswar, pinched a big wad and placed it expertly between his lower gums and lip. As the drug instantly started to take effect, Gul Nawaz relaxed slightly and, for the first time that day, allowed himself the luxury of a slight smile.

Getting Sharoon inside the bazaar with all the equipment had been posing a problem. But as if on cue, Ijaz had come up with the solution. The maulvi had filled him in on the boy's background. He came from a typical lower- to middle-class family that had lived near the bazaar.

Under the guise of the Quran Khwaani, getting Sharoon in had been surprisingly easy because the policemen at the barricades were from the area and they knew Ijaz and his family. Family ties were still strong. And besides, frisking and searching a religious procession would be inciting chaos in such a conservative community. In that aspect, Ijaz had proved to be a valuable asset to the plan. One that had saved him from a lot of hassle and bribing of people to let them into the bazaar. And anyway, nobody would dare to check a van full of madrassah students going for a Quran Khwaani, and that too on a Thursday.

Gul checked his watch; it was time. He left a twenty rupee note on the table but, on second thought, picked it up and smiled to himself. *The dead have no use for money*, he thought as he walked off. Soon he was lost in the crowd.

*

As Sharoon neared the police checkpoint, his eyes fell on a jalebi stand nearby. His mind turned to Jia. Jia always loved jalebis, smiled Sharoon as the drug-induced fog suddenly lifted from his mind.

What am I doing?

He was walking away from the bazaar when the handler pressed the button.

*

The first blast ripped through the crowded bazaar, breaking glasses in all the shops and cars parked nearby. Two streets downwards, Mustafa was knocked off his feet by the impact.

There was an immediate uproar.

As he got up, his ears ringing loudly, Mustafa walked out of the shop in a daze, not even caring to lock the door; his eyes met with Riaz. There was widespread fear in the latter's eyes. Without a word, both ran towards the noise.

Riaz had a head start on him, and after a few meters, Mustafa's smoking habits caught up to him and he could go no further, bent over, clutching his stomach. As he watched the fast disappearing back of Riaz, his eyes detected a flicker of movement further away.

He squinted in the fast-fading light and billowing smoke and saw something that sent shivers down his spine. There was no mistaking it. Even in the melee and chaos, the white robe and turban standing motionless was unmistakable.

It was another boy, dressed just like the first one Mustafa had seen. The boy stood in the middle of the wild, rushing orgy of people. Like a statue, he stood absolutely still, almost as if he did not care or as if he was drugged. One of the people around the boy noticed him standing, holding his wrist. Someone shouted and everyone began to turn.

Mustafa opened his mouth to shout.

Complete darkness enveloped him as he was lifted off the ground and thrown back through the glass into the shop.

*

Fatima had never completely severed her ties with the hospital where she had started working as a nurse during the war of 1965. She still kept in touch with the staff and pitched in to lend a hand whenever there was a shortage of help.

The day's blast had been colossal, even by liberal estimates. And the closest hospital was overstretched. So as soon as she got the call from the head nurse about the dire situation, she put away her prayer beads and asked Qasim to take her to the hospital, in spite of Jabbar's remonstrations and grunts.

In spite of the years and her work tending to the wounded and ill, the sight at the hospital that day still made her gasp for breath. People were bringing in the dead and dying in whatever mode of transport they could. Parents were carrying their kids and loved ones in their arms and then looking around for someone to take them.

There was absolutely no space at all.

Ambulances were coming and going, dumping the critically wounded on makeshift stretchers and then speeding off to bring in the next batch. The walking wounded were wandering about, lost, bleeding, some still in shock, talking to themselves.

The chief nurse saw Fatima and motioned her over.

"I'm so glad you came, Fatu, we need all the help we can get; there just aren't enough people to cope with a tragedy of this magnitude," she began.

"Don't worry about it, Noreen, I was going to come myself anyway."

"Listen, as much as I am thankful and need your help, the real reason I called you over is because I wanted to talk to you about something." She placed an arm around Fatima's shoulder and started walking her towards one of the wards.

Fatima was at once alert, this highly out of place behaviour told her that something had gone wrong. Before she could say anything, they had arrived at the ward, and her eyes zoomed in on the person lying on the bed farthest from her.

Mustafa.

Drenched in blood.

She tried to scream, but no sound came out.

Noreen caught her as Fatima's knees buckled. She sat her down on a chair and gave her a glass of water. "Relax, he is fine now, he had some shards of glass in him which explains the bloody appearance, otherwise he has been very lucky."

Fatima's heart lifted at this good news, and she looked gratefully at her friend.

"I just did not want to tell you this at home, because it always sounds much worse on the phone, and you have told me that Jabbar *bhai* already has a heart condition," added Noreen.

Fatima nodded in appreciation, and then motioned that she wanted to get up and go to her son, as she was still having trouble getting words out of her mouth. Noreen took her hand and helped Fatima to her feet. She walked fearfully to her son, who at that exact moment, as if sensing her presence, opened his eyes and looked directly at her.

And smiled.

The floodgates opened and the mother rushed forward and embraced her eldest, crying.

"I guess your premonitions were right after all," he said playfully in spite of the throbbing pain in his whole body and the ringing in his ears. Just then he remembered Riaz, and he tried to get up quickly, sending piercing bolts of pain throughout his chest where most of the shards had lodged.

Noreen and Fatima rushed forward and told him to lie down.

"What about Riaz, he ran in front of me, is he OK?" he asked frantically, he knew that Noreen had been to their house lots of times and knew all of the inhabitants.

Fatima also looked up at this new piece of ominous information. Seconds that seemed like eternity passed by. Noreen shook her head ever so slightly.

Mustafa threw his head back on the pillow and closed his eyes. A tiny tear trickled down the side and mixed with the blood stains on the bed sheet.

*

The inhabitants of the Kaleem household were all huddled over the television as the latest updates kept being relayed on the news channel. Qasim had also come back from the hospital as Fatima had told him that she would call him or get a ride herself when she got free.

Ijaz had also stayed back while the rest of the students and imam had left. Things had not turned out as he had imagined, and the reality was dawning on him. Jabbar sat on the sofa, his usual chosen place, his head down on his chest, not looking at the television. His grim expression showed all the disappointment and despair of one who had just been robbed of something he had so lovingly aspired to.

Peace.

The news reporter at the site showed the gruesome view – blood was splattered everywhere amongst the damaged and destroyed wreckage of machinery, property and lives. Estimates of the dead so far were sketchy, but the experts were putting the sum at around a hundred and rising as rescue workers frantically tried to pull survivors from under the rubble of one of the city's most densely populated and overcrowded locality.

The reporter came again to the screen with breaking news; one of the suicide bombers head's had been discovered. The gruesome and bloody image was flashed on the screen.

Ijaz felt something tightening inside him. Even death could not mask the indifference with which Sharoon looked at the world.

Ijaz felt used and manipulated. He needed answers. So far, nobody else had shown any interest in the face of the suicide bomber, so that was some comfort. But nothing could extinguish the guilt and confusion he was feeling at bringing death to his own doorstep.

*

Something woke Mustafa in the middle of the night, and as he tried to turn instinctively towards the sound, the shooting spears of pain in his side reminded him of the day he had been through. Grimacing in agony, he eased back onto the bed that his mother had dragged into the living room, within earshot of her and Jabbar's room so that she might help him if he needed anything.

He propped himself on his elbows and took a look around the room. The white sheets used for the Quran Khwaani still lay across the floor and draped over the sofas, giving an eerie ghoulish look to the whole place. The noise came again from one corner of the room; Mustafa cranked his neck and peered into the shadows.

Something welled up inside him, almost to the point of choking him.

Anisa, Riaz's wife, was sleeping in an upright position, leaning against one of the chairs, one hand resting firmly yet gently on the baby's stomach. Every once in a while, the baby whimpered, setting off a series of light pats by Anisa which seemed to soothe the kid back to sleep.

Try hard as he might, he could not take his eyes off the kid. In his mind, he felt as if he was partly to blame for the death of Riaz. The guilt of always being a failure would not let him rest. The fact that a hard-working, innocent family man had died while he had survived did not make sense to him. Mustafa felt as if he had cheated death by offering it an innocent person's body.

I made her an orphan, he kept thinking as he looked at the kid. She did not harm me and still I killed her father; I took the roof off her head. He put a hand over his eyes, trying to block out the memory of him and Riaz sharing a smoke outside the shop, only a couple of hours ago. The smiling face of Riaz kept pushing through all his defences, smiling at him with accusatory eyes.

Riaz's surprised expression seconds before the blast ripped him to bits appeared before his eyes, and Mustafa sat up in anguish. The sudden movement caused bolts of pain to shoot through his body and elicited a whimper. Anisa's eyes opened instantly, and they focused on him. Even through her own immense pain and loss, Mustafa could detect genuine sympathy and anxiety for him. The discovery absolutely gutted him, and he looked away, thoroughly disgusted with himself.

"Are you OK?"

"Yes, it's nothing – go back to sleep, I just had a nightmare."

"Can I get you anything?"

"No, it's fine; I can walk myself." Then, as he tried to stand and failed, "Maybe a glass of water."

Anisa got up and brought a glass of water to Mustafa, as he felt himself falling even more in his own eyes and could not bear to look at the woman he had just made a widow.

*

Early next morning

"Halt! Who goes there?" the policeman barked and pointed his gun at the dark figure trying to walk by the checkpoint.

The figure stopped.

"Show yourself, nice and slowly," said the policeman, pumping a fresh load into his service rifle to show that he meant business. The sound of the bolt being snapped back echoed in the deathly silence.

"P-please don't shoot." The figure threw back the cloth from over his head as a thoroughly scared Ijaz revealed himself.

"Oh! Ijaz! It's you, why are you walking round like a suspicious person at this time of the night?" The policeman was a local and knew Ijaz and his family. He pointed the rifle towards the sky and walked towards Ijaz.

The boy looked a mess.

He had been crying for quite a while, his tear-stained face bearing testimony to an anguished soul.

"*Kia hua bachay?*" The policeman had gone to school with Mustafa and knew that Ijaz was the baby of the household. He slung the rifle across his shoulder and came forward to pat the scared boy on the back, but Ijaz immediately shied away into the shadows.

"I'm not going to hurt you, Ijaz – it's me Buggy; I'm a friend of Mustafa, remember?"

Ijaz looked up at the kind face of the policeman for the first time and managed a weak smile of recognition. Buggy mistook the crying for something else and tried once more to comfort the boy.

"That's better, don't be upset yaar, these types of things happen; it's very sad that the bomb blast had to happen in our mohalla, but Inshallah, everything will be all right – Allah is with us."

Ijaz nodded and looked up. "It's not that – I'm fine. I have to go now."

"All right, take care of yourself, Ijaz, and give my *salam* to Jabbar Chacha and Fatima Chachi," Buggy shouted after the fast-walking boy as he slipped into the night.

*

Qasim awoke at Fajr to the sounds of his father getting ready to go the mosque and his mother preparing tea for the whole family.

"Maulvi *saab* time to get up, don't they teach you to pray five times a day?" He playfully slapped the bed next to him which Ijaz had been sharing with him last night. But his hand encountered only empty space.

Qasim got up and found the bed neatly made up with the quilt folded at one end and an ominous-looking note lying on the pillow. He groaned inwardly. *This can't be good at all*, he thought – Ijaz was never a man of letters.

"This is not good," he said aloud. He picked up the letter and recognised Ijaz's handwriting. As his eyes ran over the contents of the letter, the colour faded from his face, and he fell down on the bed.

"This is not good at all."

*

Ijaz located the house just as the sun was setting, bathing the whole street in its reddish hue. The building was an inconspicuous-looking double-story house with a nondescript Suzuki Mehran parked outside.

He rang the bell.

A moustached, middle-aged man emerged at the second bell. He looked at Ijaz from inside the gate, then opened the side door and motioned him inside. Ijaz hesitated, for a slight second, but then followed the man.

They entered through the side door into a long and narrow corridor, the walls of which were bare except for some posters. Ijaz could not help but notice that, almost without fail, all the posters dealt with injunctions for waging war.

At the end of the corridor, the man motioned for Ijaz to enter the room on the left. As he did so, he was met with the aroma of cooked lamb and rice, and his mouth watered at the sight of the food spread out on the floor in front of him. On either side of the cloth sat young men, about his own age, and at the far end stood Gul Nawaz.

He seemed to fill the entire room with his presence. The dark glasses were missing; instead, his blind eye seemed to suck in all the light from the room. A keffiyeh rested on his right shoulder; his shirt was open at the chest, revealing a deep, long scar running diagonally across where the heart would be. He smiled when he saw Ijaz; his voice boomed in the closed room.

"Brothers! You are all lucky, for today we have the hero of the last attack against the infidels in our midst. Welcome brother Ijaz, who took upon himself the responsibility for the success of the mission so that our two fallen comrades could fulfil their mission."

Everyone got up and started embracing a confused-looking Ijaz as he made his way towards the end of the room. His ears ringing with the shouts of praise from the boys, he found himself smiling and actually enjoying the praise.

Finally, he stood face to face with Gul Nawaz, who looked at him and then, clasping both of his shoulders, he said, "You have seen the light – welcome to the first day of the rest of your life."

*

As Fatima went about her work in the emergency ward of the Mayo hospital, she kept feeling the stares of the other hospital staff boring into her back and the buzzing of talk whenever she walked out of the room.

By midday, she had had enough. She saw the matron trying to sneak out of the cafeteria and confronted her before she could make her escape.

"OK this has to stop, Noreen, what is going on?"

"What are you talking about?" The matron would not make eye contact.

"This!" Fatima almost shouted, then, as the rest of the people in the cafeteria looked their way, she lowered her voice to a whisper. "What is going? Why is everyone avoiding me?"

The matron looked into the kind face of her oldest friend and felt a rush of sympathy. She squeezed Fatima's hands and made her sit down on one of the tables.

"OK, Fatu, these are just rumours that have been going around ever since last night. You know that the police have been interrogating people about the suicide bombers and how they entered into the bazaar."

"Uh-huh." She nodded.

"Well…" Noreen looked uncomfortable.

"Well? Come on, Noreen, what is it?"

"Well so far the people say that the two suicide bombers managed to enter the bazaar in the van that had the madrassah students that Ijaz brought to your house for the Quran Khwaani."

The colour drained from Fatima's face, and she slumped in her seat. Noreen poured her a glass of water and made her take a sip.

Fatima could not make the image of her youngest child go away. "Oh, my poor little boy, what have you done?" she whispered. She got up unsteadily. Noreen moved forward to help but Fatima steadied herself. "I have to go home."

Noreen nodded.

As Fatima walked out of the hospital, she was no longer concerned with the looks and the talking; she had much bigger things on her mind. In the last twenty-four hours, the home she had built over decades had started falling apart around her.

*

It was nearly nightfall by the time Jabbar was allowed to leave the police station where he had been held since morning. His reputation in the local community had saved him, but it had still taken a lot of convincing.

The interrogating officers had been understanding and had not used any intimidation tactics with him, even though, judging by the sounds of anguish from the adjacent rooms, some of the other suspects had not been so lucky.

But he had no reason to hide anything, and he had told the officers all that he knew. And they had believed him and let him go with the warning that they might require him in the future if the need arose. He had given them his assurance that he would come as soon as he was called. But as Jabbar left the police station, it was with a heavy heart.

All his life's work, destroyed by his two sons, he thought. One rejected from the army for drugs and the other was now wanted by the police for links with a terrorist organisation. *What did I do to deserve this?* he asked himself.

Across the street, he spotted Qasim waiting for him with a clearly worried-looking Fatima. Then his eyes made out another figure, a heavily bandaged Mustafa, who refused to make eye contact, leaning heavily on a crutch off to one side. But still, he came, smiled Jabbar to himself. There was hope yet.

*

In the middle of the night, Fatima's heart skipped a beat, causing her to wake up. She opened her eyes. Across the bed her husband snored lightly in his sleep.

A tear trickled down Fatima's creased face; she got up from bed, performed *wudu* and prayed by the light of the moon.

"Dear God, give my Ijaz the strength and courage to make the right decision; show him the way towards you."

At that moment, she looked at an old picture of the whole family hanging on the wall. She was carrying a three-year-old Ijaz in her arms. The expression of the little boy was hard to tell, like he had just come up to a fork in the road and did not know which direction to take.

Book Two

Coat of Scars

5
The girl with the broken heart

Islamabad, 2012
Asma

Most first-time visitors to the office of the National Counter Terrorism Authority, or NACTA as it was called, could be forgiven for mistaking it for just another three-storeyed residential building in the posh section of sector F-8.

But I wasn't a first-time visitor. In fact, ever since I had cleared my Civil Services exams four years ago, NACTA had been my first field posting. I couldn't make the excuse of not knowing where it was. As I parked my car outside the gate, I was acutely aware that I had, for the third time this week, missed the cut-off time for reaching the office. My boss, a cantankerous control freak at the best of times, would be just waiting to tear me a new one.

The first sign that this was not going to be my day was the shit-eating grin planted all over the face of the guard at the gate. He and I had become sort of buddies in the two years I had been at the job. Our morning routine involved shooting the breeze with the usual topics: cricket, corruption, inflation and so on.

That day, there were no words. Only sign language. With

his back towards the building and his hands in front of him, he gestured with his thumb upwards. I snuck a peek at the second-floor window.

Crap.

I saw the Turtle.

The Turtle saw me.

The Turtle must have been a handsome muscular man in his youth. However, now all that remained was a massively shiny bald plate that was fringed by the last vestiges of hair around the ear, which he was in the habit of growing long. A couple of those long strands of sideburns used to be meticulously combed over to the other side each morning. A military-styled thick moustache complemented his bushy eyebrows, giving him a stern Uncle Sargam look. But it was his lack of a neck and a metallic plate in his back from a bullet wound that had altered his posture, earning him the nickname. As I made eye contact with him, the Turtle looked mighty pissed off.

He swivelled in his chair, turning his back on me. I slumped and exhaled. No point in trying now. I was going to get it today. It had been coming for a while; today was the day. Gritting my teeth for the impending storm, I punched my card into the system and entered. The newly created NACTA building had been hastily accommodated in a residential locality of the city. The need had arisen owing to the growing frequency of suicide attacks in the country which had led to the realisation that perhaps more than a militaristic approach would be needed. Hence, with the blessings of our international friends and donor agencies, the decision had been taken to formulate a counter terrorism agency.

By the time I had joined, the authority had been in existence for five years, but you wouldn't be able to tell from its shabby and ad-hoc condition. It had seemed a good idea on paper but on ground, it refused to take off. Extremism and its radical off-shoots themselves were not a new phenomenon in the country, but people were not willing to accept that the country had a problem. Plus, on the government side, there were 'turf wars' to be fought as the other, more well-established agencies were not ready to cede ground. It was a street fight in which this new organisation had just entered armed only with a pocketknife. And all the other participants carried rocket launchers.

As I punched in my secret number at the door, I prepared myself for the inevitable onslaught which I knew was coming. Making my way up the stairs, my colleagues kept trying to cheer me up by secretively patting me on the back or giving me the thumbs up signs.

The path to the Turtle's office was the least favourite part of my office commute. And it was not just because of who sat behind the door. You see, like a majority of senior government officers, the Turtle too had family in Lahore and a huge government-furnished house there which he meant to keep for as long as he could, even after retirement. It was not an uncommon practice in a country where favours were the preferred currency. And so it was that some section officer had come up with this brilliant idea where the head honcho could keep his government mansion in Lahore and live in Islamabad on government premises simultaneously.

The house which had been turned into an office, now functioned as the Turtle's residence-cum-office with us as his half-roomies.

On any given day of the week, it was a common sight to enter the office and find the Turtle's undergarments drying out on the staircase or his pants being ironed by the staff, who also moonlighted as shorthand typists.

That morning, as I walked up the dreaded path, I was accompanied by Ziafat, the in-house chef-cum-errand boy. He was carrying the Turtle's breakfast: scrambled eggs with toast and coffee.

"How's the mood?" I asked Ziafat.

"Cloudy with a chance of thunderstorms," he grinned.

I decided to stay back while Ziafat entered the room first. I figured the sight of food would help abate the storm. As Ziafat quickly came out, followed by the sound of a shoe thudding against the door, I realised there was no avoiding it.

"Too much sugar," Ziafat explained sheepishly as he ran downstairs.

Thanks a lot, Zee, I thought to myself as I opened the door.

The room was bathed in the early morning light as I entered the office of the national chairman or NC as he was referred to.

"Does the government pay you to come to office at your leisure?"

"No, sir, my car broke down," I stammered as I tried to locate a body to go along with the voice. But the chair at the table was empty.

"Over here!" bellowed Khawaja Zaheer, and I spun around to find the Turtle sitting in front of the television wolfing down enormous mouthfuls of egg and toast.

I gave a sheepish grin.

"Asma, I hold your father in high regard, and if it weren't for him being my senior, I would've repatriated you back to your parent department by now," he hissed.

I stiffened visibly and straightened myself. "Sir please, as I have mentioned to you a number of times before, do not let my father or his reputation come in the way of my performance. If you feel my work is not up to the mark you can do as you wish, sir," I finished lamely, acutely aware that my indignation at having been reminded of my family connection had temporarily blinded me to the fact that I was talking to somebody who not only outranked me but had spent more years in the service than I had in the world.

If he had taken affront to my outburst, he did not show it. He mumbled something in-between his bite and thankfully, just at that moment, Ziafat burst in with a scalding cup of freshly made coffee.

"That will be all, Asma, please be careful in the future, and I want the Weekly Threat Assessment Report at my desk before the day is over – is that clear?"

"Yes, sir."

As I walked out of the office, I could see that all my colleagues were busy in their work. But it was all a ruse; I knew because I had done that many times when somebody else was inside, getting an earful from the Turtle. As I passed them on my way to my office, I could already hear scattered whispers of their conversation.

"…was that it?"

"I wish I was a female too."

"So unfair."

"Daddy is a big shot officer."

I flinched at the last remark. Thankfully, by that time I had reached my office and I could let my stoic expressionless guard down.

As I slumped down in my chair, I let out an exasperated sigh. There was just no escaping it. For the last two years, I had been trying to avoid my family name, but in the bureaucracy that was like trying to breathe without inhaling. Reputation was everything.

Before you got posted to a new ministry or department, the bureaucratic grapevine already had the gist of your history on their fingertips. What sort of officer you were, your idiosyncrasies, your habits, your previous postings and your reputation. For a female officer the magnifying glass got a little bigger. No matter how competent I would be, my accomplishments would always be judged in the backdrop of my father's stature.

I had entered a race I was destined to lose. I had never wanted to be a government officer. It had always been Qasim's dream. He was the one who had dreamt of changing the fate of Pakistan. Qasim…

It had been five years since he had told me that it was over between us. Surprisingly, the first couple of months afterwards had been relatively easy to endure. I had hate to fuel my resolve whenever it felt like weakening.

But spite is a fickle companion. It promises to be by your side through hell or high water. And then, one morning, you wake up to find it gone without a trace. All that you are left with is a void and an ache.

By the time my fury had abated, and I had realised that I still loved him, I had already graduated. Qasim had not come to receive his degree. I later found out that he had not finished but had simply dropped out. With that piece of news, the last vestiges of hate also evaporated; nothing short of a calamity could have stopped Qasim from his studies. He was destined for great things.

I searched everywhere for him. And that was when I realised the differences in our worlds. We both lived in completely separate universes that, although were in the same city, were totally cut off and, in some ways, antagonistic of each other. Even his friends at the university had never been to the inner city. In my desperation, I made several trips to Anarkali but to no avail.

Crestfallen, I locked myself in my room as I pondered my options. By the end of the week, I had decided to appear for the Civil Services and join the government. The decision came as a complete surprise to everyone, including my parents.

In my mind, I felt that by joining the bureaucracy and doing what Qasim had wanted, I would in some way still be close to him. What I really wanted and dreamed, and yet tried to guard tightly, was the hope that I would find Qasim also in the bureaucracy. I forced myself to believe for a fact that he would be there. Never for a single second did I entertain any other thought to the contrary.

After clearing the exams, I had no time to join in the celebrations hosted by my jubilant parents. My father saw in me a chance to relive his career while my mother saw for me even more promising marriage proposals.

But I was on a mission. I also explained to my father that I wanted to make my own mark in the bureaucracy and did not want him holding my hand and getting me all the top posts due to his name. And to prove my point, I returned my monthly allowance to my father after I joined the Civil Services Academy. From here on, I was going to make it on my own.

My first thought on joining the academy: I did not belong there. My second thought as I ran down the list of names of the probationary officers: Qasim was not there. It was as if the lights had gone out in the room of my heart. Only a tiny flickering candle remained. I vowed to protect that weak flame as long as I lived.

And so, I bowed my head and redirected all the fire, all the resolve, into my career. After finishing my Common Training Project from the Civil Services Academy Lahore, I joined the Specialisation Training Program which was another year. As soon as I finished my training, I opted for a field job away from home. In spite of my repeated requests, I was sure my father had some hand in me getting posted to Islamabad, which was always a highly sought-after posting.

I packed all my belongings in the Beetle and moved to Islamabad. After two years of trying to make it on my own, I was still being called 'daddy's girl' and not worthy of being an officer because of my gender. As I gritted my teeth at the injustice, I was brought back to the present by a knock on my door.

"Come in."

It was Khayyam, my office orderly, with a cup of tea and a sandwich from the kitchen. I relaxed and motioned for him to enter. As he set my breakfast down at the table, along with the ten different newspapers I had to finish in the next four hours, he said, "Madam, you are supposed to hand in the report by today."

I set the teacup down with a bang to show my irritation, and some of the tea spilt out on the table. Without breaking stride, Khayyam produced a rag from his jeans and, in one smooth motion, cleaned the table. As I smiled to myself, he looked up and gave me his gap-toothed grin before leaving the room.

As I munched on my sandwich, I eyed the stack of newspapers

forlornly. Every day, as Assistant Director Counter Terrorism, it was my job to scour over all the leading national daily newspapers. I had to pick out acts of terrorism and extremism from all over the country. I had a research assistant who was going over the regional language newspapers and doing the same. At the end of each day, we would sit down and collate our findings into a table which was the basic template for what had become the 'Weekly Threat Assessment Report'. The template we had come up with contained boxes for the number of casualties, the terror groups involved, the sects targeted, the location, the modus operandi, the strategy employed by the terrorists. At the end of the weekly report, we would give our analysis on any emerging patterns. We were not basing our report just on open-source intelligence but were also being fed daily threat alerts from field intelligence agencies. Every day, literally hundreds of such reports would come in with such vague contexts as 'two terrorists have entered Islamabad territory in a white Suzuki'. Somehow, we had to decipher them and make sense of them. Sometimes the reports would be more detailed and meatier. I had to admit it was very interesting work but also very dangerous, as the fate of a lot of innocent people depended on how well we were able to predict the next move of the terrorists.

And therein lay the problem. As the country continued to grapple with the threat of terrorism, I felt that the national response had so far been reactive rather than proactive. In the course of the two years spent poring over terrorism reports, I had realised, through countless interviews with jailed extremists and detained terrorists, that extremism was more of a mindset than an action and as such it had to be countered with a narrative rather than physical force. And until the minds and hearts were won, blood would continue to be spilled.

I opened my laptop and found that my associate had compiled the report from the regional newspapers and emailed it to me. I added it to my report and then got a printout of the finished version and submitted it to my senior officer for review.

*

It was five by the time the report had finally been approved after moving up and down the chain of command three or four times. That was the bit about the bureaucracy I hated the most, the unnecessary formality of it all. Why couldn't we all have just sat down in one room and thrashed it out together and just come up with the final report? In my initial days, I had voiced these views and had been met with shakes of the head and smiles.

I was told that this was the bureaucracy, and the chain of command and seniority had to be respected, and not some school science project where we could all just sit down and discuss it over snacks. Over time, I had learned to bottle in my rebuttal to those explanations.

I did not belong here.

At times I wondered what I was doing in the government. It was as if I had time travelled into the past but, instead of doing all the fun stuff, I now was stuck there and was forced to observe the rigid rules and norms that had no place in today's world. Even my father would not hear me out when I vented my frustrations to him at times. He would shake his head and explain that not everyone had had the privilege of a good and sound education like I had and thus it was unfair on my part to expect them to adapt to modern standards of work. The government was supposed to care for all its citizens equally and thus it could not make such drastic changes in its functioning which had the potential of leaving hundreds of thousands of people jobless.

That was another problem altogether. I had realised that in its effort to make up for some of its shortcomings in other areas, the government had taken on more than what it was required to do. As a result, some of its departments that had once been performing brilliantly had also become bogged down. The Civil Services exam was a prime example of this mess. In an effort to address the issue of discrepancy in the education standards of the five provinces, the government had instilled provincial quotas in the allocation of seats in the civil bureaucracy. The idea behind it had been to give equal representation to people from all over Pakistan. It was supposed to be a temporary arrangement until the standards had been improved.

That had been decades ago.

The rap on the door made me wake up with a start. It was the guard at the gate; he had come up to check up on me as my car was the only one left in the car park besides the chairman's. I looked at my watch – it was 5.15pm – an hour and a quarter over time. In the government, nobody worked overtime unless they were paid for the extra hours or if you wanted to impress your boss. In our case, my co-workers and I had realised that since the Turtle practically lived in the office, there was no point in staying overtime to impress him. So, everyone used to leave at exactly 4pm. I had stayed late that day due to the threat assessment report which had to be finalised. Once the final draft had been approved, my part of the job had been completed. The next stage involved attaching a covering letter to the report signed by the NC, detailing the gist of the document. It would then be handed over to the dispatch rider who would hand over copies of the report to the relevant departments within the ministry. The ministry officials in turn would submit the report to the prime minister's office and somebody there would go over the report and then decide on where it needed to go next or what actions needed to be taken. All too complicated and way above my paygrade for me to spend any more time figuring it out.

With one last look at my cluttered desk, I turned off the lights and headed home. Another day gone, with no trace of Qasim.

6

Love all

GHQ Tennis Club, Rawalpindi 2012
Qasim

I knew the ball was going to be out even before it cannoned across the net towards me. I could tell from the way Major Rashid had put every ounce of his six-foot-three, three-hundred-pound frame – most of it carried in his bulbous stomach – behind it.

The events of the past hour had been leading up to this moment. I had run the soon-to-be-retired, demoted major all over the red clay of the GHQ tennis court. The same clay that, Ahmed Din proudly claimed to all within earshot, came all the way from the hills of Murree. The same precious red clay that we had to cover under tarp whenever the rains came in this city of perpetual downpours.

As I soaked the precious red clay with the salty sweat of the overweight major's effort, I knew how it was all going to end. I had always known, since the day two and a half years ago when our paths had first crossed.

Me, a newly recruited ball boy, who had been taught the rudiments of tennis by Ahmed Din who, forty odd years ago, had been a ball boy like me and had been taught about the rudimentary aspects of tennis by his *ustad*.

And just like that, I had become the next in line in this

succession of sorts. Major Rashid, a cocky old bull who had been winning too often against juniors and other fellow newbies in far-flung cantonments where there weren't enough players. Over the years, this steady stream of willing losers – looking to be defeated in return for favours such as a well-timed phone call to one of his course mates who just 'happened' to be the fortunate loser's commanding officer or CO as they were called – had created in the major's mind an impression of invincibility that, on every other day, I would have let go.

All ball boys are trained the three rules of tennis:
The serve lands in the small box
Keep the ball within the big box
Lose

It was simple. Easy. After playing tape ball cricket in the narrow lanes of Anarkali, learning how to play tennis was an easy progression for me. It was a nice distraction, and it provided me an easy access to important people. And I needed to be around people who knew about things that a normal ball boy like me with no status or background could not possibly get access to.

Terrorism is a relationship breaker. I once knew a boy in college who had come from Karachi. He used to tell me about roadside muggings and how thieves would come on motorcycles in the light of the day at traffic lights. They would knock on your window with their weapons and tell you to roll down the windows and to hand over your wallet, mobile and other valuables. While this was going on, the other cars, watching this unfold, would start drifting away from you. They would still watch, but not help.

I never believed that guy.

He's just making stuff up, I would tell myself and others. *It just cannot be true.*

After Ijaz disappeared, I came to realise that terrorism, just its mere mention or association with you, was simply another form of a mugging. It happened in broad daylight. Others watched it happening to you. And they started drifting away. Until you were completely alone and exposed.

One by one, everyone left. As *Ammi* ran desperately to her relatives, friends and co-workers, they all turned their backs, shutting her off. She screamed; she shouted. And then she stopped talking.

It was like someone had turned off the light. Our house turned into a dark, empty shell. We still breathed and ate, but that was it. Nobody talked to *Abu* at the mosque or came to the shop. The only people who came regularly to meet us were the police.

Every other day they would be at the door, asking questions of my father, me and Mustafa. Soon, everyone in our street and the mohalla knew. Every day, going anywhere became this long, arduous and excruciating journey where I could feel eyes boring into my back and words and taunts being exchanged. Whenever I turned around, there would be silent, empty looks.

Ammi stopped going outside the house. *Abu* seemed to have shrunk into himself; he was a shell now. For a while, Mustafa *bhai* went back to taking drugs and remained in a haze most of the time, through which it was hard to reach him. The only people who seemed alive were me and our dead tenant's wife Anisa, who slowly started taking on the duties that *Ammi* had once done so effortlessly.

Every morning, with her little child straddled to her side, she would be up first thing in the morning, making breakfast for *Abu* and *Ammi*, going out to get the milk and groceries. Then, one day, she started leaving the kid behind with Mustafa *bhai* when she went out on her errands. And then the next day too. Slowly, she got him off the drugs again. I was grateful for her presence. She nursed all of us back into a weakened version of ourselves. As I looked all around, I realised that the world had moved on.

But we didn't.

I couldn't.

Ijaz was as much my baby as he was *Abu* and *Ammi's*. With him gone, I felt I had betrayed him, left him alone in this world so that he had nobody to talk to. I felt like someone had sat on top of me and was slowly closing off my breath.

I had to find him.

And yet, unwelcome thoughts are always the ones most desperate to visit you. I would constantly wake up in cold sweats in the middle of the night, seeing grotesque images of a bloodied Ijaz or his head flying off his body as he disintegrated into a shower of blood right in front of my eyes. I would wake up and tear my clothes off to get rid of his blood that wasn't there.

I feared that by the time I found him, it would be too late. I stopped going to my classes; I went everywhere, asked everyone. All anyone could tell me was that he was definitely not in Lahore.

So, I decided to leave the city.

Ammi barely said a word as she looked at me with empty eyes. As I bent forward to kiss her wrinkled cheek, I whispered in her ear, "I'm not coming back without him. I promise."

She shuddered slightly as if catching her breath, otherwise said nothing. With *Abu*, there were no words needed. He had seen his world crumble in front of his eyes with the disappearance of his youngest and the backlash it had created. Within a span of a few days, his identity, that had tied him to a country he had not been born in, had been shattered.

He was once again an orphan in a foreign country without any roots. Only this time, he was looking back at life instead of forward. The future did not hold much hope for him. I could feel it in his weak grip when I shook his hand. I felt the cold, clammy hold of impending doom in his skin when I kissed his forehead.

I could have stayed behind and helped. I tried. But I was not willing to give up and reconcile my fate, our fate, to destiny just yet.

If we were to be torn asunder by a random act, I would rather go down struggling than be consigned to forces outside my control. Last of all, I had talked to Mustafa *bhai* when he was in one of his sober states, which luckily had started becoming more and more frequent.

He understood my pain. At one point in my life, Mustafa *bhai* had been my ideal; he still was, the part of him that had not been tarnished by the disillusionment of life. The part that still simmered under the rubble of abandonment, disappointments and resentment, the part that flared for a few seconds at unexpected times and which I saw in his eyes when I mentioned my resolve to bring Ijaz back home.

He had got off the bed with some difficulty due to his injury; giving me the full measure of his gaze, he had nodded and then lightly brushed his hand against my chin.

And that was that. He had bid me good luck, telling me without any words needed, as is the case with siblings, that he wished me well, that he would take care of *Ammi* and *Abu* while I was gone.

On most days, I could keep the hurt and grief deep within and not let it come to the surface. But I couldn't that day. It was Ijaz's birthday. I tried to picture him as a grown-up, but I couldn't come up with an image. The realisation that I was forgetting what my baby brother looked like tore at me, and something broke inside. That day it slipped out. Against Major Rashid while playing a routine game of tennis, while he waited for his usual doubles partners, I imploded.

It was still early in the afternoon, so the courts were empty save for the young boys who came to gain access to the main courts which were off-limits for everyone except the senior crowd. The boys did not need ball boys. They were ecstatic to be playing on the special courts. They had so much energy that they were more than happy to pick up after themselves whenever a ball flew out of bounds.

As I listened to a couple of boys fighting over a line call, my mind drifted to Ijaz and how I used to play cricket with him in our street. Due to the limited space, we had to improvise and change the rules a bit.

Our bat used to be the broken arm of an old chair that had been ravaged by termites. We had been able to salvage only one armrest which had been shaved and polished and reshaped into a fairly light bat. The rules were simple: no run-up, only underarm bowling was allowed, one tip, one hand cricket. This was a fairly common game which was practised all over the city. In one tip, one hand, in addition to being bowled and caught out, you could also get out if the other team, which usually consisted of only one player who was the bowler, the fielder and the third umpire, caught the ball with one hand before it had bounced twice.

Every ball blocked by the batsman counted for one run. If he managed to block a ball that rolled all the way to a wall or any stationary, immovable object, that counted for four runs. If the ball hit any object directly without bouncing, that was considered out too. Leg before wicket (lbw) was not considered. And that was it. Matches stretched for hours, days even, with imaginary player of the series awards that included pakoras and samosas from the bakery three doors down.

Ijaz had grown up watching me and Mustafa fighting over who got to be Imran Khan or Wasim Akram. Over the years, as Mustafa outgrew the adolescent cheerful boy and turned into a sullen, lost, angry-at-the-world man, I had nobody to play with. Reluctantly, I turned to an overenthusiastic Ijaz who used to be dwarfed by our makeshift bat.

But what he lacked in size, he made up with determination. It seemed he had been born with a will to overcome the odds. And without fail, he wanted to win my approval, a fact that he would never admit to my face. Perhaps because he never got the attention from our parents, I felt bad and took up the role of both father and mother with Ijaz.

But I used to tease him a lot too. Especially during our cricket matches, I would find new ways of getting him out. I would devise rules and then tell him that these were the latest international rules, and he was too small to understand. I would get him run out in our small, cramped street. I would feint the act of bowling, and once he had swung, I would quickly throw the ball under his swing. He would go mad and charge me, and we would both go down in a heap; me doubling over with laughter, him all red-faced and pounding me with his tiny balled-up fists.

"You just wait," he would holler with tears streaking down his chubby cheeks, "when I'm twenty, I will be the captain of the Pakistan cricket team, and I will not invite you to my matches."

Today was his twentieth birthday. The last time I had seen him had been at our home five years ago. I wondered if the few straggly hairs covering his baby cheeks had turned into a full, thick beard. A sob escaped my mouth at the thought. And I seethed at the turn of events, at the world in general. At the fat figure of Major Rashid approaching me in his tiny shorts that were barely visible under his extra-large white T-shirt with 'Men at their best Pakistan Army' etched in green, with an unopened can of Wilson balls in one hand as he held a cigarette in the other.

"Game *hojaye*?"

"*Ji*, sir."

"You win three games from me and one kilo jalebi on me."

Normally, I would have laughed. Let the points go on for a bit longer, win two games, come close to winning the third but eventually lose. I would, on most days, get some jalebis anyway; he would have given me some money as well and taught me some technical aspects of the game as if he was Aisam Qureshi.

But today was not just any day. I got up without another word and went to my side of the court, the one with the sun directly in my eye. I wanted to hurt him, and I did not want my punishment to be tainted by some excuse that he couldn't serve because of the sun. I was out for blood.

As he limbered his gigantic frame through some weird version of stretching, Ahmed Din had come out of his room and climbed up the chair to officiate what he assumed would be an interesting game in which he would extol the beautiful aspects of the Major's game and perhaps, in the process, get some 'baksheesh' too.

Throughout this, I stood still at the ad-court baseline. In my mind, the person across the net was no longer an individual; it was the world with all its injustices that had ripped my family apart. That had taken my brother. That had separated me from the one person I had come to love.

Ahmed Din initiated the proceedings by opening the can with a flourish and throwing the fluorescent balls towards Major Rashid, who was going to serve. In an act of uncommon magnanimity, he threw the balls to me, letting me serve first. In tennis terms, this was considered a big handicap. It signified that the receiver did not consider the server enough of a threat to be worried about falling behind right at the start.

"Love all!"

I loved no one since everyone I had loved had been taken away from me. I was going to make the world pay for it. As I threw the ball in the air, I looked up right into the sun. I was blinded by the glare, but I stared right back, refusing to close my eyes. Three years of playing for sixteen hours with kids, grown-ups and everyone in-between had taught me enough. I met the ball in the exact centre of my racquet and sent a serve out wide. Major Rashid stretched out to return. As his return rose up from court, I met it on the rise and sent the ball back with interest towards the Major's weaker backhand. The Major, still standing in the centre admiring his forehand, was caught off-guard; he thundered towards the side and managed to respond with a weak lob. I was waiting for it. I camped under the lob; I had the whole court at my disposal as Major Rashid waited at the side, almost resigned to his fate. His face showing only mild irritation. *OK*, he seemed to say, *lucky point, you punk, I won't let this continue.*

But I wasn't interested in winning; I wanted someone to hurt

– instead of smashing the ball away from him, I gently placed it a little but not too far away from his reach. Major Rashid let out an ecstatic *Allahu Akbar* and lumbered after the ball. This time it was on his forehand, so I knew where he would put it.

"*Idher kaun hai*?!" he thundered.

I was already there by the time the ball arrived. Again, I took it on the volley and placed it towards his backhand just a little away so that he had to run. I continued this side-to-side routine for four more exchanges until, in his desperation, he lobbed one return way out of bounds.

As he glowered at me from across the net, I retuned his gaze. Ahmed Din, ever the keen mind reader, was desperately trying to get my attention, but I ignored him. I wanted his beloved clay to be powdered into mush under the Major's lumbering frame today.

For the next half an hour, I ran him from side to side. The Major, for his part, did not give up; beneath the years of comfort and flattery, there was real grit. And that spurred me on. By the time the Major was serving 0-5 down, a crowd had gathered at the sideline, including his doubles buddies. They were alternately cheering him and me too, as it was almost impossible for a ball boy to do this to a senior player, no matter how good he was. The reason having more to do with status than with skill. But they were all sportsmen, and traditions and social status or not, they admired grit.

At 15-30, the Major served. As soon as the ball left his racquet, I knew it was out. I knew Ahmed Din, sitting all the way at the top of the rickety umpire's chair, knew the ball was out. I knew Major Rashid – bent over and wheezing through his gaping mouth, the four strands of hair, that until half an hour ago had so expertly been swooped to cover his bald patch, now dripping buckets of sweat down his 'Men at their Best' T-shirt – knew the serve was out.

But someone had to call it. The honour code demanded that the receiver make the call, even though Ahmed Din was officiating. Major Rashid could not afford to go down 15-40. At 15-40 and 0-5, you realise your body has a mind of its own. And it is a panicky mind that vacillates between overcompensating and keeping it safe. In my three years of playing tennis, I had been witness to the phenomenon many times, mostly at the hands of Ahmed Din himself who, standing at a mere four foot nine inches, could hit the ball all over the court with the motion of a fly swatter and the precision of a rocket launcher. So, I knew what would happen if Major Rashid lost this point. Major Rashid knew it; Ahmed Din knew it; the whole crowd knew it.

Losing the set without winning a single game is called a *naata*. There is no greater insult in the game of tennis than a *naata*. It is the equivalent of getting your shalwar pulled down and exposing your behind to the whole world. There are two ways of dealing with it. Accepting it and moving on. Or not showing your face on the tennis court for a long time, until someone else has endured the ignobility and taken the attention away from you.

Major Rashid was the heart of soul of the club. He was the loudest, brashest, most uncouth, obscene, and therefore the most popular player at the club. You could hear his loud voice booming over the floodlit courts till 9pm as he retold various matches he had played, seen or how someone should have played. And always, the brunt of his punch lines were the losers who could not handle his prowess.

Today, perhaps for the first time, he was one point away from finding out how the subject of his punch lines spent the rest of their lives.

And all because today was Ijaz's twentieth birthday.

As everyone waited for me to make the call, Ahmed Din bellowed, "Good service, sir! *Yeh huee na baat!*"

Major Rashid got up from his position and looked across the net at me. "Qasim, was it in or out?"

"Of course it was in, *sirji*," Ahmed Din huffed. As he made his way down and quickly came to my side of the court, he expertly stepped over the mark, which had clearly been out, and pointed to one of the earlier ball spots within the service line. "This is the mark," he exclaimed.

"Ahmed Din, get off the court!" roared Major Rashid.

Ahmed Din looked crestfallen. He walked off the court but did not climb back up the chair. He knew there was no point in him getting up anyway; Major Rashid's pride would not let him win any trick points, so there was nothing he could do.

It was up to me.

"In or out?" Major Rashid said in-between breaths.

Finally, I looked over at Ahmed Din, who seemed to be shouting with his eyes, *Oye dalliya! Oh kanjraaa mat kareeen!* His eyes seemed to be pleading with me as his face remained expressionless except for the twitching of his thin moustache.

I was in no mood for mercy today. I did not care what happened. I did not care if I got fired; I had slaved away for three years as a ball boy, willing to give up better jobs because of my education, just to be near people who could help me get into the tribal areas where most of the terrorist groups were holed up. And where only the army had access to. I had spent three years trying to weed out information. And it had got me nowhere. So, I would just burn it all down and start again for all I cared.

"It was out, sir."

There were a few gasps and some of the officers laughed and cheered. It wasn't everyday a nobody, a ball boy, not even one of the good ones, would dare make a mockery of a serving Major, within a stone's throw of GHQ. This was their pride land. I was committing suicide. Ahmed Din had his hand in his hair and had sat down on the bench. This was too much for him.

There was a slight smile at the corners of Major Rashid's mouth, or maybe I was blinded by the sun.

"OK, I thought it looked out too. Anyway, OK, 15-40 match point." He got ready to serve.

Major Rashid was one of those who choose to go all out when in danger. He unleashed a bomb of a serve that I was barely able to get back. There was a smattering of applause as the seniors hushed the overexcited spectators, since the ball was still in play.

Major Rashid rushed to the centre of the court and smacked a cross-court winner. Now there was pandemonium as his friends let out loud cheers. Even Ahmed Din had allowed himself the luxury of a smile. This was the stuff of legend. If somebody wins a game at 0-5 down, it is called a *reverse naata*. In tennis terms, it's the complete opposite of having your shalwar removed. This time, it is you doing the shalwar removing.

Major Rashid's friends were suddenly applauding him for his well-crafted strategy and how it was typical of him to stage a comeback. And then Major Rashid believed them too. I sensed it in the jump in his step as he got to the service line. He suddenly had too much adrenaline in his system as his first serve flew over the net and outside the court without landing.

There was stunned silence again. And just like that, the euphoria of a remarkable comeback was gone. Reality and removed shalwars stared back. The second serve was an embarrassment. Major Rashid knew it; I knew it; Ahmed Din knew it; the twenty ball boys peeking from various points all over the courts knew it; and his friends knew it.

As I swung my racquet back to smack a return, I saw Major Rashid take a couple of steps behind the baseline, anticipating a deep return and giving himself a fraction of a second more to parry a return. I let my racquet come at full speed towards the ball and then, just at the last second, I let my wrist go limp so that by the time the racquet reached the ball, it was a feather touch.

The ball lobbed over the court in almost slow motion and landed with a gentle puff near the net. At the other end, Major Rashid was rushing towards the net, his eyes bulging with effort, his lips pulled back from his teeth as he clawed at the air with his outstretched racquet. The ball kept moving away from his reach with the amount of backspin I had put on it with my drop shot.

That he would not be able to reach the ball before it bounced a second time was a foregone conclusion by now. The more pressing question was whether Major Rashid would be able to stop himself in time before he crashed into the net.

He wasn't.

As Major Rashid slid into the net, breaking it and entangling himself in it completely, I walked off the court, heading towards the changing room, the image of a five-year-old Ijaz crying after losing a cricket match in my mind.

7
Love at first sight

Federal Lodges, Islamabad
Asma

I had never been able to make friends easily, and Islamabad and my present predicament was not making life any easier for me. Islamabad had a very eclectic feel to it; you were either a part of some group or society or you weren't. And if it was the latter, there was no way you were going to know of its existence, let alone be invited.

And so it was that the better part of my two years on the job had been spent alone after office hours. The first six months had been busy enough searching for accommodation in the priciest city in Pakistan. I soon found out that I could not afford to live in the city on my pay. I had to move out into the suburbs and then I had to rent out a portion and share it with another girl, Sameera, who worked at some bank. Father, as usual, had been livid, and only the threat of me quitting the job if he so much as got in the car had stopped him from coming to Islamabad and setting me up with a place to stay. But I had to admit, it was tough going.

Those had been really tough days: tough on the pocket; tough on the nerves. But in retrospect, those had also been the best days of my time at Islamabad, as I got to gain confidence in my capabilities and in my dealings with people. I found out about people and places. I knew where to go if I wanted to have the cheapest and best meal. On the outside, people in the government were viewed as rich and pampered officials, but the reality was much different. I was having trouble managing my expenses within my means. Each time I found myself trying to argue the merits and demerits of spending my pay on some item that I felt I needed, I found myself remembering how Qasim used to shake his head and laugh when I would give no second thought to money.

I finally understood.

Where are you, Qasim?

After six months of living in the portion, I was finally allotted a single room in the government lodges, which was a huge relief for me. Although I was sad to be separated from Sameera, the move gave some breathing space to my wallet. I could finally afford to live a little, see the city and the surroundings.

*

I dropped off my stuff in my room, showered, changed and then checked up on Sameera. Apparently, we had bonded strongly enough over those six months that we were now practically inseparable. She too was a stranger in the city, having moved here from Karachi, and like me she found the city aloof, distant and, most of all, dead.

"Hey, Sam! What's happening?"

"Hey! I was just about to text you – are you in the mood for some coffee or whatever?"

"Yes please!"

"Great! See you in Kohsar Market in twenty minutes."

"Gotcha."

They say you fall in love for the first time only once in your life. I did it twice.

The second time, while still trying to come out of the heartache and grief the first one had caused. Only this time, I fell in love with a place.

Having lived and grown up all my life in the hustle and bustle of Lahore, I took time settling into the whims of Islamabad.

And then I chanced upon Kohsar Market.

Nothing was ever the same for me again.

I had been walking along Margalla road, the last line of urban habitation before the landscape changed dramatically to lush green mountains and hidden waterfalls and springs, when I took a random turn into a side street. The more I kept going in, the less and less noisy it became, not that it ever had the potential of causing even a scratch on my Lahori eardrums.

But I kept on walking, liking the feeling of escaping into a hidden world, shrouded in mystery. At the end of the road, I chanced upon a setting that might as well have been from any place in Europe. Parallel to a children's park were roadside cafés and eateries where people were just hanging out, working on their laptops, having intellectual discussions. It was at once something so un-Pakistani-like and yet so Islamabadi that I felt myself go weak in the knees.

Dropping into the nearest chair, I ordered a cappuccino and a muffin and soaked in the atmosphere with arms wide open. I knew at that moment, just like a drowning man seeing the tip of land does, everything would be all right, eventually. Help was at hand.

And so began a ritual of sorts. Every day after work, I would make my way to Kohsar Market where, over a cup of cappuccino, I would unwind, relax, catch up. *Heal.*

Places have this hold on you at times. Like people you meet for the first time and connect, spaces too hold a special key that open you up completely when you enter them.

Initially, Sam was sceptical about the place when I took her there. One evening, at the end of our workout session, desperately hungry, I convinced her to try Kohsar Market. Being completely finnicky and rigid about her diet, she was adamant that we go to our regular place. But I begged and begged, and she finally relented.

So we came to Kohsar Market, and even though I knew there were only cafés and bakeries there which would not satisfy my friend, I had fallen so badly for the place that I felt it could and would fulfil whatever I wanted from it at that moment.

But as we walked past the line of shops and none of them met Sam's approval, I felt my faith shaking. As we came abreast the mosque right at the end, I silently prayed for a miracle. And then my eyes fell upon a young boy pushing a food cart along. In the fading light, I saw written in bright red the words 'Kabul Berger'. I nudged Sam.

"Hey, you up for some Kabul Berger?"

She rolled her eyes and looked over at where I was pointing. With a whatever-you-say shrug, she and I walked over to the boy who was literally jumping out of his worn-out shalwar kameez at the sight of probably his first customers for the day.

"Alright then," I tried to give the whole thing an air of excitement, "we will have two Kabul bergers please, but first please explain, what are they?"

The boy, a Pashtun, went into a painstaking monologue, switching into Urdu, English and Pashto seamlessly about how this was a commonly preferred street food in Kabul at that time. The burger, as it turned out, was not bad at all. It was basically a naan filled with a seekh kabab, onions, ketchup and lots and lots of French fries. The whole arrangement was doused in a healthy dosage of a fiery mint sauce that gave it an extra kick.

I had two Kabul bergers, which in the eyes of Sam, made me an honorary Kabulite.

I laughed until tears came out of my eyes, and the boy started creeping away, maybe thinking in his mind that I had lost it.

Maybe I had.

Or maybe I had finally found it again.

A replacement of sorts for what I had lost.

When Sam saw the effect Kohsar Market had on me, she made going there a non-negotiable clause in our friendship. I loved her all the more for it.

*

As I located Sameera sitting in our favourite booth outside Street 1 café, that overlooked the road and thus gave us ample opportunity to check out everyone coming and going, I saw that there was another person sitting beside her. I stiffened a bit and cursed under my breath at Sam for breaching one of our unspoken yet clearly defined edicts.

Kohsar Market was my 'Well of Rejuvenation' I had once explained to her during my bouts of verbal overdose. And so, membership to the club was limited and highly sought after but not given. I knew that a lot of people came and went there without my approval, but for all I cared, they didn't exist. For some reason, it made sense to Sameera, and she agreed to live by 'the code'.

And yet, here she was, giving keys to the city to a stranger.

I walked towards the table, telepathically asking Sam to look up and acknowledge my glare. She refused to make eye contact until I was practically past the point of return.

"Hey! You finally made it." Sam acted like nothing was out of the ordinary.

"Yeah, you too." I waited.

"Oh yeah, silly me, meet Haroon, or Harry; Harry meet Asma, the one I was telling you about."

"OK this is sounding fishier and fishier by the minute." I shook Harry's hand, as I gave my friend another glare, *this better not be a blind date set-up*, I eyeballed her. She gave me the *it's better than you think* shrug and sat down.

Oh well.

"Hey, Asma! Nice to finally put a face to the wonderful stories that Sam has been telling me about." Harry had a very Americanised accent, but I could still detect the Faisalabadi in him that kept creeping out at random syllables.

"Well, if it's all wonderful then it's definitely all true," I mumbled as I chewed on the complimentary garlic bread. I motioned to the waiter.

"Ha ha," Sam jumped in, "no, actually, Harry is a travel writer, and he wants to write about his experience in Pakistan, and I told him how you're from Lahore."

I actually choked on the bread, which froze everyone at the table. *You've gotta be fucking kidding me, Sam*, I thought, *why don't you slit my throat too while you're at it.*

I think telepathy really worked because Sam seemed to get it, word for word.

"I also told Harry about… Qasim." The last word was almost a whisper, but she might as well have used a megaphone.

I did not want to look up because of the sudden welling up in my eyes, which I was acutely aware of. At the same time, I had trouble swallowing for some reason. This was beyond sabotage. This was an ambush.

"Is this some kind of a joke?"

"Asma, you need to listen to me."

"I'm sorry, Harry, Haroon, whoever you are, but please forget whatever she told you."

Sam kicked me under the table, and before I could say anything, she added, "I told him how you lost a good friend of yours, Qasim, and how you only know that he used to live in the inner city. As it so happens, Harry has booked a guided tour of the inner city, and I thought you and I could also go. I could get to see some history after all that you have told me about Lahore and maybe you two can, I don't know, whatever…" Her voice trailed off.

What I actually heard her saying was *OK, so let's get this over with once and for all so we can put it behind us. If you can find more about Qasim, great. If not, close that fucking chapter once and for all, time to move on.* This was her telling me that I needed closure.

I finally looked up. "Have you guys ordered yet? I'm starving."

That was me saying, *let's do it.* I was all in.

Ball's in your court, fate.

8
Two of a kind

Rawalpindi
Qasim

I barely made it to the washroom before the tears came. It was as if my heart was being squeezed out of my eyes. I could feel the hot rivulets as they streaked down my face. I kept looking down as I opened the tap and splashed cold water on my face.

As I gulped a mixture of my salty tears and cold tap water to quench my parched tongue, I heard the door slam behind me.

"Oh *dallay*," whispered Ahmed Din as his eyes popped out of his face. It was the angriest I had ever seen him.

"Are you on a death wish? Do you not want to work?"

Expletives and profanities were the bread and butter of Ahmed Din's vocabulary and way of life. I had smashed teeth in for much weaker insults in my previous life. But that was then; I had nothing to defend now; I had been reduced to a nothing. But more than that, I knew Ahmed Din meant the profanities as a term of endearment.

I looked up from the sink and turned to face him.

He looked at me with my face dripping water down my faded hand-me-down T-shirt, my faded tracksuit below and my patched-together white canvas shoes. He came back to the face. His eyes registered the wound in me, and something in him softened.

Ahmed Din came up to me and raised both his hands up to my shoulders.

I stooped down and bawled like a five-year-old.

Afterwards, there were no words or explanation needed as I lay spent on the floor of the basement which served as Ahmed Din's office and bedroom.

By the time Deemu came, I had pushed the hurt and the pain back below the surface, almost. I needed to be myself now, to get away from the scene of my implosion, somewhere where nobody had seen me come apart.

There was a knock on the door. The wooden frame creaked open and Deemu marched down the stairs in his usual bouncy step; Ahmed Din got up from behind his desk and bellowed, "You need to take your friend and show him some good time, or he'll be the death of all of us."

Deemu did not say a word as he shifted his gaze from the coach to me.

He tilted his head to the side and said, "Let's go."

And so we did.

*

We passed the five-minute journey from the GHQ Tennis Club to Lalkurti in silence as Deemu zigzagged through traffic on his Honda CG125 with me clinging on.

Both of us lost in our private whirlpool of thoughts, oblivious to the shouts and squealed brakes of those he cut off. To an outside observer, it would have appeared as if Deemu had a death wish.

And he would be right.

Looks can be deceiving. Especially if you are on the ground, looking up, while being pummelled to within an inch of your life. That was the first time I got to have a close look at Deemu.

I had seen him with Raja Niaz on campus and at odd times of

the night even in my room when Niaz and I had been roommates. But those had been fleeting moments and he was always in the shadows, quiet and elusive. Gone before I could even register his presence.

Little did I know that the smudging at the corner page of my life, as it was being written, would turn out to be a central spot later on. I would have paid more attention, or would I have?

That's the thing with hindsight, you think you could have done things better, been more attentive, more receptive, more everything. But it's a lie that we keep telling ourselves when we no longer have the reins of destiny in our hands.

Sometimes I wonder if we ever do.

I was meant to get my face bashed in by this dark-skinned granite of a man, only to be reunited with him later so that he could bring me back to life.

In spite of the kind of day I was having, or maybe because of it, I smiled at the irony of life. Here I was, pushed back into the vortex of a person I had considered to be my mortal enemy. While people I held dearest to me – Ijaz, Asma, my family – had been torn away from me. By events beyond my control.

We are never in control. No matter what one might feel.

But still I clung onto a feeling that it would all add up one day. Perhaps the reason why sometimes things don't seem to make sense, like me ending up on a motorcycle hurtling towards Lalkurti with Deemu, was because I was too close to the ground to see the tapestry of life. Mine. His. All the other people who had come in and gone out of my existence so far. Maybe one day, when I would be able to look back on it, from an old and wizened age, with my loved ones, I might be able to make sense of it all.

Asma.

The thought of her caught in my throat and made me hurt with a dull ache, but I quickly brushed it aside as we rounded the bend and Lalkurti bazaar came into view.

There was something homely and timeless about the peace and tranquillity of the bazaar as it remained oblivious to the fast pace of the rest of the world. Ensconced in its own ecosystem. Muslims, Christians, Hindus all still living together in peace.

For a Lahori like myself, the slow pace of Pindi and Lalkurti especially should have chaffed. But perhaps, in another example of life's queer tricks, it turned out to be the balm for what had been ailing me.

It seemed like a lifetime ago when I had reached Peshawar according to the directions given to me by Raja Niaz. A part of me knew not to trust my ex-roommate, but I was desperate. I was willing to try anything and trust anyone so long as I had some direction in life. I needed to be doing something to find my baby brother. I needed to fill up the void that had appeared in our lives, the abyss that I saw in my mother's eyes.

And so, I left. Without a word to Asma, the person who had made me find myself. I could not face her. I had betrayed her trust. I had violated her faith in me. In us. And for that, I could not forgive myself.

So the quest to find Ijaz and heal my family had also become a sort of penance for breaking the heart of someone who had given me her fate. I felt it was the only thing I could do. Get out of her life.

Who was I to have thought I could ever have a future with her?

It was all the exuberance of youth and the idealism of first love.

As I had made my way down the bus in Peshawar and towards the bazaar, the crowd parted, and I saw Deemu. And in that moment, I knew that Raja Niaz had betrayed me.

Deemu later told me that the only thing that had saved me from being ambushed by ten hired thugs who were waiting to pounce on me, stuff me inside a van and dispose of me somewhere in the jungle, was what I did after I made eye contact with him.

I kept walking towards him.

It took me a second to resign my fate to whatever lay before me.

I had already left too much hurt and pain behind to ever entertain thoughts of turning back. Whatever lay before me could not even begin to compare. If it meant my life, so be it.

What Deemu saw was a man who realised that he had been led into a trap and yet continued to come. He recognised it and respected it. To him that spelt conviction, something he admired and held dear.

He decided then and there that it was time to part ways with Raja Niaz and the lifestyle he had adopted and to take a chance on me.

9
Ghost

Old City, Lahore
Asma

It was that time of the year in Lahore when you sweated from every pore.

Every bead of sweat pouring out of me felt like a confession of guilt on my part. Like a scorned lover, the city directed its wrath at me for having moved on to the cooler charms of Islamabad.

I wished this mad trip was over already.

Wedged in the back seat between an annoyingly sweatless Sam – "Hey I'm from Karachi, this sort of weather would qualify as a cause for celebration." – and a profusely soaked Haroon, I tried to remind myself not to think too much of what lay ahead.

Don't get your hopes up, I told myself, *this is more of a ritual where you are closing the door on one chapter of your life and moving on. Please take it like that and do not get too involved in it.*

After having been ambushed with the idea, I had time to mull it over and I had to admit, Sam was absolutely right. This was closure. I needed it.

Sensing that the uncomfortable silence had gone on too long and feeling it his chivalrous duty to do something about it, Haroon looked at me and said, "So, Asma, I am sure you must hear this a lot, but what are your feelings about working where you do?"

I flinched. I was never comfortable telling anyone about the organisation I worked for. These were confusing times. Everyone and their parents were trying to come to grips with the way the world around us was changing. I was never at ease discussing religion and its interpretation with friends and sitting in a tight horse-drawn carriage in sweltering heat was just too much.

I tried to be civil.

"I try not to let my personal feelings affect my work."

"Yeah but still, when the world suddenly shines a magnifying glass on you, as is happening in Pakistan these days, and we are witnessing the repercussions of it, one must feel the need to question if they are on the right side or not."

"Ooh big word, ow!" I yelped as I felt Sam's elbow in my ribs. The carriage driver looked back sharply and then resumed his position.

"OK, that came out too harsh." Haroon gave a shit-eating grin and said nothing, leaving me to carry on the conversation.

I took in a deep breath and then exhaled. "So you're right in a way that there are conflicting emotions at times when there are terrorist incidents and you come to find out that people behind it profess to follow the same religion as you do. It makes you wonder who is right, right? I don't know, for me it gets tiring, you know, having to justify what I feel is the right interpretation of Islam, so I just don't get into it. I keep it simple – killing innocent people is wrong; it's not what I think our religion is about, full stop."

"So how do you explain the history of this region and how it has been shaped in the last three decades? Does that explain what is happening now?" Haroon looked at me with sincere interest and I could see where he was coming from. For anyone not having lived in Pakistan in the last few decades, it was difficult to digest how the people were turning in on themselves. Like chickens that had messed up their internal compass. Chickens that had been fed on a diet of hate and extremism for too long. That were now coming home to roost.

"All I believe is that God is just. He is above and beyond emotions. Religion is a set of guidelines. The object of performing these rituals or forgoing them does not make God happy or angry. The underlying aim beyond the physical aspects of the religious obligations is to bring one closer to the reality that is God. No man is superior or inferior to another on the basis of colour, name, physical acts. There is no superior race, only a true path. Religion makes sure you tick all the boxes on the checklist giving directions to this path."

I felt Sam moving beside me; I looked at her and she was smiling. "I think that was beautiful."

I smiled. "I know."

"Vain, much?"

"I did not say that; Qasim used to talk like that," I whispered.

Suddenly, I felt bad for bringing the whole trip down by bringing up Qasim. To be fair, the whole experience had been a good one. This was our last day. In the past six days, we had been led in and around the old inner city streets, led by Mehran, the driver.

"Look guys, this trip has been wonderful, and it has all been because of you two. I realise I needed to get it off my chest once and for all. I wish it could have ended with us finding something about Qasim, but I am mature enough to know that that's not how life works. Just saying Qasim Kaleem out loud won't make him turn up in some corner of inner Lahore; that's not how life works. Shit happens. Mine happened a long time ago. Today let's just put it to rest. I hope wherever Qasim is, he is happy; I am done with this phase of my life."

With that long closing speech, I beamed at my companions, who both managed to put up fairly genuine smiles in spite of the heat and cramped space.

Ghost

Like a ghost from the past, a voice from ahead shattered the façade of my recently constructed bliss. "I know where Qasim lives."

10

Begin again

Lalkurti, Rawalpindi
Qasim

Deemu dropped me off outside Lyric Video Store. Khalid, One of the owners was seated outside the shop in his usual seat pretending to read the newspaper while he actually took in the happenings of the street.

"*Kesay hain*, Chacha?" bellowed Deemu jovially.

"*Tu bata bachoo*, what mischief are you getting this one into today?" He eyed me from behind his glasses.

I laughed nervously, confident that he could see my tear-stained face and pulled-down demeanour. Nothing escaped him.

But if he did, he didn't say anything. He never did, ever since he took me in as his part-time assistant, providing me a place to sleep at the back of the shop.

"This one's from Lahore, Chacha – we're the ones who should be learning from him."

Khalid grunted, then turned to me. "If you're free tonight, I'll show *Gunfight at the O.K. Corral* – it's the one with Burt Lancaster; you will love it."

"That *ganja* you told me about?"

"Yeah."

Khalid and his brother, who owned the video shop, had the largest collection of old westerns, something he and I had bonded over when I had first started working for him. Sometimes I wondered if he really even cared if he made money from the shop. It was just a way of life for him, something that he loved to do.

Before I could say something, Deemu said, "Actually, Chacha, Qasim and I are going somewhere tonight."

Deemu and I exchanged looks while Khalid observed us both, a hint of a smile playing underneath his silver moustache.

"You can come too if you want, Chacha," said Deemu as he got back on his bike and kicked it to life.

"No thanks, I can't deal with the headaches."

"You don't even know what I'm talking about, Chacha," laughed Deemu.

"Of course I don't," said Khalid as he buried himself behind the newspaper again.

"9pm, be ready," shouted Deemu above the din of his bike as he zoomed down the street, leaving me and Khalid in the deafeningly loud silence of his absence.

Seemingly done with his reading, Khalid wrapped the newspaper and put it in his lap as he took off his glasses and looked up at me.

"Come sit." He motioned to the chair next to him, his tone much softer.

A lump formed in my throat suddenly as I quickly bowed my head and nodded, placing myself in the chair before he could say anything else that would move me to tears again.

All these years since Ijaz had disappeared, I still could not deal with the kindness of strangers. I felt like I did not deserve it and always felt that I was betraying Ijaz by basking in the love of people while my little brother, who I should have protected, was somewhere out there. I had no idea if he was being treated nicely or not. I never let my thoughts go further than that. I could not. I had to find him before the bad thoughts found a way beyond the line I had drawn in my mind.

As I sat down and tipped the chair back on its hind legs, propped against the wall of the shop, Khalid made eye contact with the tea stall owner across the road and made the sign of two with his hand.

The tea stall owner, also called Ijaz, nodded and called out to one of the little boys serving customers inside the stall.

Presently, a boy ran across the road, expertly cradling two steaming cups of tea in one hand while in the other, he was balancing a plate of pakoras and a smaller plate of green chutney.

Khalid smiled at the sight of the pakoras. He raised his hand towards Ijaz, who beamed like a three-year-old under his bushy beard, and pressed his hand to his chest.

The little boy ran into the shop and came out with a small table which he set before us, placing the tea and pakoras on them. Khalid fished out a ten rupee note and handed it to the boy, who backed away with his hands behind.

"Ijaz *saab* said its free."

"This isn't for Ijaz."

The boy blushed and stepped forward, pocketing the note and running off in one smooth motion.

"You know I still see Ijju just like this small boy," said Khalid as he sipped his tea.

A sob escaped my mouth as I looked down at my cup.

Khalid's face jerked around to me as realisation hit him. "I almost forgot about Ijaz, *beta*," he said in a whisper.

I wanted to tell him that it wasn't his fault, to make him feel better. To tell him that I was thankful to him for being so nice to me. But all I said was, "One day, I will forget too that I had a brother called Ijaz."

Even though my eyes were on my cup, I could tell that Khalid flinched when I said that, but he didn't say anything.

After a while he said, "You know, as a kid, you never could have guessed this guy that you see now."

"What do you mean?"

"I mean the bushy beard, the tea stall, this isn't what he is, or what we all thought he was going to be."

"What did you think he was going to be?"

"He used to play cricket; we all thought it was only a matter of time before he made it to the national team."

"Then why didn't he?"

"Lots of things, who's to say? Maybe he wasn't good enough, maybe politics, maybe he lost interest."

I looked at Khalid, sensing that he was trying to tell me something.

Khalid went on, "You see, becoming a cricketer was his father's wish. And so Ijaz became one, but life eventually asks all of us one question which no one else can answer for us."

I nodded, knowing what it was already.

"And that is: is this what you want to be doing for the rest of your life? And you can no longer lie because there is no one to lie or please; it is you asking yourself. People think they can lie to themselves, but nobody can do it. It tears them apart if they try."

I started to get up, knowing where this was going to lead to. But Khalid put a hand on my arm. I settled back in my chair as my insides seethed.

Sensing my mood, Khalid's voice softened to a whisper, but he continued none the same, "What I'm trying to say, *beta*, is that there is a path for us all, and sooner or later, we find it."

But I was beyond comfort now. "So this Ijaz really wanted to be a tea stall owner instead of a cricketer?" I scoffed.

"No, *beta*," Khalid whispered, "the thing is, Ijaz never realised that he was living his father's dream. He kept trying but never made it to the national team. He never heard his heart telling him that this wasn't what he was meant to do until it was too late, and he was too old and too broken. The bearded, fat old man hunched over the tea all day is only a shell of the boy I once knew. I just wish somebody had told him to listen to his inner voice before it was too late."

I placed the cup on the table and got up. "Khalid *saab*, I am grateful for all that you have done for me, but if you are telling me that my Ijaz was meant to run off and be a terrorist—"

"I wasn't talking about your brother," Khalid cut me off. "I'm talking about you, Qasim *beta*. What are you doing with your life? You are an educated boy, working as a ball boy in a tennis court. You are wasting your life."

"How can you say that when you know my brother is missing?"

"Are you sure this is the only way of finding him? Seems to me you're more interested in a way that helps find him and punish you as well."

I knew he was right, but there was nothing I could do.

Khalid looked up at me. "*Dekho*, I'm not telling you to stop looking for your brother, but ask yourself this: if the roles were reversed and it was your brother wasting his talent and not doing what he was meant to, would you have been happy knowing that?"

"I don't even know if he is alive or not," I almost shouted. Luckily, it was drowned out by the noise of a passing truck.

Khalid grimaced at my outburst and looked down. Immediately, I felt bad for behaving this way to this kind old man.

"Look, Khalid *saab*, I just cannot get on with my life until I find out what has happened to someone I love."

He nodded, without looking up at me. "But while you're at it, what about those who love you? What happens to them?"

Asma.

It was as if I had been shot at point-blank range in the chest. I clutched at the door to steady myself. Then, without another word, I went up to my room.

11

Staring into the abyss

Asma

I felt as if I had been shot. Sensing my hesitation, Sam stepped in and told the carriage driver to pull up. As we came to a stop in the cramped inner street of Anarkali, I felt increasingly claustrophobic and out of breath.

"We're going to grab a cup of tea from that shop; you're welcome to join us," she told Mehran, as she half-led, half-dragged me off the carriage and towards an empty chair outside a roadside dhaba where I plopped onto the first chair I saw. Like a reluctant third wheel, Haroon sheepishly trudged behind us.

"OK, tell me what's going on inside your head?" asked Sam.

"You mean besides the obvious?"

"Come on, Asma! This could be a good thing – isn't this what you have been wanting for a long time?"

"Yeah, but then I got over it; I have made my peace. Now, why should I go through this again?"

"Look, you know how hard it was for you to get leave from your boss and come here. You know this won't happen every time. If you still feel like you're not up to the task, you can stay here and Haroon, me and Mehran will go check it out. Or, wait let me finish." She raised her hand as she saw me trying to interrupt her.

I slouched back in my chair, slurping my extra sweet tea.

"Thank you," Sam said theatrically. "Or, we can both stay here, and Mehran and Haroon can go and get Qasim to come meet us at a neutral point."

"What?!" I shot up from my seat, spilling some tea on Mehran who, unbeknownst to me, had sidled up to the three of us and was listening in to the conversation with total immersion. He hardly gave a second look to the stain on his white kurta and, giving me a full grin, told me not to worry.

"Are you mad? What would Haroon say? And why would Qasim agree to come since he hasn't already all these years?" I implored.

"Hmm, good point," said Sam with the faint hint of a grin. "I guess you're right; you'll have to come along with us then."

Notwithstanding the subtle manoeuvring by my best friend, I had to agree it was time to choose between fight or flight. I downed the last of my sugary drink and slammed the cup down on the table.

Haroon, who had been a silent spectator until then, also approved. "Alright! Let's do this."

And with that, we paid our bill with a decent tip for the tea boy, got back on the carriage and rode towards Qasim's house. Haroon was the first one to break our self-imposed silence. "Is it just me or does this feel like a posse riding out into the sunset to catch the bad guys?"

"It's just you," I muttered through clenched teeth as I tried not to focus too much on what lay ahead.

"Wow, somebody has been revived by the tea," said Sam as she grinned at Haroon, encouraging him to lighten the mood. For his part, Haroon seemed to be opening up and enjoying his new-found role in our group dynamic.

"OK, OK, kids," I said. "Let's not go overboard; let's act like adults here."

"Yes, Mummy!" said Sam. Before I could fix her my iciest stare though, Mehran's voice came from the front. "We are here."

I caught my breath as the carriage came to a stop in front of an old wooden door. There were a couple of potted plants on the ledge that led up to the door which was a couple of feet higher than the road. An old motorcycle was chained to an electricity pole outside the house and directly underneath a board that had seen better days. It read 'Muhammad Jabbar Kaleem (Capt)'. Someone had written *ghaddaar ka ghar* underneath it with red paint. My heart flipped.

I motioned to Mehran to go and knock on the door.

Throwing the reins of the horse onto the front of the seat, Mehran got off. As the balance shifted and the rear portion of the carriage suddenly got heavier, we were thrown forward and Sam shrieked. The sound reverberated in the deathly silence of the street, and I glared at her. As the echo of Sam's shriek echoed in the narrow street, a wooden window directly overhead opened up. I peered up to lock eyes with an old woman with flowing white hair looking down at me.

There was something about those eyes. Amidst the hurt, the anger, the void, there was something else, just beyond grasp. Something familiar. She kept looking down at me, not saying anything. I did not know what to do. By then Mehran had climbed up the stairs and was standing at the door. He looked directly up and said, "*Assalaam O Alaikum, Amma ji*! It's me Mehran, how are you?"

There was no response; she had not even shifted her glance away from me. I felt like I was being X-rayed. Mehran looked back at what the old woman was staring at and then back up at her. "These are some friends of Qasim *bhai*; they wanted to meet up with him – is he here?"

At the mention of Qasim's name, I saw a flicker in her eyes. Just for a second, and then it was gone.

"Go away! Why are you bothering us?"

We turned around to find ourselves being scolded by a bent-over man in a prayer cap and a white beard. Muttering under his breath, he brushed us aside as he went up the stairs to the house. I did not need any hints from Mehran to know this was Qasim's father. As he came abreast Mehran, the latter reverently stepped aside and touched the knee of the old man in a sign of respect.

The old man did not acknowledge the gesture and knocked on the door. "What are you doing coming here and bothering us?" he said in a gruff voice.

"No, Chacha, I was only paying my respects to *Amma ji*."

"What respects? If you came more often you would know Fatima has not talked or moved on her feet ever since." His voice broke, and he looked away. At that moment, the door opened and without another backwards look he went inside. A young woman had opened the door. And as the old man went inside, she remained there, looking at us. On her hip she cradled an infant that was barely a few months old. A little girl materialised from behind her. "Close the door and make me a cup of tea," the voice bellowed from somewhere inside the shadows.

"*Ji aye ji*," she shouted. Then she stepped outside the door and looked at Mehran and said in a whisper, "Go talk to my husband; Mustafa will tell you everything – you know where the shop is." With that, she vanished back inside. The whole incident took less than five minutes, but it had left me disoriented. Suddenly, I remembered once when Qasim had brought me to his shop. It had been late at night, and I hadn't paid much attention to the direction. I ran to the front of the carriage and grabbed Mehran by the elbow. "Do you know which shop she was talking about?"

Mehran seemed taken aback by my forwardness and was transfixed at the hand on his elbow which I hastily retracted. "Come on, Mehran, focus," I pleaded.

He seemed confused. "I know the shop where Mustafa *bhai*

works; it's their family shop. But she said her husband..." He seemed to have gone off on a tangent, lost in his own thoughts.

"Yeah so? What does that have to do with anything?"

"But her husband died in a bomb blast so many years ago, when Ijaz also ran away, that is when all the local people started the boycott of the Kaleems." Suddenly he seemed to come to a conclusion. "Oh, so she married Mustafa *bhai*!"

"Mehran, I really have no interest in any of your mohalla gossip right now." I had just about had enough.

"Can you take us to the shop, or should we just get somebody else to lead us?" I made what was a pretty weak threat. I mean, we were deep inside the inner streets of Lahore which were, at times, so narrow that the horse's flanks rubbed against the walls on either side. So that the chance of finding a cab were almost non-existent.

But it seemed to work as Mehran came out of his trance, climbed onboard and clucked his tongue, which seemed to bring his horse into life. The three of us jumped back on the carriage as it started moving along the brick-lined road.

12

Hope rekindled

Lalkurti, Rawalpindi
Qasim

Lalkurti is shaped like a bowl. On a clear day, you can stand at one end of the street and see all the way to the other end. The rickety wooden balcony outside the first-floor room I had been given by Khalid gave the perfect panoramic view of the market where time seemed to have stopped long ago.

When Deemu had first brought me here, I had been shocked at the aura of calmness and serenity in the area. Coming from the hustle and bustle of Anarkali and Lahore, Pindi seemed to be a city half asleep.

And then I discovered Lalkurti.

The Infantry of the British Army, after whom the locality had been named, might have left long ago, but it seemed nothing much had changed since then. Even an attempt to change its name to Tariqabad had been unsuccessful.

The area seemed to be an example of religious harmony where Hindus, Sikhs, Christians and Muslims were still thriving peacefully together. Then what had made Deemu leave such a peaceful life, change his name and religion and move?

I had once asked Deemu about his reason for leaving, but he had evaded it with some excuse. I had not bothered to ask him again. After all, who was I to ask someone a reason for leaving home and loved ones behind?

"*Oye*, Majnun!"

I snapped out of my reverie to see Deemu grinning up at me.

"Coming, Layla," I said.

*

Colonel Sherwin William's bungalow was the first house on the road as soon as we left Lalkurti. It was midnight. Deemu and I were standing outside the gate, which was locked. Deemu killed the engine and leaned his bike against a lamp post, circling the lock around the wheel and the post nonchalantly while he surveyed the road.

After making sure there was no other option but to scale the wall, Deemu nudged me from behind. "C'mon before Sheroo sees us, or he'll wake up the whole neighbourhood."

I nodded and quickly climbed over the wall, making sure to tuck in my clothes to avoid getting caught in the barbed wire. I was careful to land quietly on the other side, lest I wake up Sheroo, which would have been the end of our adventure.

I made space for Deemu to jump down from the wall. He landed awkwardly and fell against a trash can which made a loud noise. We both mouthed choice obscenities. And then held our breath.

Presently, there was a loud thumping noise as something huge got up and started moving inside the car garage that had been converted into a cage. Sheroo's massive frame appeared from the shadows; for a few seconds, he stood surveying us for a while, then tipped his head back and let out a huge bellow.

Instinctively, both of us shoved our fingers inside our ears to drown out the noise, but it was no use.

"AAAAOOOOOOOOOOGGHHHHHHHHHHHH!"

It was a plaintive roar, suited more for the plains of Africa than the homely streets of Lalkurti. The sound felt out of place and, precisely because of that, even scarier. The roar seemed to fill the entire sky.

"AAAAOOOOOOOOOOGGHHHHHHHHHHHH!"

It was a thick, heavy guttural sound a giant would make. It had kept me awake, scared out of my wits in my bed, for the first couple of months when I had come to Lalkurti. I would like to believe that once I had found out the truth about the noise, I had been able to sleep more at peace, but that would be a lie. I still had bad dreams about waking up being dragged through the streets by a lion.

"*Oye haramiyo*! Why did you have to be so loud?" grumbled Pitras as he emerged from his blue tent beside the cage, one hand stuffed deep inside his dhoti, scratching.

Both of us pointed to each other as we made our way towards him, cutting a wide swathe around Sheroo's cage, who by now seemed done with his roars and was spreadeagled on the cool floor of the garage, his tongue wagging out like a dog. From time to time, he'd get up and lap water from the steel bucket lying by the wall.

Pitras flashed us a grin and produced a big bottle containing a dark brown liquid. "Poured some in Sheroo's water too, *aaj donon bhai tunn hain*."

Deemu let out a huge guffaw. "So that's why!" He made his way to the bars and whistled. "Hey, drunkard."

Sheroo opened one eye and flicked his tail lazily.

I was too astonished to say much, but I quickly got over it. Making my way to Pitras, I handed him the pakoras I had brought along as snacks.

"*Haan bhai* what's happening, Raager Federer?"

"Nothing much, what's up with you, found a bride for Sheroo and yourself?"

"No such luck, brother, who's going to marry a fat Christian and a toothless lion?"

I smiled and felt bad for Sheroo. He had been rescued from a political rally as a cub where they had pulled out all his teeth and were using him as a mascot. When Colonel William had chanced upon the procession while arranging the security route, he had made sure that Sheroo went back home with him, while his handlers spent the night behind bars. Having never met him, I had only heard stories of Colonel William's exploits from almost everyone at one time or another in Lalkurti.

He had grown up in the inner streets of Lalkurti. In fact, his and Deemu's father had been orderlies in the army together and had served officers here before independence. His father had died while William had been a baby, but his officer had taken the young William in like his own son and had sent him to cadet school, ensuring that he got a good education and eventually joined the army.

After partition, Deemu's father had stayed behind, serving officer after officer who got posted to GHQ. We were in the same house where Samuel, Deemu's father, had served his last officer, a fast riser with a bit of a drinking problem. One night during a dinner at his house, alcohol bottles had been discovered by a senior of his who had threatened to report it to the authorities. This was during the eighties when the country was going through a drastic makeover.

In a bid to save his career and himself, the officer had put all the blame on his Christian orderly Samuel, thinking that would be the end of it. One day soon afterwards, a mob entered the house while the officer was away and lynched both Samuel and his wife. Deemu, who was only five years old, hid in the bushes, only coming out after the mob had left.

By then, his parents had stopped twitching as they hung from the giant Peepal tree in the courtyard. Not being able to reach up and untie them, the toddler had run to and fro, begging for help, but everyone had heard or seen what had been happening through their windows and wanted no part of it. That night, he cried himself to sleep, lying under the feet of his parents. The next morning, when he heard people approaching through the gate, Deemu had slipped out the back and ran away.

For the next decade, he had lived on the street, fighting, foraging and surviving until Raja Niaz found him and took him in.

Over the years, Deemu got to visit Rawalpindi many times, but it took a long time before he could get the courage to visit Lalkurti. He found his relatives, friends, old memories, and he realised that he still belonged with his people. Raja Niaz, ever the opportunist, had encouraged the feeling and told him to cultivate his relationships with the Christian community. It was when Niaz used his people to set fire to a Christian community in Lahore in order to occupy the land, which was located in a prime area, that Deemu got an inkling of what he had in mind.

That was the beginning of the end of his time with Niaz. And that was how it led him to meeting me in Peshawar and the start of our relationship together. After he had decided on trusting me, Deemu had brought me back with him to Lalkurti, set me up with Khalid and his brother, got me a job at the GHQ tennis club through Ahmed Din, who used to work as a dishwasher with his father at one time.

Little by little, as he opened up to me, I started seeing the orphan who had watched his parents giving up their last breath in front of his eyes. His mother and father must have known that he was nearby, hiding and watching. How they must have controlled their emotions, seconds before being strung up the tree still sent shivers down my spine. It had taken Deemu countless nights before he had finally been able to make his way inside the same house which others said was haunted. But for him, it was home still.

In fact, it had been Colonel William who had especially visited him a couple of months ago and told him that he could come anytime and that, as long as he was there, Deemu was welcome. And that is how I found out about Colonel William. He had come out of military school with honours and had distinguished himself in posting after posting. But inside, he seemed to be carrying the weight of his whole community. When he got posted to GHQ, he had insisted on moving into this old, dilapidated house.

Everything had to be big with Colonel William. If his neighbour got cable, Colonel William got a satellite dish service. If his peers did one tour in Siachen, William did two and was again on volunteer duty in Waziristan, fighting against extremists. If his neighbours had German Shepherds, William got a lion.

And if anyone complained, he let Sheroo reply on his behalf. But nobody complained really. He was an excellent officer and a shining example of somebody making it on merit. The locals of Lalkurti on their part were proud of someone from their community making it to the top and somebody they could go to with their troubles. Every Sunday, whenever he was home, William, a chronic bachelor, would hold an open 'katcheri' on his front porch and people from Lalkurti and surrounding areas would come with their problems and favours, and he would listen to them, make Pitras note them down. And he followed up on them too.

Sometimes, I used to feel a pang of sadness when I saw William and all that he had achieved and thought of my father and how he too, as an immigrant boy, had been passionate about proving his loyalty to his new home. How his life and ours would have looked if he had made it too. Ijaz would never have gone away, shattering the fine balance of our life. I would not have given up everything to come after him.

But then, I would not have realised what really mattered. And I would never have found out that somewhere deep within the recesses of my heart, this odyssey that I had embarked upon, a part of me hoped that it would also lead me back to Asma. The first time I had realised this, I had pushed it back under, into the crevices of my soul, not willing to confront it, surprised at its audacity and urgency and yet glad too. And then it kept popping up at odd times, catching me unawares. It was as if I was fighting with myself – there was a part of me that was completely out of my control, the part that belonged to the girl who had seen me when nobody else did. And that part throbbed and ached. No matter how much I neglected it, starved it, it was alive and kicking. This quest for my brother had now turned into a journey within myself. I had found out that in the end, all roads led to Asma, and if I did not find her before long, my life, my search, would not be complete.

Such is life.

You start off in search for your brother to complete your family and find that your home belongs to someone else. It had been years, and it had taken an enormous amount of effort to break off all contact with her and my friends from university. I had no way of knowing what had happened to her after I left. A part of me, the part that loathed me for leaving what had been the best thing to have ever happened to me, feared that she had moved on, had married and had settled into her new life with someone that was more equal to her status and position in society. It was my way of self-punishment, my way of atonement for what had befallen our family. I reasoned that I did not deserve happiness if my family was in tatters.

And yet. Like a piece of metal that would bend but not break, the hope for love held onto the thinnest veneers of fate. It refused to tear. I tried to break the last bond by calling it selfishness on my part to be still thinking for myself, but the heart is a dervish when it comes to matters of the soul. It sees not the bonds of blood or kin; it dances to a tune that transcends skin, levels of society, and it is unashamedly selfish. It said to me, "I may reside inside you, but I beat for someone else. And if you do not rejoin me to the part of me that has been lost, there is no telling how much longer I, and by extension you, may live."

I looked over at Deemu, who was sitting at a distance under the giant Peepal tree that had seen everything. It had been there to hear his first cries as his mother had kissed and soothed him.

It had been there when his father, tired from the day's work, had lifted him up in his arms and shown him the stars. And it had been there when he had seen the final invisible thread of life breaking from his parents' lips.

A sob escaped my lips as I realised that every time something bad happens, we feel that it is the end of the world, and life simply cannot go on. There is no coming back from this. And yet, it does.

And still the earth turns.

Another day dawns.

Like a parent wiping the tears from a child's face, life says, "There is still hope, my child. There is still time. Take the first step, even if it seems there is darkness all around. Do not be afraid, for I will be there, every step of the way, watching over you, holding your hand, even if you may not feel it. Carry on."

And so, I did. Not knowing for how much longer I could or where it would lead me. And if I would ever get back to where I was before it all started or if it would all be worth it. But I felt the invisible pull tugging at my heartstrings, and I closed my eyes and took the first step. Into the darkness. Away from everything and everyone I had ever loved. Because I hoped that one day the same path would bring me back to them.

It had to.

*

By the time I made my way towards them, the two were seated around a rickety wooden table with three legs that was leaning against the side of the garage. A lone bulb on the wall was feebly attempting to keep the darkness at bay.

I dropped into an empty camp chair as Deemu swigged straight from the bottle, draining the last drop and then throwing it behind him into the darkness where it crashed and startled Sheroo, who had dozed off, apparently.

"Nice job, asshole! I'll have to clean that up in the morning, and you just woke up Sheroo," grumbled Pitras as he got up and disappeared into the huge blue-coloured tent that had the words 'UNHCR' etched across one end.

"What exactly do you do for Sherwin?" I asked.

"He is his wife," snickered Deemu.

I could hear Pitras shouting some obscenity inside the tent but could not make out the words.

"What?" I asked. "By the way, this is a pretty impressive tent," I added.

"It is, right?" Pitras emerged from the tent with another bottle and a packet of crisps.

He had no sooner banged the bottle down than Deemu had it open and was pouring it into three glasses. Pitras eased himself into a chair.

"William *saab* got this for me."

"Why doesn't he let you use the house?" I motioned to the bungalow behind us.

"It's not like that." Pitras was defensive immediately. "I have my own servant quarter." He pointed into the darkness where there was a line of rooms at the extreme opposite end of the house.

"But it's just that it is too far from the main building, and I have to keep running back and forth looking after Sheroo and William *saab* whenever he is here in the bungalow. This is more airy, and I can watch over the whole house from here, and I get to sleep under the stars if I feel like I want some fresh air."

"And mosquitoes," Deemu mumbled from inside his glass.

"The tent comes with a mosquito netting, asshole." Pitras threw an empty wrapper at Deemu, who fell over backwards as he tried to dodge the fluttering wrapper that never reached him.

"*Chutiya*," Deemu grumbled from the ground as he got up and got back into the camp chair, dusting off the dirt.

"So, how'd you get a tent? Must have been expensive," I said.

"Of course it is, but only a *chutiya* pays for such things." A combination of the effect of the drink and being the centre of attention in the presence of his more street-smart and world-wise cousin was making Pitras feel more and more cocky.

"*Acha*? So how did you get such a tent?" I asked.

"Finish your glass and then I'll tell you."

I looked down at the still full glass in my hand. I was way past worrying about the dilemma of what I was doing. There was so much else going on in my life at that point that everything else had become numb and mute. I was beyond caring, as long as anything helped in numbing my senses and drowning out the world, I would have taken it.

I gulped down the contents of the glass, which felt like fumes going up my nostrils rather than down my throat. I winced and retched emptily as Deemu laughed in the background.

"Easy, brother, we don't want the eyeballs dancing incident again."

I banged the table with my hand as I fought to keep the drink from coming back up. Sheroo let out a startled moan.

"Assholes, you're not going to let Sheroo sleep tonight."

"OK, now tell." I opened my mouth after I was sure nothing was threatening to come out.

"Nothing comes free in this world, brother," said Pitras as he got up and went to relieve himself in the darkness.

"Don't tell me, Pitras!" Deemu was howling with laughter as he fell over backwards again.

"*Chutiya*, grow up," said Pitras. "William *saab* has a lot of contacts and influence. One of his course mates is in charge of all the stuff that other organisations are sending for the refugees from Swat that are currently camped here due to the ongoing military operation."

My body turned to stone at the mention of Swat.

I could feel Deemu's eyes boring into me from the ground.

"Did you say Swat, Pattu?" he asked, suddenly sounding very sober.

"*Haan bhai*, the Swat operation, William *saab* is there *naa*, killing all those *madarchod* killers who are shooting innocent people in the name of religion," Pitras said as he emerged from the shadows.

He stopped in his tracks when he saw the expression on my face.

"What happened? Did somebody die?"

I placed my hands on the table, trying to steady myself against the storm suddenly raging inside.

"Pitras, I need to get into that camp," I whispered.

13

Whatever it takes

Anarkali, Lahore
Asma

By the time we got out of the labyrinthian streets and out onto the main road, the sun was almost gone, and the light was fading fast. With the arrival of evening, there was a sudden increase in the humanity heading towards the old market.

As we came to an enclosure where a lot of cars, motorcycles and other vehicles were parked, Mehran brought the carriage to a halt and got off. After tethering the horse to a railing near a clump of grass, he said a few words to the bespectacled old man sitting giving parking tickets at the entrance. He slipped a ten rupee note to him and came up to us.

"It is much better if we walk from here on," he said as he marched on ahead. We fell in behind him as we made our way through the pushing, shoving mass of humanity.

"You know, Mehran, we could have just paid the parking toll instead of the bribe that you gave the old man." Sam had produced a dupatta which she had draped over her head and shoulders, in spite of the hot and humid Lahore dusk. The move made sense, and I followed suit, transforming myself from being an object of ogling to just another run-of-the-mill female going about her business.

Immediately, I could feel the eyes moving away from me. I sighed with relief and also grimaced against the hypocrisy hiding amidst the superficial façade of our society.

"Oh, it was not a bribe." Mehran turned around as he walked.

"Then what was that, because the parking ticket costs twenty rupees; I saw that on the board outside," said Sam.

"He was my father; I was just giving him some money for tea because I thought he must be thirsty." He nodded as he said it, as if that settled the matter.

All three of us shared incredulous looks; Haroon was the one who broached the topic with him as we came to a standstill in front of a line of shops running along the road.

"But, Mehran, you parked your horse in a parking spot that your father is supposed to guard and charge everyone for using – why did you not pay for it?"

Mehran looked at the three us as if we had lost our marbles in the heat. "I am his son. The parking ticket is for people who want to park their cars there. But I am his son." As if repeating his filial relation would explain everything.

I had had enough though. "Alright, you two, don't pretend like you never saw this before; this is how we roll – stop grilling the person who is trying to help us. Look at the bigger picture here," I implored.

"Spoken like a true bureaucrat," said Sam, echoing the common sentiment voiced by the community against any who held a government job but especially us *sarkari baboos* who had entered through the civil services exam. And yet, given a choice, they would give an arm and a leg to have their children join the bureaucracy and the civil administration so that they could also exploit the system which they complained about.

I was offended hearing this attitude from someone I considered very close to me. But at the same time, I also realised that this sword of hypocrisy cut both ways, and it was not always angels and saints who joined the service. People were people. The dividing line was between the haves and have-nots in Pakistan, and if some of them managed to cross that line by hook or crook, the first thing they wanted to do was to remind their neighbours, their brothers, their relations as to who wielded the big stick now.

Mehran had left us and was talking to a group of men sitting on a rickety wooden bench outside a small barbecue shop. I tried reading the lettering on the battered billboard on top of the shop, but the paint was faded and peeling off and almost indecipherable. A couple of minutes later, Mehran came towards us, followed by a gaunt, dark-toned man with deep-set eyes and a heavy stubble that was starting to show shades of white. He had a slight limp, and he winced with each step.

As they joined us, Mehran was the first to speak. Pointing to us, he turned towards the man and said, "Mustafa *bhai*, these are my clients I was telling you about. I have been giving them a tour of inner Lahore, the real Lahore, and I was telling them that if you want to have the best chicken karahi in Lahore then we have to come to your place." Up close, Mustafa seemed even darker and shrivelled, as if something had dried him up from inside. In the ensuing silence, he looked at all of us and gave a small smile, revealing tobacco-stained teeth. "Please come inside; it will be my honour to serve you a taste of the real Lahore. My family has been living in this area since the time of the Mughals."

I looked up sharply at this piece of information which I knew to be a lie since Qasim had told me about his father's family migrating from India. Mustafa noticed my reaction and he paused, then added sheepishly, "My mother's side has been living in the area for centuries; my father's family came from Kashmir."

I nodded and kept my gaze averted. Haroon clapped his hands. "OK, that's great then; let's go – I am starving." He wrapped his arms around Mustafa and led the way into the shop.

I hung back and waited for Mehran to come alongside me and

then asked him what he had told Mustafa about us. He looked at me and said, "Not much, I just told him you are here to visit inner Lahore and one of you, I have not told him who, knew Qasim and wanted to meet him, which is why we went to the house, and that is how we came here."

I absorbed this piece of information. "OK, thank you, Mehran," I said and then we went inside the shop where the other two were seated around a steel table in a curtained booth with a wall fan sending jets of hot air intermittently.

Mehran sat on the opposite side with Haroon. "Where did your Mustafa *bhai* go, Mehran?" I asked.

Mehran pointed outside through the window where Mustafa was cooking over a pan out on the main road in front of the shop. All along the road, all other shops were doing the same. In the stifling heat of Lahore, it made sense and attracted customers too, who seemed to be pulled towards the smell of barbecue.

"They hire help from time to time when there are a lot of customers. But this is not the season, plus it is still early – Mustafa *bhai's* father will come in a couple of hours after Isha prayers. So, then he will sit and take orders and Mustafa *bhai* will cook and serve the food. This is a very famous and old shop. At one time not long ago, Qasim *bhai* and the youngest brother Ijaz also used to help out their father, and this place used to be running non-stop from morning to night."

"So, what happened?" Haroon asked, munching on the carrots and salad placed on the table, waiting for the main course to arrive, ruining his appetite. I shook my head, typical tourist.

"All you guys moved to pizzas and burgers, that's what happened," said Mustafa as he entered, carrying the steaming round pan on a tray, along with a plate piled high with naan and four chilled bottles of Pepsi. He grinned at us as he set down the food.

"Please join us," I said, looking up at him.

He stopped in mid-stride and turned back to look at me; after a second he took the cigarette out of the corner of his mouth and said, "You were with Qasim at university, weren't you?"

I felt a lump forming in my throat and looked down.

"Are you Asma?"

I looked up at him, tears welling up in my eyes, blurring my image of him. "How do you know? Did he tell you?"

Mustafa lit his cigarette and took a deep puff. "Yes," he whispered.

The atmosphere around the table had gone deathly quiet; I was finally going to find the answers I had been searching for all these years.

"Yeah well," I said, brushing off a tear from the side of my eye, "that doesn't sound like somebody who marries someone else and then refuses to even meet or explain their actions."

"Marry? Qasim?" Mustafa looked startled. "You don't know?"

Sam's head shot up from her plate. "Know what? Tell us, please!"

Mustafa looked down at us and then sighed, inwardly coming to a decision. He motioned towards Mehran. "Mehran, go to the next shop and tell Altaf I need him to send one of their cooks here for half an hour, just in case somebody comes around. Tell him I sent you," he said as Mehran bolted out of his chair, a piece of chicken leg still clutched in one hand.

*

An hour later, as we paid the bill and exchanged goodbyes with Mustafa, I did not know how I felt. As I stood before him, Mustafa fixed me with a long stare at the end of which he said, "You know, I think you would have fit in with us just perfectly, in another world, in another country and in another time, perhaps."

"Perhaps," I whispered, looking down at my feet as I felt the colour rushing to my cheeks.

Placing his hand on my bowed head, as an elder brother or father figure would, Mustafa said, "Let me know if you find anything, will you? Qasim used to write and call, but it's been two years and no word from him." Then, without waiting for an answer, he went inside the shop.

I looked up to where Sam and Haroon were paying Mehran. I walked over to join them. Mehran looked sheepishly at me; I smiled at him and said, "Thank you for all your help today Mehran – is there anything I can do for you?"

Mehran blushed and mumbled something along the lines of thank you and walked off towards the parking where his horse and carriage were parked. I had called for a car from one of my batchmates posted in Lahore. I had not told my family about my visit here as I had not wanted to face that line of questioning. Sam and I were heading back to our hotel room while Haroon was off to his relative's place where he was staying.

Once back in our room, we went over the day. Qasim had not married. In the immediate aftermath of our break-up, his family had to endure the trauma of the suicide blast, which had permanently crippled Mustafa as well as tarnishing the reputation of the Kaleems in the tightly knit local community. That the suicide bombers had been visiting their house on the day of the incident and were friends of Ijaz had drawn a noose around the household which slowly but surely kept tightening as, each week, members of the household were picked up by security agencies for questioning. Qasim had dropped out without graduating as he wanted to help his father in the family business, with Mustafa laid up due to the injuries.

At the same time, they kept looking for clues as to the whereabouts of Ijaz. But it was difficult tracking someone who had been branded as a terrorist. Business and livelihood was affected as the local community ostracised the family, and interactions were restricted to a minimum.

The boycott severely affected the elder Kaleems, especially Fatima, who found herself fired from the hospital where she used to volunteer as a nurse. The humility and grief coupled with the loss of her youngest finally took a toll as she suffered a stroke shortly thereafter, rendering her wheelchair-bound and almost mute. Gradually, the boycott had lifted, and the situation was on the mend. Mustafa, the eldest who had always been a failure and a drug addict, had mended his ways after recovering from his injuries. He had married the widow of their renter who had also died in the bomb attack. The couple had a son and the introduction of new life seemed to be improving the atmosphere in the Kaleem household. Slowly, the family found its feet; Mustafa became more responsible and dependable. Only Qasim, though, refused to get over the disappearance of Ijaz.

In his blinding obsession with recovering his lost brother, he turned to his friends and colleagues from university to help. One by one, each one shut him out, preferring to cut off ties rather than be associated with the brother of a known terrorist. However, Qasim refused to be discouraged.

Finally, one day, an old acquaintance from his university days had stopped by the shop and met with Qasim. Over the next couple of days, they had met regularly until, one night, Qasim had told Mustafa that there was a slight chance of finding Ijaz, and he was leaving. And that was all that Qasim had told him before vanishing off.

The mention of someone from the university had given me some hope as I knew Qasim's friends and was hopeful of getting some lead from them. But when I mentioned all the people that I knew, Mustafa had said this person had once come to drop Qasim home and that something about him seemed dangerous and shady. Qasim had told him that he was his roommate and an influential person in the university.

"That's the part I still don't understand." Sam's voice brought me back to reality. "Why did you go completely quiet when Mustafa mentioned the guy from the university? Isn't it a good thing? Because I'm guessing this guy would be easy to track down and you would know who he is and what he said to Qasim?"

I looked at her. "I know who the person is, and he's bad news." I told her about Raja Niaz and his connections with the student unions and how they had tried to intimidate Qasim into breaking up with me and joining their organisation. I told her that things must be really bad if Qasim had willingly sought help from someone as dangerous and unreliable as Niaz.

Sam was quiet for a long while afterwards as I sat and fidgeted in my seat. Finally, she looked up at me and asked the question which I had answered already in my heart a long time back.

"You came here for an answer, for closure. Have you got closure? Will you move on with your life?" she asked as she saw the beginning of a nervous smile on my face. "Oh boy, it's not over, is it?"

We both knew the answer to that already.

"Of course it isn't, Sam!" I shouted as I jumped off the sofa. "Yes, I was looking for an answer and expecting the worst one at the same time. Though this does not change our situation, this is not closure; this is anything but closure. Nothing has changed; he did not betray me, and neither can I."

Once again, I had a path, a mission and a goal. And they all led to Qasim. If I had to walk through hell to get there, I would. So, Raja Niaz, dangerous or not, was nothing more than an afterthought.

14

Opening up

GHQ Tennis Club, Rawalpindi
Qasim

It was a sweltering August day as I struggled to keep my eyes open lying under the shade of the scoreboard at the farthest end of the tennis court. I was doing my best to stay still and block out the dazzling light from entering my head and messing with the explosive headache that was already raging inside.

The excitement of finally having a lead after months of nothing had ended in me drinking more than normal and staying up longer than I probably should have. I had a vague recollection of me being half-carried, half-dragged by a grinning Deemu and a pensive Pitras inside the blue tent and being dumped onto a soft mattress where I immediately curled up and fell asleep.

I woke up around midday to Pitras's frantic face in my immediate vision.

"What the hell?" I groaned, wincing immediately as the act of speaking sent a million needles shooting inside my brain.

"You need to go Qasim *bhai*; William *saab* is here – he will be coming out to check on Sheroo in a bit." Pitras was literally crying, and I felt bad for having overstayed.

I gathered my stuff and crossed the empty road over to the

other side. I half-leaned, half-walked my way alongside the wall of the National Defence College as it curved downwards into Lalkurti. I managed to take a quick shower and down a scalding cup of tea in two gulps before I had to leave for the tennis courts.

The sound of a ball hitting a racquet brought me back to the present. I held a hand against the glare of the sun to look who it was playing at this time. It was the middle of the monsoon season, and not only the heat but the humidity was such that even schoolkids, who were usually the craziest and the first ones to come to the courts, had not yet arrived.

Presently, as my eyes adjusted to the light, I made out the unmistakable shape of Major Rashid practising serves on an empty court. I could not suppress a grin. You had to hand it to the guy. His enormous girth notwithstanding, he was fully dedicated to giving everything he had on the court. I respected that. In spite of our encounter last time, I felt myself warming up to him.

I picked up my racquet and was about to get up when I heard Ahmed Din's voice from behind me. "I'll break your fucking legs if you even dare to get up."

I turned around. "I won't do anything like last time – I promise."

Ahmed Din was already putting on his tattered tennis shoes that were three sizes too big for him, donated by some foreign player who had last visited Pakistan during the Davis Cup fixtures and given them to a young Ahmed Din. He was sentimental that way. It was what had got me the job as Deemu had told him that him and I shared a common home: Anarkali.

But today, he was having none of it. "*Na bhai*, if I let you play today and you again pull such a stunt, you will make me lose our clients and the money we make from letting these officers win against us. You think I could have put my two kids through school only on the wages I get as a coach… marker, OK, OK marker." He corrected himself when I grinned at him.

"No, you're right Ahmed Din Chacha; I only felt bad for the

last time, and since Major *saab* was playing alone, I thought I'd go play with him a little."

"That is great. I am happy that you are acting more maturely, but let me go now; I've already put on my shoes." He patted my shoulder as he passed me by. I slouched back against the cold cement bleacher seat and flung the racquet against the seat a little harder than I had intended. The loud clang of graphite against cement reverberated and hung in the air. Across the width of the three clay courts, Major Rashid and I locked eyes. I could have sworn he smiled, but it was hard to be sure in the glaring sun. I groaned inwardly as Major Rashid said something to the bobbing shape of Ahmed Din and then motioned with his head towards my direction.

Oh, this can't be good.

I shouldn't have made myself more visible after what I'd done the previous day.

Ahmed Din, to his credit, was still trying to entice Major Rashid. He had rushed over to the other side of the court. He had even told the ball boy to give the major a three-game lead on the scoreboard.

He was pulling out all the stops.

In tennis parlance, the trick of giving your opponent a head start is one of the oldest tried and tested hustling moves. But you have to be sure not to overdo it. Give too big of a lead and any novice can suddenly start playing like the next Aisam Qureshi, and there goes your easy money. Give too small of a lead and the 'fish' wont bite.

In this case, a 3-0 lead was very generous by Ahmed Din, considering the physical shape he was in and the major's prowess. Ahmed Din, in his day, could have come back from a 0-5 deficit but, sadly, those days now came very few and far between. And I had played with the major; he wasn't half as bad as he seemed. Then I figured Ahmed Din was playing the long game; he planned on letting the major win the first set, to salvage his wounded pride, maybe even the second. At least, he would get to keep a satisfied customer.

Nice one, coach, I thought as I settled back into my seat.

"Love all, *sirji*!" Ahmed Din bellowed as he got into his service stance which was more like someone about to take a dump while swatting a mosquito with a newspaper.

But the major was not taking the bait. He turned sideways. Towards me.

He motioned me to come.

I saw Ahmed Din, still frozen in his service stance, watching, horrified at what was about to unfold. I walked up to the major.

"*Salam o Alaikum*, sir."

"*Haan bhai*, champ, how about a rematch?"

"Sir, I am not feeling well."

"*Acha*? Ate too many jalebis and pakoras?"

"Something like that."

"It'll be fine; I'll go easy on you."

I smiled. I had to hand it to him. Whatever he lacked in skill, he covered it with loads of self-confidence.

The next hour and a half went by in a flurry of shots and shouts. My mind was only half on the game. The Major too, it seemed, had come with a game plan, and he stuck to it throughout. He kept going to my weaker backhand and coming to the net on the approach.

At 4-4, he finally broke my serve with a blistering inside-out forehand that caught me flat-footed. I grinned at him as I saw the ball scream by.

"Shot, sir!" I clapped my hand against the racquet in appreciation. He barely nodded, still locked in on the mission, which was not complete. I felt myself warming up to this guy. He had grit; he had resolve. I respected that.

If he wanted to win so bad, I had to respect it by making him work for it. On the last changeover, I threw off my tattered cap, poured a glass of tepid water over my head and, ignoring the dull throbbing pain, went over to receive the first serve as Major Rashid bounced the ball a couple of times, waiting for me.

The Major had a flat serve that relied more on placement rather than anything else. He had been consistently putting me on the defensive from the start by going for my backhand. I could have gone with my double hander, which was more of a cricket style swat, but it was always a half-chance. The slice was more reliable and less threatening.

But I had had enough with playing it safe. It was time to see how badly the Major wanted this. Just as he threw the ball in the air for the serve, I stepped sideways so that I was almost outside the gallery. But this time, I would be taking the ball on my more reliable and stronger forehand. As the ball came across the net, I was ready.

I let rip a perfect down-the-line forehand winner that screamed into the back curtains before the Major had completed his service follow-through. We both locked eyes across the net. This time it was Major Rashid who smiled.

Game on.

The next point was right in my arc; I knew where I wanted to put the ball even before I hit it. I could visualise the winner as it whizzed by. I walked into the shot, taking the ball on the up and hitting it flat and hard, cross-court.

I saw the Major's shoulders slump as he realised that he would never reach the ball in time. And then it happened. The ball clipped the top of the net and bounced three feet in the air. I saw the major's eyes light up as he charged.

The ball sat up in the centre of the court as he smashed it hard and true.

"*Aethay kaun aye?!*" he bellowed as the ball passed my outstretched hand for a winner.

I laughed.

Major Rashid was also laughing. We were at war. We were comrades. We had pushed each other to the brink. In the process, we had bonded.

The next couple of points were a see-saw affair in which we both lunged and stretched and drained the last ounce of energy left. On match point, we had a sizeable crowd along the side lines, cheering us both on.

He finished with an ace, down the middle, where I had least expected it. I ran up to the net to shake his hand, smiling, my headache gone. Major Rashid clasped my hand and met my gaze. "Ahmed Din, lemonade and jalebis for everyone on me," he shouted to loud cheers from all around.

He punched me in the shoulder playfully and, still holding onto my hand, led me across the net and onto one of the player's chairs. He motioned me to sit.

I hesitated. We were not allowed to sit on the players' chairs as a mark of respect. Major Rashid, who was guzzling down water from his bottle, prodded me in the back with his racquet and motioned me to sit down.

So I did.

The Major also slumped down onto the chair next to me.

"Good game, sir."

He looked at me and just nodded. I held his gaze for a while, expecting him to say something, but he just kept staring, as if trying to look through me. He had the typical army haircut, parted at the side. There was a lot of greying at the temples, and the hairline was starting to recede. The standard military moustache was starting to get flecked with white hair. He would have once had a strong protruding jaw as a young man; now years had added a layering of fat and given it a more rounded shape. It was common knowledge around the court that he had been passed on for promotion one too many times, and now he was just waiting for retirement. But the eyes still retained the spark and fire. Which is why, according to the grapevine, instead of opting for a nice comfy posting which many of his course mates in senior positions could have offered him, he still volunteered for 'hard postings' in the field.

"Why are you here?" he asked finally, breaking my train of thought and bringing me back to reality.

"Sir?"

"You don't belong here."

"Sir, I don't understand what you mean."

"What I mean is, there are many ball boys and coaches here who play much better than you. Because they have been playing for years. But knowing how to play is not the same as actually knowing what to do when the game is on the line and handling pressure. That comes from a sharp mind that can look at the big picture and can strategise. Sadly, most of these boys can be great hitting partners, but it's precisely due to this inability to look at the big picture that keeps them limited to being just ball boys. You, on the other hand, don't play as well, but you are more aware and can size up the situation. This tells me that you have had some education. Which just does not add up."

These were more words than we had ever exchanged over three years. I had misjudged him; there was more to him than met the eye.

I sighed and looked down.

Nabeel, one of the ball boys, came holding a tray with two glasses of lemonade and a plate of dripping jalebis. He gave me a sideways smile and, placing the tray on one of the empty chairs between us, scampered away giggling to himself.

I smiled, then looked up to see the Major still waiting for my response. I took the lemonade glass and handed it to him and then took the second one for myself. I took a sip; the sweet, salty taste felt amazing on my parched tongue.

"I was doing my master's at Punjab University," I said, visualising my future in the swirling ice cubes.

Major Rashid whistled. "I knew there was something about you," he said. "I have a son who has been trying to get admitted in their undergraduate programme for over a year. I have been spending thousands every month on tuitions, and here I am playing tennis with a Punjab University graduate ball boy." He laughed to himself. "Me, an FA pass, playing with a ball boy who is a graduate." He shook his head as he drained the lemonade in one go.

"I am not really a graduate, sir – I left in the final year."

He said nothing, waiting for me to go on. I kept looking into my glass, not willing to meet his gaze. Just wishing that the ground would open up and I could disappear. But it had been three years, and I had kept waiting for the ground to burst open. But it had not. And in the process, I had lost my moorings, my sense of purpose; I had lost my one true love.

Each year that I spent trying to find Ijaz, trying to put my family back together to the way it was, I felt the memory of Asma getting dimmer and fading. The thought of losing her had always clawed at the back of my mind, but I had been putting it off, constantly telling myself that I was not right for her, that this would be over soon and then I could give my full attention to her. I had shut out everyone from the university in order not to find out about her or for her to know what I was doing. And I had managed to dull the pain. But since yesterday, when I had heard about the camp, the spark of hope had risen inside me. If there was a way to finish this search quicker, that meant I could still maybe, just maybe, try to go back and see if Asma would still have me. If she still felt the same way about me. In spite of my own admonitions, like a resilient drug, my love for Asma, I realised, had never really died. It had just lain dormant all these years, hibernating, but alive.

There was no getting over it – I had to find Ijaz, bring him home so that I could go and try to start my life over. And all roads led to Asma. I don't know what it was; maybe it was the lack of energy left in my drained body; maybe it was the realisation that I needed all the help I could get, that I could no longer go it alone, but I found myself opening up to Major Rashid.

Right there – on the side lines of the tennis court where, a couple of minutes ago, we had been mortal enemies, edging each other to the brink of surrender – I reached inside and let down the walls. I told him everything, from the start: Ijaz, the blast, the note left behind, my parents, me, trying to find him and how I had found out about the camp last night.

Throughout it all, Major Rashid had listened silently, nodding when I explained my reasons for giving up everything and the need to find my brother. He did not say anything, just looked at me over the smoke of his pipe, as he puffed away, both of us oblivious to the shouts and sounds of life going on around us.

By the time I had finished, I felt lighter and more at ease. If for nothing else, I felt like I had given words to all that had been boiling and churning inside me. And now that it was out, I could understand it better and maybe even handle it.

I looked up at him, all spent and exhausted. He tapped his pipe against the chair, dumping the ash onto the ground, then stood up. I also stood up. His face was completely closed, expressionless for once.

"I am going to shower and change; I suggest you do the same – change into clean clothes – then come have dinner with me."

I did not know what to say. "*Ji*, OK, sir," I said, trusting the moment and surrendering to it.

"Good, I'll see you here in half an hour then, OK?"

"Yes, sir."

15

Hoping against hope

Lahore
Asma

After tossing and turning most of the night, I woke up at the crack of dawn with a spring in my step. Life finally had a purpose and direction once again. I showered, changed and went down to the lobby for breakfast. I let Sam sleep in – she deserved it. Plus, I also needed time to think and plan what I needed to do.

Some people like to brainstorm and think things over. Not me. I am more of an unconscious thinker. I like to absorb all the details and specifics and, once I have gone over them, then I switch to autopilot. Let the facts marinate and swim around in my head, away from the glare of focus and scrutiny, that's what has always worked for me.

I loaded up my plate with pancakes, poured a healthy helping of maple syrup on top and two dollops of Nutella on the side. I poured myself a piping hot cup of cappuccino from the counter and then found myself a seat right at the corner of the breakfast buffet, where I could think and eat in peace.

There was no doubt in my mind that I had to help Qasim. My feelings for him to one side, as a friend, he needed me. The fact that he should have but did not contact me when Ijaz disappeared was typical of the stubborn Qasim I knew. What I had presumed to be a happily married and moved-on person was in fact the same old-school, principled and obstinate boy I had fallen in love with. So completely had he cut himself off from our shared world of acquaintances and friends that he had no idea that I had even joined the government.

As I polished off my plate of pancakes and settled back in my chair to enjoy my coffee, I lined up my options. I had started off with the aim of finding Qasim and getting some answers. After last night, I sort of had an answer, which explained most of what had happened. But it made finding Qasim all the more important for me. The last person to have known the whereabouts of Qasim was someone I knew more through his reputation and that one terrible incident. And the third individual crucial for me was Ijaz, the young religious student who had disappeared after a suicide attack and had most probably joined an extremist organisation.

These three individuals were linked together through the invisible chain of connectedness. If I managed to reach any one of them, it would help me in locating the others. I was not interested in finding Raja Niaz at all, except for the fact that it was my guess that he would be the most visible and easy to track of the three. As a leader of a student organisation, he had operated on the fringes of what constituted as legal. As much as his affairs were clandestine, he also had to make appearances and meetings with influential personalities in political circles who would hire him for his 'services'. This was a well-known fact during our time at the university. I was hopeful that there might be some way to dig him out through my friends and connections in the government. And from him, I might be able to find out where Qasim had gone. I would worry about making Niaz give up that information to me after I had located him. No need to worry about that for now.

And then there was Ijaz. Given the number of terrorist organisations and splinter groups and sectarian factions that were operating in the country at the time, it would have been very easy for a young, impressionable boy to be picked up by any one of these entities. There was no way of telling whether Ijaz was still alive or not. Although, as somebody whose job it was to track and assess terrorist and extremist cases, I realised that the fact that Ijaz's name had not cropped up in the list of victims and perpetrators – in almost all suicide bomb cases, the head of the bomber is completely severed from the body and intact so that it can be used in facial recognition to identify the person – in the cases over the last three years, meant that he might, most probably, still be alive.

The question of the whereabouts of Ijaz was also a tricky one. Most, if not all, of the terrorist organisations had sleeper cells in major cities like Lahore. These operated on a skeleton crew and functioned like line agencies, providing tactical and logistical support. What was even more appalling was the fact that these organisations worked in a decentralised form of hierarchy that enabled individual cells to function even when the rest of the chain was broken. Moreover, there was proof of a thriving terrorism economy within the country, which specialised in the market for products as well as services. Suicide bombers were mostly minors, from impoverished backgrounds but not necessarily always. There were cases of brainwashed kids from urban locations also being trained as suicide bombers. They were a high-priced commodity, and they were bought and sold on the terrorist black market. Our analysis had shown that the training of suicide bombers was conducted far away from the city, in the rugged, mountainous border region between Pakistan and Afghanistan, which was inaccessible most of the year.

In my personal estimate, Ijaz did not fit the description of a suicide bomber, mostly because of his age but also his urban background. According to Mustafa, the boy was definitely a teenager, and that reduced the chances of him being kidnapped or brainwashed. Terrorist sleeper cells are lean operations, and they would not bother carrying a screaming and kicking boy along with them. They would either kill him or dispose of him at the earliest opportunity. If Ijaz was still alive, that meant he had gone of his own free will. Mustafa had told me about the letter, which meant that at least until the time he disappeared, Ijaz had not gone over to the side of the extremists. However, the fact that he had not come back or been heard of in the ensuing years was not good news. A terrorist camp was no place for debates and arguments. There were two broad chances as to the fate of Ijaz: he was dead or alive with the caveat that he had been brainwashed into seeing the world from the viewpoint of the extremist. Only a family member could still hold a third option in their heart: that he was still alive and not an extremist.

If he were still alive, that opened up more intriguing areas. A terrorist organisation is just like any other organisation in the sense that it has different roles with specific job descriptions. It has a media wing, a procurement wing, a tactical and strategy wing, a human resource wing that recruits applicants, a screening process, training processes, promotions, transfers and so on. Ijaz could be placed in any of those roles. For his sake, I hoped that Qasim reached him before the government did, because for us he was a terrorist and an enemy of the state. If I wanted to help Qasim, I had to make sure that we got Ijaz out before the noose tightened around the last remaining terrorist stronghold in the mountainous area around Swat. Whether he wanted to go back to his family or not was a question that I preferred not to get into for now. I hoped when the moment arrived, the answer would be a happy one. But my experience so far had taught me not to have high hopes. The best thing to do in the meantime was to keep my eyes peeled on the ground and move forward, one step at a time.

16
This too shall pass

Westridge, Rawalpindi
Qasim

The journey to Major Rashid's home was largely uneventful as we both sat, lost in our private thoughts. Having had no time to rush home, I had taken a quick cold shower in Ahmed Din's quarter, which shared a wall with the tennis practice so that, at all times of the day, there was a dull thud in the background as someone pummelled the ball against the wall. I wondered how Ahmed Din and, even more so, his wife, whose face I had yet to see, and their two kids, had managed to keep their sanity against the constant monotonous thudding of the balls.

But then that is the curse and the gift of being a human being. We are capable of adapting to anything if forced to endure it for long enough. Thoughts like these always made me break out into cold sweats. What if the monotony of living amongst people whose whole ideology was centred around a violent and misguided doctrine had finally broken through the years of Ijaz's loving and tolerant upbringing?

Was it already too late? Would I even recognise him anymore when we finally met? Would he want to go back?

I fidgeted uncomfortably in my seat. The shalwar kameez that

I had borrowed from Ahmed Din did not help much as they were at least two sizes too small. The shalwar barely reached my ankles, and the kameez was so tight that I had to give up trying to button up for fear of shredding the dress.

The Major, on the other hand, seemed completely at peace with the world. He was drumming one hand on the steering along to the tune of a slow song playing on the stereo, with the other arm resting on the window, which was rolled all the way down.

As we passed by a large gate, behind which I could see a large field filled with rows upon rows of tents, he turned towards me and motioned outside my window. "That's the Rawalpindi Polo Club."

"*Ji*, sir" I said, lost in my thoughts, not even bothering to look.

"That's where some of the Swat IDPs are camped," he explained.

My head shot back so fast it made a cracking sound; I craned my neck trying to peer into the gloomy darkness.

"You can just drop me here, sir!" I said frantically as I watched the ground diminishing in my rear-view mirror.

"Please just stop here, sir." I was panicking now.

Major Rashid slowed down and pulled over to the side of the road. As I was about to get out of the car, he put a hand on my arm. "*Beta*, relax."

An uncontrollable sob escaped my lips. I shielded my face as I felt the hot sting of tears on my cheeks. I hadn't been called that in so long that I had almost forgotten that I was once someone's beloved.

"There is no use trying to go now." Major Rashid's tone was one I would never have associated with his persona on the court. It was patient, tender and fatherly.

"Even if I drop you off, you will not be able to enter the camp – you will not be allowed – it is under military control," he reasoned. "Come home with me; we will talk this over. I think I can help you. If nothing else, you now know where it is. Does that sound reasonable to you?"

I nodded.

"Good, let's go – I'm starving."

Ten minutes later, we arrived at the gate, which was opened by an orderly wearing white starched shalwar kameez and a black Jinnah cap. Before I could get out, a large jet-black dog reared up with a low growl outside my window. I almost fell backwards with fright.

"Smoky! No!" Major Rashid shouted as he got out. Immediately, the dog whimpered and vanished from sight, its tail tucked between its legs.

"Come out, Qasim; he won't say a thing."

"I'd rather not, sir."

Major Rashid chuckled then, turning to his orderly, "Nawaz, tie him up."

"*Ji*," said Nawaz as he walked away. Smoky got up and bounded playfully beside the orderly as they both disappeared out of sight.

"OK, now you can come out."

I gingerly opened the door and then bounded inside the house to the sound of Major Rashid laughing. We made our way to the lounge where Nawaz was already standing with two glasses of Rooh Afza. I took one and sat down on one of the sofas.

Major Rashid took the other then said to Nawaz, "Go check if Uzair is home and tell him to come downstairs; we have guests."

"*Ji*, sir."

"*Aur suno*," Major Rashid shouted to Nawaz, who was almost out the door, "see if dinner is ready; we're both starving."

"*Ji*, sir."

Major Rashid looked at me. "What?" he asked as he noticed me smiling.

"Nothing, sir, I just found it amusing how, with just two words, Nawaz can reply to all your questions, only with a change of tone. I don't know what I'm saying, sir," I finished, feeling my face go red.

Major Rashid kept looking at me for a while. Then, clearing his throat, he nodded and said, "It's loyalty is what it is."

I nodded my head, not knowing what he meant but pretending to do so.

"Loyalty is the only truly worthy thing in anyone, be it humans or dogs," he continued, warming up to the subject. "You saw Smoky outside? I got him as a pup. I've fed him, bathed him, cared for him like my own son. He will lay down his life for me at a signal from me. That kind of trust and faithfulness cannot be bought."

I nodded.

"Nawaz, on the other hand, is a human being. He has been with me since he was a young boy of eighteen. Everything about the world that he knows, I taught him, since he was an orphan when he came to me. I got him married; I was at the birth of his child. So, I think he should be loyal to me and feel the same way about me. But does he? I can never know for sure."

I looked up at him. "Sir, what are you saying?" I asked as I felt a knot tightening in the pit of my stomach, knowing full well where this was going.

Major Rashid leaned forward in his chair and said, "What I'm trying to tell you, *beta*, is that we humans are complex beings. We are never the same. We are always changing. You have a father, a mother, another brother, a family that you have forsaken, all on the hope that you will find your younger brother. These are terrible times for our country. There is no guarantee that your brother will, God forbid, still be alive."

I winced. "Please don't say that, sir," I almost whispered.

"I'm sorry, but like your elder brother, I must prepare you for what you must already know but are not accepting." In my mind, I could see Mustafa looking at me. All of a sudden, I felt like a three-year-old.

I shook my head, trying to clear the memories that Major Rashid was bringing up.

"Look, sir, I have thought about it all."

"I don't think you have."

"Believe me, I have, three years of living in poor conditions away from any sort of companionship gives you lot of time to think, mostly bad things. But I will do this; I cannot go back without my brother, even if it kills me. I need to make my family whole again." I was almost out of breath, surprised at my own outburst.

Major Rashid too had a shocked expression. He twitched the end of his moustache, lost in thought. "Look at these people who are carrying out these suicide attacks," he said suddenly in exasperation, "killing their own brothers and sisters! People they had gone to school with, played with, neighbours suddenly becoming enemies, what is happening to our world?" He sighed.

"Where does it end, sir?"

For the first time, he looked old and lost. "To be honest, I don't see it happening in my lifetime." He looked forlorn. "I hope my son and his son don't get to inherit this world that we have created. But it will take more than one generation to cleanse this mindset of hatred and violence."

I looked down. "Yes, but that also depends on which side wins."

Major Rashid perked up. "Never lose faith, *beta*; truth and peace will always prevail, as it should – that is what we have been told, and that is my faith."

"*Ji*," I said, seeing *Abu's* optimism in him. *What was wrong with me?* It was like a dam had burst inside and all the longings and nostalgia I had been pushing underneath had suddenly broken free.

I could feel tears welling up again, threatening to spill. I think Major Rashid saw it too. He got up and came to stand over me; I lowered my head and looked at the carpet. Presently, a big tear fell.

I closed my eyes.

"This too shall pass, *beta*," he almost whispered as he squeezed my shoulder.

"I really hope so."

Just then, Nawaz entered to announce that dinner was ready.

*

"Hmmm, let's see what we have here." Major Rashid lifted the lid off one of the pots. The steam that escaped carried the unmistakable smell of biryani made well.

"That smells just like home," I blurted before I could stop myself.

Major Rashid stopped mid-stride as he was about to help himself to a healthy serving. He beamed at me. "Hand me your plate."

"*Nain*, sir, you go ahead; I'll help myself."

"Shut up," he boomed in mock anger while his eyes twinkled. "Hand over your plate."

I smiled and held out my plate which he proceeded to heap with mountains of biryani.

The door slid open and four children, ranging in ages from five to eighteen, entered the room. They all resembled Major Rashid in different aspects, but the similarity was there.

"Mmmm shabash, come say *salam* to *bhai* and then dig in. Where's *Ammi*?" he asked the eldest one.

"It's Tambola night at the ladies club, Baba."

"Well, let's hope she wins – ice cream for us then!"

"*Ice cream!*" squealed the youngest one with unrestrained glee. We all laughed.

One by one, they all came to me, holding out their outstretched hands, with Major Rashid doing a background commentary while eating at the same time.

"That's Saima; she's five, our ice-cream monster." Saima smiled bashfully and twisted herself into a knot when I shook her hand, then quickly ran away and took the seat closest to her dad.

The next one was a boy with long hair that kept going into his eyes as he walked towards me with both eyes on a handheld device. He walked into the table with his outstretched hand.

"*Oye*, Adil! What did we decide about tabs during dinner?"

"Sorry, Baba," he murmured as he turned it off. Then he looked up at me, gave me a bored look and said, "*Assalaam o Alaikum*, uncle," and shook my hand.

"Uncle? Am I that old, Adil?" I asked in mock indignation, holding his hand as he tried to squirm free. Major Rashid guffawed in the background.

Next up was Sara who had not come in with the other children. She emerged with Nawaz from the kitchen, carrying a tray of pink custard. Placing the dish on the table, she wiped her hands on her dress and smiled at me and shook my hand.

"Sara is our chef in training. So, Nawaz, how did she do?"

Nawaz beamed and patted the top of Sara's head benevolently. "*Mashallah choty bibi* will soon put me out of a job."

"We'll see – then you will sit with us, and she will cook for all of us."

Last of all came the eldest boy, Uzair. He walked towards me with the confidence of someone completely aware and in control of himself. He was the age Ijaz would be now. I put down my spoon and got up to meet him. He towered above me. He resembled Major Rashid, or how he would have looked when he was young.

I held out my hand. "How are you, Uzair?"

He shook my hand warmly. "Did you win today?"

I smiled. "No, your baba crushed me today."

"Nonsense, Qasim is being too kind; I got lucky today," Major Rashid chimed in with his mouthful.

"Why don't you play, Uzair?" I asked as I sat back down.

"Nawab *saab* is too busy bodybuilding," piped Major Rashid.

Uzair smiled. "Maybe one day I might," he said as he helped himself to the biryani.

The rest of the dinner passed by in a flash of good-natured talk, laughs and giggles. For a while I felt myself transported to a time where there were no worries, and nothing was missing. I felt the warm embrace of a family again. And then I saw my mother's vacant face when she found out that Ijaz had gone.

And just like that, I was back in the lonely cold again. My family was scattered and disintegrating. I was clawing at the wind again, searching for the missing piece to our salvation.

"*Alhumdullilah*," said Major Rashid as he let out a loud belch which set Adil and Saima off into uncontrolled bouts of laughter. Major Rashid grinned at me as he rubbed his bulging stomach. "Yaar Qasim excuse me, but this happens when I have good food and good company," he said as he pushed back his chair and got up.

"No need to worry, sir, I haven't had such delicious food in a long time," I said as I followed him out of the room. We made our way back to the drawing room as Major Rashid started filling his pipe with tobacco and lighting it. Uzair joined us, closing the door to the dining room behind him where the three children were laughing and shouting about something.

"So, Uzair, sir tells me you plan on going to Punjab University," I said as Uzair eased himself into his chair.

"*Ji*, how did you know?" He looked over at his father who was busy puffing.

"Sir told me. It's a wonderful university."

"Qasim is a law graduate of Punjab University," said Major Rashid through clenched teeth as he puffed on his pipe.

"What?" Uzair's jaw almost dropped to the floor as he looked at his father, then at me.

I sighed. "Yes, I am or was at one point."

"But then, what, I mean how, I mean," he stammered not knowing how to phrase the sentence that would sum up the abyss that defined my current situation.

"I know," I said, placing him out of the awkward situation. "It is kind of a long story, and your baba tells me that you can help me."

He nodded as I gave him a general outline of the story of my life.

Two hours later, when I brought him up to speed, Uzair finally eased back into his chair. His eyes were popping out of their sockets, and his mouth was still open.

"I can't believe this has all happened and you, your family, are managing to go through all this," he whispered more to himself than to any of us.

"Never stop being grateful for all that we have been blessed with, *beta*," said Major Rashid in a sombre tone. "Look at Qasim, a brilliant student, a promising career, and look at what life had in store for him."

I felt a little uncomfortable at how my life and family was being used as a cautionary tale while I was present, but I said nothing.

I looked up at Uzair. "So, Uzair, the question is, can you get me into the camp so that I can look for my brother?" I asked.

Uzair pursed his lips as he went deep in thought.

"*Haan* yaar, you must help Qasim; we have to do something," said Major Rashid.

Uzair looked at both of us and then thought some more before finally clapping his hands together as he reached a decision in his mind.

"It is on!" he said, getting up from his chair. I also got up to embrace him, the spark of hope burning brighter in my chest.

"We will do it Inshallah, you don't worry," Uzair said as I hugged him. "I will get you on the list of volunteers that are visiting the refugee camp tomorrow. You just pray that Ijaz is in that camp."

"Inshallah, I have a very strong feeling that he is there," I said through tears of hope.

"Inshallah," said Major Rashid.

17

The tiger's stripes

Lahore
Asma

When I went back up to my room, Sam had already changed and had ordered breakfast. She raised her buttered toast at me accusingly. "Thanks for waking me up."

"I didn't want to since we slept so late."

"Anyway, what is the plan for today? Haroon called and said he can join us wherever we decide."

"OK, let's get some things clear," I said as I sat down on the couch. "This is no longer an adventure trip. This is serious business that we, I mean I, am now entering into. So, I really cannot ask you guys to come on board and help me out."

"Hold on there! That's a little unfair, wouldn't you say so?"

"OK, my bad, you I can understand, and I appreciate, but Haroon? Come on! It doesn't make sense – what is he doing with us still? This guy needs to get a life."

"Ouch! That's harsh."

"So he did the whole chivalrous thing and tagged along, but I thought he would tactfully disappear after last night."

"Maybe the universe still has some plans for him in our adventure."

"Touché, but please stop calling it that; we're not the Famous

Five, and this isn't going to be an Enid Blyton sort of adventure, where we have ginger ale and mysterious islands and tunnels and the sort."

"Darn!"

"I know."

"How about some rabri falooda then?"

"Maybe, I'll think about it." I smiled.

By 9am, we were back on the road. I had sent back the official car my batchmate had given me for the day, along with the armed guard, much to the dismay of Sam and Haroon and the consternation of my batchmate.

But I was sure it would prove to be a hurdle rather than a help in what I planned on doing and would draw too much unwanted attention towards ourselves.

I had finally decided that the logical next step was to locate Raja Niaz. The most obvious way to do that would be to go to Punjab University and try to locate his address or phone number from their alumni services. In case that did not work out, there was always the option of contacting the current student president of the federation and asking him. I knew that would be a tall order given the federation's stance on interacting with females on campus. But since I was no longer a student, I figured that rule could be circumvented around. If nothing else worked, I had convinced Haroon to pose as an old friend of Niaz, although I had my doubts about him holding up under the resulting cross-examination.

But these were the best plans I could come up with at the moment.

Entering the university proved to be harder than I had imagined. Every place on campus reminded me of the time I had shared with Qasim and how all that had disappeared. I tried to maintain my composure and blocked out everything else.

As we made our way up the stairway, I was hit by an overwhelming feeling.

Life is fleeting.

In our desperate attempt to hold onto something permanent, to make sense of our time in this world, we build bridges through relationships and alliances. For a while, they fill the nagging void inside. And we smile, thinking we have solved the puzzle. Cracked the code. Until one day, we are forced to confront our loneliness again. All our relationships with the people we find and try to hold onto are finite. Nothing really lasts. They are also just as lonely as us. For a brief moment in time, we find solace in each other from our fear of hurtling through space all alone. And then it's gone.

I caught my breath, trying to force back the tears welling up suddenly. Thankfully, just at that moment, we reached the office of the alumni person who was at that moment about to engorge a steaming bite of samosa at his desk.

As the spoon wavered in mid-air, dripping potatoes and gravy down his shirt, he looked at me intently. I smiled. Recognition dawned eventually as he put the spoon down and laboured to get out of his chair.

"*Arre* Asma bibi! What a pleasant surprise!"

Waryam. How could I have forgotten that my father had got his personal secretary a post-retirement job after decades of service. As I half-grimaced, half-grinned my way towards his fast-approaching outstretched hand, my mind was simultaneously working on coming up with an excuse for the inevitable phone call that I was about to receive.

I had a lot of explaining to do to my father.

*

If you go far enough back, you can always find the origins of anything. Life is like an elephant that never forgets. You might think you have put lots of miles between the event you are trying to forget but, sooner or later, it will confront you. Just to throw it in my face, fate had once again reminded me of my past by making me run into Waryam.

When I was twelve, my father got posted to a different city. New city meant new school, which meant having to make new friends. At school, I quickly identified the 'Queen Bee', the daughter of a local industrialist. She had the teachers, as well as the students, in the palm of her hand, and she wasn't willing to share her throne with anyone. Being my father's daughter, neither was I. Something had to be done. I needed to topple her empire from the inside, which meant that I had to find an ally in the school administration.

I turned to my father, the master strategist.

It wasn't something I was proud of even then, but at that time, I had no name for the uneasy feeling I got whenever I used my father's position and influence to sway people's decisions. Growing up in the house of a bureaucrat is a powerful drug. One that intoxicates you without you even being aware of how long it's been in your bloodstream.

I grew up thinking it was normal for people to be meeting my father at all times of the day with fake smiles plastered over their faces. I believed it was normal for the traffic to be stopped whenever me and my mother went out for shopping in the local markets. And for the shopkeepers to give us special discounts.

I thought it was my right.

Just like it was my birth right to be the most popular girl in whichever school I went to. And so, I turned to my father. To this day, I am not sure of what he did exactly. But having had years of introspection, and having worked in the public sector myself, I had a fair idea.

My father was a chess master. He looked for weaknesses in the structure that he could exploit. In my school, that weakness proved to be Waryam. I had seen him previously but had never given him a second look. Apparently, neither had the school.

For three years, this rail thin boy with the protruding front teeth had been the gatekeeper. Sitting just outside the main gate, his duty had been to call up the kids when their rides arrived.

One day, I was sent on an errand to the administration block by my teacher. On the way back, I heard somebody calling me. I turned to find Waryam smiling down at me. In-between praises for my father, he stuffed a packet of candy in my hand. A week later, I was made prefect of my class. Nobody saw it coming, not even me.

For the next three years, two things were a constant: I never lost a class or school election, and Waryam kept rising up the grades. By the time he had reached the post of an assistant director, I knew something had to give. Over time, I had discovered that my father, ever the strategist, had placed Waryam not only to keep an eye out for me but also on me.

Realisation runs on its own time and terms. You cannot fast-track it. I should have seen it coming, but I didn't. I couldn't. Another thing about clarity is that once you see it, you can never look away.

I finally saw what I had been all those years and what I had done to get my way. For days, I refused to eat or come out of my room. I couldn't bear to look at myself.

For the first time in my life, I was questioning my perception of the world, of my parents and myself. And I was not liking the answers I was coming up with. I felt undeserving. I felt sly. I felt snobbish. But most of all, I felt betrayed by my father. And yet, it was something I could never think of consciously, let alone utter. It was a thought that sneaked in whenever I was distracted.

It found nooks and crevices in my mind where it made a home for itself. Over time, it became my constant companion. Now that I look back upon it, I think it was this feeling of having cheated and deceived people out of what they deserved through my position that I was able to notice Qasim for the person that he was.

It was the cross I bore that made me look beyond the layers of status, class and power and see him for who he was. For the first time, I was realising there was grey too, besides the black and white. And that people I loved and looked up to were covered in it. My father most of all.

But I was still not giving up on my father and my concept of the universe. A part of me still argued with my better judgement. Maybe my father was not aware of what was happening, I reasoned to myself.

Each evening, for the next week, after dinner I would find excuses to linger in the living room. Trying to muster up courage to talk with my father. But even if I could find the time, I never had the words or the vocabulary to let him know the dilemma I was undergoing. I just could not come up with a coherent explanation for all the wrongs that I felt had been done and were weighing me down.

I remember that day as clearly as if it was only yesterday. It was a Friday. After school, I asked the driver to drop me off at father's office instead of taking me home. I had gone to his office from time to time, whenever I needed to make a special request which I did not want my mother shooting down. Since it was a Friday, I knew my father would have just come back from the Jummah prayer and would be having a smoke in his office.

Father was staring out the window, deep in some thought as he dictated a letter to his assistant. On seeing me enter, his eyes lit up, and he took out his cigarette and gave me a huge grin. I jumped headlong into the purpose of my visit. I told father that he had to get rid of Waryam. I tried to explain how it was wrong and that Waryam was not a nice person and that he was using unfair means. All through my case, Father had a half-bemused, half-tired look on his face.

In the end, I made my pitch: either Waryam was to be let go or I was going away from home.

With a genuine look of surprise, Father assured me that he would set things right and that he would get rid of Waryam.

And he did. I never saw Waryam again. Until today. In my

university, where he had been keeping an eye on me. Just like he always had been. My father, ever the strategist, had not lied to me. He had just hidden his pawn better.

We never really change; we only learn to mask and cover ourselves better.

*

Kot Lakhpat Jail, Lahore

My father was nothing if not a man of his word. He might not have agreed with my life choices, but when he had seen that I was determined, he had agreed to help.

Later in the evening, I received a call from Father's personal secretary telling me that my meeting with Raja Niaz had been arranged.

The next morning, around 9am, I was picked up from home in an official car and taken to Lahore jail. Raja Niaz was as awful as I had imagined. He was as powerful as I had imagined too.

And he was in jail. But you would not have known from his demeanour or from the way he was being treated by the inmates and the jail staff. Sipping my delicious cappuccino, I had to remind myself that I was in a jail and not some fancy café. I looked up at the behemoth of a man sitting opposite me. He had the same beaming face, now decorated with a long, straggly beard.

"How do you like your *kaafee*?"

I looked up; Niaz grinned at me as two muscular men massaged his arms which were stretched across the length of the leather sofa on which he half-lay, half-sat.

"You know this is actually very good – how did you get to order it?"

"Order?!" He threw back his head and roared. "No, no, I don't order – I do not eat outside food; it is not safe for me." He was dead serious. He motioned with his head to the muscular man on his left. "Bhola here used to work in a fancy restaurant on MM Alam Road, didn't you, Bohla?"

Bhola nodded and kept on kneading Niaz's arm.

"Yeah, he can cook you a pizza right now if you want. *Jaa oye, bana ke laa.*" He shoved Bhola, who straightened and started walking out the room.

"No! Please, there is no need, thank you, Bhola."

Niaz shrugged and waved him back. Bhola resumed his massaging.

"So, Raja *saab*, you know why I am here?"

"Yes."

"You do?"

He smiled. I felt violated. Exposed.

I looked down at my hands in my lap. They were trembling. I tried to cover it up by holding the coffee mug.

Niaz said nothing; he just kept looking, torturing me under the same gaze with which he must have overpowered many other lost souls. But I was not lost. On the contrary, I was finding my way back. To Qasim.

I looked up and met his gaze. And held it.

The smile froze. He nodded. With a snap of his fingers, the two men were dismissed, and we had the room to ourselves.

He sat up straight.

"OK, let's talk."

*

It had been an hour after Asma had left. Raja Niaz sat in his jail cell, deep in thought as Bhola came back in with a steaming plate of nihari, naan and a jug of cold lassi. Bhola placed the food on the table and then remained standing until Niaz noticed his presence and looked up.

"Something on your mind?"

'*Ustad ji* is this the same Qasim? From Anarkali? The one who used to study with you."

"*Haan.*"

"Why did you tell the girl that he is in Swat when you had actually sent him to Peshawar?"

Niaz's head shot up, the naan dripping with nihari suspended inches from his mouth. Some of the meat had dripped and was lodged in the stands of his straggly beard. He fixed Bhola with a steely cool look.

"If you want nothing to happen to your mother while you're in here *madarchod*, then stick to what you are told to do."

"*J-ji Ustad.*"

"Get out of my sight now."

As Bhola left the room, Niaz munched on the nihari and downed the lassi in one go. Running a finger through his beard, he took out his mobile and dialled a number.

"Hmm, it's me. She is coming."

Placing his phone back in the pocket of his shalwar, Niaz nodded to himself. It was true that there was nothing he needed in the jail that he could not get. He might be in jail, but it was a temporary stop. It came with the territory. He had bigger plans for himself; he was not going to get old just screening out potential recruits and watching them become MNAs, MPAs and ministers while he, the one who had groomed them, remained a big frog in a small pond. It was time that he made a name for himself.

If it meant cutting off some of his old connections, so be it. If it meant some people being removed. So be it. It had to be done.

Niaz stroked his beard. Times were changing.

18

Clutching at straws

IDP Camp, Rawalpindi
Qasim

Ijaz wasn't at the refugee camp.

As I wedged myself in-between Uzair and his colleague in the back seat of the Suzuki, I had a sinking feeling that I was drifting away from Ijaz again. All day we had walked in the makeshift refugee camp that had been set up in the empty space beside the Rawalpindi Polo Club.

I had carried cartons of food, clothes, tents and bedding and given them to families all day. I had searched all over the camp for any sign of Ijaz. Had tried talking to some even in spite of the language barrier between us. All to no avail.

We had all tried, even Uzair and his friend who had got me on the list. I had seen them earnestly talking to families in the camp, looking for someone who would meet my description. Or would at least resemble what Ijaz would look like after five years.

For all our efforts, we had nothing to show besides sweat-caked shirts, sore arms and legs from having carried heavy cartons and muddy shoes that had slipped and stumbled in the sludge created in the heavy monsoon rain.

"It can't be." Uzair seemed to have taken it to heart.

I threw one arm around him in the cramped space. "You did all you could, Uzair; I am grateful."

"You can't give up like this," he said with a quiver in his voice.

"I won't. I can't."

"What will you do then?" Uzair's friend Mansoor, who had got me on the volunteer list, asked from up front.

I looked at him and shrugged. "I honestly don't know right now, but I can't just give up and pretend to go back to my life. I have no life as long as my baby brother is missing. I just can't…" I trailed off.

"Well, there is still a slight chance," said the driver, who had been quiet the whole time and whose name I had missed in my excitement during the morning introductions.

We all looked at him expectantly.

"The polo ground refugee camp is not the main camp; it only holds the refugees that were unable to be accommodated in the main site for the IDPs."

My heart skipped a beat. We all looked at each other and then back at the driver.

I could tell just by looking at the back of his head that he was also grinning.

"The main refugee camp is outside Rawalpindi; it is on the Peshawar Road, along Golra Mor."

I felt Mansoor clutch my arm and squeeze it.

"Can we get inside Ishaq *bhai*?" Uzair asked the driver.

"*Massla nai hai*, anyone can volunteer and provide rations for the families. It is a huge camp; the government needs all the help they can get," said Ishaq. "My brother-in-law is taking a truck of supplies there tomorrow; I can ask him to take you along as volunteers," he added.

This time, none of us said anything. Each of us having already been bitten by the fangs of bad luck and not wishing to pin too much on this slim chance that fate had provided at the doorstep of despair.

The next morning, over two plates of naan channa and hot scalding tea at Ijaz the cricketer's shop, I had brought Deemu up to speed. It did not surprise me at all when he said that he would come with me to the camp. I would not have expected anything less from him. When the chips were down, he was someone you could always count on to stay with you.

I smiled at him. "Life sure is funny," I said, raising my third cup of tea, "who would've known that the person I fought with and hated would one day help me when it mattered the most?" I wondered aloud.

Deemu had a serious look. "I'm not proud of everything I did during that time. Sometimes it seems like another lifetime. The way I see it, life's a journey that we're on. Who I was did help me become who I am right now," he looked at me with a mischievous glint in his eyes, "and to be fair, you were a *chutiya* too back in those days."

I laughed, spraying a mouthful of tea on myself. "In any case, I'm glad you gave me another chance; we could have been brothers in another lifetime," I said, getting up and wiping my clothes.

"*Kal kissne dekha hai bhai?*" said Deemu as he got up to clasp my hand in his. "Let's be brothers in this one."

*

Half an hour later, we were seated in the back of a Suzuki pickup truck as it made its way through the early morning traffic towards the refugee camp at Golra Camp. There were piles of packed rations crammed in the pickup truck. So much so that accommodating Deemu, who had not been included in the initial calculation, had been a problem. But we were able to squeeze him in as the NGO was short-staffed and they needed as many volunteers as they could get.

Uzair had not been able to come, but his friend Mansoor greeted us, and once we reached the entrance of the camp, he handed us over to one of the administrators who was overseeing the distribution, then went off with his team of volunteers. After giving us our instructions, Deemu and I teamed up to distribute the cartons amongst the refugees.

The camp turned out to be a city in itself with really cramped mud streets that had become a treacherous sludge due to the recent rains. There were thousands of tents stretching as far as the eye could see. Tents of all sizes and all colours, some of them the same blue as the one Pitras had. Everywhere we turned, there were outstretched hands, protruding from behind burqas, or tiny, malnourished arms held up. The camp was conspicuous in the complete absence of males ranging in age from roughly eighteen to sixty-five.

I stopped dead in my tracks when I came to the realisation: this was a camp of those left behind. In our next trip back to the truck, I said as much to the administrator, who shrugged and agreed. He said that the army was wary of some of the extremists entering the camps under the guise of refugees. The ones who fit the age range were being screened and interrogated in separate secluded locations. Added to that was the fact that an overwhelming majority of men had died under the Taliban regime, and a large number were still holed up in the mountains fighting against the military.

I sat down on the ground with my head in my hands. "I'm never going to find him," I whispered as Deemu came and sat on his haunches beside me.

He lit a cigarette, took a couple of puffs and handed it to me. I took a deep drag and passed it back, exhaling the smoke slowly through my nostrils, like I'd seen him do countless times. I started coughing violently.

Deemu smiled and thumped me on the back a couple of times

until the coughing fit had subsided. After finishing his cigarette, he stubbed it under his toe, got up, picked up the carton and started off back into the camp. That was the thing with Deemu, he would put his life on the line for you, but words held no meaning for him. He was a man of action.

As if on cue, just as I was about to follow Deemu into the camp, I saw him drop the carton and take off into a narrow dark alley between two overlapping tents. One second he was there, the next he was gone. I put my carton down and ran forward. As I came to the opening of the alley, I saw the back of Deemu sprinting towards a smaller figure that was bobbing and weaving in-between people and tents.

He was chasing a boy.

That made no sense at all. But I had no time to think. The alley dipped downwards, and I was standing at the top of a gently rising knoll, giving me a bird's-eye view. I could see where the boy was leading Deemu into. It was the centre of the camp where another, much bigger, organisation was distributing supplies from an open truck. There was a sea of humanity there. Once the boy reached that mass, he would disappear. I quickly scanned the path and saw that he would have to pass through a lane that was perpendicular to the camp centre. That was my chance; I could cut him off there.

I made a mental note of just where I had to go, then entered the alley and set off at a dead gallop. As I skidded and splashed through the mud, my heart was beating like crazy, threatening to burst out of my chest. I watched the faces of people flash by as I ran headlong towards the lane.

A couple of seconds later, I saw the small boy also running straight towards me from the left. He was looking back at the rapidly advancing figure of Deemu. The boy must not have been older than eight, and I wondered again at what Deemu must have seen that made him chase him. I had to trust his instinct.

We will find out soon enough, I thought as I ran towards the unsuspecting boy with my arms outstretched. I looked up at Deemu to give him a grin, but for some odd reason, he had stopped, and his eyes were bulging out of his head as he opened his mouth to say something.

That's odd, I thought. The next second, I felt something crash into the side of my face. As I went down sideways into the mud, I remember the boy looking directly into my eyes as he jumped over me, his shoes sending a spray of mud into my face. I tried to raise my hands to protect my face, but my arms refused to move. That was very odd indeed. I heard a flurry of activity and shouting around me before everything was enveloped in the warm embrace of darkness.

*

I woke up to a brightly lit room. I raised my hand to the side of my face which felt swollen to twice its size and was soft to the touch. I got up gingerly and felt a bolt of pain shoot through my body. I groaned and fell back.

At my sound, I felt the door opening and people entering. Presently, I saw Deemu's battered and bruised face looming over me.

"Good to have you back," he said. I had never seen him worried before.

"What happened?" I croaked and then winced in pain. My throat felt like it was on fire.

"You were hit with the butt of a rifle by one of the soldiers guarding the camp," said a voice that I recognised as belonging to Major Rashid. I raised myself on my elbows slowly so as not to start off the shooting pain again. As the room gradually stopped spinning, I saw the pensive face of Major Rashid sitting on a chair.

"Hi, sir."

"What were you doing chasing a refugee?" he asked, ignoring

my greeting. "And then your friend attacked the soldier who hit you." He looked at Deemu, who met his gaze unflinchingly. I looked at Deemu. One side of his face was a red pulp; his clothes were torn as if he had been thrashed like a rag doll. I saw his knuckles – they were bruised and raw, with the skin peeled off at some places. *Well at least he gave as good as he got*, I thought, smiling.

"You kids don't know what I had to do to get both of you out; you weren't even on the list of volunteers, and then to go off and expose yourselves like that," said Major Rashid, his voice softening. I saw my opening.

"Sir, I will always be grateful for what you are doing for me, what you have already done, but it will all count for nothing until I find my brother, and right now I am at the same place I was yesterday. I will do anything to find him."

"And what does chasing an eight-year-old boy have to do with all that?"

I had no response to that; I looked at Deemu, but he wouldn't meet my gaze. He was examining his tattered clothes, straightening them out and dusting off the mud onto the carpet.

I looked back at Major Rashid and shrugged. Major Rashid nodded, as much to himself as to anyone else.

"Very well then. Have it your way."

"No, sir," I began, then stopped. Whether it was the injury or the effect of the rifle butt, suddenly I had no more energy left. I flopped back on the bed.

"Please excuse me," said Major Rashid, his voice all distant and aloof. "Nawaz will serve you dinner; I'm afraid I won't be able to join you, but I wish you all the best."

"Thank you for the dinner, but we will be leaving now, sir," said Deemu as he jerked me to my feet and then half-dragged, half-walked me out with Major Rashid looking on.

Once outside the house, Deemu led me to the footpath where he made me sit down.

"Those *madarchod* broke my phone," he grumbled as I eased myself down onto the pavement.

"I see a shop up front. Wait here; I'll be right back," he shouted as he ran off. My body still felt like it wasn't in my control, and my skull felt like it was made of tissue and even the slightest wind would cave it in. I leaned against a pole and closed my eyes.

I must have dozed off because the next thing I knew, Deemu had returned; he was puffing on a cigarette with another tucked behind his ear. After wiping the pavement with his hand, Deemu sat down beside me and offered me the cigarette.

I looked at him incredulously and shook my head. "Are you crazy or what?"

"What?" he was smirking, showing his bloodstained teeth.

"Your clothes are caked with mud and are in tatters, and you are dusting the footpath before placing your arse on it?"

Deemu craned his head back and let out a huge roar of laughter, then immediately doubled up in pain, clutching his ribs. "I think they broke my ribs."

Despite my pain and our situation, I could not help laughing. "Well, it serves you right for trying to run away from the soldiers."

"I wasn't running away," he said.

"Then?"

"Then what?" Deemu looked uncomfortable. "They were about to carry you away to who knows where, and I saw how that *bhaindchod* smashed his rifle into the side of your face, so I just went over and let it be known that you weren't alone. I've lost enough family members; I wasn't going to stand and lose another one."

"Thanks, brother." I held out my hand.

Deemu clasped it in a firm grip. "Anytime."

"You haven't told me why you were chasing the boy," I asked.

Deemu went quiet again, and for a second, I thought he wouldn't say anything, but then he looked up. "I knew the boy; in fact, it was me who had found him on a garbage site and brought him to work for us."

"Brought to whom? Work for whom?" I asked as a part of me realised the answer even before Deemu uttered it.

"Raja Niaz."

Raja Niaz, the student federation leader. My one-time roommate and the one who had told me that Ijaz would be in Peshawar. No matter the hundreds of miles and days I had tried putting between my past and the future, I was suddenly face to face with everything I thought I had left behind.

There were so many questions that were clamouring in my head, but there was no time as Pitras arrived on Deemu's bike. If Pitras looked shocked at our condition, he did not show it. Deemu sat at the back with Pitras almost straddling the fuel tank, leaving me wedged in-between. Both of them had one arm around me, perhaps still worried that I wasn't fully in control of myself due to the concussion. I felt an overwhelming outpouring of love for these strangers who, in a small time, had managed to forge bonds that were as strong as blood. As we made our way through the evening rush-hour traffic back to Lalkurti, each of us lost in our private thoughts, I felt weary and downcast. Just when I had thought that the ordeal was about to come to an end, the road had forked and opened up to another long and mysterious detour. And if Raja Niaz had anything to do with it, it was going to be full of unpleasant surprises.

19

Dead end

NACTA, Islamabad
Asma

There is something about public offices. The work is never enough to make you go crazy. And it never stops either. It's a slow trickle that goes on forever.

It's waterboarding, with inane files, papers and correspondence. I could not believe that it had been three days since I had come back from my meeting with Niaz. If he was to be trusted, and that was a big if, Qasim was somewhere in Swat at this moment.

My heart had constricted to a knot when Niaz had mentioned the place, which in recent times had become a hotbed of radicalism and extremism. According to Niaz, Qasim had approached him to use his network and find out about Ijaz.

It was not much to go on. Considering that his information was at least three years old, Qasim could be anywhere. Or. No, I willed myself not to even think of the alternative.

After the initial tongue-lashing from Turtle on how I was not a good officer, normalcy had returned. In the sense that I avoided him, and he pretty much acted as if I did not even exist.

Good enough for me.

I had realised pretty early on that I was not my father. And the sooner my bosses realised that, the better it would be for everyone. It got rid of the incessant coffee, tea, club invitations, the small talk and the effort to interject my father somewhere in there. I had to convince them that I could not get them a meeting with my father, let alone a favourable posting.

Nobody would believe it when I told them Shahzad Zafar's daughter could do nothing for them. And so now I let my actions precede me. I no longer cared.

Here I was. In a career that I did not want. In a posting where no one liked me. Willing myself to slog through another day in the hope that I would be able to find something about Qasim.

At that moment, just as I was about to shut down my laptop and leave, I heard a noise outside.

I got up and looked outside my door. Saeed, who was the section officer in the administration wing, was talking to his subordinate while coming out of the office of the chairman.

"Saeed *saab*, how are you?"

"Asma *bibi*." He smiled and changed his direction and kept coming straight towards me. I backed into my room and opened the door a bit wider. Saeed had risen through the ranks, starting from the post of a typist. He ate, slept and breathed the Pakistani bureaucracy, where nothing was as important as gossip over a cup of tea.

He plopped himself in the chair opposite my desk. With a snap of his finger, he had the subordinate run off downstairs to continue doing whatever task they had been assigned. Another good thing about the public sector: there were always ten people for any task that could have been done by one. Getting a government job, or a *pakki naukri* as it was called, was the best way to earn votes by the politicians. As a result, the public sector had become a behemoth, an underworked and overextended dinosaur.

"What's going on, Saeed *saab*? Coming out of the chairman's office this late? Isn't it time for golf?"

Saeed smirked as he sipped his green tea; he still had the inherent mistrust of the gazetted officer who would blame all the crime on the assistants and lower-grade staff. In his mind, he was still the typist; he did not how to shed off that skin.

"*Ji* Asma *bibi*, we just got the approval from the ministry."

"What approval? Are we getting the pay rise or the new laptops and the Suzuki Cultuses?"

This time, he really laughed. So much so that some of the green tea spilled on his kameez. I nudged the tissue paper towards him.

"Nothing like that, although do not worry, any day now. The admin at the ministry is trying to delay our file; they want the pay rise to be applied to them too. I will go and talk with them."

"*Kia* Saeed *saab*, I have heard you saying that for the last three years. *Humara time kab ayega.*"

He smiled.

"Anyway, the approval is for the visit to Swat."

I froze.

If somebody had punched me in the gut at that second, I would not have reacted any differently.

"What trip to Swat?" I asked on my third attempt at getting my voice to go above a whisper.

"Oh *ji* you were away last week. The chairman put up a summary to the minister for a team from NACTA to visit Swat in the aftermath of the military operation and to produce a fact-finding report. He feels it will put our organisation more in the limelight."

I tried to say something, but words would not come out.

"Don't worry, Asma *bibi*, your name was on the list, but it has been taken off now. It is still dangerous, especially for a woman. Civilians have returned to the area, but there is no telling if the terrorists have also returned with them. You should count your lucky stars that you don't have to go."

"Who else is going?"

"The chairman, Uroosa *bibi*, her husband, Rafay and myself."

"Even Uroosa is going?"

Uroosa was an English teacher who had been hired as a consultant. According to the grapevine, the chairman and Uroosa were a couple. Which made the presence of her husband, a local lawyer, on the same trip weirder. I tried to keep myself away from the gossip because of my gender, my father's reputation and because I just felt it was none of my business. But even I could not help but feel indignant at being excluded from what was, even if I disregarded the fact that I wanted to go there to find out about Qasim, a very important trip. And to top it all off, I was being replaced by a lady whose only claim to the position was her tolerance for a bald and fat old geezer.

I had to talk to the Turtle. I decided to take Saeed into confidence. No matter what anyone else might say of him, he was committed to the code of the public sector. And the code said that helping a fellow colleague out was religion.

"Saeed *saab*, I need your help; I need to be on the team."

"What? I thought it would be too risky for you."

"Saeed *saab*, if I were scared of risks, I would not have volunteered for this organisation. You do know I could have got any posting I wanted." I realised that recently I was using inferences to my father's influence a lot. But I was beyond caring.

"*Ji ji* of course." Saeed got it.

"I want you to sit on the file for a day."

In government lingo, sitting on the file or *file dabana* meant to delay its journey up or down the command chain. How one decided to do it depended upon the expertise of the officer and the nature of the urgency.

Expectedly, Saeed was alarmed, or at least made a pretty good show of it. He would undoubtedly leverage it for some other favour. It was to be expected. In fact, it was the accepted thing to do. If somebody did you a favour without asking for anything in return, watch out.

"Asma *bibi*, it is impossible – you know how the chairman *saab* is; I absolutely must process it today."

We both looked at the clock – it was 5.10pm. Although the official timings were 8am to 4pm, they were never observed. The officers were required to stay back until the boss left, which was usually after 6pm or 7pm at the very least. There was a skeleton crew of the boss's favourites who would remain behind, putting in the extra hour in hope for a favourable annual performance report or some lucrative assignment.

I had never conformed to that unofficial rule. Which was another of my many flaws in the eyes of my peers.

In any case, getting a dispatch rider from here to carry the file to the ministry would have taken an hour, and I did not think Saeed would have sat for tea with me if he were really in a hurry.

We had us a deal; I just needed to seal it.

"Saeed *saab*, you are a tremendous asset to this organisation. I am sure you can do it; you will be an asset wherever you go."

That got his attention.

"Why would I want to go?"

"No, obviously not, but I met my father last week, and he was complaining how there aren't enough competent administration officers in the new project that he is heading in the Punjab government."

Punjab was the jewel in the crown of the public sector. Getting posted there was like being given the keys to the kingdom. And obviously, only the favoured few got those keys. Nobody without connections and pedigree, certainly not somebody who had risen through the ranks like Saeed, could hope for such an opportunity on their own.

His eyes lit up. I had dangled a diamond in front of him. Now it was his turn to play it cool. He sipped his green tea. Looked at it intently. Placing it very carefully in the saucer, he gave me the full measure of his grey eyes.

"OK, Asma *bibi*, I can hold it till 12pm tomorrow."

I had until tomorrow to somehow get myself on the list.

*

The next morning, I was the first one in the office. Well, technically the second one since Turtle actually lived here. As I parked my car and got out, I saw the guard, whose name I still did not know. Silently, I rebuked my snobbishness for not having asked him his name. But our interaction had never been for more than a minute as I was always running late.

However, this time the roles had been reversed. It was I who had caught the guard with his pants down. My incessant honking of the horn had awoken him enough to finally open the gate, but in his haste, he had forgotten that under his uniform shirt he was still wearing his shalwar.

As he nodded at me, I grinned and pointed downwards. He looked down, did a double take and burst out with a hearty laugh. Beneath the gruff exterior, he was a simple boy.

I joined in.

"Asma *bibi*, how are you here so early?" he panted as he jogged back inside his tent just inside the gate.

"I thought for once in my life, I should be on time and see what it's like."

He grinned as he emerged from his tent, tucking the shirt in his pants.

"I'm sorry, I never got your name."

"My name is Qasim Ullah."

I caught my breath. If that wasn't a sign, I don't know what was.

I held out a thermos I had brought with me. "Here, Qasim, I brought you some tea – pray my work goes well."

He came forward and, grabbing the thermos, said, "Inshallah, all will go well, *bibi*."

I tiptoed my way inside the building. Ziafat, the cook, was ironing Turtle's clothes for the day. Beside him on a small handheld radio, an old Pakistani Punjabi song played.

The sound of the door being closed made Ziafat look up. He flashed me a surprised look as I climbed up the stairs. I took this as a good sign. That meant breakfast had been served without anything happening that might have triggered the Turtle's legendary short fuse.

I went to my office, placed my laptop bag on the table and then did a little walkabout in the space by the window. Khayyam, my office assistant, had not as yet arrived as he, like everyone else, was more accustomed to me coming late. How I wish I hadn't given my tea thermos to the guard in a moment of vulnerability. I could really have used the caffeine to calm my nerves.

I guess I was going to have to do it on my own.

I decided since I was taking a chance, I might as well go all in. Instead of meeting the chairman the conventional way, which involved first going to the personal secretary who would then see the chairman's schedule and try to fit me in, I just burst in.

Khawaja Zaheer had once been a muscular person. Over the years, the muscles had given way to layers of fat, accumulated from sitting behind a desk. He still missed the excitement and thrill of being out in the field, and it showed in his famous short temper.

But time catches up with everything. And now, on most days, the Turtle took out his anger on the golf course or on mounds of samosas and sandwiches.

My first image of him, as I barged into the Turtle's office before the personal secretary could stop me, was of him about to engorge a mini sandwich in one bite.

He stopped his hand midway, clamped his mouth shut and considered me for a second. I could see the lines along his fat-layered cheeks clenching as he fought to control his initial reaction. In the ensuing uneasy silence, Zafar, the chairman's personal secretary, opened the door slightly and knocked.

The Turtle had put down the sandwich and was looking at me over his hands, which were now holding up his head by the chin. His eyes went to the door and motioned for Zafar to enter.

"Asma *bibi*, you didn't tell me that you wanted to meet sir." Zafar was practically whining as he tried to clear his name from this kamikaze mission I had just attempted.

Still with his chin resting on his hand, the Turtle shifted his eyes back to me. There was no excuse for what I had just done. I was beyond the point of concern. I shrugged. "Sir, I'm sorry but I really needed to talk to you about something important."

Khawaja Zaheer sighed then stood up. He still had not uttered a single word, which was somewhat a record considering his reputation for always speaking first and thinking later. He motioned Zafar to leave.

As the door closed behind him, I locked eyes with the chairman, who had walked around from behind his table and was now standing a couple of feet away from me.

He looked me up and down, taking in my trainers, jeans and kurta and hair tied up in a sloppy ponytail.

Uh-oh.

And he then let me have it.

As soon as he began with a mention of my father and how I was disgracing his name, I went into automatic shutdown, and the internal sound system in my head drowned out the ensuing tirade. It was like I was witnessing a mime.

The old Asma would have run off crying by now, not to be seen for days. I was surprised at how calm and indifferent I was feeling at the moment. But I had no option. I was committed to the cause and everything else had to take the back seat.

"Are you listening to what I'm saying?"

I could feel a distant smile on my lips, which I quickly controlled. "*Ji*, sir, I am listening," I blurted.

"You are not even listening." Turtle sat himself down on the sofa.

He was panting.

I went to the door and told Ziafat, who had his ear pinned to the wall, to get a glass of water for the chairman. He was still frozen in his act of having been caught eavesdropping by the time I had slammed the door in his face and walked back to stand infront of the Turtle.

"*Beta* Asma, I am sorry if I have been harsh on you this morning." Turtle had recovered some of his breath, and the colour was slowly creeping back to his face.

"No, sir, I know you are right, and I deserve it."

"What happened to the go-getter who volunteered for this post and blew everyone off their feet with her determination and spirit?"

"Sir, I am still here."

"No, you're not! Is this how an officer behaves? Is this how an officer dresses? You look like a student or a researcher for God's sake!"

And there it was. Everything was judged on how it looked and not on merit. This was my biggest complaint with my father whenever we got into an argument over how far the bureaucracy had gone down the drain. He, much like Turtle, would not see my point that we were encouraging a culture where superficiality was being replaced by actual worth.

I squirmed my toes in my Adidas trainers.

"Sir, I am sorry; I was just too caught up in my work, and there weren't any official meetings on the schedule planned today and—"

"Don't give me that bullshit."

I looked up and made eye contact with him. He softened his gaze. I could feel my vision clouding, and I quickly looked down.

"*Dekho* Asma, I had to give you this lecture; it is for your own good."

"*Ji.*"

"You have a long and, Inshallah, successful career in front of you. You need to grow up."

I sighed. Not the long-career sermon. It was time to make my move. Now or never.

"Sir, I agree and am very sorry for not living up to your standard."

"Shabash! I know what you are capable of."

"*Ji*, sir."

"Just last week I was talking to the Interior Minister and praising you to him for the excellent work you had done in preparing that report on the Swat Operation."

I knew for a fact that he was lying. I had two witnesses in that meeting who had told me of how he had taken credit for the whole report. But that was nothing new; everyone did it. I had got used to it.

But this was my opening.

"Thank you, sir – you are very kind. I will make you proud again, I am confident, when I write about what I observe on the trip to Swat."

And there it was. He narrowed his eyes. He knew that I knew that I was not on the list. The question was, would he be man enough to own up to my face or send me off with a lie?

To his credit, he decided to be upfront with me.

"You're not going." He walked back to his desk and eased his considerable frame into the chair which groaned and squeaked on its wheels.

"But, sir, I wrote that report; I know everything there is to know, and I have been working on it all these months."

"And you have done a good job. Now your part is done."

"How can it be done, sir? What about the trip and the findings there? Who will deal with them?"

"Zaidi is going, and the staff are going; they will record everything and then you will have them to prepare your report.

You don't have to be there; it's not a safe place for a woman."

I stiffened, and Turtle realised his mistake.

"Sir, with all due respect, let's not go there."

This time it was the Turtle who stiffened; he knew who I was dangling in the air, his mistress.

He looked me up and down for a few seconds more and then picked up the remote and turned on the television.

"You're not going, and that's final."

20
All roads lead to Swat

Qasim

"You seem awfully quiet," I said to Deemu as he sat cradling a hot cup of tea, gently rubbing it against the now bandaged side of his face. We were all sitting upstairs in my room, me, Deemu and Khalid. After dropping us off and parking the bike, Pitras had run back, saying that he had to feed Sheroo.

Khalid had been deep in conversation with a customer, probably telling him the whole story in detail about some western that he was convincing him to rent. Sometimes I envied him his persistence in harping the virtues of a bygone era. How he kept the shop open and running was beyond me, since all he had were a handful of loyal customers, old-timers who came each week more out of habit than anything else.

Khalid had taken one look at our battered faces and, without another word, had taken out his first-aid kit from the medicine cabinet and followed us up the stairs. He tended to my wounds with a professional hand, which immediately brought back memories of my mother and how she used to come home after volunteering all day at the hospital and still not complain when some little kid in our street used to be brought in by their parents after some minor scrap or accident.

Having patched me up, Khalid quickly moved over to Deemu, who avoided making eye contact with the elder man. Khalid kept making clucking noises with his tongue and shaking his head side to side as he cleansed and bandaged Deemu's face, arms and hands. At one point, he held the bandaged face of Deemu in both his hands and said, '*Desmond beta*, if only Samuel were alive today, he'd have whipped those soldiers for laying a finger on his baby."

Deemu still wouldn't meet his eyes; he looked away and said laughingly, "Yeah, and he'd have made fun of you for being a grown man and crying mama *ji*."

That had been an hour ago. Since then, Khalid had ordered dinner, special fried daal tarka with naan, topped up with scalding cups of tea. Throughout it all, Deemu sat off to one side, nursing the cup, taking occasional sips while deep in thought.

"Come on, yaar, it was just a phone," I chided him, trying to coax him to talk. Khalid, who had given up trying long ago, looked up.

Deemu put aside the half-empty cup and faced us. "You know all those years I was with Raja Niaz, do you know what my job was?"

Khalid looked down and shook his head, not wanting to find out.

"You were an enforcer for him, beating people up into submission, like you did with me. Do you know, Khalid *saab*, how we first met?" I said good naturedly.

But Deemu wasn't in the mood; something really serious was on his mind. "No, that was an added advantage; I liked beating people up, and it suited Niaz to have a wild animal on his leash who could bend people to his will. But that wasn't my job."

He kept looking at us until I couldn't take it anymore.

"Then?"

"I was a recruiter. I used to pick up kids, boys as small as four, five, orphans mostly, street kids who had grown strong on the streets like me. Because I could connect with them; I knew what they were going through; and they saw in me a ray of hope, that they too could make it out of the streets. And I built up that dream, and then I used to bring them over to Niaz."

Khalid fidgeted in his chair uneasily. I shrugged. "So you had to do some unpleasant work; you didn't know – it's not your fault."

This time I saw tears in Deemu's eyes. "You don't understand, Khalid *mama* – those were kids, just innocent kids with their whole lives still in front of them like a blank paper, and I tricked them into coming with me and then fed them to a monster."

Deemu wrung his hands, clearly in agony. "And I cannot forget the boy I saw today, Ramiz – he was so sweet; I couldn't believe how he had survived on the street until I had found him. He was working at a balloon factory and living with some other bunch of kids, and I talked him into coming with me…" He trailed off as if gasping for air.

I walked over and placed my arm over his shoulder, trying to console him, but he brushed me away.

"I knew Niaz wanted an army; I knew he was ambitious, but I never thought his dreams would make him partner with extremists and terrorists."

Suddenly, a chill went up my spine. "What do you mean?"

"Can't you see it? The kid was there, which means Niaz placed him there, which means Niaz is involved with the terrorists."

I sat back down in my chair, too shocked to say anything.

"We used to train kids to be our eyes and ears on the ground. To find out what was being planned, what were the weak spots. He probably has an older handler in the camp too. There must be more than just one in there. If the extremists have people like Niaz partnering with them, this thing is far from over."

"*Yaa meray Khuda*," whispered Khalid. "What makes people do such things?" he said more to himself than either of us.

"Death and power, Khalid *mama*, people like him cannot be

reasoned with; they only understand the language of power or death," said Deemu, as if coming to a decision.

I too had made a decision: Rawalpindi was no longer my home. I could no longer stand by the side and hope for fate to throw me a bone. I had to enter the fray and make my way into the thick of action come what may. I was done waiting; I needed to find a way to get into Taliban territory. All roads led to Swat.

*

The next morning, I woke up with a sense of unease and restlessness. I wanted to put Rawalpindi and Lalkurti behind me and just get on the road towards Swat. I had overstayed my welcome and now nothing seemed worth doing. I thought about going to the tennis court, but I didn't want to face Major Rashid and Ahmed Din, both for very different reasons.

I had never been good at farewells, and I knew that if I went, I wouldn't be able to explain myself to Ahmed Din or thank him for the love and care he had shown me in his own way. So, I spent all morning in my room, packing my belongings in a bag and placing it by the door. Khalid and Hanif both came upstairs in-between, just sitting for a while, not saying anything and then leaving. Around noon, I went down, had lunch with them, and then Khalid put on an old favourite film of his, *The Searchers* starring John Wayne, which I had watched many times with him previously but, somehow, he still wanted me to see it. Perhaps it was his way of saying goodbye.

I tried Deemu's number a couple of times, but there was no response. He had seemed restless since yesterday and had left during the night after I had fallen asleep. I wanted to go check up on him but right now I had to focus all my energy and time on getting myself to Swat. I still had no idea how I was going to do that. Although the military operation had ended successfully and all the terrorists had either been killed or driven back into the mountains, the area was still closed tightly, and entry and exit was subject to background checks and clearances.

Public transportation had resumed though, and I was hoping that I would be able to enter without too much trouble. But I had been waiting for this moment for so long that now I had doubts and fears. *What if the military deemed me a threat since I was the brother of a fugitive and locked me up? Would I be able to talk my way out? What if I got there too late? What if?*

Where was Deemu?

It was in moments like these that I realised how much I had come to depend on him and his connections. These past three years, he had been as involved in finding Ijaz as I had been. Just yesterday, he had put himself in harm's way to protect me. I owed my life to him. More importantly, I needed his help, but he was nowhere to be found.

I went outside and sat down on one of the empty chairs. I needed to clear my head and think. Presently, Khalid appeared at the end of the road; he seemed to be walking really fast and motioning towards me.

I got up and went up to him as he stood with his hands on his knees, doubled over and out of breath. I patted him on his sweat-soaked back. "Khalid *saab*, is everything OK?"

"Come… come… with… me."

"Come where?"

"He will meet you."

"Who?"

"Sherwin."

Khalid finally straightened up and, taking my hand, led me around the bend and to Colonel Sherwin William's house, where he was holding his weekly durbar.

21

Resolve

Asma

As I sat nursing a mug of hot chocolate at Street 1 café at Kohsar Market, I went over the recent setback in my mind. The confrontation with Turtle had been many months coming.

How was I supposed to know I would be needing his approval for something that mattered so much to me?

As I brooded, the waiter came for the third time and stood over me, willing me to look up. I let him stew for a few seconds.

I was sitting on one of the outside seats; it was a beautiful summer evening. The café management obviously wanted to avail their best seats for people who would be coming here to enjoy the ambiance and order more.

Not someone who would sit around for two hours holding a cup of hot chocolate.

I was a sunk cost.

A gone case.

Not someone they would want to be associated with their fine establishment.

"Is it the way I dress?" I asked the waiter.

"I beg your pardon, miss?"

"It can't be my trainers – they're Adidas!" I knew I was losing it, but there was too much momentum behind the breakdown that I realised I was having. "Look!" I lifted one foot off the ground and pointed it towards the retreating waiter as he bumped into a group of smartly dressed people waiting to be seated.

"Ma'am, is there a problem?" someone was whispering behind me. With one foot still in the air, I turned around to see the manager bent over the table, with a look of sincere warmth in his eyes. He knew I was a regular, and we used to exchange pleasantries at times.

His eyes seemed to be begging me to take a hold of myself, for old time's sake, and not create a scene.

I planted my foot down.

I looked down at the table, boring holes in it with my eyes.

"I'm so sorry." And I was. I wished I could disappear inside the ground.

He placed a fresh cappuccino and a plate of nachos in front of me. A peace offering.

"That's OK, on the house." He smiled and walked away.

"Can I have another cappuccino and a hot fudge brownie too please, Akhtar *saab*?"

I whipped my head towards the voice.

Oh no.

Sam. She was grinning from ear to ear as she walked towards my table. I hid my head between my hands. I had not responded to her calls since coming back from Lahore.

She nodded at the manager, who greeted her by pushing out the chair opposite me for her and motioning towards the waiter to bring her order.

"Oh wow! So, you're alive." Clearly Sam was enjoying this.

"I'm sorry, Sam."

"I was looking at the obituaries or the classifieds for a rogue government officer."

"I got busy."

"Asma Bourne."

And just like that, over a plate of half-eaten nachos, I bawled like a three-year-old as Sam wrapped an arm around me and glared at whoever dared look at a fully grown woman sobbing up a storm. I was glad to have my friend back.

Half an hour later, as we polished a second bowl of nachos, Sam's expression was more serious, and mine, spent.

I had regurgitated the events of the time in Lahore, from my meeting Niaz in the jail, talking to my father, to the Swat trip, to finding out that I had been dropped and, finally, the day's confrontation with my boss.

Sam was unusually quiet as she toyed around with the last nacho. "Hmm, that is a bit of a pickle." Her best impression of a British accent sounded more Jamaican.

"Yaaah maaan." I put on my best Rastafarian accent.

It never failed. The cloud lifted from Sam's face instantaneously, and she grinned.

After paying our bill, we walked to our cars. Sam suggested that we drive together, so I decided to leave my car in the parking. It was a safe place, and I could pick it up any time.

"OK, let's go over the plan again," I said as I got into the passenger seat.

"The plan is that we are going to Aabpara Market where we shall get our disguises. Then we shall call Daewoo bus services and book two tickets for Swat. You already know where the team from your office will be staying. We will go meet them. Your boss might scold the crap outta you, but he won't send you back again, not two girls by themselves, after all."

The plan had sounded better a couple of minutes ago. Now hearing it again, I could see a number of things not going the way we hoped. Going to Swat by ourselves was a risky move. Notwithstanding the successful military operation, there was no guarantee on there not being any terrorists in the area. The government and the army had been projecting it as a major success and sending the residents back into the area from the camps. But in the ensuing flood of humanity, it was impossible to separate peaceful civilians from extremists.

Sam and I were about to put my theory to the test. Getting the burqas had been a piece of cake. We could not believe it had been that easy. After trying on our black head-to-toe coverings, we decided to keep them on. I thought it would make us invisible.

I was wrong.

It was like the eyes of everyone were constantly on us as we made our way through the crowded market. I felt claustrophobic. I felt like I was on display. Finally, I couldn't take it any longer. I nudged Sam. "Let's get out of this shit."

"Yeah, I'm sweating like crazy."

We made our way to our car which was parked across the road. Throwing our burqas in the back seat, I rolled down the window and stuck my head out to grab whatever wind there might have been blowing.

There wasn't much.

"Let's have some Muzaffargarh karahi, like old times." Sam felt that we needed to reward ourselves for getting the burqa. She honked until one of the guys from across the road looked our way. He squinted for a second then broke into a huge grin. He turned and said something to Rab Nawaz, who was standing over the barbecue grill, turning the chicken tikkas over.

At seven feet tall, Rab Nawaz towered over the landscape no matter where he was. He looked up from the fire, flicked a bucket of sweat from his forehead, then grinned at us. He held up two fingers and Sam nodded and then shouted, "And Coke!"

He nodded and mouthed something to the waiter who had spotted us.

Sam looked pleased with herself. She looked at me and smiled. "Just like old times."

I had to agree. Sam, me and Muzaffargarh karahi went back a

long way. It was the place of our first meal when we were getting to know each other. One night, three years ago, at 1am, I had a hankering for chicken. I had called Sam and, without another word, she had come over, picked me up and we had come to Aabpara. Since that night, we had struck up a friendship with Rab Nawaz, who owned the place with his brother. We had never gone more than a week without coming here in the initial couple of years.

Then, as happened with most things in life, slowly other distractions kept crowding in and slowly, I had stopped coming as often.

"You know, I haven't come here for a while now," I said to Sam.

"Mmm, I know," she said as she wrestled with a stubborn slice of chicken. "Rab Nawaz and I used to talk about how you had become a big government officer now."

"What?!"

"Yeah, he still would not hear a bad word about you though; dude considers you his little sister."

I was touched.

Yeah, it felt good. Why did I close myself off from people who cared for me? It was not their fault if I had been hurt by others. I had to keep reminding myself not to let what happened to me influence me or change me.

I was about to say something to Sam when I felt the words pushed backwards into my mouth by a sudden violent tremor. It was like being thrown and having the wind knocked out of you.

A couple of seconds later, we heard the sound of the blast. It was deep and ominous. Like a giant beast, growling.

We both looked at each other.

"Oh my God."

"Turn up the radio." I could see the whites in Sam's eyes. Having grown up in Karachi, the terror of the current moment was striking much closer to home.

I fumbled with the dials. After surfing all the channels, we couldn't find anything.

"It's probably too soon."

"Let's just get out of here." Sam was practically shivering now.

"Sam, look at me, look at me." Reluctantly, she met my gaze. "Don't worry; everything will be alright, OK?"

"Yeah, I know; I'm sorry. It's just…"

"I know."

When Sam had been seven, she had lost her older brother in a bomb blast. The family had been coming back from a day at the beach when they got stuck in traffic. There had been a political rally that was passing through. Some motorcyclists had come in from a side street and attacked the party leader's motorcade. In the ensuing fight, somebody threw a hand grenade which blasted pretty close to Sam's car.

Although she and her parents were unhurt, one of the shards of glass had penetrated her brother's neck, and he lost a lot of blood. By the time they were able to get out of the melee, Sam had lost her brother. The image of him lying limp in her hysterical mother's lap had turned Sam into a mute for the next few years.

It was only after she had left Karachi to go to college, that she realised that the city would never be her home again. It reeked of blood for her.

Sam had seen the look of loss in my eyes when we had first met. It was that look that had bonded us together. We both had lost somebody essential to our identity. She had brought me out of that dark period. She had held my hand and guided me through those days and weeks when I questioned my existence in this sorry excuse of a life that meant nothing anymore.

"It's going to be OK, Sam. Here, let me drive." I got out of the passenger seat and came over as Sam climbed over the gear box to vacate the driving seat.

"Yeah, good idea."

I got in, adjusted the seat a bit, then took a U-turn and stopped in front of Rab Nawaz, who was still grilling chicken tikkas as if nothing had happened.

I passed him the plates, along with a five hundred rupee note. He took the plates but wouldn't touch the money.

"Big government officer, your money is no good here."

I blushed. "It's not like that, Rab Nawaz *bhai*."

"Are you OK?" He was looking at Sam, who still looked pale.

"*Ji*, I'm fine."

"What was that noise?" I asked.

"Bomb blast at Kohsar Market," he said matter-of-factly as he kneaded a piece of meat and then threw it on the big pan by his side.

"What?!" we both shouted.

"Yeah, some big shot political guy's security detail was attacked. A constable who was sitting here heard it all on his walkie talkie."

"We just came from there."

"You guys should give *Sadqah*; you two were lucky."

"My car is still there."

Rab Nawaz paused. "I don't think there's anything left for you to go there – this constable was saying that the first respondents who got there were reporting the whole area is a big hole, lots of cars destroyed."

I remembered the second blast. "There were two."

"Yeah, this has become the new strategy of these killers who think they're doing God's work," Rab Nawaz said through gritted teeth.

"What strategy?"

"People come here and talk. So, I listen. Someone was saying about this terrorist incident that happened in Tollinton Market, Lahore last week."

I nodded. I had read about it – sixty people had been killed in two bomb blasts that had ripped through the famous colonial-era marketplace.

"This person lost an aunt. So, he was telling me that after the first blast, people would rush to help those killed and injured. And as more people would run towards the spot, a second bomber, who had been waiting in the crowd, would detonate himself."

"*Ya Allah.*" I felt my throat constricting.

Throughout this time, Sam had not said a single word. She kept clenching and unclenching her fist. Her knuckles had gone white.

"Who are these people?" I could not imagine hatred that had the power to turn humans into these callous, calculating killing machines.

"People, just like you and me," said Rab Nawaz.

"Not like us," said Sam for the first time, more to herself than to anyone else.

Rab Nawaz looked at her and kept quiet.

"Take care, sisters. *Fi aman Allah.*"

"*Allah hafiz*, Rab Nawaz."

We peeled out of there.

I was going to find Qasim, whatever it took.

*

Kot Lakhpat Jail, Lahore
Raja Niaz

Raja Niaz was into his second helping of haleem when his eye fell on the news about the Kohsar bomb blast on the television playing in the background. Something about it made him sit up and reach for his mobile.

Bhola picked it up and brought it to him.

"Dial your brother."

"At this time, *Ustad*?"

"*Kyun bhonssree ke*?! Is he a prime minister?"

Bhola started stuttering and dialled the number.

Ziafat picked up on the second ring.

"*Ji* Raja *saab*, how are you?"

"I'm good. What's this news about the blast? Have you heard anything?"

"Raja *saab*, I just served tea to the chairman *saab* and his guests," Ziafat whispered. "They were from the Interior Ministry. The trip has been postponed due to the blast. I did not hear much, but one of the guests was saying how the army might be mounting another operation real soon."

"Hmmm."

"There is something else too, Raja *saab*."

"*Bol.*"

"As you saw on the news, it was a huge blast and, besides damage to the building, it is impossible to recognise the bodies."

"Yeah so?"

"Asma Zafar's car was found in the wreckage. It was instantly recognised because one of our guards at the gate was in the area, and he was the first one to arrive there. He told me a while ago when he came back."

Niaz grunted and hung up. He threw the mobile in the direction of Bhola, who caught it at the second attempt.

As Niaz dove back into his plate of haleem, his mind wrapped itself around the death of Asma and how this affected his equation with her father.

So much for leverage.

Book Three

Echoes in Eternity

22

The long night

NACTA Office, Islamabad
10pm

It had been a hectic couple of hours for Ziafat. Minutes after making the call to Niaz, he had been called back to help clean up the chairman's office, who had rushed to the bomb blast upon learning that one of theirs was on the victim list.

After he had cleared up the dishes, Ziafat came downstairs to the kitchen and sat down by the window for a smoke. Presently, the face of the guard on duty appeared, along with that of Khayyam.

Both of them were grinning.

"Khayyam, what are you doing at this hour?"

"I heard about the blast and rushed here to find out."

Ziafat fished around in his breast pocket for a match and then lit his cigarette. "I thought Asma *bibi* was nice to you," he said as he took a deep drag.

"She was," nodded Khayyam, still grinning.

"Then shouldn't you be just a little sad?" asked Ziafat, getting irritated by the second.

"Oh, didn't you hear the good news?" gushed Khayyam, now literally poking his head into the kitchen through the window. "Asma *bibi* is not dead; we just heard over the wireless from chairman *saab's* driver. Her car was there, but all the dead bodies have been recovered, and she isn't among them."

Ziafat froze.

"Oh, that is good to hear."

"Allah be praised," said the guard. Khayyam nodded vigorously and continued, "What's more, they have one of the suicide bombers in custody as his vest did not go off. Chairman *saab* is trying to get the authorities to hand him over, but most probably the army will get the bomber; still nobody gives a shit about us." Khayyam shrugged.

I have to inform Raja saab, thought Ziafat as he realised that the piece of information he had conveyed to his leader a few minutes ago was no longer true. And he knew what happened to people who misled Raja Niaz. Ziafat owed his job to Niaz. In fact, he owed both his and Bhola's life to the student leader. It had been Raja Niaz who had provided the two brothers with the money to pay for their mother's cancer operation. In return, all he had asked for was loyalty. It was the reason Bhola had got arrested on a false charge so that he could protect him from enemies inside the prison. Keeping a nose out for developments had been Ziafat's task for which he had been placed in Islamabad. Raja Niaz had tried getting him placed inside the Interior Ministry, but the best he could manage was in NACTA.

It was a good job; it paid well, especially after the new allowances and bonuses that had been added to the salary in light of the rising incidents of terrorism and the law enforcement agencies being in the frontlines. However, for Ziafat, that meant preparing the sandwiches just the way his boss liked and washing and ironing his clothes. It was the easiest money he had ever made. If Ziafat were to have his wish, he would have wished for more bombs and killings so that he could get another hefty allowance in his pay. But for that, he had to keep this job so that he could save enough money to bring his mother from Gujranwala to live with him and find him a nice suitable girl to settle down and have kids with.

Ziafat jerked out of his reverie at the sound of static on the guard's wireless handset. He moved off to a distance and spoke for a couple of minutes, then rushed to the gate, straightening his uniform instinctively.

"*Saab* is coming back," said the guard, looking back at Khayyam and Ziafat. "Khayyam, you better disappear before he returns, you know that *Saab* doesn't like day staff at the office beyond official hours."

Khayyam nodded and slipped out the side gate.

With both of them gone, Ziafat stubbed out his half-finished cigarette under his foot and rushed out of the kitchen and to the back of the house. There was a tiny side lane which was wide enough for one person to pass through. Ziafat expertly moved through it, stepping over the backup generator and the pipes jutting out from the underground water storage tank. He stopped outside a small side door and pushed it open. The tiny room stank of sweat, stale food and cigarettes. Without turning on the light, Ziafat moved past the chair, piles of clothes and newspapers strewn about the room until he was at the bed.

He bent down and dragged out an old trunk from under the bed. He opened the lock and fished around the inside of the trunk until he found the mobile phone. The phone had been given to him by Raja Niaz, and it had only one number: that of Bhola, who was with Raja Niaz all the time. Ziafat dialled the number. On the third ring, Bhola picked up. Without waiting for him to say anything, Ziafat said, "*Raja saab naal gal kara.*"

Bhola grunted into the phone, and Ziafat winced. His elder brother had always been a man of few words. The first four years, his parents had been worried that their first child was a mute. But as it turned out, what he lacked in words, he more than made up with his strength and size. At ten years, Bhola was already six foot two and could lift his parents clean off the ground on each arm. The two brothers perfectly complemented each other; one knew when to speak and when to keep his ear to the ground, and the other knew how to break bones when needed. Both were qualities that Raja Niaz knew how to appreciate and use to his advantage.

"This better be good," grumbled Niaz. He seemed to be in a bad mood.

"It is, Raja *saab*," beamed Ziafat. "Asma *bibi's* body has not been found from the blast site; she is still alive."

There was a moment of stunned silence and then he could hear the happiness in his master's voice. "Shabash," he said then hung up.

Feeling pleased with himself, Ziafat did a small impromptu bhangra in the dark. *This calls for a celebration*, he thought to himself. Putting the mobile on the bed, he moved to the small stove in one corner of the room. He turned it on and poured a cup of milk and some tea into a pot and placed it over the stove. It was then that he turned on the light.

"Hello, Ziafat."

Ziafat froze. He knew that voice even before he turned around. As he did, his fears were confirmed.

Standing in the corner of the room was Deemu. He was smiling as if glad to see an old friend. In his hand he held a pistol aimed at Ziafat.

*

Kot Lakhpat Jail, Lahore
10.30pm

The luxury-sized cell, that had been especially built by tearing down the walls of three normal cells in order to accommodate Raja Niaz, was drenched in pitch-black darkness. Presently, a cigarette glowed in the corner, throwing one side of the infamous student leader's face in sharp relief. As his henchmen snored and slept around him, Niaz was deep in thought.

Throughout his life, Raja Niaz had been nothing if not a cautious man. Never a gambler, he loathed people who took a blind chance and plunged ahead without calculating every move.

Niaz believed in survival, everything else, such as emotions and morals, mattered little to him. His people, even Bhola, who sat guard outside his cell at that moment, had begged him to reconsider his plan, to think twice before going into business with the extremist groups; there was no knowing what they would do. But Niaz recognised a business opportunity when he saw one, and he knew that this was his chance to strike big. He had wasted enough time rotting in a cell waiting for the right moment. He had to make his move if he wanted to be someone.

After the second call from Ziafat, Niaz had called his informant to verify the news, which he had, calling half an hour later to inform him that Asma was in fact still alive and was with her friend Sameera – he had bugged both Asma and Sameera's mobiles – in her friend's car and that they had booked bus tickets for Swat. Niaz had told his informant to stay close by and keep updating him on their movements regularly. The second call Niaz had made had been to his contact in Swat to let him know that the plan was in operation and that the 'package' would be arriving the next day.

Satisfied that everything was in place and moving just as he wanted, Niaz stubbed out his cigarette and told Bhola to come in and give him a customary neck and shoulder massage before going to sleep.

*

NACTA Office, Islamabad
11pm

It had not taken Deemu long to get all the information out of Ziafat. After all, the younger of the two Butt brothers had never been known for keeping his mouth shut. Ziafat had always been more of an opportunist and relied on his ears and nose to pick up important information which he could then pass on to whoever his bosses were at the time. It was the elder Bhola who held up the physical end of their enterprise, breaking bones where required and enduring punishment while not uttering a word if the situation called for it.

In fact, Deemu had been surprised to find Ziafat alone and without his behemoth of a brother at his side. It was a recipe for disaster as, without the other by their side, both were vulnerable to manipulation. It also gave Deemu an indication to the dwindling fortunes of his ex-boss.

Deemu lounged on the single bed, the revolver dangling from his hand as Ziafat sat frozen in the chair in front of him, beads of sweat dripping from his nose, eyes and forehead. He knew too well what Deemu was capable of.

Presently, Ziafat's phone buzzed silently on the table, breaking the silence. Ziafat made eye contact with Deemu and, after receiving the slightest of nods, tentatively picked it up.

"*Haan* Bhola," he said with more confidence than he actually felt. He listened intently for five minutes then hung up. He turned to Deemu and told him about Niaz's conversation with the terrorists. If the news of the kidnapping surprised Deemu, he did not show it. He had been around Niaz too long to know that the worth of human life to him mattered only as far as it could benefit him.

He had to tell Qasim and alert him about the danger Asma was in. When he tried to call on Qasim's number, he got no response. It would have to wait, he decided as he punched in another number.

When somebody picked up at the second ring, Deemu said, "*Haan bhai* Sheeday, give the phone to *Amma ji*."

Even before Deemu handed the phone over to him, Ziafat knew who would be on the other line.

"*J-j-ji Ammi ji*," Ziafat stammered as his eyes welled up at the sound of his blind and frail mother living all alone in Lahore. Ziafat replied through half-controlled sobs to all the routine queries of his half-deaf mother as she shouted into the phone, asking him about his and Bhola's health and if they were eating properly and looking after themselves. Ziafat had never had the heart to tell her that Bhola was in jail. In his mind, the less she knew the better.

After she had finally hung up, Ziafat handed the phone back to Deemu, who had stood up and was languidly stretching himself like a big feline.

"How long have we known each other, Laddoo?" asked Deemu, calling him by the nickname he had been given as a kid when he used to be fat and round.

"More than twenty years."

"And in that time, have you ever known me to not honour my word?"

"Never."

"Good," said Deemu more to himself as he tucked the revolver in the waistband of his shalwar and pocketed the mobile. He approached Ziafat, who flinched as he felt Deemu's hand on his shoulder. "Nothing will happen to *Amma ji*; I give you my word," he whispered as he squeezed past Ziafat towards the door.

Ziafat merely nodded, still shaking because he knew that there was more to come.

"But you will have to do something for me," said Deemu with his back towards Ziafat.

"Anything."

"Before the night is over, Bhola must kill Niaz," he said as he turned around to face Ziafat.

"Can I count on you to do what is right and save *Amma ji's* life?"

"Y-yes," whispered Ziafat.

Deemu nodded. "I'll be waiting for your call; if it doesn't come by morning, please accept my regards for the death of your mother," he said matter-of-factly and then slipped away into the night.

*

Lalkurt, Rawalpindi
11.15pm

Lt. Col Sherwin William was a man of bold statements. Throughout his storied career, his motto in life was '*Gajj ke Wajj*'. Sitting atop the garage which housed Sheroo, his pet lion, William twirled the ends of his freshly waxed massive moustache and surveyed the sea of humanity sitting below him.

Pitras, carrying cups of tea and biscuits, scurried between the rows of people, seated a safe distance away from the sleeping Sheroo, who had seen too many of these meetings over the course of years to be bothered anymore. Two pedestal fans at either end droned incessantly, attempting to bring some much-needed respite to the people, who sat intently and without complaint, despite the stifling hot and humid August weather.

There was a hushed silence, broken only by the occasional murmurs of hopefuls when they saw their turn to meet William and narrate their request. As William listened absent-mindedly to the toothless John, who had retired as a caretaker at the nearby CMH, about the unpredictable supply of water to his quarter, his eyes came to rest on Khalid standing at the back of the crowd, whispering something in the ear of Pitras. There was another young boy standing beside Khalid who did not seem familiar.

William raised his hand at John, who had been droning on about how he had not been able to clean up due to the lack of water for a week now.

"*Ji*, Baba, *ji*, I have heard your problem – leave your details with Pitras, and I shall see what can be done," said William in a deferential tone as he got up and helped the old man down the stairs. After handing him over to Pitras, William kept on walking, extending his arms as his face broke into a wide grin.

"Khalid Chacha, why did you not just send a message? I would have rushed over myself," he said in a young boy's voice as he warmly hugged his childhood hero. The elder man hugged back and kissed William's shoulder before holding him at an arm's length and looking him up and down.

"I can still see the little boy who used to skip school to watch the latest John Wayne film with me," said Khalid as he brushed away a tear at the edge of his eye.

"Your William is now John Wayne himself, Chacha, thanks to all those lessons you taught me about being good and helping the needy."

"I know, *beta*, I am so proud of you. What's more, I'm sure your father up in heaven would be looking down proudly too."

William blushed at the praise. In the ensuing silence, his eyes wandered over to the boy standing beside Khalid who had been silently watching the whole thing.

Finally, Khalid broke the silence. "*Beta*, this is Qasim. I came to you for him; he needs your help."

Qasim still did not say anything as he stared back stoically at the Colonel, his face a mask. At that moment, Sherwin had the feeling that he was being sized up and not the other way around. William found himself smiling as he held out his hand. Qasim grasped it firmly.

"Let's go inside," said William as he led Khalid and Qasim inside the house.

*

Kot Lakhpat Jail, Lahore
1.45am

Constable Sakhawat Chauhan had almost dozed off on his chair when he came to with a start. Something had woken him up. It was a noise that seemed out of place with the normal night sounds of the jail. Sakhawat recognised all too well the usual sounds that he had come to familiarise over the years walking, sitting and generally killing time during the graveyard shifts. He knew all the different types of snores and burps. He was even accustomed to the farts and coughs. Most of the inmates had been in his jail for so many years and so many times that he knew their sleeping habits as well as he did those of his wife.

And then he heard it again. Faint but unmistakable; it was a gurgling sound. As if someone had left a tap open and air accompanied with water was escaping from it with a whooshing sound. As Sakhawat groaned out of his chair, he went over to the entrance of the corridor and craned his neck into the creamy darkness, trying to see where the sound was coming from.

With a chill that sent shivers down his whole body, Constable Sakhawat Chauhan saw the light coming from the last cell at the furthest end of the corridor. The cell that housed the 'special VIP' guest of the jail, Raja Niaz.

And then, as his eyes adjusted to the darkness, Sakhawat saw the foot protruding from under the cell door and the dark puddle surrounding it.

With a start, Sakhawat fumbled for the keys and unlocked the door. He ran with every ounce of energy he could muster from his fifty-five-year-old body, knowing in spite of himself that whatever had happened was beyond salvaging. As he skidded and slipped on the slippery floor in front of the cell, his worst fears were confirmed.

The first thing he saw was the spreadeagled body of one of the bodyguards who used to shadow Raja Niaz everywhere he went inside the jail. As his eyes travelled up the length of the corpse, he saw the mangled pulp of what once had been the face. The cooking pot that had been used to crush the skull lay nearby with the bottom shimmering red, with bits of bone and brain clinging to it.

Then he heard the gurgling sound again. Transfixed with terror,

Sakhawat walked closer to the cell entrance to make out two bodies deep in the darkest recesses of the room.

"Bhola?" whispered Sakhawat. He had grown to be fond of the quiet behemoth who had the mannerisms of a child and the size of a giant. Many a time, he had shared a steaming plate of biryani with the gentle giant and swapped stories and gossip.

At the mention of his name, the gurgling sound stopped and there was a cough as a form emerged from the shadows.

It was Bhola. There was blood all over his shirt front, and more was oozing from the side of his mouth, but the expression in his eyes was as if he were just waking up from a deep and content sleep.

"*Ji* Chauhan *saab*," he said in his childlike voice. "How are you?"

"*Mein theek aan puttar.*" Sakhawat was having trouble matching the calm demeanour being shown by the convict.

"What happened?" he finally stammered.

Bhola looked back blankly. He shrugged and said, "I killed Raja *saab*."

Sakhawat's eyes went wide with shock as he recognised the inert form of the local strongman lying in his own pool of blood mixed with urine. His eyes were bulging out of their sockets with a shocked expression, and his hands were crimson with caked blood on his nails. Then Sakhawat looked closely at Bhola and saw the bloody claw marks on his face and torso.

Raja Fiaz had not gone down without a fight.

"*Bhaindchod* Bhola, what have you done, *puttar*?" whispered Sakhawat more to himself as he sat down on his haunches in the corridor. Around him he could feel the eyes and murmurs of the other convicts who were now also craning their necks to get a view of the carnage.

It's going to be a long night, thought Sakhawat as he handcuffed the docile Bhola and gingerly led him over the stiff bodies and the pool of congealed blood. *It's going to be a long, long night.*

23

A second chance

Hindu Kush mountains

An icy-cold breeze, which was uncharacteristic for this time of the month, blew in from the north, making Ijaz shiver in his threadbare shalwar kameez as he waited in the open courtyard of the makeshift mosque for the people to come in so that he could lead the Fajr prayers.

As he made his way to the pulpit, he ran a hand over each of his arms, wringing the last droplets of water and rubbing them up and down to bring some circulation back into his body. Finally, satisfied that he had dried himself as much as possible under the circumstances, he rolled down his sleeves and covered himself with the woollen shawl that had been a wedding present from his wife.

He sat himself down on the rickety old pulpit and looked up at the sky as the first shards of light began to sneak in from the edges of the horizon. Ijaz absent-mindedly wrung out his straggly beard and pulled it tight until a few droplets dripped down onto his lap.

A grin crossed his face, transforming his weathered and rugged features to those of the boy he had been. Despite living there for years, he still found himself marvelling at the majestic beauty of the mountainside and the serene beauty of the village which had come to be his home.

He still used to wake up at odd times of the night, surprised by the sounds of the night. It had taken him many months to get used to the openness of the landscape, the sights and sounds of his environment and the healing powers of his new adopted home.

He was finally home.

It wasn't the home he had wanted or could ever have imagined. But it was the one fate had prepared for him. And slowly but surely, after many failed escape attempts, after countless days chained to the wall inside a black pit, he had finally surrendered to his situation.

The first couple of months had been jarring. He had found himself in a camp inhabited almost exclusively by men. Rugged, bearded men who spoke multiple languages and carried more weapons and ammunition than Ijaz had ever seen.

Ijaz had been handed over to an Afghan, a Soviet-war mujahideen who preferred to use his hands and feet to give orders rather than his mouth. Over the following days and weeks, it dawned on Ijaz that he was being trained to be a suicide bomber. With no other option at his disposal, Ijaz had gone about his duties in a trance, learning how the explosives were prepared and how to strap them on his body. Until the day finally arrived when Ijaz and another boy had bathed, put on their cleanest clothes, strapped on the explosives and got into the jeep that would take them to their target.

The target had turned out to be a military outpost near a village where the army doctors had been administering vaccines and providing supplies for the local community. Once they had come within range of the checkpoint, their handler, a towering Uzbek with one arm missing, had pointed out to them the locations where they were supposed to blow themselves up.

As Ijaz and the other suicide bomber joined the trickling line of locals that had heard about the army doctors in the area and were bringing their families for a check-up, the handler had remained on his bike, away from the checkpoint but within range so that if the detonator strapped to the hands of the suicide bombers malfunctioned, he could still remote detonate it.

As they neared the checkpoint, Ijaz slowed down and fell back. The plan was for the first suicide bomber to blow himself up when the guards approached him. In the ensuing melee, Ijaz was supposed to wait until more people, preferably soldiers, rushed in to care for the wounded, and then to blow himself up. The aim was to take as many lives as possible. Anyone who was not with them was an infidel and worthy of death.

It had been the sight of a young boy, not more than ten years old, carrying a toddler on his shoulders that had broken the spell. In a wild rush, the memories of him and Qasim, playing and frolicking in the streets, had flooded back. Suddenly, Ijaz found his feet getting heavy, and he came to a halt. In a panic, he looked back at his handler.

What he saw sent shivers up and down his spine.

Their handler was talking to a soldier and pointing straight at them. What occurred next happened in mere seconds, but in Ijaz's mind, it was as if time had stood still and everything was moving glacially. The soldier was talking on his walkie talkie and pointing towards him.

Ijaz was on the bridge, a mere twenty yards away from the checkpoint. The other suicide bomber was almost at the checkpoint when the soldier raised his rifle and shot him point blank. The bullet lifted the boy off the ground and threw him backwards, almost at Ijaz's feet.

Miraculously, the explosives strapped to his chest did not go off. In his hurry, the soldier had shot him through the collarbone, luckily away from the explosives. Both boys locked eyes and, at that moment, realisation came all at once.

It was a set-up. Their handler had sold them out.

At that moment, Ijaz finally realised something: it wasn't a holy war; it was just business, and he was just an accessory. His life meant nothing to anyone.

As he saw the soldiers rushing towards him, trying to disperse the crowd of frightened villagers, Ijaz had a decision to make. If he gave himself up, there was no guarantee that the soldiers wouldn't shoot him dead before he got a chance to reveal his story. And even if he did, there was no knowing how much of it would convince the army, keeping in mind that they would rather believe the word of his handler, who had seen Ijaz readily volunteer to blow himself up.

Even though Ijaz had just realised that he wanted no part of this war which he had been brainwashed into believing, he also knew that now was the time for survival, and that meant sticking with the known.

He quickly helped his wounded companion, who was still alive, to his feet and then half-dragged, half-pulled him to the side of the wooden bridge as they both jumped into the thrashing icy-cold waters of the Swat river.

It had taken all his strength to hold onto the limp and lifeless body of his companion as they were carried with the current. Finally, they were able to reach the bank a couple of miles downstream. Shivering uncontrollably, he stripped himself and his companion, whose name he found was Aqeel through one of his delirious mumblings, of the explosives.

For the next day and a half, Ijaz and the semi-conscious Aqeel hid in the jungle during the day as the sky overhead was blotted out by army choppers flying at low altitude, scouring the terrain for them. Ijaz had accompanied his mother to Mayo Hospital as a kid, and he had seen her tending to wounds enough to know how to clean, bathe and bandage it with what he could find. During the night, Ijaz carried Aqeel on his shoulders and made his way back to where he vaguely remembered the camp to be.

On the second night, just when his last reserve of energy was about to give in, Ijaz spotted one of his fellow camp members walking away at some distance. Knowing that he was down to his last ounce of strength and risking being caught, Ijaz mustered all the strength he had and shouted at his startled companion who was about to shoot when he recognised them.

Back at the camp, he was met with hostility and suspicion. He tried to explain how the handler had sold them out, but the language barrier proved to be an obstacle. The fact that nobody really knew him that well worked against him. Aqeel, by that time, had slipped into a coma and was barely clinging onto life.

After two days of being chained to a post and barely being fed, he was handed over to a man who, he later found out, was Aqeel's father. He had become a prisoner. In those dark days, Ijaz wondered what or who it was that was stopping his captors from just doing away with him. He would later find out that Aqeel's father had been impressed by the rudimentary medical expertise Ijaz had shown on his son. It had helped in convincing him to let Ijaz live for the time being.

The three of them had moved to a village deep in the mountains where Aqeel's family lived. It was a village occupied by women, children and men, deemed too old to fight. It was where the families of most of the senior fighters in the camp lived. During the day, Ijaz was mostly chained to a post in the basement, except for a couple of hours in the evening when he would be allowed to relieve himself. Otherwise, for the next month, he saw very little of the sun or people, except for a thin figure who used to bring him food and water.

One night, as the figure was bending down to put his food in front of him, they both heard the shrill sound of a missile from a drone coming closer and closer. The figure shrieked and fell as the missile landed close enough to make the earth under them shudder and tremble. Soon the house all around him was crumbling in the dust as Ijaz pulled and tugged at the chains until they came loose.

As he inched his way blindly through the dust and smoke, he saw a hand protruding from the rubble. It was the girl who had been bringing him food all these days. At that moment, Ijaz feared for his life, knowing the whole building could topple on top of him at any moment, burying him under mounds of earth. There was also the very real threat of another missile hitting even closer this time.

And yet, something about the helplessness of the hand waving feebly for help made him stop and rummage through the rubble until he located the rest of the girl. As he pulled her out from under the earth, the first thing he noticed were the eyes that were bulging from their sockets with fright. At once his heart went out to the frail creature. Surprised at his own strength, he lifted her in his arms and carried her out of the building and away from the village towards a clearing where the rest of the villagers were standing.

Aqeel's mother was the first one to recognise them. With a shriek she ran towards Ijaz and snatched the girl away, covering her with a shawl and hugging her tightly. The father also joined them. Both cried and hugged their daughter fiercely as Ijaz stood at a distance, the chains still dangling from his hands. Suddenly, he was reminded of his own family and how he too had once been loved.

Aqeel's father had dragged his wife and unconscious son out of the house as soon as he realised what was happening. Once he saw the house collapsing, they had reconciled themselves to the fact that they had lost their daughter.

Nobody had given a second thought to the prisoner in the basement.

That night changed a lot of things. Ijaz was no longer chained to anything but allowed to move freely in the village. And Ijaz, for his part, suddenly felt a sense of belonging with his fellow villagers and the family of Aqeel in particular. He helped in rebuilding their house. He assisted Aqeel's father in tending to the wounded. It was as if he was suddenly visible and welcome again.

A month and a half after being shot, Aqeel finally regained consciousness. He retold how the handler had apparently switched sides and how he had been shot and how Ijaz had saved his life. The next few days were a blur as Ijaz found himself being welcomed and hugged everywhere he went.

In time, Ijaz became a member of the family with his own room. There was no further talk of him being sent back to the fighter's camp where Aqeel left for again after regaining his strength. But before he went, there was a large celebration in which all the villagers and most of the fighters from the camp participated.

It was the wedding ceremony of Ijaz with the small girl he had saved.

Her name was Fatimah.

Ijaz had finally come home.

Over the next year, Ijaz settled into his new life in the village. He built a small school where he taught the village children how to read and write. He rebuilt the village mosque that had been destroyed and became the de facto imam. He also tended to the sick and wounded both from the village and the fighter camp. Sometimes, he would be awakened in the dead of the night by Fareed, Aqeel and Fatimah's father and his father-in-law, and they would leave wordlessly for the camp or some other location where their services were required.

Life was hard, but all things considered, it finally seemed like he could heal.

After nine months, Fatimah gave birth to a healthy baby boy.

Ijaz named him Qasim, after the first ray of light that had shone on him as a boy and helped and guided him throughout his childhood. He hoped this other Qasim would again provide the illumination that would guide him towards salvation.

As if on cue, Ijaz was brought back to the present by the sight of the three-year-old Qasim holding hands with his grandfather as they made their way to the mosque.

Ijaz smiled as he blinked back the tears.

Yes, he was home.

24

Into the fray

For Asma and Sam, the last twenty-four hours could not have gone any slower. Ever since she and Sam had boarded the bus, Asma had been having second thoughts about her decision to venture into what, until a few weeks ago, had been the epicentre of a bloody, door-to-door battle between the security forces and hardened terrorists.

Two hours later, as they made their way off the bus, Asma could feel her skin crawling as the eye of every person in the vicinity seemed to be focused on them.

There were not many people in the station. As Asma looked around, she saw only the familiar faces of some of the passengers she had travelled with. They all seemed to be leaving off with people who had come to pick them up or were haggling over fares with the local transport drivers.

In a couple of minutes, they were the only two people still standing in the station, along with their bags, as even the bus drove off.

"What do we do now?" Sam whispered through gritted teeth as she attempted not to be freaked out by the line of bearded and unkempt men who were lounging in various stages of indifference. They stared unashamedly with the complete rapture that comes easily to people not accustomed to the norms of cities with regards to personal space and intrusion.

"Asma!" Sam was practically growling with anger now. That seemed to unfreeze Asma as she came to with a start.

"Oh right, right, I need to call my office colleague and we'll find out where they're staying, and they'll send somebody to come pick us up," she said in a rush as she noticed one of the onlookers breaking away from the pack and coming towards them. He seemed slightly cleaner and more presentable, but still the sight made both Asma and Sam turn around involuntarily as they started walking away, dragging their bags along the ground.

Behind them, they could hear the wolf whistles and claps of the crowd.

"I thought the army was supposed to be here."

"There's no army for catcalls and wolf whistles, Sam," whispered Asma as she flipped open her mobile and searched for signal.

There was none.

"What the fuck," whispered Sam in a tone that made Asma whip her head around sharply. The man had reached them and was calmly cleaning his teeth with a toothpick. Once done, he put it between his teeth and smiled.

"There are no signals for most telecom providers in the area as the military has jammed them, except one or two," he spoke in impeccable Urdu.

Asma and Sam stood transfixed, not knowing what to do.

He stepped forward, causing Asma to jump back as Sam caught her breath and raised her hands as if to fight. The man stopped in mid-stoop, looked up, smiled and picked up their two bags. "I have a taxi; I can take you wherever you want. You will not be able to speak with other cab drivers as they do not understand Urdu that well."

With that, he picked up the two bags and started walking away.

Sam and Asma exchanged worried glances that seemed to say, *I have a bad feeling about this.*

They both followed the man.

INTO THE FRAY

*

Being cramped inside the stifling heat of the armoured jeep as it bounced and tossed over the gravelly road had given Qasim a raging headache. It was the thought of finally getting some clue as to the whereabouts of Ijaz that prevented him from clawing the face off of the gnarly and sweaty soldier sitting opposite him who kept bumping the barrel of his G3 rifle into his ribs.

And then he would smile each time afterwards, revealing an uneven row of brown tobacco-stained teeth beneath a five-day stubble.

It had been a few hours since the meeting in Colonel William's house. After listening to his impassioned plea and giving in to the demands of Khalid, who seemed to have a strong hold on him, William had nodded once and that had been that.

"Fine, you're coming with us. We leave in five minutes."

Matter closed.

In a matter of seconds, Pitras had handed him a jacket. "It gets cold there," he had added gruffly as he bounded away at the call of his master. Qasim had not had the time to even rush back to his room to pack some clothes or to get his toothbrush.

When he had stepped out, the ground had already been cleared of all the chairs and most of the people had also left or had been herded away to make room for two army jeeps and an armoured vehicle that resembled a giant bug.

"Make room for one more," William said to the driver of the armoured bug as he saluted smartly and clicked his heels. As he got into the front passenger seat of the second jeep, William had looked at Qasim and motioned with his head towards the bug.

At that moment, if he had been told to ride a live giant bug, Qasim would have gladly done so. As the rear door opened, Qasim reeled backwards as he was assaulted by the force of the sweat and heat that rushed out. The soldiers guffawed as Qasim regained his footing and climbed inside.

Three hours later, the stench and heat inside the armoured vehicle had morphed into a living thing that was pressing on Qasim's nerves and his resolve. The smell of sweat and farts and breath hung in the air like a mushroom cloud that was making his eyes watery and stinging his nostrils.

Every second stretched for an eternity as Qasim tried to block it all out, telling himself that it would soon be over. Each time he would be reminded of the frailty of his beliefs as the barrel rammed into his ribs followed by a sneer or a snort.

Finally, when it happened one time too many, Qasim couldn't take it any longer. As he cocked his hand back to ram it down the throat of the soldier so hard that he would be shitting teeth for the next week, the armoured jeep lurched to a complete stop.

Qasim was thrown completely off-balance and fell into the lap of the soldier who had a genuine look of panic in his eyes as he lifted Qasim up and then peered through the grimy glass divider to the driver for any information. There was a muffled exchange of words between the driver and his companion, and then he motioned to the soldier to get out.

Qasim was shoved to the back of the jeep as his two companions opened the rear door and got out, suddenly all business. His tormentor, the grizzled soldier, looked at him and gently said, "*Bacha* stay behind me. Don't worry, *theek hai*? Shabash."

Not waiting for any confirmation, the soldier moved out and to the left of the jeep, flanking it while his partner did the same on the right side.

Qasim saw the two army jeeps come to a halt behind as Colonel William took off his sunglasses and spoke into the wireless handset while more soldiers poured out of his and the other jeep. As they rushed by him, fanning out into the surrounding fields, Qasim turned around and peered from behind the armoured jeep to look at what had caused the stoppage.

As he peered outside, Qasim saw that an army convoy had

got off the road and taken up positions as far as the eye could see. Smoke and puffs of dust still hung in the air and over the lush green mountainside. Off to the side of the road, a car was on fire with something resembling a charred hand protruding from the front seat.

A commotion drew Qasim's attention towards the other end where two men suddenly got up with their hands held up in the air as they started walking towards the soldiers.

"Halt! Stop right there!" shouted the soldiers as the two figures kept approaching, muttering something indistinct.

"Stop or we'll shoot!" shouted the soldier in Pashto this time, but again the figures kept walking forward. As they came closer, Qasim could definitely make out that they were boys, not much older than Ijaz.

The thought of his brother made Qasim gasp. Suddenly, he rushed forwards towards the two boys. *They must know something – maybe they know about Ijaz*, he thought as he started running towards them.

The next instant, he had the air knocked out of him as someone yanked him back by the scruff of his neck and hurled him sideways into the road. As he lay there gasping for breath, the clear blue sky was suddenly filled with the frame of his sweaty and grizzled companion.

There was genuine fury in his eyes. "What the hell do you think you are doing?" he whispered through gritted teeth.

The sound of two rifle shots broke the calmness in the air and made Qasim's ears ring. As he got up and looked, the first thing his eyes froze on were the inert bodies of the two boys lying on the ground. There was a faint puff of dust trailing upwards from the body of one of the boys as he twitched slightly, the ground beneath him darkening with blood.

Something welled up inside him at that moment that made him want to get up. As he dug his nails into the ground to lift himself up, the butt of a rifle came swooping down out of the corner of his eye and crashed with a dull thud against his jaw.

The force of the blow sent Qasim sprawling sideways. As he opened his eyes, his mouth suddenly felt full of something hot and gravelly. Qasim got up again, this time slowly, spitting out blood and sand as he locked eyes with the soldier.

There was no remorse, or hate, just complete alertness.

"Stay down; this is not over," he whispered while his eyes scanned the area.

Qasim nodded and got up gingerly, holding his jaw that already felt twice its size. He brushed his clothes and looked behind him where a ragged line of cars, motorcycles and carts had stopped. Some people had got out of their cars and were looking curiously ahead. There were even a couple of women covered in burqas, which seemed odd and out of place to Qasim as he nursed his jaw.

Qasim returned his gaze to the front where the soldiers were now approaching the two dead boys. Both were now completely still.

Something clicked in his head, reviving a long-forgotten memory and making him turn his head around so fast that he heard his neck crack and put the nerves around his jaw on fire. Qasim's eyes screened the crowd until they came to rest on the two burqa-clad women who were now being herded back into a Suzuki Mehran.

There was something oddly familiar about one of the women. As the seconds ticked, Qasim's mind raced into the blind alleys and ravines inside his memory, searching for the clue that had triggered the feeling. Time seemed to stand still as he kept searching for something.

And then she turned. In spite of the prodding of the man who seemed to be physically pushing the two into the car, the woman turned around. At that distance, there was no way of seeing anything more than a figure and yet, Qasim could feel those eyes travel over the distance and reach into his soul, making their way to a part that had been closed off. A soft spot that had been coated over with a hard shell.

A part of him that he had told himself would never heal.

Asma.

At that instant, Qasim did not need to hear her voice – he knew that it was her, and he knew that she had heard him too. He was about to turn around and walk towards her when he saw, out of the corner of his eye, the grizzled soldier crashing into him.

As he went down under the weight of the soldier, there was a split second in which Qasim saw one of the dead boys twitch and his hand move. In that short span of time, everything moved in slow motion as soldiers dived and took cover while one kept firing into the boy, trying to prevent him from doing whatever he had planned to do all along. As he lay there bleeding his life out on a dusty and broken road, the boy had waited and waited, willing the soldiers to come closer until he could see the whites in their eyes, until he could see the shiny tips of the bullets lodged into the barrels of their pointed rifles.

Qasim tasted sand for the second time as he fell face first into the ground. There was no time to shout for Asma or to tell her that he would never leave her again. In the next instant, there was a muffled blast and then Qasim felt the weight of the world press against him as he was rammed deeper into the soft earth.

And then everything went black.

25

Wheels in motion

Kot Lakhpat Jail, Lahore

Constable Sakhawat Chauhan looked down at the angry red welts on his hands that seemed to visibly throb with pain as he leaned against the wall of the cell. As his sweat-soaked shirt slid against the wall, his legs gave way, and he fell with a thud on the floor.

The incident had no effect on his senior, Nadeem, who continued to thrash the upside-down suspended body all over his exposed torso and buttocks with a long whippy leather tongue. Both of them had fallen into a sort of sadistic rhythm which seemed to have them in a trance.

Nadeem was still dressed in the vest and shalwar in which he had been sleeping in the bedroom in the back of the police station, which in good times had seen prostitutes and 'desperate damsels' willing to do whatever it took to curry favour with the senior.

As if the memory had just resurfaced in his mind, resting like an angry boil, refusing to burst but throbbing with a vengeance, Nadeem bellowed as he gave the leather whip an extra flourish before bringing it down on the glistening buttocks of Bhola, who whimpered slightly through sealed lips. His once white shalwar was bunched around his knees and torn to shreds over his buttocks where most of Nadeem's focus had been for the past one hour, after Constable Sakhawat had given up due to the welts on his hand.

"*Oye bhaindchod bol!*" panted Nadeem as he leaned against

Bhola, who swung away from the weight of the officer. As he came back into range, Nadeem grabbed hold of the front of his shalwar and got down on his knees so that his face was inches away from the drenched face of Bhola.

"Open your fucking eyes," hissed Nadeem as he poked his fingernails into Bhola's blood- and sweat-streaked face until, howling loudly, he opened them.

"They will kill you and not even think twice," said Nadeem as he caught his breath. "Your name will be buried under piles of paper; nobody will give a fuck. Do you know who Shahzad Zafar is *bhaindchod*? He is a monster; he will destroy everyone in your family, your mother—"

"*Amma Ji?*" whimpered Bhola, the first words he had spoken after two hours of whipping.

Nadeem exchanged glances with Sakhawat, who cracked a smile.

"*Allahu Akbar!*" shouted Nadeem as he lay down on the wet and slippery floor of the cell which, until a couple of hours ago, had been covered with the blood of Raja Niaz, the feared student federation leader.

"Yes *chutiye!*" said Nadeem with renewed vigour. "For the sake of your *amma ji*, don't put her through this over nothing; just tell us why you did it so that you can go home to your *amma ji*."

At the mention of his mother, the huge giant convulsed into loud sobs and wept uncontrollably. Finally, he was able to muster enough strength to say, "Ziafat. Call Ziafat *bhai*."

*

An hour later, Nadeem knocked and entered the office of the superintendent. He had taken time to scrub himself clean and was wearing a newly ironed uniform.

He saluted and then approached the warden, taking in the

individual seated in the shadows. He was halfway towards the superintendent when the individual got up from his seat and cut him off, coming to stand in his path.

Coming face to face with the legendary Shahzad Zafar had been the dream of most government officers, and Nadeem was no exception. Many were the times they had recounted tales of how a young AC Shahzad had walked out into the thick of a raging mob and held them off.

Or how he had thrown the son of a sitting MPA in lock-up for harassing a poor local lady. Or how he had made under-the-table deals with both sides of the aisle so that no matter which party or government came into power, Shahzad Zafar was indispensable.

All those tales always came to end on one point: you did not take Shahzad Zafar lightly.

Standing inches away from the legend himself in the flesh had the effect of turning the experienced Nadeem, a seasoned officer of two decades, into stone.

"*Ji*," said Shahzad calmly, running his eyes over the nameplate of the transfixed officer. "What can you tell me, Nadeem *saab*?"

Hearing his name out loud brought the blood back into his legs. Nadeem saluted and came to attention stiffly. Shahzad nodded impatiently. "Just get on with it," he said, the slightest hint of irritation.

"Sir, he has a brother who works in the National Counter Terrorism Authority in Islamabad. We have him under arrest too, and he told us that this was ordered by an old accomplice of theirs, somebody by the name of Deemu. We are looking into his background."

Shahzad Zafar had turned his back while Nadeem had been speaking, and he was pacing the room. Finally, he came to a stop in front of the superintendent.

"Well, this has been a total waste of time," he said, mincing no words.

The superintendent nodded and then indicated to Nadeem that he was dismissed.

Nadeem clicked his heels and saluted, leaving the room echoing with the sound of his steps.

In the ensuing silence, the superintendent remained frozen in a half-standing, half-sitting pose, not knowing what to do. He had been hoping that they would be able to glean some vital information from Bhola. He had told Nadeem not to worry about leaving torture marks.

As long as he pleased the people in power, these sort of things hardly mattered. And there were only a handful of people who were more powerful than Shahzad Zafar at the moment. His tentacles started all the way from the bottom of the workforce, where he had spies and agents in every department, and reached all the way to the top of the bureaucratic food chain.

After all, it had been Shahzad Zafar who had got him this cushy job in the first place. He could just as easily take it away. Finally, when his arthritic knees could take it no longer, the superintendent sank into his soft leather chair and cleared his throat. Shahzad Zafar broke from his deep thought and looked at him, as if seeing an insect trying to climb its way out of a hole.

"It will be hard to contain this news for much longer, sir."

"Just make it look like a case of political rivalry. God willing, it may very well turn out to be that way."

"But I heard that he had been banished from his party." Shahzad's eyes lit up at this, and he gave the superintendent the full scale of his glare.

"That's what I read in the news and rumours, sir," whined the superintendent meekly.

"Your job is not to read the news or rumours, Wasim," said Shahzad icily, "and your job sure as shit is not to make decisions based on the news. If you feel your intellectual capabilities are being wasted here, we can always look for a posting more suited to your analytical needs, say Balochistan perhaps?"

The superintendent shrank back into his chair. He tried to say something, but his throat was too dry to form any words. Shahzad let him stew under his steely gaze for a couple of seconds more, before he nudged the glass of water on the table towards the superintendent, who construed it as a sign of release. Gulping the contents of the glass in one motion, he wiped his mouth with the back of his sleeve and said, "No, sir, I apologise, profusely."

"Hmm, good," said Shahzad, turning his back and pacing the room. "Make sure this does not get out until I tell you to."

"It will be done, sir."

"Can your subordinates also be trusted not to leak this news?"

"Absolutely, sir."

"For your own sake, I hope so, because if I hear of a little bird crapping on the car of a journalist and the journalist deciding to analyse the contents of that shit, only to find that Raja Niaz, the infamous student body strongman, has been brutally murdered in your prison…"

"On my child's life, sir, it won't."

Shahzad Zafar nodded once, then looked out the window at the full moon that was waging a personal battle against the darkness.

"I need to get to Swat," said Shahzad to no one in particular.

26

So close, so far

Swat

Sometimes when you have been on a quest for too long, you lose track of the destination and begin to think that the journey is the destination. Asma had spent many sleepless nights worrying about what would happen when she finally came face to face with Qasim.

Would the same spark be there between them?

Would they recognise each other?

Would they be able to start off again from where they had left off?

Never in a million years had she imagined that she would be cloaked head to toe in a burqa with two slits when she would finally get to lay eyes on the destination towards whom she had dedicated the last half decade of her life.

And yet, even in that moment, her fluttering heart had the presence of mind to hone in on the rough-looking, gaunt figure that was lying in the grass and being pummelled by the butt of a soldier's rifle. In that instant, without even being aware of it, Asma saw the layers of time, losses and heartbreak peeling off from the visage of the stranger until it was stripped down to its truest actual form.

She saw her Qasim.

Just as she had last seen him.

She wanted to shout out his name at the top of her lungs. She felt like ripping off the burqa and running towards him, but she hesitated. *Would he reciprocate? Did he feel the same way?*

Even while her heart told her that he would and it didn't matter, Asma's eyes covered the distance between them and willed him to look up and see her.

And he did.

It was just them in the whole world, and there was no one around. There was no need for words. All was said and heard. As Asma's heart fluttered and she blinked back her tears, she was suddenly almost knocked off her feet as the driver whipped around and pushed her back.

She crashed into Sam and they both collided against their cab.

"*Jaldi! Jaldi!*" said the cab driver in a frantic pitch, the whites of his eyes betraying the fact that he knew something that nobody else did. She could see people moving and shouting around her, but in that moment, she was existing in a vacuum that was filled only with the sound of her panicked heart bursting against her chest.

"What's going on?" whispered Sam in a little girl's voice that sent a shiver down Asma's spine as they were both manhandled into the back of the cab. The cab driver squeezed them in and slammed the door shut.

Asma was about to shout when her head snapped back from the force of the speed with which the car accelerated, the tires tearing up the ground and sending plumes of dust and gravel in its wake. She realised with a start that they were making a run for it. Asma squirmed and twisted to get a look outside the window to get another glimpse of Qasim.

The last image she had was of Qasim struggling to get off the ground before a thunderous explosion violently lifted their tiny car and sent it crashing back on the ground. There was a moment of lucidness and clarity in Asma's mind as she smiled inwardly with the hope that the period of trial and tribulation was over. They had found each other, and everything was going to be fine.

Then, all thoughts evaporated into thin air as her head crashed into the roof of the car. A million tiny needles exploded before Asma's eyes as she fell unconcious.

*

It was early morning when Qasim opened his eyes. He immediately closed them again as the tarpaulin roof overhead did nothing to block out the sunlight that attacked his vision, sending bolts of pain throughout his body.

He instinctively reached up to shield his eyes and was alarmed when he saw a heavily bandaged arm come up. Slowly, as the room came into focus, he looked around gingerly, careful not to make any hurried motion that would set off the pain shooting up and down his whole body.

The scraping of a chair against the rocky ground made him open his eyes and search for the origin of the noise. Presently, the silhouette of a soldier came into focus. Qasim peered closely and recognised him as one of his two companions in the armoured vehicle.

He was mud-streaked, and there was a wild gash across his chest which glistened with a mixture of sweat and blood. If he was hurt, he seemed not to care. His tear-stained face was stoic and impenetrable as he returned Qasim's gaze.

Qasim could not hold his stare. As his eyes dropped, they fell on the soldier's nameplate.

"Javed," he whispered in a hoarse voice that he had trouble recognising as his own.

If there was any response in Javed's eyes, it was gone in a flash.

"Javed," Qasim tried again, attempting to raise himself on his elbows as a fresh bolt of pain shot through his body, making him fall back on the bed.

"Your partner..." he panted as he lay staring at the roof of the tent.

"Aslam Khan." There was a visible tremble in Javed's voice as his face twitched violently, trying to maintain the calm façade.

Qasim raised his face again to make eye contact with the soldier, searching his eyes for any clue.

"Aslam Khan," he whispered as the image of the grizzled leathery face who, in spite of his rough exterior, had never wavered from shielding him from danger.

This time it was the soldier who was the first one to break eye contact. Turning his back to Qasim, Javed convulsed as he sobbed silently.

Finally, managing to contain himself, Javed turned and said, through bloodshot eyes, "Aslam Khan embraced *Shahadat*, trying to save you."

Qasim's heart fell.

Javed raised his hand, as if to console Qasim, then thought better about it. "He may have seemed a hard and uncaring soul, but he was like a father to me and to most of us sepoys whom he raised like his children."

Qasim fell back on his bed again. Tears streamed down the side of his face to merge with the sweat-soaked pillow.

"He would not have had it any other way," continued Javed. "Aslam Khan longed for *Shahadat*, and he got what he wanted. So, do not cry for him or his children; we will protect them just like he protected us."

There was a long pause then as Qasim gulped back his emotions and Javed fidgeted nervously, perhaps surprised by his own outburst.

"Anyway, I am glad you have regained consciousness – we and Colonel *saab* were worried about you," he mumbled.

"How long have I been unconscious?"

"Two hours. When we removed Aslam Khan's body from you, there was so much blood that it was hard to tell if you were alive."

Qasim nodded, not knowing what to say.

Javed cleared his throat. "Anyway, Colonel William *saab* wants to talk to you," he said as he slung his rifle over his arm and approached Qasim, helping him off the bed.

27

Scorched earth

Hindu Kush mountains
5pm

Ijaz stood at the edge of the protruding rock that jutted out the side of the village mosque and acted as a natural courtyard for prayers and activities when it got too hot.

It was the height of summer and yet still cool in the mountains. For Ijaz, summers meant monsoon rains and humidity, and it had taken some getting used to when he had first come here. The wind soared, sending the prayer cap flying off his head and whipping his shoulder-length hair across his face. As Ijaz brushed the hair away from his eyes, he eyed the valley spread out below him and noticed the small dot bouncing and zigzagging across the rough terrain, making a beeline for the camp which was a mile away from the village.

The location of the camp and the village was such that it never had many visitors. It was nestled into the natural labyrinthine trails of the countryside so that nobody could find it unless they knew where they were going. The way the car was leaving a cloud of smoke in its wake meant that the driver not only knew where he was headed, but he was also in a hurry.

That was never good.

No matter how long he had been living in their midst, Ijaz had still not been able to accept the reality of his world and the people he had come to call his family. He had learned to push his own family deep down into a crevice inside his memory where it lay buried, only slipping out at odd times, catching him unawares. But mostly, he had locked that time. And just like that, he had turned his back on the reality of his life with the people he ate, slept and talked with. Over time, he had willed himself to learn the rhythms of the mountain and the village. He had come to learn that nothing was permanent, and change was always cyclical. Little by little, he had honed his instincts into believing that time only mattered as far as each day was concerned. The sun came up over the mountains every day, bathing life in its warm glow until it dipped behind the ice-capped mountains. If the sun appeared the next day, it was a good omen. It was a good start. Winter was followed by spring. There was no need to look any further. It was better to be content with what he had in his grasp rather than pining for something that lay beyond reach.

A fresh gale of wind whipped up, sending a chill down the back of his neck. It was an icy-cold wind, unusual for this time of the year, even this close to the mountain. It was as if the snow-capped mountain, which overlooked their village, had reached down and clasped his heart in its deathly cold grip.

The small dot had grown larger, and in the clear mountain air, Ijaz could clearly make out the inhabitants of the car as it sped over the terrain, inching ever closer to the camp. He looked frantically at the camp as he remembered that his son had accompanied his grandfather there that morning. He scanned the valley, desperate to see any sign that would ease the beating of his heart. Down below, the valley still seemed undisturbed, serene.

For a moment, he hesitated, looking up at the heavens, unsure of what to do. He wished it not to be true, daring, pleading with his *kismet* to not break the peace and tranquil façade that he had so carefully built over the tumultuous uprooting of his past.

In that moment, time seemed to stand still. In the valley, the long grass danced with the wind; the long, slender pine trees swayed gracefully along with the gentle quivering of the sage and thistles as nature danced to the slow melody being played by the icy-cold gale of the mountain. The area between the village and the camp had been used by the women to sow wheat, which sparkled in the sun, reflecting gold rays of light. Each step swooned in harmony with the wind as the gusts whistled over their golden heads.

As he still hesitated, Ijaz saw the car screech to a sliding halt in the central open area of the camp, momentarily engulfed in a plume of dust. He peered closely, squinting his eyes to make out what was happening. By now, people had started gathering around the car. As he looked on, his heart fluttered – standing at the head of the crowd was his father-in-law, with his son riding on his grandfather's shoulders.

Ijaz did not even bother to put on his shoes as he flew down the mountain, scrambling over rocks and brush, silently praying.

*

Terrorist camp
5.10pm

Asma was glad when the car finally screeched to a halt. For the past two and half hours, her heart had been in her mouth as the car had swerved and careened over hair turns and slid close to the edge of roads that were almost indistinguishable from the rest of the mountains and rocks. If there were any tracks in the jagged and broken-up terrain, only the driver could see them as he never took his foot off the accelerator, preferring instead to make last-minute turns that nearly tipped the tiny car over the edge a couple of times.

As Asma gulped her heart down her parched and dusty throat, she looked across the back seat to Sam, who lay crumpled against the door like a rag doll. She had not moved for the last hour and a half. The blood that had gushed out the side of her head where the butt of the gun had hit her had congealed and hardened into a thick, dull maroon, caking the burqa to the side of her head.

The bomb blast and the ensuing hour of high-speed and death-defying turns had been too much for the already frazzled nerves of Sam, and she had gone hysterical. No amount of threats and pleadings on the part of Asma had helped in calming her. Finally, the man sitting in the back seat between them had raised his gun and hit her with the butt repeatedly until Asma had thrown herself over him to stop him from hitting anymore. That had been almost two hours ago. Since that time, Sam had been a silent passenger on the remaining part of the journey, being tossed and jostled quietly like a burlap sack. The thought of Sam being seriously hurt was beyond comprehension for Asma. She could not imagine going through this ordeal without her best friend.

Despite the danger she was in, Asma still had the presence of mind to pick up little details about the situation and their abductors, which she knew could prove crucial. For starters, she had noted that both her abductors were careful not to hurt her. That told her that they had a plan in store that did not involve them disposing of her and Sam just yet. There was still time. Asma knew that she had to keep her wits about her and to ensure her and Sam's survival in the meantime and to keep a lookout. The thought of escape had crossed her mind countless times during the bumpy ride. She had seriously contemplated crashing through the car window or ramming her shoulder against the door in the hopes of pushing it open.

But those were low-reward choices with dismal chances of survival. First of all, she had to think of Sam too. She was not leaving her friend behind. Any plan of escape had to work for both of them. Secondly, she was in an alien landscape. This was Taliban territory. The army might have wiped them out and driven them back into the mountains and forests, but they still held sway in pockets and patches. Two lonely women out in the open with no idea where they were stood no chance. Her experience told her that while her current abductors were careful to keep her alive, she could not rely on the same fate befalling her if she fell into the hands of another group. She willed herself not to make a hasty decision that would put their lives at any further risk.

Asma was yanked back to reality as she felt rough hands dragging her outside the car and throwing her on the hard, dusty ground. As she fought to catch her breath, her burqa was ripped off violently, leaving her feeling exposed. Asma shrieked and instinctively covered herself, even though she knew she was fully clothed. The last thing she saw before they blindfolded her was the crowd around her closing in and the limp body of Sam being thrown out from the car.

Then her world went dark.

*

Army forward post
5.15pm
T minus twelve hours to attack

Thick cigarette smoke hung over the room like a cloud, making Qasim's eyes water and stinging his throat. If the other occupants shared his symptoms, they dared not express them. Lt. General Fakhar Ali paced the room, the cigarette dangling absent-mindedly from his mouth, burning dangerously close to the filter and leaving a trail of smoke in his wake.

At one end of the room, a map of Swat had been placed with a portion of it highlighted in red. Colonel William stood in front with a long stick. A long, rectangular table was in the middle of the room, which was flanked on both sides by rows of senior officers. There were multiple plates and ashtrays placed at various intervals on the table which were stacked with mountains of cigarette butts.

As Qasim, sitting at one extreme end of the table, closest to Colonel William, eyed the cigarette mounds through bloodshot eyes, he had the feeling that they represented the funeral pyres, and the rising smoke were the ashes of time being wasted while Ijaz and Asma's lives were in danger.

They had been in the stifling hot room since last evening, poring over the maps as strategies and counter-strategies had been presented and then quashed for one failing after another. The fact that the Corps Commander had personally flown in on a chopper in the middle of the night to oversee the operation had galvanised the entire force and alerted them to the direness of the situation. For the past twelve hours, the only breaks had been for meals and drinks which had been served by the waiters, coming in to place the dishes and to clear up the empty plates and glasses. No one had dared to leave the room. The smell of smoke and sweat of officers not willing to make a bad impression on the Corps Commander and his guest, who had accompanied him, hung thick over the room.

Sitting at the other end of the room, the guest looked down at his hands that were spread out over the table. He dragged on his cigar, the hollows of his cheeks stretching the skin inwards and bringing into sharper focus the dark lines under his eyes.

He tugged at his already loosened tie, betraying the sense of calm he had mastered over the years. As his eyes met Qasim's across the room, there was a flicker of helplessness and worry that washed over them, and Qasim saw the father worrying for his child. And then the mask was back on again as he pushed back the chair and got up.

The loud scraping noise echoed in the close room, bringing everyone back to attention and worsening the throbbing headache that had been pushed back out of focus by Qasim. He winced as Shahzad Zafar rolled up his sleeves and joined General Fakhar on the floor. The back of Shahzad Zafar's shirt was plastered with sweat and clung like a second skin to him.

"So, partner," said Shahzad as he clapped the General on his shoulder, referring back to their time together in the Neelum Valley when Shahzad Zafar had joined the Civil Services Academy and was posted in Fakhar's regiment as part of his military attachment. The young bureaucrat and the captain had quickly bonded in their shared passion for trekking and birdwatching. Over the years, as their careers had taken them to different parts of the country, they had maintained this bond and relationship and had made an effort to reach out and connect whenever their paths crossed.

So, when the General had been awoken in the middle of the night by a worried-sounding Shahzad, desperate to find his daughter, Fakhar's first thought hadn't been to check what time it was, it had been to call his second in command and make sure that the chopper was ready to take both of them to Swat as soon as possible. It was while they were still in the air that he had been informed of the ambush on Colonel William's convoy and the possible sighting of a pair that could link up to the description of Asma, and this had made him decide to go there instead of the camp headquarters in Swat city.

Things had quickly spiralled from there as Colonel William had recounted his own experience and then introduced them to Qasim, who was known to Shahzad and who had only reinforced Fakhar's gut feeling that the attack was a diversion to get Asma out of the city and into the mountains where there were reports that the Taliban were planning for another attack.

Lt. General Fakhar could understand the strain his friend was under. He had experienced it first hand. He still carried the weight of the loss of his young son, who had been killed while leading a party against entrenched terrorists in Waziristan three years ago. He had

had to keep a brave face and pretend to carry on, but whenever he was home with his wife, the empty home that would never hear the loud laughs of his twenty-year-old only son or the giggles of the grandchild that could have been, a part inside him quivered and cried.

As he looked at his friend, Fakhar vowed that the same fate would not fall on Shahzad, not if he could help it. Fakhar smiled at Shahzad and then looked at Colonel William, gesturing for him to continue.

Colonel William cleared his throat. "So, sir, as I was saying, we have fairly accurate reports of the area of the Hindu Kush range where large activity has been reported by our sources for the past couple of days. This is where we will concentrate our attack."

"Attack?" echoed Shahzad.

"Yes, sir, we are going scorched earth."

Shahzad stared at William then looked at Fakhar. "What am I missing here? What have we been going over for the past twelve hours? How does this scorched earth all-out attack guarantee the safety of my daughter?" said Shahzad, his voice rising by a couple of octaves with each sentence.

This time it was Fakhar who clasped his arm around Shahzad and brought him back towards the map.

"Relax, yaar. We will bring Asma back alive and unhurt; I give you my word," he said with more confidence than he actually felt. But he knew now was not the time to reveal his own doubts about the success of the operation.

"What Colonel William meant to say," he continued, "is that our sources and spy drones have confirmed the presence of a camp in the mountains, which has seen increased activity recently. Firstly, there is no indication that there are women or children in the camp, as usually these camps are only for men. Even if there are captives or prisoners being kept, they would be hidden in bunkers or basements and our troops would be warned beforehand to look out for anyone who matches the details."

"There has got to be a better way," whispered Shahzad exasperatedly. "What about the Mehran car that Qasim saw?" He turned towards Qasim, their previous animosity having dissolved once their shared concern for the one both loved had come to the fore.

"Sir, I saw the car too," this time it was Colonel William who spoke up, "and while I agree with him, we have come up with nothing on it so far. It happened so fast that we weren't able to note any details, and there have been no sightings of it either. Our best guess is that it is somehow linked to the terrorist camp which is an ominous thing, I know," he conceded as he saw Shahzad catch his breath, "but we must be realistic. And knowing what we know about the logistics and linkages of these groups, all of them know about and are in constant contact with each other. If what you have told us about the call made to you from the student leader is true, then this is most probably a case of kidnapping for ransom."

"Go on," said Shahzad as he slumped back in his chair.

"Sir, you have to think of it from the point of view of these kidnappers – ransom and extortion is one of the biggest booming enterprises right now in these areas under the guise of religion. All these local thugs have got crews in major cities who are picking up rich and influential people, and then they have networks that transport them into Taliban strongholds which are currently inaccessible to local law enforcement. However, in picking Asma and coming to this area, they made their first and last mistake, sir; we will flush those bastards out and recover the hostages," said Colonel William to thunderous applause from his colleagues.

I really hope so, prayed Qasim as he placed his head down on the table and prayed for his brother, who had been forgotten in the new ordeal. Throughout the last twelve hours, Qasim had tried to catch Colonel William's eye to get him in a corner and ask him how the new situation affected his search for his brother.

Two hours later, when the operation had been okayed and the finer details were being hashed out, the General and Shahzad and some of the other senior officers retreated to relax. This was the moment Qasim had been waiting for. He slid his chair over to where Colonel Williams was sitting with another officer, poring over some maps.

"Sir, can I speak with you?" he said.

William looked up and saw the question in Qasim's eyes. He motioned to his officer who nodded, got up and went outside.

"Sir, what about my brother?"

"Qasim, this situation just came up out of nowhere, and you know this is top priority."

"I know, sir, and I agree. I know Asma too, and I want her to be safe as well." He paused and looked down at his feet. "I just don't know what to think right now; I want my brother to be found, and I want Asma to be brought back to safety. I just don't know," he finished weakly.

"I know, buddy, I know; I understand." William reached out to pat Qasim on the back. "I tell you what, we will still look for Ijaz once this is over; I will provide you with all the help you need – how does that sound?"

Qasim looked up with genuine tears of relief in his eyes. "Sir, I do not have the words to express my gratitude."

Colonel Williams smiled and gave his moustache a twirl. "No worries at all." He turned around to focus on the map again.

"Sir?"

He looked back again at Qasim, who still had not left.

"Yes?"

"Sir, can I accompany you on the operation?"

Colonel Williams stared back at him, a vein throbbing visibly in his jaw.

"It's just that I want Asma to be safe, and I feel like if I am there, I might look around for Ijaz too," he said, clutching at straws.

Colonel William exhaled, then began, "Look, Qasim, first of all, this is not going to be a field trip or a picnic where you can look for your brother," he hissed angrily. "Please respect the risk I am already taking by bringing you here; there will be bullets flying, and I cannot have another casualty on my hands. I do not want to lose anyone." Qasim felt the thinly veiled allusion to the death of Aslam.

He flinched.

"Look, son," said Colonel William, his tone visibly softer. Qasim opened his eyes and nodded, trying to hold back his tears. "Even if I wanted to, I cannot take you along; you are in no position to walk. You needed help just to walk from your tent to here."

Qasim nodded, knowing that William was right.

"I promise you that I will help you look for your brother. Who knows, if this operation goes well, Inshallah—"

"Inshallah," said Qasim.

"Inshallah, who knows, we might get some leads as to the whereabouts of your brother; although for his own sake, I really hope he is not in the area."

Qasim nodded quietly, his mind racing to a million different scenarios, none of them good.

"In the meantime, you get your strength back, young man, and you pray for us, for your brother and for the success of this operation."

"*Ji*, sir, I will," he said.

*

5.30pm

Asma!

The name screamed in his mind as a huffing and panting Ijaz made his way through the throng of onlookers to the opening. He saw the two captives being dragged out by their burqas and being dumped on the ground. Then, as the burqa was removed from the first one, a gasp escaped his lips.

Despite the years having hardened the edges of her lips and the corners of her eyes, there was no mistaking it. It was the same girl he had peered at from inside the shop when Qasim had come unannounced one night for sehri.

This is the girl I'm going to marry.

Those words rang in Ijaz's ears, drowning out the outside world and his own thoughts as he stood transfixed, watching the men blindfold and lead her away while two men picked up her other companion and followed.

As if on cue, the other Qasim in his life, his son, was suddenly at his side, pulling his shirt with his little fingers and stretching his arms up, begging to be lifted up. It was as if two different worlds were pulling at him, stretching him beyond his control.

Ijaz smiled and lifted his son up and threw him up in the air. Qasim squealed with delight. He was about to head back to his hut when he heard his name being called. Ijaz turned around to see one of the Uzbek commanders walking towards him.

"We need you," he said in Pashto.

His father-in-law, who had been accompanying Ijaz and Qasim, also stopped.

"Why?"

"These guys are from your part; they don't understand us."

Ijaz stood still and thought for a moment. He had committed his life to a new surrounding and had made peace with the cards that fate had dealt him. But he had always maintained a safe distance from what went on in the camp. Because of the social standing of his father-in-law and the fact that he helped around the camp tending to the wounded, doing odd chores, kept to himself and had never tried to escape once, restrictions on his movement had relaxed; the Taliban had also allowed him to remain within their midst and not bothered him.

Ijaz felt all that changing.

As if sensing his distress, his father-in-law stepped forward and was about to say something, but Ijaz stopped him. Prying himself loose from the desperate grasp of his son, Ijaz placed Qasim in his father-in-law's arms and shrugged good-naturedly. "Don't worry," he said. "I'll be back soon."

He watched them disappear over the mound that dipped into the valley. Across the wheat crops was the village, where he could close his eyes and see his wife, Fatimah, setting the table and preparing dinner.

Presently, Ijaz and the Uzbek arrived at the house where the meeting was being held. They entered through the main door, then went down a staircase that led to a basement which further led to a tunnel. A pair of Afghan guards sat at the entrance; they nodded and gestured at them to enter the path on the right which led inside the base of the mountain.

Ijaz had heard about the existence of these tunnels, which were numerous and ran for miles inside the mountains and served as safe passage across the border into Afghanistan and also prevented important commanders from being targeted through drone attacks. After walking for about half a mile in near pitch-black darkness, they came to an opening inside the mountain which was lit by a kerosene lamp flickering against the granite walls, throwing half the area into light and the other into shadow.

The two strangers were seated on the recently swept and cleaned floor, drinking qahwa with a very senior commander whose name Ijaz did not know but whom he had seen countless times in the camp. The commander looked at Ijaz and gestured to him to come sit with him.

Ijaz nodded and took a seat close to the commander, who nodded towards the two strangers while looking at Ijaz. "Tell me what they say," he said in a mixture of Farsi and Pashto. Ijaz nodded and turned to the two who had been watching raptly, knowing full well that their safety and life also lay in a successful relay of information and that information being of some use to the fearsome-looking mercenary sitting in front of them.

After an hour of back and forth, the picture cleared. The two were part of a small-time Lahore-based gang that specialised in kidnap for ransom. They had been instructed to kidnap the girl and to hold her until further orders. However, they had run into unforeseen trouble. First, they had stumbled upon an army convoy that had blocked their way, due to which they had to switch direction and look for another place to hide. Secondly, upon calling their handler, they had come to know that the person who had placed the order, Raja Niaz, a name that rang alarm bells in Ijaz's mind as he recalled meeting him on that night when there had been a suicide attack on the Sufi shrine, was not responding.

With nowhere else to go, they had been advised by their handler to head for the camp and to offer them a deal.

"And so that is why we came here," said the shorter of the two Punjabis who appeared to be the leader and decision-maker. He had a fast way of talking and moving his hands in the air for emphasis after every sentence.

Ijaz nodded and turned to translate the last bit of the conversation to the commander. As he was finishing, he felt an urgent tug on his shirt. He turned around to find the short guy leaning over.

"Also, tell your leader that in exchange for giving us shelter and safe passage, we can give him a portion of the ransom money." He winked conspiratorially. Ijaz was about to speak when the short one interrupted him again. "Or you could just buy the girl from us, yeah." He nodded, happy at his own genius. "I can set it up with my boss, and you can pay him and buy the girls, well, girl actually, the second one we will give you for free." Again he winked. "Will you please tell him that?"

Ijaz sighed and nodded, then turned and was about to open

his mouth when the commander rose from his seat in a flash and whipped out a pistol from within the folds of the shawl. For a split second, there was a pause in which everyone was frozen in their poses: the short one still had a smile on his lips; his companion had his mouth pursed over the cup; and Ijaz was still in the process of speaking at the spot where there the commander had been sitting only a second ago.

Then the moment was shattered into a million pieces as the cave walls reverberated with shouts closely followed by a staccato of shots that bounced off the walls and set Ijaz's ears ringing.

And just like that, it was all over. The cave was enveloped by silence once again as Ijaz felt something warm and sticky on the back of his neck. He reached back to feel it and the hand came back dripping with blood. He fell backwards as he frantically tried to wipe off the remains of the person he had been talking to a moment ago.

He looked over at the two still bodies that lay sprawled in a fast-spreading pool of their own blood. Smoke was coming off the spot where the bullets had entered their bodies. The front four teeth of the short guy had been obliterated by the bullet that had entered through his mouth. The other three bullets had been more generous, leaving relatively smaller holes in his neck, shoulder and thigh. The second guy's face was a complete mess as the bullet had entered from the base of the cup. The shattered pieces of glass had accompanied the bullet on its journey to the left eye and on to the skull. The second bullet had hit him in the toe of his boot as he was flying backwards.

As Ijaz took in the whole scene, the commander had thrown off the shawl and was standing over the two corpses, taking in his handiwork. He slid the pistol into a shoulder holster and then bent over the short guy and fished out something from his pocket. Without looking at him, the commander threw them at Ijaz, who caught them instinctively – it was the keys to the car the kidnappers had driven in.

"Do you know how to drive?" he asked in perfect Urdu.

A chill went through Ijaz's body. "Yes, I do."

"Good, take the car over to the village and hide it for now."

Ijaz nodded, getting to his feet unsteadily. The commander came closer until they were almost touching noses, and he could smell his breath, which reeked of opium. The combination of the smell and the close proximity with the commander was terrifying for Ijaz, and he staggered backwards, but the commander reached out and caught hold of him, bringing him back in.

He smiled and patted him on the cheek. "You are in charge now, *bacha*, take both the girls back to your place, lock them up, keep them safe and find out who they are, where they're from and then let me know, OK?"

Ijaz nodded, while inside, his mind was screaming no.

"Shabash," yawned the commander sleepily. "Now go."

Ijaz half-ran, half-stumbled out of the tunnel.

The voice of the commander followed him outside. "You have two days."

*

12pm
T minus five hours to attack

When he could toss and turn no more, Qasim finally got up from the camp bed and looked out from the mosquito netting, under which he lay at the rows of sleeping and snoring sepoys on either side. He wished he could have their peace of mind for just one night.

But sleep would not come. He could not shut his mind off when he knew that his brother might well be within arm's reach somewhere out there. In the past five years, he had never been this close and yet so far. And then there was Asma. Her appearing out of nowhere had completely knocked the air out of him. As much as seeing her, what had surprised him even more was the effect that she still had on him after so many years. All this while when he had been thinking that he had pushed her out, she had been living in his heart, waiting and biding her time.

Qasim smiled and then grimaced as he got up, gingerly putting pressure on his injured left leg. The pain was excruciating, but he felt that he could take it. Plus, he needed to get some air. Parting a side opening in his mosquito net, he picked up a chair and hobbled outside the long hallway-type dormitory in which he had been told to bunk with the soldiers. As he made his way through the long line of camp beds on either side, he glanced at the soldiers, barely boys, some sound asleep, others in various stages, catching a brief period of rest and calmness before they would again be called on to put their lives on the line for the safety of total strangers. At that moment, Qasim's heart went out to the innocent boys, some of them barely old enough to sprout facial hair. Silently, he prayed for their safety.

There was no breeze outside, and the temperature was only slightly cooler. But the open night-time sky and the stars made it worth the effort. He dragged his chair down the landing and tipped it against the back of the building, so that it was balanced on its back legs, and then sat down.

"You'll fall and further hurt your leg."

The sound of the voice from the shadows scared Qasim, and he brought the chair crashing down on the ground, jarring his injured leg and causing him to wince in pain. He looked behind and recognised Shahzad Zafar's face in the red glow of the cigarette when he gave an extra-long drag on it.

"You scared me," said Qasim as he gingerly rubbed his leg.

Shahzad said nothing as he gave a final puff on the cigarette before flicking it against the side of the building. The embers sparked into a million red dots as they collided against the building and then disappeared into the blackness.

"She came here for you, you know."

Qasim gave no response, as he continued to massage his foot. He was bemused by his own reaction to meeting Shahzad Zafar after all these years. Where previously he would have been nervous and anxious to make a nice impression, now he felt indifferent and uninterested.

Something seemed to be bothering Shahzad. He came and stood in front of Qasim, who still would not look up to meet his eye.

"How is your family doing?"

"I don't know." There was a noticeable heaviness in Qasim's voice.

"How come?"

"I have not talked to them in a while."

"But, *beta*, why would you do that? When they were already dealing with the news of your other brother joining the Taliban." Shahzad saw Qasim's body stiffen instinctively. "I'm sure it's not true; I'm only saying what I heard."

Qasim laughed to himself. "You heard, so it must be true."

"You think it's not true. I can understand that – he is your brother – but how do you explain his absence?"

"I don't; I only know my brother."

"We sometimes think we know someone more than we actually do."

"I agree."

Shahzad stiffened, then smiled ruefully.

"Asma tried a lot to look for you, despite me telling her not to."

Qasim looked up at the sky, still not willing to make eye contact.

"You know, I have had a lot of time to think and go over stuff in these last couple of years after I saw my family being torn apart and having to give up the one person who really understood me," he said. "I have realised that one of life's greatest ironies is that the chain of narration of life that we grow up listening to is downwards

– it goes from our grandparents to our parents to us. The world as we know it is shaped by that narration which has nothing to do with what we feel or believe in. It is as it is, and we accept it. But as we grow up, we go out in the world, experience feelings, emotions, for the first time. And we accomplish things on our own. But what is stopping us from relishing those milestones? We need validation, and that chain of validation, in life's strangest twist, goes upwards, from children to parents. Until, and unless, they approve our choices, our life and achievements amount to nothing. And that is the irony of life. Parents forcing their failed dreams onto their children and not appreciating their children due to their own fears and shortcomings, and this keeps on happening until someone breaks the cycle. But if you choose to do so, you run the risk of being all alone and without anyone to steer you to shore," he panted, surprised at his own outburst.

Shahzad stepped forward and placed his hand on Qasim's shoulder. "Son, stop blaming yourself and others; it was not in your control."

"Who said I was talking about myself?" he said as he got up and looked directly at Shahzad, the tears in his eyes mirroring the helplessness and regret in Shahzad's.

Somewhere in the night, a lonely jackal howled; its plaintive call stretched across the starlit sky, followed by deathly silence as the darkness enveloped everything in its shadowy embrace once again.

*

By the time Ijaz emerged from the back, along with another man, dragging the two girls along with them, Fatimah's father and their son had also come out. Without another word, her father handed over Qasim to her mother and went to help the two men who were having a hard time dragging the unconscious woman.

Together, the three men led the two captives inside the house and into one of the rooms where Asma was chained to a bolt in the wall. Sam was placed on a blanket on the floor. Fatimah's father checked her pulse and pursed his lips but said nothing. Asma could feel the presence of people around her, but she had seen what had happened to Sam, so she did not resist or shout while she was handled and tied. Her breathing was coming in rapid, short bursts, and she felt that her lungs were about to explode. The blindfold was making it worse by not allowing her to see and, in effect, letting her imagination run wild with scary thoughts. The blindfold was stretched across her face so tightly that it left tiny slivers of sight where the cloth stretched over the bridge of her nose so that Asma's vision had become limited to what was immediately before her on the ground. When she was being led into the room, a pair of small feet, like those of a female, came into her limited vision. This was the first time in a long while since she had seen or heard from anyone who was not a man.

"Please! Help me! Sister!" she shouted with renewed vigour as she fought against the chains.

In-between her cries, Asma's ears were peeled for any response. But there was nothing. After a couple of seconds, Asma heard the sound of feet going away.

"No!" she shouted, "please don't leave me." She ended on a tearful note as she heard the door close. Then, for a long time, there was nothing. The chain was long enough for her to sit on the ground with her hands stretched over her head. As she craned her neck and shouted till her voice grew hoarse, she could hear people talking in muffled voices in the distance.

A couple of hours went by in which Asma had nothing to do except pull against her chain or try to pry the blindfold off by scratching the back of her head against the wall. But try as hard as she might, the blindfold would not budge, and she only ended up giving herself a headache.

Sometime in-between her struggles and cries for help, the exhaustion of the journey finally took over and she fell into an uneasy sleep that was broken by the noise of a glass falling over and the sound of water being spilled. Asma realised that someone had come in the room while she had been asleep and placed the glass of water beside her.

As she licked her parched lips, Asma weighed the possibility of shouting to her captors for help. But before she could come to a decision, the door creaked open. This time the footsteps were heavier and more purposeful.

Asma stood up and backed herself against the wall, expecting the worst as she felt the invisible figure bend down near her.

A steel plate filled with lentils and a roti slid into her view. Asma relaxed and reached for it. She felt hands on her head, and she recoiled and shrieked, desperate to get away.

"Relax, I won't hurt you," said a young-sounding voice.

Asma froze. The voice had spoken in Urdu.

"Please help me," she whimpered, the effect of hearing someone speak in her mother tongue breaking down the walls behind which she had been keeping her emotions locked. "*Bhai*, please save me; I will tell you who I am."

"I know who you are, Asma *baji*."

Suddenly, the tears dried up, and Asma felt her body go numb. Realisation dawned upon her just as she felt the hands reach behind and untie the blindfold. As the cloth dropped from her eyes, she found herself face to face with a lean and thin boy with large eyes that seemed to burn out of deeply sunken sockets. A scraggly and wispy beard covered the long, bony face in patches, giving it the appearance of a boy pretending to be a man.

"How do you know who I am?" she whispered as the boy unchained her and nudged the plate of food closer to her. Her mind raced in a thousand different directions. The boy said nothing and got up. "I'll be back in an hour to take away the plates."

Perhaps it was the manner in which he spoke or his body language, but as he turned around and walked away, suddenly the veil was lifted from Asma's vision.

Her eyes went wide. "Ijaz? Is it you?"

The boy stopped and his shoulders stiffened, then relaxed. He turned his face sideways so that Asma could see his profile. "I will be back in an hour. Please eat," he said and then, in a whisper, "Qasim *bhai* would not want you to starve."

28

Worlds colliding

3am

Once the initial awkwardness had worn off, they had talked for three hours straight. For Ijaz, meeting someone from his past had opened up a space that he had forever closed in his heart. And he had found that in shutting out his previous life, he had turned his back on a large part of his identity that had shaped and defined him. For Asma, seeing the boy whom she had never met but who had taken a central role in her life and the relationship she had with the memory of Qasim these past five years had been cathartic.

Later, when it was all over, both of them sat lost in their own thoughts. Ijaz had his head in his hands, his entire body convulsing with uncontrolled sobs. The empty plate and glass lay forgotten on the floor. Asma had surprised even herself by eating ravenously in spite of the dire situation she was in.

She banged her head lightly against the wall, staring pensively at the lone bulb hanging from the ceiling. She was trapped in a situation that she had no idea how to get out of. And to top it all, she had brought this not only upon herself but had brought in her friend too who, at that time, was fighting for her life. Ijaz had told her that Sam was still breathing but unconscious.

For his part, Ijaz had taken the news of his family falling apart badly. Asma could see that the years of living amongst hardened militants had not affected the innocent little boy inside Ijaz. He had completely broken down when Asma had told him about meeting Mustafa and what he had told her about their parents. The news of his mother had shattered him, and he had been sobbing ever since.

"You can still change things, Ijaz," Asma tried again.

Ijaz shook his head and said nothing, as he continued to sob.

"Ijaz, we have to get out of here – you don't belong here. Please, listen to me."

Finally, he looked up. Asma was alarmed at the effect her words had had on him. The calm, stern-looking man of a few moments ago had given away to a boy who seemed completely helpless and scared. His eyes were bloodshot and mirrored his anguish.

"What have I brought upon my family?" he wailed.

"*Shhhh*, you'll wake everyone up," Asma pleaded with him.

Ijaz nodded and composed himself. "I never wanted this to happen, you know."

"I know. Qasim knows that; your parents know that. This isn't your fault."

"But I brought those killers into our house; my family is now associated with those killers!"

"You did not know, Ijaz; it wasn't your fault. Everyone makes mistakes, but your family loves you; they care for you – Qasim has been looking for you for all these years."

The mention of his brother calmed him considerably, and he sighed and looked at her. "You love him," he said.

If they were in a different situation, in a different time, Asma might have blushed at such a blatant enquiry about her emotions, but now, she merely shook it away. "It's too late for that, and it has nothing to do with you."

"He loves you too, you know."

"I know," she said quietly.

"That's the thing about Qasim *bhai*," Ijaz smiled, "he will never give up on those he loves; he will keep coming back; he will keep trying, even if it kills him." Ijaz's voiced trembled as his lips quivered. "And this is how I repay his love." He buried his face in his hands and wept.

The realisation that the situation was too big for Ijaz suddenly dawned on Asma and hit her like a ton of bricks. He was still a little boy, looking for his big brother to help him out. He had never grown out of his childhood.

"I'm going to die here," she said with more calmness than she felt inside. Ijaz looked at her blankly and said nothing. He had told her about what had happened with the kidnappers. From there on, she had been able to piece together enough information to know that her situation had deteriorated considerably.

She and Sam might have been picked up by one of the many low-level kidnapping groups that had sprouted up all over Pakistan, especially the Punjab over the last couple of years due to the volatile situation. While that in itself was tricky, based on what Ijaz had told her, she and Sam had now become the possession of a militant commander who could not be expected to play by the same rules. With local small-time kidnap for ransom groups, law enforcement agencies were able to trace their networks and work around them. However, once outside the jurisdiction of the urban centres, specifically Punjab, the scales shifted heavily in favour of the rogue elements. Asma and Sam were now well out of reach of the law. She knew that in the border region, the writ of the state was almost non-existent due to the inaccessibility and porous nature of the terrain which gave the local militants an advantage.

As she looked back at Ijaz, she realised that her best and only hope of walking out of here alive lay on the shaky nerves of the teenager. Knowing that her own and the life of her friend lay in the balance, Asma ventured again, this time using a different approach.

"Do you have children, Ijaz?" She remembered that he had told her of his ordeal and how he had got married to the girl he had saved in the drone attack.

The transformation in Ijaz's countenance was remarkable and instantaneous. "Yes." He smiled. "Qasim."

Asma looked up, startled, and then smiled. Ijaz smiled back and shrugged. "Growing up, first Mustafa *bhai* and then Qasim *bhai* were everything to me. I watched the world through their eyes and atop their shoulders. And then, when Mustafa *bhai* got into drugs and drifted away, it was just Qasim *bhai* who cared for me, looked after me. If there is goodness and love in the world, I only saw it through Qasim *bhai*."

Asma's eyes welled up, and she bowed her head as two crystals fell in her lap. "Yes," she said.

"So, when Allah gave me a son," he continued, "there was no doubt in my mind, he had to be Qasim, the shining light in this dark moment."

"What did your wife think of the name?"

Ijaz chuckled. "Fatimah? What was she to say? She is a good wife; she knows that when the husband makes the decision, the wife has to follow."

Something inside Asma recoiled, but she did not let it show. "So, is she only like your mother in name?" she asked playfully.

Ijaz smiled absent-mindedly. He picked up the empty glass and spun it in his hand. "No, *Ammi* was not a timid or quiet person at all." He perked up suddenly. "In fact, Qasim *bhai* and Mustafa *bhai* used to tell me stories of *Ammi* when she used to fight with *Abu* and have her way all the time. She stood up for what she felt was right and backed down from no one..." His voice trailed off as his eyes fixed on some distant image of a memory long gone.

Suddenly, he broke out of his thought and looked irritably around, his eyes resting on Asma. The change in his demeanour was instantaneous and startling. He was no longer the crying, crestfallen boy. He threw the glass at Asma, which missed her and crashed against the wall, breaking the serene calmness in the air as the room reverberated with the sound.

"Stop trying to mess with my head," he shouted as he got up.

Asma tried to get up but slipped. "Ijaz, please listen to me," she pleaded. "This is not you; you have to help me get out."

Ijaz smiled derisively and looked at her. "Help you get out? You modern women think you can have everything, don't you? This western education has corrupted your mind," he said through eyes that seemed to have gone into a trance.

Asma could not believe the transformation, but she knew that time was slipping. She had to break through to him before it was too late.

"Ijaz, your mother will die if she doesn't see you soon!" she shouted. Ijaz stopped in his tracks. The mention of his mother had breached his walls and the cloud lifted from his eyes, revealing the scared, hurt boy again.

He looked at Asma and then at his feet. He stepped forward towards her as she shrieked and cowered in fear.

"I would never hurt you, Asma *baji*," he said in a small voice. "I don't know what comes over me sometimes; this is not me," he said as he picked up the shattered glass pieces from the floor. "You see, I am not the same boy, I have become this violent beast who thinks such thoughts. How can I ever let *Ammi* or *Abu* see me like this?"

"You are not this," said Asma. "That pure, innocent boy is still inside; you have to believe he is there, and you have to protect him."

"I have to prepare for Fajr now," he said in a tone of finality as he moved towards the door. "You need to get in touch with your father and do as you are told."

"Ijaz, please listen to me," she pleaded. "Think about your son; think about Qasim," she said as Ijaz left the room, slamming the door on her words.

*

5am

"I wish I was going with you, sir." The night's sleep had not been able to wash away the unease that clung to Qasim like a second skin. He had the feeling that he was about to let slip an important chance to reach Ijaz.

He was leaning on a crutch, talking to Colonel William who sat in the early morning sun, cleaning his Colt 357 Magnum with a piece of rag cloth and oil. "Don't worry, Qasim," he said as he rammed the piece of oilcloth down the barrel and pulled it out from the other side. "I gave you my word – we will find your brother, and I," he stood up as he dropped the bullets in the cylinder and placed the revolver in the holster on his hip, "I am nothing if not a man of my word," he finished with a flourish.

"*Bhai kesa lag raha hai*?" he asked with a sly grin as he cocked an eyebrow and slung one hand over the butt of his revolver. He was dressed in his battle gear, head to toe in camouflage and itching for battle.

Qasim grinned in spite of himself. He brought his forefinger and thumb together and said, "Superb!" Colonel William nodded. "*Yeh cheez!*"

"Sir," Qasim continued, "I was talking to some of your men. And they were saying you always lead from the front, even now when you are a Colonel and do not necessarily have to be the first one."

Colonel William looked at him, the hint of a smile playing beneath his moustache. "And?"

"Are you never afraid, sir?"

Colonel William threw his head back and gave a loud guffaw. "Truth be told, every second of it, I'm shit scared," he was laughing, "but that's the kick, yaara. Rising above your fears and staring death in the face, like all those cowboys that I'm sure Khalid Chacha showed you too."

Qasim grinned. "He showed them to you too?"

"Why else do you think I have this?" he asked as he theatrically drew his silver colt and twirled it in his hand before dropping it back in the holster.

"OK, but seriously," he said in a sombre tone, as he worked the ends of his moustache into fine tips, "life comes just once. Why live it being scared and afraid?" he asked. "This is my country; I swore to defend against these thugs and thieves who give my country a bad name," he continued suddenly with a fire in his voice.

"These mercenaries who lead little boys astray and destroy families," he said, looking at Qasim. "No, I give you my word; I will not let that happen."

"*Fi Aman Allah*, sir'" said Qasim, remembering the words his father said every time he left the house.

"Ameen."

Colonel William playfully punched Qasim on the shoulder as he climbed into the driving seat of his jeep. From the back of the jeep, Javed poked his head out of the window, raised his arm in the air and shouted, "*Allahu Akbar!*" Qasim gulped back the large knot in his throat as he raised his fist in return and mouthed the war cry.

He watched as the jeep merged into the long convoy of armed trucks carrying soldiers that had been driving down the road towards the mountain strongholds of the Taliban for the past hour. Overhead, military gunship helicopters hovered in the air like giant insects as they accompanied the troops. Since morning, fighter jets had been streaking across the sky. They had been pounding the mountainside, destroying all entrance and exit points, practically boxing in the militants in a large area of the mountain, leaving only one way for them to flee which would be straight in the face of the oncoming Pakistan Army.

Colonel William was leading an advance guard that would reach the militant camp before the main force. The strategy of air bombing the mountain was to drive the militants inside their bunkers so as to make them vulnerable to a sneak search party led by Colonel William. Their aim was to look for Asma and to leave quickly with minimum contact with the militants before the main force arrived. The success of the whole operation hinged on them reaching the camp undetected, locating Asma and getting out without engaging with the militants.

Qasim was still mumbling all the prayers and verses he had heard his mother and father incant during times of crisis when Shahzad Zafar came up to stand by his side. Qasim looked at Asma's father. There were dark stains where the sweat had dried and caked on his clothes from yesterday. His hair was unkempt; there were visible lines of worry around his eyes. For the first time, he looked his age.

Shahzad felt the eyes on him and turned sideways to face Qasim. There was no need for words as, in that second, both men shared a bond of love. For the first time in his storied career, the old bureaucrat, who had single-handedly broken up bloodthirsty mobs, negotiated with crafty criminals and held his own against aggressive politicians, wavered and felt at a loss for words.

Qasim reached up and wrapped his arm around the shoulder of the taller Shahzad Zafar and hugged him sideways. "Don't worry," he said. "Everything will be alright; Allah is watching over them," he said.

Shahzad sighed as his whole body relaxed, and he leaned back against his younger companion. Both stood there for an hour, motionless, silent, watching the receding convoy disappearing over the horizon, carrying their hopes with them.

29

Blaze of glory

He was seven years old and back in his home. It was raining outside as he lay on his bed beside the window, overlooking the street below. Ijaz giggled and closed his eyes each time the rain splashed on the window pane and sent tiny droplets crashing on his face.

He turned around to see his mother coming from the kitchen. She had an expression that made him smile. Her face seemed to be angry with him for getting wet, but her eyes laughed with him, enjoying the respite from the heat of the day. He giggled again as she came and sat down beside him on the bed. She stretched her arm out through the bars of the window to catch some of the rain droplets on her hand, which she then flicked on Ijaz.

He squealed with delight and got up to run with Fatima chasing him. As he jumped off the bed, he opened his eyes to find himself face down on the hard courtyard of the mosque. One side of his face was caked with dust and tiny pebbles from the ground. As he rubbed his eyes and tried to clear his head, Ijaz tried to make sense of the knot in his stomach. Something did not feel right. Something had woken him up. He was still trying to figure it out when it happened again. A gentle rumble that seemed to be coming from deep within that grew steadily until he could feel the ground vibrating.

Ijaz's eyes bulged out of his face with fear; the mountain was being bombed. When the bombing had started early in the morning, Ijaz had been sleeping in the courtyard of the mosque. Sitting up all night talking with Asma had left him drained, both emotionally and physically. After finishing the Fajr prayer, he did not have the energy to walk all the way back to the village. Instead, he had sat down in the courtyard and leaned against one of the pillars, and the next thing he knew, the whole ground beneath him was shaking and quivering like a frightened animal.

He sat up and waited for the trembling of the earth to subside. In the intervening silence that followed, he could feel his own heart crashing against his chest. As he was about to relax, he heard the sound before he felt the earth shudder under him. A chill ran down his spine.

Occasional shelling of the mountainside was not unusual during ongoing military operations. In fact, in the five years since he had been here, there had been only few air bombings or drone attacks, owing to the inaccessible nature of the camp and the village. Ijaz stood up slowly, still groggy from his lack of sleep and not willing to believe what his fried nerves were telling him.

Then it began again, a low rumbling, deep in the belly of the mountain, like a nervous twitch. Ijaz saw tiny pebbles in the courtyard gently vibrating with each rumble. As his eyes drifted upwards, in the distance behind the nearest rise of mountains he saw clouds of smoke rising up in the early morning air.

Ijaz ran down the mountain towards the village, his heart in his mouth, praying with each step. In the distance, the village resembled an anthill, with people running about everywhere. As he neared his house, Ijaz saw young Qasim running towards him with his arms outstretched and tears streaking down his sleepy eyes. His wife Fatimah came up to him, followed by her mother and father.

Unlike the camp, the village did not have bunkers to hide

inside during air strikes. The only recourse for the villagers was to come out in the open to prevent being buried under debris. Some of the families had even started heading for the road leading out of the mountain. Ijaz fell in with his family as they ran along with the other villagers towards the open countryside.

He had gone a few steps when he spotted three men headed towards his house. In the front was the Afghan commander. Ijaz knew as soon as he saw them that they were going to take Asma and the other girl. Ijaz saw his brother's face for a split second. He knew what he had to do.

He saw that his wife and family had already got lost in the mass of humanity that was now rushing away from the village. Still carrying young Qasim in his arms, Ijaz separated himself from the crowd and ran back towards his house. As he looked up at the billowing smoke on the mountain, he saw that the bombs were starting to land closer and closer to his village.

Ijaz cut through the wheat field that lay between the camp and the village. In a small patch where the wheat had not grown that tall, he sat Qasim down on the grass and looked at him. "Qasim, can you do a small thing for Baba?" he asked, his heart racing.

Qasim looked up at him solemnly and nodded. "*Ji*, Baba."

"I want you to hide in here until I come back, OK?"

"Where are you going, Baba?"

"I left something in the house; I will be back quickly."

"I want to come too, Baba. I left my toy gun; I will protect you."

"No, *bacha*, you stay here, and I will bring your gun. Can you be brave for your baba?"

"Yes, Baba."

Ijaz kissed his son and took off the tawiz from around his neck and placed it over his son's head. "I will be right back," he said as he ran towards the house.

*

Inside the house, Asma had awoken to the sounds of footsteps and shouts outside her door. Then, she had felt the dust and debris fall from the roof as the ground rumbled with each shell crashing into the mountains close by.

Asma had shouted and cried for someone to come and untie her, but no one came. She had shouted out for Ijaz, again and again, but had only been met with the sounds of the house as it groaned and creaked under the effects of the shelling.

After an hour of trying, she only had bruised and raw wrists to show for her effort. Her throat had gone hoarse from all the shouting, but still she persisted.

"Help!" she shouted, as she again pulled on her chain. As she opened her mouth to shout again, she heard something heavy being dragged on the floor outside her room. Before she could say anything, the door opened and a heavily bandaged Sam walked in, dragging an axe behind her.

At that moment, Asma could not have been prouder of her friend, who had willed herself to get up from her injury and come to her rescue. Tears welled up in her eyes as she reached out and guided Sam towards her. It seemed as if Sam had used up every ounce of her energy in getting to her, because as soon as she reached Asma, she crumpled in a heap on the ground.

Asma took the heavy axe from her limp hands and got up. She aimed for the point where the chain was bolted into the ball and swung the axe back over her shoulder. She brought the axe crashing down at the spot.

She missed.

The axe hit two inches above. The force of the hit made Asma lose her grip on the axe and it fell with a loud clang on the floor. "Son of a bitch," she muttered under her breath as she bent down to pick it up. Again and again, she tried, getting closer and closer to the mark. She knew she was running on borrowed time as she could feel the bombings coming closer. The house shook with each rumble, dropping a thick cloud of dust on both of them each time.

Perhaps it was her persistence; perhaps it was the soft material of the wall, but on her twentieth swing of the axe, Asma felt something give way, and she fell backwards with the momentum of her swing.

She looked up at the wall where the chain had been. An ugly gaping hole looked back at her.

She was free.

But there was no time to rejoice. She grabbed Sam and tried to raise her to her feet, but it proved harder than it seemed. Sam's eyes were open, but they had a glazed look. She was making gurgling sounds, but no words were coming out.

"Sam, I need you to get up," she pleaded. "We have to get out of here, come on, please."

Her friend smiled back wordlessly as if to say that she was at peace.

"If you think I am going to let you stay here, you are out of your mind. Now come on!" she shouted as she heaved with all her strength and dragged Sam to her feet. Asma draped Sam's arm around her neck and, with her other arm around her back, they stumbled out of the room. As they inched their way out through the narrow gallery, they were faced with two doorways. Asma chose the one on the left. She opened it to find herself in the open courtyard facing the road leading out away from the mountain. But before she had a moment to smile, her eyes fell on the three men fast approaching towards the house.

Towards them.

Asma recalled what Ijaz had told her about the Afghan commander from the night before. They were coming up the road and had not seen her as she was hidden in the darkness of the doorway. She dragged herself and Sam back inside and closed the door. She retraced her steps back into the room where she had been locked. She needed to find another way out. Time was running out.

There was a sound of glass breaking and then something dropped onto the floor. In the next instant, Ijaz appeared in the doorway. There was a split second when their eyes met; no words were spoken.

"What took you so long?"

Ijaz smiled and shrugged. "Come on, this way," he said as he picked up Sam and slung her over his thin, bony shoulders. Asma was surprised by the strength in his slender frame. "Your brother would be proud of you," she said as she ran beside him down the corridor and towards the kitchen.

"Don't thank me yet; we are not out of danger," he puffed.

"The Afghan you mentioned is coming," Asma said.

"I know."

He pointed towards the window. "Go, now!" Asma peered out; it opened into the mountainside. She looked back at Ijaz. "What about you?"

"Just stay close to the mountain. Do not come out in the open until you are well away."

"What about you?"

"Go! Now. And don't look back," he said as he helped Asma over the ledge, lifted Sam over the threshold and gently placed her beside Asma.

"Ijaz, why are you not coming?" she shouted, but it was too late. Ijaz had closed the window and had turned around. The last image Asma had of Ijaz was of him taking out a pistol from his waistband and running away, deeper into the shadows of the house.

Asma dragged Sam beside her as they made their way away deep into the mountain. The sound of shots being fired made her stop dead in her tracks. She looked back, waiting, praying for Ijaz to emerge.

Nothing.

Come on, Ijaz, she prayed, but he did not appear. As she kept looking, the sound of shots being fired started growing louder and appeared to be edging closer and closer. There was no time to lose. Asma turned around and started moving away.

She did not look back again.

*

The operation had been a success in terms of surprise. The bombing that had been going on since morning had made the militants retreat and hide in their bunkers, which had given Colonel William and his men the cover they had needed to approach the camp undetected.

As he surveyed the line of villagers stretched out on the road, Colonel William knew that if Asma was among them, she would be identified and rescued at the military checkpoint that had been placed at the road, which was the only remaining exit point.

However, the success of Colonel William's operation had hinged on the chance of finding the girls in the camp. But as their team went through the abandoned huts and tents, it was quickly apparent that the militants had retreated deep inside their hideout, along with their captives, leaving Colonel William with two options: either to wait for the rest of the force to arrive or to forge ahead and follow the militants into their bunkers. As much as he himself wanted to charge in with guns blazing, William had to think of the safety of his men, and he knew that they were not enough to take on the full militant force. Plus, there was no guarantee of the safety of the girls in the event of a firefight.

As he scratched the light stubble on his chin, the flash of sunlight on the barrel of a gun caught his eye. He peered into the distance and could barely make out three dark dots moving across the land. Without another word, he ran in their direction, with his team following closely behind.

As he came up the bend, Colonel William noticed a young boy grappling with a much larger and older man. Blood was streaking down his face, flecking his sparse beard. One arm hung limp by his side, almost severed from the shoulder joint. As if immune to his state, the boy stood blocking the doorway in front of the larger man, empty shell casings and a pistol strewn at his feet, testament to the valiant but losing battle he had been waging.

In his other hand he was holding a knife with which he kept making lunging attacks at the Afghan, who seemed to be toying with him, staying just out of reach. Two other soldiers stood at either side of their leader, their guns aimed at the boy, waiting for the order. The boy had put up a fight – one of the soldiers was hit in the leg and the other also had a deep gash in his shoulder. The sound of running feet made all four turn towards him. Colonel William locked eyes with the boy and sensed something familiar as the boy smiled and then suddenly lunged with his arm outstretched at the Afghan who had been distracted. The knife made a gurgling sound as it pierced the neck and went into the hilt. The Afghan was hurt mortally, but he did not go down as he turned around and fired five rounds point blank into the boy.

Colonel William roared as he fired from his hip, emptying his Colt 357 at the first soldier, who flew backwards from the impact of the shots. By then, he was almost on top of the second soldier who was bringing up his AK47 as Colonel William rammed head first into his chest. The two went tumbling backwards into the dust. As both came up simultaneously on their feet, Colonel William realised that his revolver was empty.

Colonel Sherwin Francis William had lived a life of no regret. He had lived every day believing that if he put his mind to something, he could achieve it. And that had been the belief he had instilled in his men too, by leading from the front. The last image Colonel William took in was that of his men running towards him with his orderly Sepoy Javed in the lead, shouting something unintelligible, his face a mask of worry and determination. Colonel William smiled and then charged, with his teeth bared, into the hail of bullets, his hands clawing for the throat of the militant.

*

Army forward post
Swat
12.15am

It was midnight when the first convoy returned back to camp. Qasim had sat by the wireless set, catching reports of the progress of the operation. He had been stunned to learn of the death of Colonel William. Walking out of the communication room, he had felt his sadness magnified manifold in the eyes of the men who had worked under William. All the way to his room, Qasim had not seen one dry pair of eyes as the news of the brave demise of the flamboyant Colonel had spread through the camp.

A part of him had also worried about his own personal agenda and the promise the late Colonel had made to him regarding Ijaz. Qasim had tried to rebuke himself for thinking of personal gains in that moment, but there it was; he could not help himself. As he tossed and turned on his camp bed inside the stifling hot tent, Qasim's mind had raced to countless paths and possibilities as he tried to see the way forward. Sleep had mercifully come just when he had run out of answers.

It was the feeling of being watched that woke him with a start.

Sepoy Javed sat on the edge of his bed, looking out of eyes that seemed to say more than words ever could. As he got up to sit on his bed, Qasim saw other soldiers who had accompanied Colonel William on the operation sitting on their camp beds. Some, like the Colonel, were conspicuous with their absence.

"You know when I was told that I would be his stick orderly, I was about to quit," said Javed as he looked down at his feet. "There was no way that I was going to be that close to a non-Muslim," he continued in mock disgust as a tear fell down his face. His expression did not match that of someone sad; he was serene and seemed at peace.

"It was Aslam Khan who convinced me not to," he continued. "He told me not to base my opinion on someone's faith. 'He's a lion.' That's what he had said, and I had smirked, but I had not quit and became William *saab*'s stick orderly." He fought back tears as Qasim got up to stand beside him and pat him on the shoulder.

"I had to beg him to let me come with him, because he said it was too dangerous, and I had just got married. 'Who will look after your family if you die?' he had said. When I had asked him the same thing, he had said, 'I already have a family; you all are my *bachay*.'" By now, other soldiers had gathered around, and they nodded and murmured. There was not a single dry eye in the group of soldiers who had seen countless deaths and had fought through many life-threatening encounters.

"When I picked up my *saab*," said Javed to the gathering, "he had his hand around the *nafarman*'s throat and his knife deep in his gut," he said with genuine pride. "He charged like a lion straight into the hail of bullets. Not one bullet on his back; he took all of them in the front." He beamed proudly.

At that moment, a sepoy entered the tent and stood before Qasim. "2IC *saab* would like you to come to his office right now," he said and then waited while Qasim buttoned his shirt. His heart raced at the thought of what he was about to hear. There had been news about the success of the operation, but nobody had mentioned anything about Asma being found. There was no sign of Shahzad Zafar also to find out anything.

Qasim followed the sepoy to the small, dark room of the second-in-command officer Major Shakir, who sat behind a desk stacked with documents and maps. Major Shakir was a broad man, with a face that resembled that of a banker with his neat moustache and centre-parted oiled hair.

"Please have a seat, Qasim." Major Shakir motioned towards the chair in front of him.

Qasim sat down. His heart was so loud that he was pretty sure that everyone could hear it. "I am really sorry about the death of Colonel William. He was a brave man, a good man," he said.

Major Shakir nodded. "Yes, but this is what we soldiers call a glorious death," he said. "He died fighting to protect his homeland against those who are using it for their own nefarious designs."

Qasim nodded.

"Anyway," Major Shakir cleared his throat. "I have some news," he began. Qasim could feel the ground moving underneath as he grabbed onto the chair to keep himself from toppling over. "As you know, the operation is still ongoing with the terrorists being entrenched in their bunkers and tunnels under the mountains, and it is going to be a long time before we can get a final tally on the dead and their identities."

Something did not feel right; he had thought that he had been called to be informed about Asma, but the major had not even mentioned her, talking instead about death. Qasim felt the room move as his eyes clouded over. "Wait a minute," he said shakily. "Please tell me that Asma is alive."

"Please pay attention to what I'm saying, Qasim."

"No, no, tell me Asma is alive," said Qasim, standing up.

"Calm down, please."

"Just tell me, damn it! Don't tell me to calm down!" shouted Qasim as he stood up suddenly, sending the chair flying backwards.

Major Shakir remained seated. "Please, Qasim," he implored in a tired voice. "I beg you, sit down. This is not about Asma."

Qasim turned and picked up the fallen chair and sat down again, facing the major across the table.

"Thank you."

"Now please can you tell me what this is about?"

Major Shakir said nothing as he looked back at him for a second. Then he reached inside a drawer and pulled something out. He extended his hand over the table and kept it suspended in the air until Qasim reached out and placed his open hand under it, his heartbeat thundering in his ears.

Major Shakir opened his hand and a shiny, heavy object fell in Qasim's palm. Even before he looked at it, Qasim knew just from the feel. He could see it before he saw it.

As he brought it close to his face and opened his eyes, Qasim's worst fears were realised – it was the tawiz he had placed around Ijaz's neck when he was a toddler and had made him promise never to take it off.

"Ijaz," he whispered as he brought it close to his face and kissed the gnawed and worn out leather pouch.

"This was not found on a grown man who matches Ijaz's profile." Major Shakir's voice seemed to be coming from a distance as it dragged Qasim back to reality.

"What?"

"Well, you know as the operation began, villagers ran away from the area, and we are still interrogating them as we feel that some terrorists might have infiltrated with them. But the person this was found on was not among them. He was all by himself, alone in a wheat field. We would like you to identify him for us."

Qasim nodded, too scared to trust his voice.

Major Shakir pressed a bell on his desk.

The silence of the room was shattered by the howling of the wind outside as the door opened and the sound of heels clicking as the soldier entered the dimly lit room. He closed the door behind him and stood stiffly at attention, waiting for his next command.

The Major motioned towards Qasim who had his eyes focused on something on the mud floor. In one fluid motion, the soldier bent down, dropped the piece of paper in Qasim's lap, straightened, clicked his heels, saluted and left the room.

Qasim looked down at the piece of paper in his lap. Even in the near darkness of the makeshift bunker, and in spite of the grimy and smudged quality of the black-and-white photo, there was no mistaking it.

Qasim could spot that smile in a crowd of thousands.

From miles away… Ijaz.

Qasim looked up. "I don't understand," he lied.

"His name is Qasim; he is Ijaz's son," replied Major Shakir. "Miss Asma has also verified that Ijaz had mentioned him when they talked."

Qasim's head shot up. This was the first mention of Asma. Major Shakir smiled. "Yes, we have good news – Colonel William lived up to his promise – Miss Asma is alive and well, as is her companion."

Qasim fell back in his chair and closed his eyes, his mind racing with a million thoughts. He sat back up and looked at Major Shakir, wanting to ask a question, the answer to which he had already known ever since he had seen the tawiz which he had asked Ijaz to never take off.

"My brother," he began feebly.

Major Shakir got up. "Ijaz died while helping Asma escape," he said. "He did not have to, but he came back and faced armed terrorists so that Asma and her companion could get away. He died a brave man. You should be proud of him. He did not die a terrorist; he is a *shaheed*. Hold your head up high, son."

Later, Qasim found himself walking all over the camp, lost in thoughts, clutching the tawiz in his hand, his head bowed. Finally, he sat down on a large rock and wept. All the years and moments that had been missed came rushing back to him as he looked back on the times they had spent together. Again and again, he wished that he could go back and do something different so that Ijaz would still be alive.

He heard the sound of the mobile ringing before he felt the vibration in his pants pocket. *Who could be calling at this hour?* he thought as he fished the mobile out and looked angrily at it. It was an unknown number. Qasim answered the call, wanting to shout at someone, anyone, but the voice on the other end cut him off before the words had left his mouth.

"Hello? Qasim? How have you been, brother?"

It was Deemu.

Qasim closed his eyes as he felt the tears welling up again. "Qasim, speak up – I can't hear you. Are you alright? I'm so glad Asma is alive and well; I just found out."

Qasim nodded and then sighed. "Ijaz is dead," he said.

There was silence at the other end; then he heard Deemu again – this time his voice was softer. Tender.

"No. Oh my God, Qasim."

Suddenly, the tears he had been holding back erupted, and he could not control himself any longer. In-between his sobs, Qasim told Deemu everything that had happened in the last twelve hours.

"I failed him, Deemu," sobbed Qasim. "I failed my beautiful baby brother; I could not save him."

Deemu's voice on the other end came strained and heavy. "Listen to me, Qasim – there are no second chances in life except for the ones that we give ourselves. This is your second chance – embrace it."

Qasim fell silent.

"Ijaz named his firstborn after you," whispered Deemu. "You did not fail him; you were the only thing that kept him alive through those times. Look at this as proof of the positive effect you had on your brother; you saved him."

Qasim nodded, the thought brightening up the darkness that had engulfed his soul.

"Yes," he whispered.

"Ijaz made up for all his faults and mistakes by sacrificing his life for your happiness. He saved Asma because he knew she mattered to you. If that is not love, then I don't want to know what else is."

"He used to run away from fights; he never liked confrontations," smiled Qasim through tears.

"And yet, he faced his fears for you."

"Yes."

"And he did something more than that, brother." Deemu waited, letting the moment sink in. "He has given you a second chance to help raise his blood, his son, just as you raised him. He has given you the glue that will hold your family together. Ijaz has given you the balm for the wound that ripped your family apart. His son will be your salvation."

After Qasim hung up the phone, he looked up at the sky. The first drop of rain felt cool on his parched skin. As he walked towards the infirmary where the survivors were being kept, he felt good for the first time in a long time. He walked towards his nephew Qasim and the love of his life Asma, the two people who had brought him back from the edge of the abyss.

It was time to start living again.

*

In the dim light of the infirmary, the silhouette of a gaunt man straightened as the sound of scraping feet on the hard mud earth woke him. Shahzad Zafar smiled when he saw the tear-stained face of Qasim in the lamplight.

"How is she?" asked Qasim.

Shahzad got up and squeezed Qasim's shoulder. "I'm sorry about your brother," he said. "He saved my daughter, thank you." With that, he motioned towards the bed. "Why don't you ask her yourself?" He walked out of the makeshift infirmary.

Qasim was suddenly aware of his hands, and he did not know what to do. He was scared to look at the bed.

"Why do I always have to make the first move?" said Asma in a weak voice, breaking the spell.

Qasim exhaled and smiled as he looked at her; she looked beautiful. He dragged the chair close to the side of the bed and sat down. Asma reached out and grasped his hand.

Still, the words would not come. Qasim held her hand close to his cheek. He closed his eyes and a tear fell down.

But he was smiling.

*

Anarkali Bazaar
One year later

"I have walked these streets for so many years," said Jabbar as he waved his hand to a young kid who greeted him, "but never before have I felt more at home than I do now."

Qasim walked quietly beside him. They were coming back from the mosque after Zuhr prayers. The colour had returned to his father's face in the last year, and he had started eating again.

"I know, *Abu ji*," he said as he clasped his hand. His father squeezed it hard.

They stopped outside their home, which had a new board outside with the words: 'Shaheed Ijaz Kaleem's House'. A horse-drawn carriage was parked outside the house. Mehran's face emerged from the front seat. "Are we ready, Qasim *bhai*?"

Qasim nodded and placed his father's hand in Mehran's hand. "Yes, you help *Abu ji* up, and I will go check."

He shouted, "*Ammi*, let's go," as he started for the door. As he was reaching for it, the door opened, and the two Fatimahs emerged. Qasim grinned widely as he saw his mother walking gingerly down the steps. He stepped forward and held her hand as he helped her onto the carriage.

"*Chal* shabash, Mehran," she said. Mehran cracked his whip, and the horse trotted forward, his hooves beating a loud tune on the cobbled street.

"Where is little Qasim?" asked Jabbar.

"Asma is picking him up from school and will bring him there," said his mother. Presently, the street opened up into a wide road that led to a spacious three-story building that had been recently erected. As the horse carriage stopped in front of the building, Qasim got out to help his mother down. Mustafa appeared at the other end and held his father's hand as Jabbar got down.

Both men looked at each other for a brief moment, their eyes conveying more than words ever could. Mustafa smiled and said, "It is ready."

"Shabash, Mustafa, I am proud of you." Jabbar patted his eldest son lovingly as they walked towards the building. The five of them walked up to the gate and looked up at the board which read: 'The Sherwin William Orphanage'.

The idea had come to Qasim one day as he had gone back to Rawalpindi to bury Colonel William. Pitras had shown him the late soldier's will, in which he had left all his possessions and inheritance to be used for the betterment of children who had no one to care for them. From there, the idea had grown, and everyone had come together.

Deemu, who had helped Qasim in securing the position of student federation leader after he had gone back to finish his degree, had also helped in arranging to buy the plot of land on which the building had been built in less than seven months. The army and the civil administration had pitched in together to provide labour, materials and infrastructure. Mustafa, who had a son of his own, had volunteered to take over the charge of the orphanage that provided a safe shelter to homeless children.

Qasim grinned as he saw Deemu coming from inside the building. As he reached them, he looked at Qasim and said, "Remember what I told you?" Qasim nodded, recalling the talk they had the night he had found out about Ijaz's death.

"Was I not right?"

Before he could answer, they heard the sound of tires on gravel as a car stopped behind them. Assistant Commissioner Lahore,

Asma Zafar, got out of the back seat. She greeted everyone and then paused for a second as she made eye contact with Qasim. There was no need for words. Qasim smiled and nodded at her. Asma smiled back.

The silence was broken by the pitter-patter of small feet as young Qasim burst into view, followed by his mother, carrying his school bag. Both mother and son came to a screeching halt as Fatimah, out of breath, adjusted her dupatta, and young Qasim ran out and wrapped his arms around his grandfather's legs. "*Dadi ji!*" he shouted gleefully.

Jabbar beamed as he picked up his grandson and threw him up towards the sky. The air was filled with the child's squeals of delight as Qasim looked back at Deemu, who was grinning.

"Yes," said Qasim. "A second chance."